Kang hed
across the 　　　　　　　　　　 of
the wood li　　　　　　　　　 ds
distant. Th　　　　　　　　　 d,
hidden in t　　　　　　　　　 d
expectation, hands clutching their weapons, fangs
bared, tails twitching.

Notoriously shortsighted, the squint-eyed goblins
were slow to notice the seven-foot bozak draconian that
had just risen in front of them. They kept marching.
Then one of the goblins turned its piss-yellow face in
Kang's direction. He saw its squinty eyes widen in terror, its mouth open.

"Regiment . . . charge!" Kang shouted.

Margaret Weis and Don Perrin

THE DOOM BRIGADE

BROTHERS IN ARMS

DRACONIAN MEASURES

by Margaret Weis

THE SOULFORGE

DRACONIAN MEASURES

Don Perrin
with Margaret Weis

DRACONIAN MEASURES
©2000 Wizards of the Coast, Inc.

Cover art by Daniel Horne
First Printing: November 2000
Library of Congress Catalog Card Number: 00-101966

9 8 7 6 5 4 3 2 1

ISBN: 0-7869-1678-8
620-T21678

U.S., CANADA,
ASIA, PACIFIC, & LATIN AMERICA
Wizards of the Coast, Inc.
P.O. Box 707
Renton, WA 98057-0707
+1-800-324-6496

EUROPEAN HEADQUARTERS
Wizards of the Coast, Belgium
P.B. 2031
2600 Berchem
Belgium
+32-70-23-32-77

Visit our web site at **www.wizards.com/dragonlance**

Dedication
To the 30th Field Artillery Regiment
(the Bytown Gunners), Royal Canadian Artillery,
who showed me how a regiment works in the field.

Editor's Note

Several past events in the history of the First Dragon-army Engineers are referenced in this book. Kang and the rest of the troop were first introduced in the story, "The First Dragonarmy Bridging Company" by Don Perrin in the DRAGONLANCE® anthology, *Dragons of Krynn*. The story of the catapulting minotaur can be found in, "The First Dragonarmy Engineer's Secret Weapon" by Don Perrin and Margaret Weis in the anthology *Dragons at War*. The story of how Kang discovered the female draconian eggs is told in the novel *The Doom Brigade* by Margaret Weis and Don Perrin. The tale of Kang's trek north, pursued by goblins, is told in "To Teach the Righteous of the Right" in the anthology, *Heroes and Fools*. The episode of the wicker dragon can be found in *Dragons of Autumn Twilight* by Margaret Weis and Tracy Hickman.

Chapter One

Kang lay flat on his belly, his huge scaled body crushing the long grass beneath him. He gripped his battle-axe in his clawed hand. He had spread his wings to cover his arms and his torso so that no errant beam of sunshine would flash off his armor or his scales to reveal his location. He could see nothing except grass, and because he'd been lying here over an hour, he'd come to know the grass really well. It was long and brownish green and slightly sticky and it made an irritating clicking sound when the wind blew.

Kang had come to know all the sounds of his surroundings quite well, too, in these past slow-moving minutes. He'd thought the late summer's day silent when he had first taken up his position, but now the noise drummed in his head. Cicadas buzzed frantically, for no good reason that Kang could tell, perhaps trying to find some way to avoid the coming of winter and death. Crickets chirped mindlessly; no sense, crickets. Tree frogs burbled and gulped. The dry grass rustled in the wind. Kang lay there, hating them all collectively and individually and fighting against the urge to yell at them, demand that they all shut up. He was listening for two sounds—the flapping of goblin feet and the rattle of goblin armor, and he couldn't hear a thing with the flora and fauna making this blasted racket.

Kang couldn't see the other members of his command group. He couldn't hear them, either, which pleased him but did not surprise him. Slith lay several paces to the right. The sivak draconian was Kang's second-in-command. Slith could have also worn the ranks of Best Friend, Adviser, and Confidant, if such ranks had existed among the First Dragonarmy Draconian Engineers. Granak, the newly promoted standard bearer, lay behind Kang. Granak was a giant sivak—huge even by draconian standards. He would be holding his sword in one hand and the precious standard in the other, the standard that bore the symbol of the First Engineers—a black field with a mailed fist holding crossed pick and hammer. Other draconian warriors lay close by, waiting, listening.

Late afternoon. The sun was starting to slide down the bowl of the sky, but it was still hot. Lizards basked in the hot sun, dozing, sleeping. Draconians are not lizards, although they have some resemblance to lizards—big seven-foot lizards that walk humanlike on two legs and wield sword and spear with more skill than most humans. Born of the eggs of the metallic dragons, which were perverted by evil magic long ago during the War of the Lance, draconians had been Queen Takhisis's shock troops, her best and most feared soldiers. The draconian armies had confidently believed that they were going to win the War of the Lance and it had come as quite a shock to them when they didn't.

Not only had they lost, but after the war, they had been abandoned by the Queen's commanders. Abandoned to be harried and hunted by the cursed Solamnic Knights, the thrice-cursed elves and the other so-called races of Light, with no help from those on the side of Darkness. Strong, powerful, gifted with the intelligence and magicks of their unwitting parents—gold, silver, bronze and brass dragons—the draconians had been viewed as a danger to all of mankind since there was no longer a use for them in the war.

Some draconian bands had turned to robbery and murder to make their way in the world. Kang had predicted what would happen to those who tried to live that sort of life and his predictions had proved true. They were slaughtered. If the war had taught Kang anything, it was that life was precious and fleeting. He had kept his command together and he led them into the Kharolis Mountains, far from civilization. He had hoped that the world would leave them alone.

After all, their race was doomed. They were dying out, and after them there would be no more. A race created by magic, brought forth from the stolen eggs of metallic dragons, draconians could not breed, they could not reproduce, due to the fact that there were no draconian females. Only males had been born from the dragon eggs, or so it was believed; the Dark Queen's commanders having reasoned that such powerful beings as draconians should be around only as long as they were needed. They could be easily removed when their usefulness had ended.

The world owes us this much, Kang thought. Just to be left alone . . .

"Sir!" came a hissing sound.

Kang's eyes blinked open. His body jerked with the alarmed, panicked feeling experienced by those who fall asleep and don't mean to.

"Sir," came Slith's smothered whisper and Kang thought that he heard a suspicious chuckle, "you were snoring!"

Furious at himself—Kang would have tongue-lashed and demoted the tail off any of his men caught snoozing in such a situation—Kang concentrated grimly on the task at hand. He could make excuses for himself. He couldn't recall the last night he'd had a really good sleep. But he would not have accepted such an excuse from any of his men, and he damn well wouldn't accept it from himself. To make matters worse, a fly landed on his snout. Kang twitched his snout, and the fly flew off. The blamed insect continued to buzz around him, however, adding its irritating sound to the cacophony of rustles, clicks, buzzes, and blurps.

Kang had been dreaming of their home in the mountains, the draconians' fortress home that had gone up in smoke. He had been dreaming of the pesky dwarves, who had been their neighbors—the draconians' bane at the beginning and, in the end, the draconians' blessing. The dwarves raided the draconians. The draconians raided the dwarves. Back and forth for years. Then came the Chaos War. The First Dragonarmy Engineers had marched out to offer their services to the Dark Knights of Takhisis. Their services had been accepted. They had been put to digging latrines. Angry and insulted, Kang and his engineers had left the army. They had returned to their home, only to find that in their absence, the dwarves had set fire to their dwellings.

But out of the ashes of that tragedy had risen a blessing. Through a series of odd circumstances that Kang, looking back on, now saw were the result of the guiding hand of his Dark Queen. The dwarves had led the draconians to a treasure worth more than all the jewels in the Dark Queen's navel. Only a few miles from where Kang and his men lay in the long grass, waiting to ambush the goblins that had been following them and harassing them and killing them for months now, was a group of twenty draconian females.

Over a year old, they were almost full-grown, as near as Kang could tell. They were not yet of breeding age and he had no idea how long it would be before they were. He seemed to recall hearing that female metallic dragons did not start to breed until they were over fifty years old. Kang hoped that female draconians would be somewhat quicker to develop, else there might not be any males left alive to do their part. But he knew full well that there were some things that could not be hurried. Meanwhile, the females were the salvation of his race, the future of his race. He kept them as he would have kept any valuable treasure—under close guard, confined to quarters, watched day and night.

It had all seemed so simple, in the beginning. Kang had decided that they would leave the Kharolis Mountains and travel north to found their own city. They had a map, given to them by a dwarf, that showed an abandoned dwarven stone city named Teyr just ready for the taking. Once inside Teyr, a city with walls and guard towers and gates, a city that could be defended, the draconians would be safe from attack. They would be free to breed and raise their children, free to set up shops and taverns, smithies and mills, free to live as every other race on Krynn lived—looking to the future.

The draconians had left the Kharolis Mountains and traveled across the Plains of Dust, covering the first hundred miles in just two weeks. Then, out of nowhere, came the goblins. Kang's small force was attacked by hordes of the accursed creatures. Descending out of the north, the goblins hit the draconians hard. For a month, Kang and his soldiers and the precious baby females were pinned down, holed up in a farmstead that they had fortified. They remained there until the food ran out and winter began setting in. They could leave or starve to death.

Breaking out of the siege, they had traveled no farther than twenty miles when winter weather forced the cold-susceptible draconians to seek shelter for the remainder of the season. The goblin attacks abated during that winter, but never ceased entirely. Goblins were always on hand to ambush draconian patrols, pick off draconian hunting parties. Spring dawned late in the south that year. Kang moved his force north ten miles at a time. They had little food, were forced to forage for extended periods just to find enough for them and their oxen, who hauled the now nearly empty supply wagons.

The First Draconian Engineers had been on the move for over a year now, but they had traveled only a few hundred miles in that time.

Other military units would have broken under the strain. Kang's draconians held together. Kang had sworn an oath to the rest of his command that he would keep the females alive and provide a safe home for their children. The rest of the regiment had sworn the same. To a draconian, they had kept that oath.

The regiment was now south of Kari-Khan by some fifty miles, or so his ancient map indicated, in the foothills of the Khur Mountains. Their destination was another hundred and fifty miles beyond that. Kang's current objective was to reach a road that led northeast and then east, exactly the direction that they were heading. Kang could move his forces along at an accelerated pace on the road and possibly even put some distance between him and the goblins.

The rolling foothills and plains of tall grass would give Kang his chance to halt the goblins, drive them back, allowing him to make dash for the road fifty miles north. The draconians had taken casualties in the fighting during the past year. For every draconian that had fallen, ten goblins had died, but still they hung on, like starving wolves to a bloody haunch. Kang had never known goblins to be so persistent, so dedicated to a cause.

Someone more feared than draconians must be behind the goblins. Someone holding a whip of flame. Kang just wished he knew who that someone was. He'd take that whip and shove it up . . .

Kang raised his head a fraction, sniffed the air. He shook his head ruefully. He needn't have bothered straining his ears. The smell of goblin—like rotting, maggot-covered meat—tickled his snout, much like the fly. The smell was close and coming closer.

Kang saw Slith lift his head cautiously, look toward his commander. Kang touched his nose. Slith nodded, pointed south, toward the tree line some fifty yards away.

Kang waited. An ambush works only when the prey is in the trap and not before. He forced himself to be patient when what he really wanted to do was to rise up, screaming, and launch his attack.

He began to count silently to himself. "One, two, three . . ." His hand gripped the shaft of his fighting axe. The wood was warm in the sun. His count continued. He wondered, idly, if it was true that gully dwarves could not count past two. "—one hundred ninety-nine, two hundred."

Kang hoisted himself out of the grass. He looked

across the glade. A hundred goblins had crossed out of the wood line and were no more than twenty-five yards distant. The other draconians of his command squad, hidden in the grass, stared up at Kang in glittering-eyed expectation, hands clutching their weapons, fangs bared, tails twitching.

Notoriously shortsighted, the squint-eyed goblins were slow to notice the seven-foot bozak draconian that had just risen in front of them. They kept marching. Then one of the goblins turned its piss-yellow face in Kang's direction. He saw its squinty eyes widen in terror, its mouth open.

"Regiment . . . charge!" Kang shouted.

Draconians sprang up like fast-growing weeds. Lethal weeds, as far as the goblins were concerned. To the right of Kang was First Squadron, numbering nearly seventy draconians. Second Squadron was to his left with sixty. Together, the two squadrons and Kang's command group charged the startled enemy.

Goblins fight with spears and scythe-like swords that are crudely made. The draconians had learned that an ugly, rusted, notched goblin blade could kill just as surely as the finely polished blade of the most spit-and-polished Solamnic. Goblins also use short bows to fire arrows as long as they can maintain range on their opponents. Goblin archery was not the most accurate in the world, but a volley of arrows that fills the air like wasps from a plundered hive is bound to hit something. Kang had lost over fifty draconians during their running battles with the goblins. He had not come to respect the goblins. He had come to actively hate them.

Kang ran ahead of his bodyguard, lunging to attack the still stunned goblins. One of the yellow-skinned, splayed-legged, slobbering-mouthed creatures jabbed at him with a spear. A blow from Kang's axe split the spear in two and a well-placed kick caved in the goblin's chest and sent him flying. Kang's axe caught a second goblin in the ribs. Blood gushed and the goblin crumpled like a wet sack.

Then Kang's draconians were all around him, slashing with sword and axe, battling with claws and fist, tail and feet. The clash of steel on steel, pierced by the screams of the dying, were sounds that Kang knew well. Though the racket was deafening and he couldn't have made himself heard if he'd wanted, these sounds didn't seem as loud to him as the incessant buzzing of the locusts had only moments earlier.

Kang saw Slith to his right only five yards away, fighting two opponents at once, but having no trouble with either of them. A single stroke of the blade decapitated both goblins simultaneously. Slith caught sight of his commander and grinned before carrying on with his attack. Kang was glad to see Slith resist the temptation to assume the image of those he had just killed, one of the magical powers with which sivaks are born. In some circumstances, changing from draconian into a goblin would have been an advantage, but not in a close hand-to-hand brawl. Too easy to get confused and find yourself battling for your life, all the while trying to convince one of your fellows that, Hey, I'm a draconian too, you dolt!

Kang dodged sideways to avoid a spear thrust. He swung his axe at his opponent but missed. Closing the gap with two hasty steps, he brought his axe down again. The goblin tried to block the swing with his spear, but the spear's haft split in two. The goblin jumped to the side and drew his sword.

Kang was about to sweep the goblin's head from its scrawny shoulders when his foot slipped in goblin brains leaking out of a cracked skull. He lost his balance.

The goblin, red eyes gleaming with the kill, leapt at

him. Granak strode in front of the fallen Kang. Granak held the Regiment's standard high in his left hand. In the right he brandished a longsword. He thrust the sword clean through the creature, held the goblin spitted on his sword for a moment, then, using his foot, pushed the body off his weapon.

Kang regained his feet and pivoted to face the next threat to find that none existed. The goblins were in full retreat. Kang's men brandished their weapons and yelled wildly.

Kang glared at them. "Less cheering and more fighting, men," he shouted. "After them! I don't want a single goblin left alive!"

The baaz and sivak draconians that made up the line engineer squadrons chased after the enemy, whooping and hollering and shouting out gleefully what terrors they were going to do to the goblins when they caught them.

Kang hobbled after them. He had never been a swift runner and he'd twisted his ankle when he slipped.

"Go!" he shouted to his bodyguard. "I'll catch up!"

His troops swept around him and soon passed him. He lumbered on and had just reached the first row of trees in the wood line when he heard what sounded like a vicious battle being waged in front of him. He could hear his men shouting, swords clanking. The sounds startled and worried him. The goblins had turned tail and run and he had expected them to keep on running until they ran off the face of Krynn. Those he didn't kill would think twice before they attacked the First Draconian Engineers again. That's what he'd expected. He didn't expect a fight.

An enormous figure stepped out from behind a tree and stood in front of Kang. The figure had the same yellowish skin as the goblin, but it was taller, wider, stronger. Its eyes were cunning and clever, not squinty and shortsighted. It was clad in heavy armor and it wielded a sword with skill.

Hobgoblin! That damn thing's a hobgoblin! was Kang's first amazed thought. The second was, There aren't any hobgoblins around here! This second thought was, unfortunately, quickly dispelled by the first thought.

The hobgoblin attacked, slashing with its sword. Kang swung with his axe. The hobgoblin deftly parried the blow and returned with a skilled slice that very nearly took off Kang's sword arm.

Shaken, Kang fell back a step to recover. The hobgoblin pressed the attack, swung again. Kang parried the blow with his axe, then whipped his tail around, caught his foe in the knee, sweeping his leg out from under him. The hobgoblin lost his balance and staggered back against a tree trunk. Kang smashed his axe through the hobgoblin's breastplate, drove the axe head into the creature's midriff. He didn't take time to see if his enemy died or not. He'd stopped the hob for the moment and that was all that counted. Kang had to find out what was going on.

His bodyguards were around him, extracting themselves from their own fights to return to protect him. Ahead in the trees, he could see fighting and hear the sounds of a much larger battle.

Slith came crashing out of the trees. The sivak was covered with goblin blood. He had a gash on his arm and one on his thigh.

"Sir!" Slith shouted. "It's an ambush!"

"I know it's an ambush, damn it," Kang thundered back. "We planned it to be an ambush—"

"We didn't plan this one, sir," Slith said grimly.

Kang finally realized what Slith was saying. The

draconians had meant to ambush the goblins. Instead, it happened the other way around. The goblins had ambushed the draconians.

"There must be five hundred hobs in those woods!" Slith said, panting, his lizard-tongue flicking. "And at least a thousand gobbos."

Kang swore roundly. His plan to hit the enemy and then steal a march on the goblin troops lay in bloody ruins at his feet. It had been a good plan, too, damn it. It was hard to let such a good plan go, but it was obvious to Kang that the plan had failed, and if he didn't do something quickly, the plan wouldn't be the only thing in ruined tatters.

Kang turned to his bodyguard, motioned to the nearest draconian, a bozak named Harvah'k.

"Go find Gloth," Kang ordered tersely, pointing ahead into the chaos. "He's in the fight somewhere. Tell him to take First Squadron and retreat with all speed back to Support Squadron. We'll fall back under their covering fire.

"Leshhak!" Kang called out to another draconian. "Find Yethik in command of the Second Squadron and tell him the same thing.

"Slith, run back to tell Fulkth to get Support Squadron in position at the bottom of the ridge to cover our withdrawal. He's got to buy us some time until we can reform ranks and get the hell out of here!"

Slith didn't say a word. He began to run. Kang watched the sivak flit through the forest, swift, silent, deadly. If anyone could get the word through, it would be Slith.

Kang turned to the rest of his command staff. "We're going to give the regiment a place they can fall back to. Granak, I want that standard held high so that the men can see it. You know the drill."

Ten minutes later, both Gloth's and Yethik's draconians began pulling back from the forest. They formed a battle line with the troops drawn up in proper alignment centered on Granak's standard, which he held high just as Kang had ordered, and began to fall back across the field of long grass, their faces to the enemy. Behind them was a high ridge. Fulkth and Support Squadron were posted at the top of the ridge, guarding the females and the supply wagon. Kang was already forming a new plan.

The goblins did not pursue them out into the grass, but stopped at the tree line. A few goblins fired arrows at the draconians, but otherwise they did not attack—a bad sign. Normally in a situation like this the undisciplined, rapacious goblins would have rushed headlong after their enemy, their thoughts on slaughter. Someone was holding them in check. The same someone who had planned that clever ambush. Someone smarter than goblins had coordinated that attack. The same someone who was maintaining the goblin army in disciplined order. The same someone who had brought in hobgoblins to strengthen his forces. There was someone new in command across the glade. Someone who stood between Kang and the road to his dream.

Kang had only one option, an option that he had never before now considered, an option that brought bitter bile flooding to his mouth.

Retreat.

Chapter Two

The rolling plains stretched from the wood line to the foothills. Beyond, the Khur Mountains thrust jagged teeth into the soft underbelly of the blue sky. Before reaching the foothills, the ground dipped to form a shallow valley, large enough and just barely deep enough to conceal the four ox-drawn supply wagons, the small group of female draconians and their protectors. The presence of the valley was the main reason that Kang had chosen this ground as suitable for ambushing the goblins. He had stationed the wagons, the females, and Support Squadron at the south end of the valley, far enough from the fighting to be safe and yet near enough should they be needed.

The twenty female draconians sat or laid in the long grass, doing nothing. The bozaks dozed in the hot sun. Four of the baaz played at mumble-the-peg, in which one draconian, using her teeth, pulled out a peg that the others had driven into the ground with blows from a knife. Sivak twin sisters quarreled over a rabbit pelt that one had and the other wanted. The quarrel between the two had been dragging on for months, so long that by now everyone had forgotten which sister was in the right. Almost nothing was left of the pelt, which had traded hands several times, one stealing it from the other. Fonrar looked forward to the day when the pelt disintegrated completely, except that she knew the sisters would just find something else to quarrel over.

Fearing that if she listened to them any longer she'd end up throttling both of them, Fonrar left the group and took a walk up the small rise that would carry her out of the valley to the level grasslands beyond.

"Just stretching my legs," she said to the draconian guard, who had been staring straight ahead. At sight of her, the guard had left off trying to see the battle and snapped into alert attention.

The female draconians were over a year old now and had attained their full growth. The casual observer would not be able to distinguish the males from the females at first or even second glance. Male and female draconians have dragon snouts and are covered in scales whose colors vary depending on the color of the unfortunate parents. Auraks have a golden sheen, sivaks are silver, bozaks bronze. The baaz have a brassy finish, and the kapaks are a rich copper. Most have wings, some larger, some smaller, with the exception of the auraks, who have no wings at all. Draconians have clawed feet and hands, long tails that are more like the tails of lizards than dragons. An astute observer might note that the female draconians are smaller in girth and height than their male counterparts, that their bone structure tends to be somewhat finer and lighter, that their wings and tails tend to be larger and longer.

There were other differences between the sexes, differences that were subtle, yet far more important. These had yet to be revealed to the world at large and to the draconians themselves. Males and females of races that had been on Krynn since time began had trouble understanding each other. Small wonder the draconian males were bemused and baffled by the female draconians.

Fonrar peered out at the battle. Although the long grass made it difficult to see exactly what was going on, what she could see alarmed her. A glance at the nervous guard confirmed her dismay. She shifted her gaze to Support Group and their leader, Fulkth. He too was staring grimly out across the plains, toward a large dark mass moving among the rippling grass.

"What are they doing?" Fonrar asked the guard, a baaz named Cresel. "I never saw our troops march backward before."

Cresel twitched, his scales clicked. His eyes flicked toward her and then flicked away again. His tongue slid nervously out from between his teeth.

"The . . . uh . . . commander does that sometimes. Marches . . . er . . . backward. Good for . . . for discipline."

Fonrar's eyes narrowed. At that moment, a sivak soldier appeared, flying along just above the grass. Fonrar recognized Slith, Commander Kang's second. Slith ran straight to Fulkth, began speaking urgently to him. The subcommander was undoubtedly relaying commands, explaining the situation. Fulkth, leader of Support Squadron, listened intently and nodded once.

Fonrar took a step toward them. She didn't get far.

"Uh, miss," said Cresel, moving to block her way with his body, "you shouldn't be here, miss. The commander wouldn't like it. You best go back with the rest of the girls."

Moving with every appearance of meek obedience, Fonrar turned and, using her own wings, glided back over to where the "girls" lazed or dozed near the supply wagons. The females did not wear armor—they were never permitted anywhere near a battle.

As she came to a landing near the supply wagon, Fonrar cast an envious glance at the oxen, who were munching on the long grass. They, at least, had something to eat. Her empty stomach grumbled so much it seemed to have developed language skills. She knew very well that the females had been given the majority of what rations the draconians had left. She could only imagine how hungry the males must be.

And it didn't look as if they were going to be feasting on goblin this night, as the commander had promised.

Fonrar walked to stand in the center of the small group of females.

"Troops," said Fonrar, "something's up."

Thesik, the only aurak in the group and Fonrar's best friend, lifted her head with her jerk. She punched the slumbering bozak beside her, who woke immediately. The game of mumble-the-peg ended. The quarrel over the rabbit pelt was forgotten. Within seconds, all the females were awake and alert, intent upon Fonrar, a bozak, who had become the unofficial leader among them.

"Something went wrong," she said, lowering her voice, although she did not think they would be overheard. Their guards were clearly preoccupied with whatever was happening on the other side of the ridgeline. "The ambush failed. Our men are in retreat. We need to learn more about what is going on." She looked at one of the twin sivaks, the sisters who'd been quarreling over the pelt. "Shanra, you know what to do."

"Why does Shanra get to go all the time?" her twin,

Hanra, grumbled.

"You went last time," Fonrar said.

"No, I did not. It was Shanra last time. You always pick her. You like her best—"

Fonrar was in no mood for whining sivaks. She fixed Hanra with a piercing gaze and the sivak mumbled and fell silent.

Shanra entered one of the three large tents given over to the use of the females. Her sister, still grousing, accompanied her. Inside the tent the argument picked up again.

"Ouch! That's too tight! You're pinching me!" and "Quick wriggling! I can't buckle it if you're squirming around like a toad!"

Fonrar would have put a stop to the argument if she thought the two were wasting time because of it. Knowing that this was the way they worked best, she kept silent, maintained patience. Within a few moments, Shanra emerged, her silvery scales covered by a breastplate, her head and face concealed by a helm. The females learned early on that the male draconians, in an effort to protect the young females from the harsh realities of life, would often lie to them. The females had resorted to spying upon the males in order to learn the truth. After sending in various sorties, Fonrar had discovered that using sivaks as infiltrators into the ranks of the males provided the best results. The female sivaks, it appeared, possessed an uncanny ability to blend with their surroundings. In a crowd of males, the sivaks were taken to be just another one of the guys. In a stand of fir trees, the sivaks could be mistaken for just another tree, so long as they didn't move.

Accoutered in armor, even to the point of carrying a sword in a belt on her hip (the sword blade was broken, but she kept it in the sheath), Shanra could easily be mistaken for a male draconian.

Fonrar glanced over her shoulder. Their male guards were craning their heads, trying to follow the battle.

Keeping one eye on the guards, Fonrar looked Shanra over critically. "Good. Even I couldn't tell the difference. Get going. The moment you find out something, hurry back!"

"I make a much better male," Hanra said, pouting.

Fonrar pretended she didn't hear.

Shanra grinned with pleasure at her commander's praise. Saluting in an imitation of the males, she departed, heading for the ridgeline. Head up, wings folded, she walked with speed and confidence as Fonrar had taught her.

"Look like you're supposed to be where you are and no one will give you a second glance," Fonrar had instructed.

Fonrar could hear Fulkth shouting orders. He was deploying his archers along the top of the ridgeline. The one hitch was that if any of the guards decided that now was the time for a head count, they'd come up one sivak female short. Never mind goblins then. A missing female would send the camp into an uproar. Fonrar was fairly confident that the guards wouldn't be doing much counting now. Still, just in case . . .

"You know what to do, girls," Fonrar said briskly. "Into the tents. When one of you has been counted once, dash out the back of your tent and into Hanra's and Shanra's."

That way, the males would always come up with twenty females.

* * * * *

Shanra walked boldly and confidently among the male draconians, who were dashing about in orderly chaos, some running to fetch their weapons, others racing to form ranks. Archers were already there, arrows nocked, waiting for the enemy to come within range. Their supply of steel arrowheads and shafts was running low. On the run from the goblins, they hadn't had time to forge more arrowheads or cut more shafts. They had been hoping to pick up arrows from their enemy on this raid, but that hope appeared now to be a forlorn one—unless they yanked them out of the dead.

"Make every shot count, men," shouted the sub-commander.

The archers nodded grimly. They did not need to be told.

Shanra's objective was Squadron Leader Fulkth. He was standing in the middle of a knot of officers, issuing rapid-fire orders. She intended to join them, to hear what they were saying, when suddenly the meeting came to an end. The officers departed, hastening to carry out their commands. Fulkth remained, talking to a single draconian—Slith.

Shanra halted in alarm. She had not seen Slith standing there. Her view of him had been blocked by the wings of some of the bozaks. She turned quickly sideways, using her own wings to conceal her face. If Slith looked at her too closely, she feared he would recognize a fellow sivak. Slith talked as if he were about to depart, so Shanra lingered, keeping her head down, pretending to be adjusting one of the leather straps on her armor.

"I've got to go back to my command," Slith was saying. "Get your men moving!"

"Wait a moment." Fulkth detained him. "You can tell me the truth, Slith. It's really bad this time, isn't it?"

Slith's expression was tense. "There must be a thousand goblins in those woods. Not to mention hobgoblins. Maybe a thousand of them, too. We didn't hang around to count 'em." His tail lashed moodily. "It was as neat and slick an ambush as I've ever seen. Had to be, you know, for the commander to tumble into it."

"A thousand gobbos," Fulkth was counting. "And a thousand hobs. We're each of us good for three, maybe four, gobbos, but, after that—" He shook his head.

"After that comes the hobs," said Slith practically. "And they're hard to kill, those bastards. They just don't know how to die."

"But the commander has a new plan," said Fulkth.

"Of course, the commander has a plan," Slith returned.

"And he'll get us out of this," Fulkth said.

Slith didn't respond to that. Lifting his wings, he caught a breeze and used it to carry him across the grass.

"A thousand goblins!" Shanra repeated softly, horrified. "And maybe that many hobgoblins."

All her brief life, they had been running from goblins, or so it seemed to Shanra. She was terrified of them, especially because the exasperated males, in an attempt to control twenty, playful female children, had often used the threat of goblins to scare their young charges into behaving. "Don't wander off into the woods, little girl. The gobbos'll get you for sure!" "What are you doing up this time of night? You want the gobbos to get you?"

She'd actually seen a goblin once, close enough to smell its hairy, yellow flesh and see its gobbling mouth with its rotted, yellow teeth. Goblins had raided their camp one night when the females were about six months old. She and Hanra had been on

21

their way to the latrine when the goblins had come crashing out of the woods. Slith himself had rescued the two females, grabbing them up—one under each arm—and dashing away with them while the male draconians rushed to the attack. Shanra still had nightmares about goblins and now there were a thousand heading this way.

She drew in a choked breath. At the odd sound, Fulkth glanced around, saw her. Fulkth squinted, eyes narrowing as if trying to place this draconian. Shanra, remembering Fonrar's training, looked as confident on the outside as was possible with her insides quaking.

"Yes, soldier? What do you want?" Fulkth demanded. "Make it quick."

"Waiting for orders, sir," Shanra said, giving a salute. She'd practiced for weeks to achieve just the right snap to her wrist. "What's to be done with the females?"

"They're to accompany the supply wagons to the north end of the valley," Fulkth replied, pointing. "Commander Kang wants them on the opposite side of that ridgeline. The commander's retreating across the valley to make our stand there. Make sure the females keep together. Don't let any of them wander off. And don't alarm them. Tell them it's a drill."

"Yes, sir," Shanra said, saluting again.

Someone began shouting for the squadron leader. Fulkth turned away and Shanra thankfully escaped back into the confusion.

* * * * *

"What's that fellow's name? Fulkth asked one of his soldiers.

"What fellow?" The draconian glanced around.

Fulkth turned, looked, but couldn't find him. "I keep

seeing this sivak trooper around camp and I can never think of his name."

"We've only been together thirty-eight years," said the soldier wryly. "You'd think you'd know our names, by now."

"You'd think so," Fulkth said to himself. He was about to leave when he was stopped by a voice. "Sir, what are your orders regarding the females?"

Fulkth whirled, scowling. "You have my orders, soldier! How many times do I have to give them?"

"Sir?" Cresel stared at him.

"Subcommander Fulkth!" shouted another soldier. "Support Squadron is in position! Whenever you're ready, sir!"

"Fine! I'll be right there! Look, Cresel, I gave the orders regarding the females to the sivak!" Fulkth said impatiently.

"Sivak?" Cresel repeated, puzzled. "Which one, sir?"

"You know," Fulkth cried, dashing off to take his place in the front of his squadron, prepare to lead them into battle. "What's-his-name."

Support Squadron, giving a defiant shout, marched out of the valley to provide covering fire for their retreating comrades. Cresel, baffled, returned to his charges.

* * * * *

Whoever that unknown goblin commander was, Kang hoped that the draconians' sudden retreat had caught the bastard off guard. He and his men had stumbled into an ambush, but they hadn't stayed around long enough to let the net settle over them. Faced with a reversal of fortune, Kang had halted his advance, pulled out of the woods at a run, heading

23

back across the plains toward the valley where he had left Fulkth's Support Squadron. Always mindful that even the best plan rarely survives contact with the enemy, Kang had deliberately held Support Squadron out of the fight to use as a reserve unit for just such a dire occasion.

Once out of range of goblin arrows, with no signs of pursuit, the draconian regiment turned and sprinted across the plains. Having been on short rations for weeks, the draconians couldn't keep up the demanding pace for long, and, at Kang's order, they slowed to a fast jog, their pounding feet keeping the cadence. They saved their breath for breathing. They had cleared the first of several small hills when they heard braying horns, coming from the woods they had just left. The goblins were advancing.

Kang looked ahead to the small valley where Fulkth had chosen to conceal his command. Perhaps only fifteen minutes had passed since Kang had sent Slith off with Fulkth's orders, but already the sixty draconians were in ranks, twenty with longbows.

"Well done, Slith!" Kang said, when his second returned.

Slith glanced back at the advancing goblins. "There sure are a lot of 'em."

"There sure are," Kang agreed.

"Orders, sir?"

Kang pointed. "Move your command to the north side of the valley and hold there. You're fighting a delaying action, nothing more. When you're hard pressed, pull back. By that time we'll be in position to cover you."

"Do you know where we're going, sir?" Slith asked. "Is there some defensible position ahead—a cave or something where we can hole up?"

"I wish I could tell you, Slith," Kang said and hoped he didn't sound as defeated as he felt. He shook his head. "I thought we were advancing, so I sent the scouts to search out the terrain *ahead* of us. Not behind."

"Something'll turn up, sir. It always has," said Slith and, giving his commander a reassuring grin, the sivak dashed off, shouting orders to his command.

"It always has," Kang said glumly to himself. "But, by the law of averages, there's bound to be a time it doesn't."

Support Squadron marched past, the draconian warriors fresh, rested, and ready for battle. Kang and his men had a breathing space. Support Squadron would hit the goblins hard, hopefully hard enough to drive them back in disorder. He called a halt to let his men rest.

Throughout his military career, Kang had been an engineer. Engineers fought when they had to, but they were meant to support the infantry. The infantry fought and the engineers provided fighting support. That's how it was supposed to work. Having someone else do the majority of the fighting was a luxury that Kang had not known for many, many years, however.

Wearily, he lifted his head, looked to the objective. A mile beyond them the ridgeline rose to form a barrier to the north. Kang summoned his standard barrier and pointed out the feature to Granak.

"We'll make our defense at the base of the ridge. When the enemy hits us, we'll fall back, moving steadily uphill. We'll have the advantage of height. We'll be able to fire down on top of them, while they'll be forced to fight an up-hill battle. Granak, take two men and go to the top of the ridge. That will be our objective. Plant your standard at the top, and light a fire with lots of smoke. Fulkth and Slith will use that to guide them when they pull back."

Granak nodded, saluted and sprinted ahead. Kang sent Harvah'k and another of his bodyguards with him.

Kang looked over his troops. The draconians were exhausted. They stood in ranks, leaning on their spears, panting, their tongues lolling. Between the two squadrons, they had lost eighteen draconians either dead or missing. Twenty-two more were wounded, but they could still fight. They all looked at him, wondering what he would do. Kang thought he might say a few reassuring words, then decided against it. The men knew the situation was bad, the worst they'd ever faced. He'd never lied to them before and he didn't intend to start now. He looked back, anxiously, at the ridgeline.

Fifteen minutes passed with no sign of movement, then he saw the four supply wagons from Support Squadron lumbering across the glade a half-mile away from him. Behind them came the group of twenty female draconians, marching in parade step as he had taught them. Watching, he realized the oxen would have trouble dragging the wagons up the steep incline.

"Gloth, send a troop to help them out. I want the wagons and the females moved to the top of that ridge."

Gloth nodded and saluted. He motioned for Celdak, one of his junior officers, to take his command. The bozak took his twenty draconians and headed off to aid the wagons.

A loud explosion echoed across the glade, followed closely by another. Kang looked to the north end of the valley to see two pillars of black smoke rising into the air.

Yethik grinned. "Slith's using some of his keg bombs on the gobbos. That'll slow them down."

"Slow 'em down," Kang said dispiritedly. "That's about all it will do."

26

Yethik looked at his commander in concern. "Sir, are you all right?"

Kang shook his head, turned away. He couldn't let the men see him this way—despairing, defeated. He had to be the strong leader they could rely on. Rely on to do what? Die nobly? He was helpless to do anything else. He couldn't even pray to his god. Takhisis had forsaken him, forsaken the whole of Ansalon. But before she had departed, she had given the draconians a great gift. She had given them the females, the future of their race. She had entrusted Kang with this precious gift, and all he had to do with it was keep the female draconians alive.

Kang knew as well as if he'd been flying on the back of a dragon and could see the whole terrain spread out beneath him that the scouts would find no defensible position. They would fight and fall back, fight and fall back, and keep fighting and keep falling back until there was no place left to fall back to and there was no one left alive to fight.

Kang heard shouts and yells and a great clash of steel against steel. Support Squadron had hit the goblin's front lines like a battering ram. With Slith harrying their ranks from the north, flanking them, and Fulkth bashing heads in the front, the goblin charge was halted. But the cessation was only momentary. Wave after yellow wave of the creatures pounded against the wall of draconian soldiers, like a stinking, obnoxious sea. Support Squadron's advance ground to a halt.

Kang looked back over his shoulder. A bonfire blazed. Smoke rose from the top of the ridge. The draconian standard fluttered bravely in the wind. The wagons were crawling up the ridge, draconian soldiers pushing and shoving them from behind to give the thin and half-starved oxen what help they could.

A couple of the females hastened forward to help

with the wagons. Kang watched in concern. A wheel might slip. One of the heavy wagons might roll back on them. He was relieved to see Gloth come racing up, order the females back. This was work for grown-ups, not children. One of the females appeared to argue. Fonrar, he bet. It had to be her. She was the trouble-maker, the rebel. And, he had to admit, she was his favorite. Gloth would stand up to her, though. He had the fear of Kang's wrath in his heart if he didn't.

Fonrar marched back reluctantly to rejoin the females. Kang could tell by the set of her shoulders that she was furious and the sight raised his spirits. He didn't know why. Fonrar was certain to try some other wild and crazy scheme, just to get even. He loved her for it. He loved them all. They were his charges and, by the gods that were no more, he would find a way to save them.

Grabbing hold of the feeling, he locked it in his heart.

"You are what keep this regiment together," he said, berating himself. "You must always remember that. Keep the soldiers alive, and they will do the same for you."

The sun was disappearing behind the tall peaks of the Khur Mountains. The shadows of the mountains slid over the valley, bringing an early nightfall. Another explosion echoed across the foothills. Both Fulkth's and Slith's squadrons were in orderly retreat, marching back to the base of the ridgeline.

Kang turned to his men.

"This is it. We're going to fight our way to the top of this ridge, and if there are any of those slimy gobbos left by the time we get there, we'll charge them and clear them from the face of Ansalon. Are you with me?"

The men cheered. They were hungry, wounded, exhausted. The odds were against them, they were outnumbered five to one. They had no cover, no place to hide, no place to defend. But Kang led them and, so long as he had confidence in himself, they had confidence in Kang.

Chapter Three

"Drill, my ass!" Fonrar muttered, fuming. She stood on the top of the ridgeline, gazing down into the valley below. The draconian squadrons had met at the base of the ridge and were fighting a pitched battle with the goblins. "Does Commander Kang think we're stupid?"

Fonrar would have never spoken of the adored and revered commander in disparaging terms to anyone other than the females. Certainly to none of the males. But Thesik was Fonrar's best friend, and, as such, Thesik shared Fonrar's thoughts, hopes, dreams, and frustrations.

"No, he thinks we're still children," Thesik said. "That we have to be babied and protected. You can't blame him, really, I suppose."

"I can," said Fonrar. "I'm tired of having to sneak around to find out the truth about what's going on. I'm tired of having to steal bits and pieces of armor, of being ordered not to handle swords because we might cut ourselves! I—"

She paused, her tongue clicking against the roof of her mouth. Thesik caught hold of her friend's arm, squeezed it tight.

"Fon, do you see! The goblins are retreating!"

"That's what it looks like," said Fonrar, skeptical. "I wonder why? Maybe it's a feint."

"No, no!" Thesik was hopping from foot to foot in excitement. "Look, there they go. Run! You slimy bastards! Run!" she shouted, forgetting herself.

"Hush!" Fonrar warned, then groaned. "Now you've done it!"

Hearing Thesik shout, Gloth looked around. His eyes widened. Alarmed, he came dashing over.

"What are you two doing here in arrow range!" he scolded. "Standing in the firelight, no less!"

"We were not! We have more sense than that!" Fonrar retorted indignantly, but Gloth wasn't listening.

"Get back to the other side of the ridge." He waved his arms, driving them like sheep. "Get back! Hustle! Now, before the commander sees you! He'd have my hide! Cresel!" he bellowed down at the draconian guard. "Keep these females on this side of the ridge!"

"Sorry, sir," Cresel said, climbing up to retrieve the lost members of his flock. "It won't happen again."

"See that it doesn't," Gloth growled, glowering. "You're on report, draco. I'll be speaking to the commander about this."

Cresel marched Fonrar and Thesik down the opposite side of the ridge from where the battle was taking place. The females had not been allowed to pitch tents, since the army might be on the move at any moment. But they had been permitted to spread blankets on the rocky ground.

The female draconians stood huddled together in a group, not out of fear, but—Fonrar recognized—because they were deep in discussion. Eighteen pairs of bright eyes turned her direction, and she knew immediately that something was up. Two of the baaz began making oblique hand gestures, motioning for her to hurry.

Thesik hadn't noticed. She was talking to Cresel.

"I'm sorry we got you into trouble with the commander," Thesik was saying.

She had a soft spot for Cresel. All the females did. He'd been their guard ever since they were little and, unlike some of the other males, he was always extremely patient with them. They all remembered him allowing them to clamber up his back and ride on his broad shoulders, tweak his wings, play jump-over with his tail. Their esteem for him had grown when Thesik had overheard him say once that he felt more like their prison guard than their bodyguard. Now he looked dejected and cast down. Fonrar assumed his depression was due to the fact that he was going on report.

"I'll tell the commander it was our fault," Fonrar offered. "That you told us to stay but we disobeyed."

"It's all right," Cresel said with a smile that he was obviously having to work to produce. He glanced back up the ridge. "To tell you the truth, Fon, I wouldn't mind going on report. Not a bit. I'd welcome digging crap holes. I'd dig them for a year and never complain once. Do you understand?" He shifted his gaze, looked at them meaningfully.

"Yes," said Thesik quietly. "I understand."

Cresel took up his position between them and the ridge line. Fonrar and Thesik returned to their waiting, impatient sisters and cousins.

"Well, I don't understand!" Fonrar whispered. "Is Cresel saying he likes digging latrines?"

"No," said Thesik, "he means he wouldn't mind digging them because at least he'd be alive. You know Cresel. He's never lied to us. He's telling us the situation is bad, Fon. Very bad."

"But we saw the goblins retreat!" Fonrar protested.

"I know." Thesik said, sighing. "I don't get it."

"We may have to send Shanra off on another fact-finding mission," Fonrar said.

"Hanra," Thesik corrected. "It's her turn."

"Right," said Fonrar wearily. "I'd forgotten. Yes, troops," she said on reaching the knot of females. "What's up?"

"We saw flashes of light," reported Riel, the leader of the baaz females, the largest group among them. She pointed a clawed finger out into a boulder-strewn canyon that separated the ridge from the foothills. "Down there. Among all those rocks."

"What kind of light?" Fonrar asked. "Wizard-light? Torchlight? What?"

"Sunlight off steel," said a second baaz immediately. "You can't see it now," she added, noting Fonrar's intent gaze staring that direction. "When the shadows fell across the canyon, we couldn't see the light flashing anymore."

"That's why we figured it had to be sunlight reflecting off a breast plate or a helm or something," said a third. "If it was a torch, we could still see it."

"Any movement? Any goblin troops?"

The baaz all shook their heads. "No, nothing."

"What do you think, Fon?" Thesik asked. "Should we tell Cresel? It could be more goblins. Sneaking up behind us."

Fonrar turned the problem over in her mind. They

could tell Cresel. Cresel would tell Squadron Leader Gloth. Gloth would have to pass it up the line to some other officer. The males related stories of the time when they fought with the Dragonarmies back in the War of the Lance, back when the horror was bureaucracy, not the enemy. It was always the dreaded Staff Officer who was the evil incarnate in the story, not the White Knight of Solamnia. In fact, the story goes that the White Knight of Solamnia was easily handled with a well-placed pit trap, but it had taken two weeks of wrangling to get permission to dig the pit. Fonrar didn't have two weeks and, from the sounds of it, neither did any of them.

And that wasn't the worst case scenario. The worst would be for Gloth to tell Cresel to go back to his duties. He wasn't getting off report by listening to the wild tales of boojum in the night dreamed up by adolescent females. Fonrar knew Gloth would say that because she'd heard him say it before. He and the others. Even the honored and much respected Commander Kang, who seemed like a god to the girls, treated them as if they'd just been newly hatched and still had eggshell stuck to their bottoms.

"I'm not going to tell anyone," Fonrar decided. "What would I tell them? That we saw flashes. And that we can't see them now because it's dark. You know perfectly well they'd just pat us on the head and tell us to go back to playing mumble-the-peg and leave the grown-ups alone."

"So we don't do anything?" Thesik said, astonished. "That isn't like you, Fon."

"Oh, we're going to do something," Fonrar stated. "You and I are going to go see for ourselves."

Everyone started talking at once. Everyone wanted to go. Fonrar lifted her hand, jerked a thumb in the direction of their bodyguards. The females hushed instantly, everyone understanding. Fonrar began issuing orders.

"You bozaks stuff our bedrolls to make it look like we're safely asleep. You know the drill. We've done this before."

The last glimmers of the setting sun illuminated the ridge. In the afterglow of twilight, the guards would look down to see twenty slumbering figures, their wings wrapped around them for warmth. Only very close inspection would reveal two of those figures to be piles of rocks covered with blankets and Fonrar considered it unlikely that anyone would come to inspect them closely. For one, the males would never imagine that the females would take it into their heads to slip off in the night and, for two, the males were all far more concerned with what was happening on the opposite side of the ridge.

The females settled in for the night. Lying on their blankets, Fonrar and Thesik waited for the brilliant reds and golds in the sky to fade into pinks and grayish yellows. When those colors had faded to gray and then to blue-blackness, the shadows on the ridge were deep and dark. All that could be heard were the sounds of wings rustling as the females settled themselves. There came no sounds of battle, but Fonrar could feel the tenseness that pulled the air taut like a rope in a tug-of-war. Cresel and their other guards were nervous, restless. They paced the top of the ridge to see if they could see anything and conversed in low tones with other draconians. No fires were lit. Even the signal fire had now been doused. The stench of goblin fouled the air. They were out there somewhere. Perhaps circling around behind them.

Night drew her dark wings over the ridge. Fonrar

waited until her eyes had adjusted to the darkness, shifted over to night vision, then she motioned to Thesik. When Cresel made a trip up to the top of the ridgeline, the two rose from their blankets and crept out of the female encampment. They moved carefully over the rocky surface, taking every step cautiously, fearing that a scrape of a claw or the dislodging of a stone would betray them. Back in camp, two of Fonrar's bozak sisters would be quietly sliding rocks under the blankets, artfully forming the blankets around the rocks to look like two sleeping draconians.

Thesik was a good companion for a mission like this. Thesik was an aurak, the only aurak among them. More slender than Fonrar, Thesik was naturally graceful, naturally stealthy. Fonrar—larger-built, more muscular and bulky—was clumsier. She slipped and slid, scrabbled and blundered among the rocks. It seemed to her that she was making more noise than the goblin army and she expected any moment to hear Cresel shout and come racing after her. Thesik glided silently among the rocks, never placing her foot wrong, never disturbing so much as a bit of gravel.

The aurak was intelligent, the most intelligent of all the female draconians. She had been quick to catch the import of what Cresel was really trying to tell them, while the more practical and literal-minded Fonrar had thought only that the man liked to dig latrines. But, though smarter than Fonrar, Thesik was not a leader. She was quite content to allow Fonrar, the bozak, to take that role.

"You're good at making decisions, Fon," Thesik had told her friend. "You're good at taking on responsibility. When the two of us walk through a forest, you concentrate on the path. You look right straight down it to the end. You don't see anything else but the goal and how to reach it. Me—I get distracted by the trees and the birds, the plants and the animals. I want to see everything. I'd wander around lost in that forest forever, Fon, if you weren't along to help me find the way out."

"Yes," Fonrar had replied. "But someday a tree's going to fall down on top of me or something's going to jump at me from that forest and I'd never see until it was too late. You, on the other hand, would be watching for it."

Which is why, Fonrar said to herself, we make such a good team.

The two continued on their way down the ridge. No one heard them, no alarm was raised. The camp that they were now leaving far behind them was quiet. The stillness wasn't peaceful. It was tense, waiting, watching.

* * * * *

Night settled far more quickly over the side of the ridge opposite from where the females slumbered. The darkness brought a hush to Kang's command. The goblin's sudden withdrawal had taken them all by surprise. No one cheered or celebrated, however.

"They're not gone," was the word whispered through camp. "They're still out there. You can hear them."

They could not only hear the enemy rustling in the tall grass down below, hear the creak of leather and the clank of mail, they could smell him—the foul rotted-meat stench of goblin. But even with their night vision, the draconians couldn't get a sense of numbers or what the goblins were doing. All they knew was that the sounds weren't coming any closer.

Kang had taken the opportunity provided by the unexpected lull to move his troops to the top of the ridge.

The draconians crouched on their haunches, thankful for the respite. They drank water sparingly from waterskins that were running low, cleaned their weapons, made what repairs they could to armor and weapons that were in some cases past repairing. No one slept.

The waiting, the silence, the smell began to tell on their nerves.

"You want me to go and take a look, sir?" Slith asked. "See what the slime are up to?"

Kang shook his head. "No, they'll come to us. I'm certain of that. It's just a matter of time, and we've got all the time in the world. We're not going anywhere and they know it."

"So we just sit here and wait to die," Gloth muttered.

Slith poked the Squadron Leader in the ribs. "You're speaking to the commander," he said severely.

"No, I wasn't," Gloth returned, aggrieved. "I was speaking to myself. It was my own private thought. A fellow's got a right to his own private thoughts, doesn't he?" He looked uneasily at Kang.

"We are *not* going to die," Kang said, raising his voice, not only to halt the argument, but so that other soldiers could hear him. Morale was low, as low as he'd ever seen it, and he blamed himself. He should be inspiring confidence, not fomenting doubt. "We can win this fight! We know goblins, damn it. They used to be our allies before they turned on us, the filthy scum. Just now, we gave them a bloody nose."

Some of the men cheered raggedly. Kang was heartened.

"That's why they skulked off," he continued. "Their commanders are out there trying to whip some fighting spirit back into them. The next time they come, we'll give them a bloody nose *and* a good ass-kicking into the bargain. And while they're holding their behinds and crying for their mamas, we'll take off running and put a good ten to fifteen miles between us and them before they can find the nerve to chase after us. We'll find somewhere to hole up, hopefully better than that place we tried to defend last time."

The draconians laughed, as Kang had intended, and several, hooting, nudged Slith. They had taken refuge against the goblins inside an abandoned granary. The goblins had stormed the granary in the dead of night, hoping to catch the draconians off guard. Goblins bashed in the doors, swarmed through the cracks in the timber walls like rats. During the vicious melee that followed, Slith, aiming for a goblin, had accidentally sliced through a weight-bearing timber that was holding up the ceiling. Down came the roof of the granary. The walls collapsed.

The draconians, with their tough hides and heavy helms, managed to escape the wreckage with no worse hurts than a few scales missing, a broken wing or two and one severely mangled tail that had to be amputated. The females had not been injured at all, due to the fact that Kang had stashed them underneath a large pile of hay. The smash-up had killed a number of goblins, however. The shaken goblin commander, who more than half believed the draconians had endangered themselves simply to kill more goblins, had withdrawn. But although they had won the battle, the granary was no longer defensible and the draconians had been forced to move on.

Rising to his feet, Slith took a mock bow. The soldiers jeered and tossed rocks at him until he sat down. He squatted next to Kang.

"Good speech, sir," Slith said softly. "But you and I both know that these gobbos out there aren't acting like any gobbos we've ever fought before."

"You're right," said Kang worriedly. "I can't figure—"

"Excuse me, sir," said Gloth, apparently hoping to take his commander's mind off his own infraction by casting aspersion on another, "I've had to put Cresel on report. I think you should reprimand him, sir."

"Cresel?" Kang recognized the name of one of the females' bodyguard and was suddenly alarmed. "What's happened? Nothing wrong with the females, is there?"

"No, sir," said Gloth. "But no thanks to Cresel. I found two of the females, a bozak and that aurak, standing on top of this ridge, not far from where you are right now, sir, watching the battle. They were cheering and everything." He looked extremely disapproving.

Kang had no trouble guessing which two. "Fonrar and Thesik?"

"Yes, sir. Those two."

"Cheering, were they?" Kang couldn't help but smile.

If Fonrar had been a male, he would have marked her out as good officer material. A born leader, she was courageous, decisive, and, most important, exhibited common sense. As for Thesik, the aurak, Kang didn't know what to make of her. He'd been extremely disconcerted to discover that one of the eggs had produced an aurak draconian. The auraks came from the eggs of golden dragons and were extremely rare among the draconian species. Kang had known few male auraks in his time and he had disliked and distrusted those.

Auraks dislike taking orders. They have no use for anyone, including their own kind, and they tended to be loners, holding themselves aloof from other draconians whom they considered inferior. Ambitious, secretive, extremely powerful in magic, auraks had been known to slay their inferior brethren without compunction. Due to their dire magicks and ruthless natures,

auraks are feared and distrusted by all other draconians. They did not make good soldiers and were rarely
to be found in the armies of draconians.

Kang had watched Thesik closely to see if she
showed signs of developing a bent and twisted person-
ality like male auraks, but so far all he had seen in her
was an unfortunate tendency to daydream when she
should have been concentrating on her engineering
studies.

Kang had been concerned when he'd seen a friendship developing between Thesik and Fonrar, but now
he was grateful for it. He hoped such a friendship
would keep the more obnoxious qualities of an aurak
from coming to the surface, if indeed, such qualities
were even present in a female aurak.

"Sir," said Gloth, reprovingly, seeing his commander
smile, "the females were standing in the firelight! In
arrow range! And Cresel didn't even know they'd gone
missing!"

"Oh, um, yes," said Kang, banishing his smile.
"You're right, Gloth. We can't have the females near the
front lines. I'll speak to Cresel. A week of digging
latrines should make him more attentive to his duty."

"My thought exactly, sir," said Gloth, gratified.

He walked away, pleased, and Kang sighed deeply.
What a farce. Cresel on report. In a few hours, less perhaps, Cresel might be battling for his life against a thousand goblins, with all his other comrades dead or dying.
And what would become of the females then? As a last
resort, Kang decided, he might send them away, send
them north. But only as a last resort. They were in
unknown territory. The few scouts who had ventured
out to try to find a safe place to hole up had not
returned. They were past their time and Kang was
forced to conclude that they'd been captured or killed.

He couldn't believe that his dream, his hope, the promise of a new life, was going to end ignominiously on top of this ridge. He couldn't accept it. He and his men had come so far. They were so close to their destination—a city of their own, a city with thick walls and tall towers. In such a city, the draconians could stand against all the goblins in the world with a few Solamnic Knights thrown in for good measure! But that city might have been on the other side of the strange new moon for all the good it was going to do him. He was going to die out there in the long grass and unless he could find a way out for them, his Queen's gift was going to die with him.

"Don't give up, sir," said Slith. "Don't ever give up. If you do, you're finished before you start."

"Thank you, Slith," said Kang, recognizing his own words coming back to him. "You're right. If we do go out, we'll make it a fight that they'll sing about for generations to come."

"Only one problem with that, sir," said Slith, with a chuckle, "draconians can't sing!"

Kang slugged his second in the shoulder and immediately felt much better.

A good thing. From out of the long grass came a familiar thwacking sound—the sound of hundreds of arrows being nocked. This was it. The beginning of the next attack.

"Shields!" Kang yelled.

Each draconian raised a small buckler to protect his face. There was a buzzing like a thousand angry wasps and arrows came raining down all around them. The goblins' aim—poor at best—was hopeless in the dark.

"Steady, boys. They'll soon quit this nonsense. They'll be rushing in to try to carve us up like mutton in a minute!" Kang yelled. "They'll find we're sheep all right, sheep with fangs!"

The soldiers laughed, although the joke wasn't a very good one. Humor, even bad humor, calmed the men and reminded them that they weren't alone. They could all rely on each other, but most of all, they could rely on their commander.

Kang continued talking, letting them hear his voice. Now that the battle was coming, he shed his fear and his anxiety like a snake sheds an old skin. Draconians had been bred for fighting. This is what they did best.

"Tighten up your lines, there, First Squadron. We aren't in some damned cotillion! You're not choosing dance partners for my lady's first ball! Now close up those ranks!"

The soldiers knew the drill. They had lived and fought together for years. Kang had once kept a chronicle of the deeds of their regiment. He had been quite proud of the book and had carried it with him in his knapsack. The book had even saved his life, having taken a spear thrust meant for him. Although he had survived, the spear had effectively ended the life of the book. Looking at the mangled pages, Kang had decided it was all a waste of time. Their deeds would be remembered in story and song. Except that draconians couldn't sing.

Kang chuckled again appreciatively, but the laughter died as he watched rank after rank after rank of goblins rise up out of the long grass where they'd lain hidden. To make a bad situation worse, the goblins marched forward in disciplined unison, spears leveled, quick-stepping toward the draconian position.

"Not ordinary gobbos," Slith said with a curse. "No, sir. Not ordinary at all."

Slith was right. Normally the goblins would have charged in no order whatsoever, attempting to overwhelm them by numbers alone. Cowards by nature—undisciplined, slovenly cowards at that—goblins could be counted on to break and flee the moment they met fierce resistance. Not this time. The goblins were advancing in good order. They appeared to be disciplined and determined. Kang was shaken to the core.

Once again he wondered as he had wondered before, who was behind this? Who wanted them dead?

The draconians held their position, waited grimly for the lines to collide. The lead rank of goblins dashed forward, jabbing with their short spears. The draconians fought with hammer, axe and sword and the front line of goblins disintegrated into a bloody pulp. But more ranks were behind, all pushing forward. Here and there a draconian fell. On the left flank, a goblin arrow pierced a bozak's scaly hide. He died instantly and, as customary after death, the bozak's bones exploded. He took out ten goblins, but he also damaged his comrades, who had been unable to get out of the way.

Kang was fighting two of the vermin, when he saw a third aim a spear at him. He could not defend himself, but he trusted his bodyguards would deal with the gobbo and he was right. A blow of the baaz's sword splintered the goblin's spear and cut off his hand. Another goblin, jumping up from behind, thrust with his own spear, caught the baaz right below the breastplate. The spear found its mark, and slid into the draconian's vitals. The baaz died. The body turned to stone, trapping the goblin's spear in its body. Having dealt with his own opponents, Kang kicked the goblin in the teeth, fracturing its jaw and breaking its neck. He sliced yet another goblin to death with his axe in the same action. On the ground, the baaz's corpse turned to dust.

Fighting alongside Kang, Slith reached into a leather pouch he wore slung over his shoulder and brought out a slow-burning fuse that he had lit prior to the battle. The leather was well-oiled so that the fuse didn't set it ablaze. Inside another pouch, Slith carried what he called "keg bombs"—small barrels filled with the mash that remained behind after the distillation of a liquor known as "dragon's breath."

Slith had discovered that the distillation of corn produced a powerful liquor. He named it dragon's breath and he had been intrigued to find out quite by accident that the mash left behind by the distillation process would, under the right conditions, explode.

"Dragon's breath is wonderful stuff," Slith had observed to the commander. "Not only does it render you pleasantly comatose, but it will conveniently blow up your enemies for you, as well."

Slith inserted a length of fast-burning fuse into the keg and held the slow fuse to the fast fuse. Sparks flew. The fast-burning fuse sizzled. Slith began to count. On three, he heaved the keg into the mass of goblins who were threatening the command group. The keg bounced off a goblin's head, fell to the ground, and blew apart. At least thirty goblins went down. A huge hole opened in their ranks.

"Charge!" Kang yelled. Swinging his battle-axe above his head, he cleaved into the goblin's front rank, bashing and battering, hacking and hammering. He did not stop to see if he had killed or merely wounded his enemy. Draconians coming along behind him would finish the job he started.

His troops surged after him, yelling savagely. The goblin lines held for a moment, wavered, then broke. Shrieking in terror, the goblins turned and ran, those in front striking down their own comrades in their efforts to escape the doom sweeping down on them.

The draconians pushed to the bottom of the ridge. Eager for blood and to avenge their fallen comrades, the draconians were all set to pursue the goblins, killing as many as they could. Kang ordered the recall. Horns commanded the draconians to pull back. They obeyed, retreating up the ridgeline. The goblins vanished into the night, out of the draconians' line of sight.

Draconian soldiers slumped to the ground. There was no cheering, no laughing, no boasting of their exploits. A bad sign. They were worn out. Already weakened from lack of adequate food, they had been on the march for weeks, constantly harried and attacked. The battles this day—battles intended to drive the goblins away for good—had not succeeded. The fighting had taken a severe toll on Kang's forces, weakening the soldiers, slowly grinding them down, breaking their morale. And although they had killed and wounded a vast number of goblins, there always seemed to be more where those came from.

Kang found Slith slumped on the ground, head down, flanks heaving.

"You all right?" Kang asked, concerned.

"Yeah," Slith managed, sucking air. He peered into the darkness. "They'll clear out now, won't they, Commander? Hell," he added, frustrated, "we must have killed five hundred of the bastards! They won't stick around to take any more."

Kang let his axe fall from aching fingers and sank wearily to the ground.

"What do you think?" he asked

Slith didn't answer. He could hear—they both could hear—the rustling in the long grass.

Chapter Four

Fonrar and Thesik reached the canyon floor and began picking their way among the boulders that lay at the foot of the ridge. Behind them, on the other side of the ridge, they heard a voice raised in a bellowing shout.

". . . carve us up like mutton . . ."

The two could make out those words, but the rest were lost in laughter and cheering.

"That's the commander," said Fonrar, pausing to look back. She couldn't help but admire Kang to the point of worship. All the females felt the same about the bozak who had been a father to them when they were little and was now not only father but commanding officer. "He's making a joke."

She looked fearfully at Thesik. "You know what that means."

"They're in real danger," Thesik said.

The commander's jokes were legendary. Kang never cracked jokes except right before a battle. The soldiers claimed that they could judge a situation by the commander's jokes. If the jokes were good, so was the situation. If the jokes were bad, so was the situation. The mutton joke was one of the very worst.

"Next he'll be telling them that they're not going to my lady's ball," Thesik added, alarmed. "Do you think we should go back?"

"And do what?" Fonrar asked sharply. "Laugh at the commander's stupid jokes like the rest of those ninnies!"

"Fon, you shouldn't talk that way!" Thesik said, shocked. "He's . . . he's . . . the commander." In a world the gods had abandoned, she could think of no higher authority.

"I know," Fonrar said, half-ashamed and half-defiant. "It's just . . . I've been having these strange, hateful feelings. I can't understand myself. One minute I want him to put his arm around me, like he did when I was little and scared of the dark. Then the very next minute, he'll say or do something that makes me so mad I could take that scaly arm of his and twist it off."

Fonrar sighed deeply, shook her head. "I've begged and pleaded with Commander Kang to give us military training. I've asked him to at least teach us how to use weapons, teach us how to fight to defend ourselves. He won't even consider it. Engineering studies! That's what we get from him. All we know how to do is to build a floating pontoon bridge over some blasted creek! Do you see any creeks that need bridging around here? Do you?"

"You're right there," Thesik conceded. "If I have to bisect another lateral triangle or whatever it is you do to those wretched things, I'm going to puke."

The two stood in morose silence. They could hear the sounds of battle now, shouts, screams, the clash of metal. The sounds were as familiar to them as a nightly lullaby.

"So we've come this far," Thesik said at last. "Do we go back or go forward?"

"Forward," Fonrar said firmly. "We have to find out what those flashes were."

"And if they are goblins, what do we do?" Thesik demanded. "We can't fight them."

"No, but we can run," Fonrar said. "We'll do what the scouts do—we'll spot their location, count their numbers, and run back to tell the commander."

The sounds from the other side of the ridge grew louder. Goblins shrieking, horns blowing. Something exploded.

"We'd better hurry," Fonrar said.

* * * * *

With the rising of the full moon, the goblins no longer bothered to keep their movements secret or silent. Standing at the top of the ridge, Kang looked down on the goblin sea and saw it heave and surge with the approach of the coming storm. He could hear their officers giving commands, hear hundreds of goblin feet stomping to obey, the thump of their spear butts on the ground. His night vision let him see hundreds of slimy bodies glowing an incandescent red, as if they had all caught fire.

He wished fervently and desperately that they all would catch fire. In the old days, he would have said a prayer to his Queen to that effect, with some hope that she might be listening. In the old days, he would have been on his knees, requesting his magic spells of her, feeling her touch, hearing her voice—dark and tinged with smoke—as she granted his request. Those days were past and gone. He had not cast a magic spell since she had fled the field, retreated, left him. He had hated her for abandoning him then, but now he had no more hate left. He didn't even hate the goblins. He only felt very tired. Just so very tired.

Someone touched his arm. Slith was pointing.

"Look there. The hobs."

"I see them." Kang was riveted by the sight.

The smaller goblins were being shoved aside, in some cases trampled, by ranks of the larger, fiercer, bolder and better-trained hobgoblins advancing to the fore. The gobbos had done their part. They had weakened the enemy, worn him out. The hobs would lead the assault this time. They meant to finish the job.

Slith said, very quietly, "Sir, we're not going to live through this one."

Kang struggled against the truth, but he couldn't struggle long. The truth was out there, a thousand strong.

"I know," he said at last. He didn't mind dying so much. It was the death of his dream that tore his heart with grief. "I just wish I knew why!" he said softly, furiously. "I just wish I knew why someone was doing this to us!" He shook his head in bitter frustration and despair.

"Would that make the end easier?" Slith asked.

"I don't know," Kang returned angrily, angry at whoever was out there wanting to kill his troops, angry at himself for failing to save them. "It might."

"Sir," said Slith, "I think you'd better send Dremon on north with the females. It's their only hope. We're not going to hold against another concerted attack, but we could at least hold long enough to buy them some time to get away."

"There may be—probably are—goblins to our rear," Kang pointed out.

"Yes, sir," said Slith. "But the females are fast runners. They could outrun any goblin."

"They're splendid runners," Kang agreed, his anger slipping away from him at the thought. He'd held footraces for them, races that not only strengthened their limbs, but instilled in them a competitive spirit. Once he'd offered a fine rabbit pelt as a prize. One of the twin sivaks had won. He couldn't recall which.

"Sir," said Slith respectfully, but insistently. "It's not much of a chance, but it is a chance."

"Yes, all right," Kang said gruffly. He turned to Granak.

"Pay very close attention to these orders. You will follow them exactly. When the next attack comes, you will wait until the fighting begins, and then you will take Dremon, the security troop and the females and head north at your best possible speed. Don't stop for anything. If you're attacked, don't stop to fight, keep running. Your job is to get the females to a place of safety. Take the standard with you. It represents us."

"Sir, I won't—" Granak began, but at the sight of Kang's grim expression, Granak fell silent. He was a seasoned officer. He could see the hobgoblins advancing to take their places at the front of the line. Moving with deliberate slowness, he came to attention, raised his hand in a respectful salute. "I won't fail you, sir," he said. Glancing up at the battered standard, he added, "Or the regiment."

"I know you won't, Granak," Kang said. "Good luck."

"Good luck to you, sir," Granak said. He wanted to say something more, seemingly, but, after a moment's hesitation, he turned in silence and, bearing the standard, disappeared over the top of the ridgeline.

Kang awaited the final battle. He had done what he could. Now he had to make a fresh plan, one last plan. He had to figure a way for his forces to remain alive and fighting for as long as possible. Every five minutes they held off the enemy meant another mile for the females and their guards.

"Slith, how many of those keg bombs do you—"

"Sir!" Frantic shouts behind him. "Commander Kang! Sir!"

Certain that it was goblins attacking the rear, Kang whipped around.

Fulkth came dashing up over the ridge.

"Well? What is it?" Kang demanded.

"Two of the females are gone, sir!" Fulkth gasped.

Kang stared at him. "Gone? Gone where? How long?" He shifted his stern gaze to the shame-faced Cresel, who came running up behind his commander. "By the gods, Cresel!" swore Kang, forgetting that there weren't any, "I won't just have you digging latrines! I'll bury you in one! How did this happen? Didn't you take a head-count?"

"Yes, s-sir!" Cresel stammered. "At sundown, I counted twenty of them sleeping away as quiet as dead kender."

"Well?" Kang demanded.

At that moment, one of the females, one of the sivaks, Shanra, came running up.

"Sir," she began.

Kang didn't have time for childish nonsense. He waved her to silence.

"I asked you a question, Cresel."

"It seems that there were only eighteen, sir. Two of them turned out to be . . . piles of rocks with blankets draped over them."

"Sir!" said Shanra urgently. "If you'd only—"

"Who's missing, Cresel?" Kang asked, though he had already guessed the answer.

"Fonrar, sir. And Thesik. It seems that some of the baaz saw flashes of light down in the canyon. They thought it might be goblins and Fonrar and Thesik went to investigate."

Kang's heart sank. "Of course, it was goblins!" he said in frustration. "Why didn't they come tell one of the officers?"

"Because you never listen to us, sir!" Shanra shouted, glaring at him in exasperation.

"All right," said Kang. "I'm listening now."

Shanra's defiance ebbed a bit at his tragic expression.

"Fon and Thes should have come back before this," Shanra said, her voice quivering. "They weren't supposed to have been gone this long. Something must have happened. Don't you agree, Commander?"

Kang could have sat down on the ridge and wept. Tears were a luxury only the Soft-skins possessed, however.

"Get her out of here," he growled to Cresel, who obeyed with alacrity, grabbing hold of Shanra's arm and hustling her out of the way of the commander's wrath.

"Fulkth!"

"Sir!" Fulkth saluted.

"I've given Granak his orders. He knows what to do. You're going to take the females—the rest of the females," Kang added with a sigh, "and try to escape. Granak is in charge. You are to obey him as you would me."

Fulkth waited before answering. He waited for his commander to countermand that dire order, waited for Kang to reconsider, tell them that he'd been hasty, that they didn't need to take such drastic measures. Fulkth waited in vain. He could hear defeat in Kang's voice, see defeat in the commander's slumped shoulders and bowed head, see defeat in the ranks of hobgoblins assembling at the foot of the ridge.

"Go!" said Kang, glowering.

Fulkth shook his head, not disobeying, just disbelieving.

"Go, Fulkth," Kang repeated. He laid his hand on the draconian's shoulder.

Fulkth rested his own hand briefly on his commander's and then, forgetting to salute, he turned and dashed up the ridge.

Horns sounded out of the long grass.

"Here come the gobbos, sir," Slith warned.

Here comes the end, thought Kang.

* * * * *

Once down among the rocks, Fonrar discovered to her chagrin that the canyon was much wider than it had appeared from the top of the ridge. The surface of the canyon floor was not as smooth as it had looked either. The ground was marred by deep cracks and crevices, some of them so wide that the wingless aurak Thesik could not jump across and the two were forced to make long detours to find a way around. Jagged points of rock thrust up from the floor like miniature mountains. A veritable forest of boulders surrounded them. They could no longer hear the battle raging on the ridge.

"How far do you think we've come?" Fonrar asked, taking a moment to stop and catch her breath.

"About five miles," Thesik guessed.

Fonrar glanced around. Surrounded by mountains on all sides, she had long ago lost track of which ridge was their ridge. "I'm completely lost," she admitted.

"I'm not," Thesik replied. She pointed a clawed finger. "That's our army's location. Right there. To the left of that tall peak. You can see the moon rising just over it."

Fonrar regarded her friend in admiration, never doubting her. Thesik had proven her accuracy in direction-finding many times before now.

"How do you do that?"

Thesik shrugged modestly. "I don't know. Just something I'm born with, I guess. Like your wings." She glanced enviously at Fonrar.

"Maybe they'll grow," Fonrar said.

Thesik shook her head. "Cresel says they won't. He says auraks don't grow wings. He says that makes me special. I say it makes me a freak."

"Right now your sense of direction is of more use to us than my wings," Fonrar said wryly. She looked again over her shoulder.

"We should go back, Fon," Thesik urged. "They've probably discovered we're gone by now. We'll be in no end of trouble."

"I'm not going back until I've found out what those flashes were," Fonrar said with characteristic stubbornness. "As for being in trouble, we already know what's going to happen to us. We'll get a lecture from the commander and we'll be confined to quarters for a week. Staying out a little longer won't make that any worse."

The moon rose, a silver orb, shining bright enough to cause the boulders to cast dark shadows.

"Look at that," Thesik said softly, awed. "The mountain peaks look like the mane of a dragon. The horizon is an enormous dragon lying stretched out, basking in the moonlight. Do you see it, Fon?"

"No," said Fonrar shortly. "All I see are mountains. And what would a dragon be doing basking in moonlight anyway? The moon doesn't give any warmth. It— Wait! Look, Thes, look!" Fonrar grabbed hold of Thesik, dug her claws into Thesik's scales, turned her bodily around. "I saw a flash! There! Look!"

"What? Where? Ouch! You're pinching me!" Thesik shook off Fonrar's hand, peered ahead. "I don't see anything."

"It's gone now," said Fonrar, disappointed. "Wait. There! There! Did you see that?"

"I saw it!" Thesik was excited. "A definite flash!"

"It was moonlight reflecting off metal. I'm certain of it. The gobbos are out there, Thes. We've found them. We just need to get a little closer to make certain. You know what the commander says. 'Verify. Always verify.' "

The two crept forward, hunching among the shadows, fearful that moonlight glinting off their scales would reveal them to the enemy. Thesik glided along the broken, uneven ground as silently as a moonshadow. Fonrar tried her best to move silently, and succeeded fairly well until a large rock turned under her foot. She managed to maintain her balance, but not without considerable wing flapping, tail lashing and scrabbling. Alarmed, Thesik looked back at her companion.

"Are you all right?" she started to ask when another voice boomed out of the darkness.

"Halt! Who goes there? Stand and identify yourself!"

Fonrar grabbed Thesik, dragged her down behind a boulder. The two froze in place, not daring to breathe.

"I know you're out there," the voice said again.

"Do goblins speak draconian?" Fonrar whispered.

"Not that I know of," Thesik returned. "Goblins barely speak goblin."

"Whoever it is spoke in draconian." Fonrar paused,

then raised her voice. "*You* stand and you identify yourself!" she called out in a creditable imitation of Commander Kang.

"We can smell you, if we can't see you," was the answer. This second voice sounded very unimpressed. "And it's only because you don't stink like humans that we haven't spitted you already. You have five seconds to identify yourself or we'll be identifying your corpses."

"They do talk like draconians," Thesik said doubtfully.

"Yes, but they might just be speaking our language to fool us," Fonrar returned. "The commander says that some of the cursed Solamnics speak draco. Maybe that's who they are. Solamnic spies."

A sword rattled. They could hear metal sliding against metal and the sound of clawed feet scraping against rock.

"Advance on my order, men," the first voice said.

"Don't attack! I give up," Fonrar shouted. Lifting her hands in the air to indicate that she held no weapons, she jumped out from behind the boulder. "You keep hidden," she whispered hastily to Thesik. "If anything happens to me—"

"I will *not* keep hidden!" Thesik returned indignantly. "If anything bad happens it's going to happen to both of us."

Thesik reared up from behind the rock and, defiantly, before Fonrar could stop her, the aurak female stepped out into a patch of moonlight. Argent light sparkled on her golden shining scales. Her slender body was poised, her movements graceful. She held herself with dignity and without fear.

From out of the moonlit darkness came gasps, exclamations, in-drawn breaths and whispered blasphemies.

The voices no longer sounded threatening. They sounded awed, even afraid.

A large bozak rose up from out of the rocks not twenty feet away from them. At his signal, four more draconian soldiers materialized, moonlight flashing on their helms and the buckles on their sword belts.

The bozak advanced a pace, staring at Thesik. He suddenly sank down upon his knees.

"Great aurak!" he said, his voice and his wings quivering. "Forgive my threats. My rash words. I had no idea. I meant no disrespect. If I had known . . ." Bowing his head, he spread his arms wide. "Great aurak! Command me. Command my men. We are in your service."

Two other draconians dropped to their knees. Two fell flat on their bellies.

"Command us, great aurak!" they cried in unison.

"Now *this,*" said Fonrar exultantly, "is more like it!"

* * * * *

The ranks of hobgoblins marched forward. The hobs were fresh. They had taken no casualties. Their morale was high. They had probably just waken from a sound sleep after eating a good dinner. The draconians had not had a good night's sleep in months. They had not eaten properly in at least that long. They had fought three major engagements this day alone. Almost every one of them was wounded, some severely. They'd seen their comrades die beside them. They were outnumbered and had no where to run.

The hobgoblins marched forward chanting a battle song. The draconians stood grimly, gripping their weapons. They were dead-tired, the battle they faced was hopeless. Kang more than half expected to see his men lay down their weapons and die where they stood. He would not have blamed them.

And then one of the baaz raised his voice in a shout. The baaz had been wounded. One arm hung useless. He could no longer carry a shield. But he could still wield a sword.

"For the commander!" he yelled raggedly and he dashed forward to meet the oncoming hobgoblins.

"For the commander!" shouted the draconians and charged after him.

Kang's heart swelled with pride. No one would sing about this final moment, except maybe the victorious hobgoblins. But Kang would. In whatever afterlife awaited him, he would carry this moment, his pride in his men, with him.

Slith pounded on Kang's shoulder armor.

"Sir! Look there!" Slith pointed to a small knot of hobgoblin warriors who were larger and stood taller than the rest, wore chain armor criss-crossed with bright red sashes. In the center stood an enormous hobgoblin—the biggest hob Kang had ever seen. He wore a leather helmet decorated with elk horns and with the horns added on, he stood eight feet tall, at least.

"Their general." said Slith.

"Any keg bombs left?" Kang asked urgently.

"No, sir." Slith shook his head. "Sorry, sir."

"Never mind. We'll take him on hand-to-hand," Kang said, holding his battle-axe in one hand and drawing out his dirk with the other.

"Something to sing about, sir," Slith said with a lopsided grin.

"With my last breath," Kang returned. He glanced back at his command group. Only two warriors were left with him. Granak, the standard bearer, had vanished over the ridgeline. Kang took a single shining moment to imagine the females racing away to a safe haven they were sure to find. He imagined them keeping the standard a treasured artifact, imagined them telling their children of the First Dragonarmy Engineers who had proudly fought and proudly died beneath that standard. Holding that single shining moment in his mind, Kang lifted his hand, pointed at the huge horned hobgoblin. "That's our objective, men. Let's go!"

Kang battled his way into the first ranks of the hobgoblins. A spear sliced into his ribs. He swung his axe and decapitated the hob before he could attack again. Slith fought at his side, wielding sword and dirk with dispatch and efficiency. The ranks of hobs opened up before them. Kang's two bodyguards were bogged down in the battle. Kang lost track of them. He and Slith continued to push forward, their objective in sight.

The general saw them—Slith's shouted insults, spoken in excellent goblin, made certain of that. The hob general paid scant attention to the two attacking draconians. Continuing to guide the disposition of the battle, he left the annoying dracos to be dispatched by his bodyguard.

Kang faced off with one of the red-sashed hobgoblins. The hob was nearly as tall as Kang, and well-muscled. He swung a huge broadsword with ease, brought the blade slashing down on Kang. Kang deflected the sword with his battle-axe and sideswiped back. The hobgoblin lifted his leg to kick Kang in the stomach. Thrusting his dirk between his teeth, Kang used his free hand to grab the hob's leg and upend the warrior, sending him sprawling onto the blood-covered ground. Slith plunged his sword into the hobgoblin's chest.

"Duck!" Kang roared.

Slith crouched low, avoiding a vicious swing from the sword of the second bodyguard, a blow that was meant to separate Slith's head from his shoulders. Slith stabbed his dirk into the hob, burying the blade up to the hilt in the flabby stomach where it protruded from beneath the breastplate. The hob doubled over, went down with a grunt.

"You stinking Solamnic flunky!" Kang bellowed. "Look at me, you bastard hob!"

Now, at last, the hobgoblin general glanced around. Seeing his two bodyguards wallowing in their own gore, he scowled with irritation.

"Just a moment while I deal with pests," he told a messenger who stood waiting for orders.

Kang charged, wielding his axe. The general lifted a great two-handed broadsword to meet the draconian's furious onslaught. Kang's axe crashed down on the broadsword. He hoped to snap the weapon in two, but the hob's blade was a fine one and held true. The two closed, heaving and shoving, each hoping to force the other to break.

"Who hired you?" Kang demanded. "Who paid you to kill us? Answer me, you slimy gobbo turd!" he added, shifting into draconian in his frustration.

"No matter to you, lizard. You be dead," the general returned, sneering, showing his yellow, rotting fangs. "I tell you this. I almost sorry kill you skinks. You make me fortune while you alive." He shrugged and gave a great heave with his muscular arms. He easily pushed Kang backward. "But when you dead, I collect bounty. So is all right."

"Blast you to the Abyss!" Kang swore, leaping back to the attack. "I'd almost let you kill me just so I'd blow up in your ugly yellow face."

The general laughed and raised his broadsword. But

at that moment, another of the red-sashed bodyguards threw himself in front of his general. Kang was forced to fight the bodyguard.

"You coward hob!" Kang shouted, so angrily that spittle flew from his mouth. "Fight me, damn you!"

The hobgoblin general sneered. Turning his back, he resumed giving orders.

The hobgoblin bodyguard sliced the greave off Kang's right leg, took a hunk of flesh with it. The hob was an excellent swordsman and Kang was forced to give his full attention to battling the bodyguard.

Still more hobgoblins surged forward.

Kang defeated the bodyguard, cleaving its head in two, but two more loomed up behind that one. Kang was so tired he did not think he had the strength to lift his axe. Slith fought valiantly at Kang's side, but Slith was wearing out, too. He made a mistake that opened him up to his opponent. Only a desperate lunge on Kang's part saved his friend.

The two had no breath left to exchange words, but they managed to exchange glances.

This was good-bye.

Kang fought on, still hoping to reach the general, if only to die at his feet. He was dimly aware of a breathless hobgoblin messenger dashing up to make a report, a report that appeared to take the general by surprise. The hob listened and looked intently out to the west. He issued orders. A horn blast went off right in Kang's face, half deafened him.

"What the—" Kang began, but he was drowned out by horns that blared all around him.

Officers shouted commands. The hobgoblin general took to his heels. The rest of his staff ran alongside him, their feet pounding down the long grass. Kang stood panting, looking around him in dazed confusion.

Where before he had seen a thousand hobgoblin faces slavering for his blood, now all he could see were a few hundred hobgoblin backsides.

"What'd I miss?" Kang asked, bewildered. "We were losing, right?"

"Yes, sir," said Slith. "In a big way."

"Am I dead?" Kang demanded. "Is that it?"

Slith eyed him. "You don't look all that good, sir, but you're not dead."

"Then what the hell is going on?"

Slith stared out at the hobgoblin army. "It looks to me like they're running away, sir."

Kang shook his head and glanced behind him. The remnants of his army were scattered all over the field, most wounded, many dead. No answers to be found there.

"By the Dark Queen's grace!" Slith breathed. He touched Kang's arm. "Look, sir. Look there!"

A phalanx of draconians came charging across the plain. They hit the hobgoblin's flank like a lightning bolt flung from the heavens. The hobgoblins' retreat dissolved into a rout. The draconians lifted their voices in a fierce war cry and chased after them.

"That must be Fulkth's squadron," Slith growled, annoyed. "He was never one for obeying orders."

Kang stared until his eyes burned. He rubbed them, stared again. The vision didn't go away.

"It's not Fulkth," he said at last. "I don't know who that is, Slith. There aren't that many dracos in Fulkth's squadron. Hell, there aren't that many dracos in our whole damned regiment!"

Slith blinked. "You're right, sir. Where'd they come from then?"

In answer, Kang heard giggling behind him, giggling he recognized.

Slowly, as in a dragon's breath dream, he turned around.

Fonrar snapped to attention, raised her hand in a brisk salute. Beside her stood Thesik, also saluting, and behind her were the sivak sisters, Hanra and Shanra.

"We brought draconian soldiers, sir," Fonrar said proudly.

She cast a rebuking glance at Shanra, who had a most unfortunate tendency to giggle in tense situations.

"And I showed Fonrar where to find you," Shanra added.

"No, *I* showed Fonrar where to find them," Hanra said, glaring at her sister.

"Thesik and I thought you might be able to use the help, sir," Fonrar hurriedly intervened. "Not that we feared you might lose." She carefully did not look at Kang, who was battered and bloodied, gasping for breath and grasping at what was left of his sanity. "We brought these troops just to give you and the others a rest."

A kapak draconian officer strode out of the moonlit darkness and saluted Kang.

Dazedly, Kang returned the salute. There were no kapak draconians in the First Dragon Army Field Engineers. There hadn't been for over thirty years. The kapak was accoutered in splint armor like that worn by draconian heavy infantry. He wore the rank badges of a subcommander.

"I am Prokel, subcommander of the Ninth Infantry." The kapak eyed Kang. "Are you injured, sir?"

Kang was too dumb-founded to reply, his brain having apparently decided to go off to dance a cotillion. Seeing his commander momentarily incapacitated, Slith returned the kapak's salute.

"First Dragonarmy Engineers," Slith said, adding incredulously, "Where in the Abyss did you spring from?"

The kapak continued to look with concern at Kang. "We have a fortress about ten miles from here. We're the last remnants of the draconian race, or so we thought until these two valiant warriors"—he motioned toward Fonrar and Thesik—"intercepted one of our patrols. We were investigating your signal fire on the top of this ridge. We thought you might be Solamnic Knights." The kapak looked at the retreating enemy. "Instead we find draconians being attacked by hobgoblins."

"Commander Kang, sir!" came a shout.

The tall sivak Granak appeared, waving the standard proudly.

"Sorry to disobey orders, sir," Granak said. "But we ran into these draconians and I knew you'd want us to come back."

Fulkth was there, pounding Slith on the shoulder. More of the females arrived. Gathering around Fonrar and Thesik, they all began chattering at once.

Fonrar managed to extricate herself from the crowd, came over to Kang. "We hope you're not too angry with us, sir."

"We've already confined ourselves to quarters, sir," Thesik added meekly, "just to save you the trouble."

Kang looked out over the field. The goblins had disappeared into the night. For the first time in over thirty years, Kang saw more draconians than he could count. Draconian soldiers were everywhere, jogging past in company columns, picking up dead, dispatching wounded goblins, tending wounded draconians.

Looking back at Granak and the standard, Kang began to laugh. He fell to his knees, laughing, and then he pitched forward face-first into the long grass. As consciousness slipped away, he heard Fonrar cry out in a fear that was very sweet to him. He heard Shanra or Hanra—bless them both—still arguing. He heard the kapak officer shout for a litter-bearer. Last, before he sank into a blessed oblivion, Kang heard Slith.

"The commander's wounded, but not badly, sir. He's like the rest of us. He'll live. We'll all live," Slith stated triumphantly.

Chapter Five

Kang hurt all over. Goblins—giggling goblins—surrounded him, jabbing him with their spears, sending flashes of pain through his body. Kang fought the goblins, slicing off their giggling heads, but for every one he killed, six more sprouted in its place. Then horns began to blow and he looked around to see draconians charging straight into the giggling goblins. Kang was angry. He hadn't ordered a charge! He struggled to call the soldiers back, but the ship on which he was sailing was lurching wildly and every time he tried to stand up he toppled overboard and drowned in a yellow sea.

Kang woke with a gasp and start. Completely disoriented, he was afraid to move, afraid to even wiggle lest he fall off that blasted ship and tumble down into that yellow water again. He dared not even turn his head, but stared straight up above into blue sky. Blue sky that was floating. No, he was floating. He was lying on a bed and his bed was on a ship that was floating along on the air.

I'm dead, he thought. I'm dead and my soul is drifting through the ethers.

But if that was the case, why did his back ache abominably? Why was his shoulder stiff and immovable and why did his leg burn like it was on fire?

Kang was angry. A fellow should get some reward for being dead, if only that he didn't hurt anymore. This was intolerable. Kang was going to speak to someone about it. Someone in charge. He just had to find out who. Who was in command? Who was trying to kill him?

Kang sat up.

His sudden and unexpected movement caused his floating bed to tilt. All around him, draconian soldiers began shouting and cursing. He experienced a wild moment of intense confusion during which he had the feeling he was being juggled like a ball and then he was unceremoniously dumped onto the rock-hard ground.

Lifting himself on his elbows, Kang looked above him at an upended litter and at the four stricken baaz who had been carrying him. Kang closed his eyes, sighed in relief. He wasn't dead. His soul wasn't floating. He was being carried on a palanquin on the shoulders of four strong baaz, when his sudden movement upset the whole contraption and dumped him on the ground.

"Are you all right, sir?" one of the baaz gasped.

The four bearers bent over him. Two began attempting to raise him to his feet, while two argued that he shouldn't be moved. Other draconian soldiers crowded near, offering their own helpful advice.

Slith appeared out of nowhere. "Give him some room,

you men. I'll take care of the commander from here. *Move!*" he yelled.

The soldiers departed at once, running to catch up with the long column that was marching past. The litter bearers lingered, wanting to help, but Slith waved them on.

"How are you feeling, sir?" Slith asked, squatting down beside Kang. "Can you sit up?"

"Yes, I can bloody well sit up!" Kang snarled.

He didn't like anyone fussing over him. He not only intended to sit up, but to stand up as well. Unfortunately, he was forced to reconsider that notion when his head continued to float and his legs let him down completely.

"Don't take it too fast, sir," Slith advised. "You've been chewed up and spit out."

Kang's left shoulder was bandaged. Another bandage was wrapped around his thigh. He twisted his head to try to see why his back hurt.

"One of the slime got you from behind, sir," Slith said. "Just missed the spine."

Kang had never even felt that one. Squinting his eyes against the blazing sun, he watched the long column of draconians march past where he and Slith sat by the roadside. The head of the column snaked through a pass cut between two hills. Kang had never seen so many draconians, not since the War of the Lance. Where had they come from? How had so many survived for so long? He had been thinking he had dreamed them, but these draconians looked pretty darn real.

"You remember anything, sir?" Slith asked.

Kang nodded, as much to clear his head as to acknowledge Slith's question. "I remember the last onslaught of gobbos, and then the right flank charge.

I remember wanting to know who ordered that charge because I hadn't and there was going to be hell to pay."

"There was hell to pay." Slith grinned. "Hell for the gobbos. That was the Ninth Infantry that came in on the right flank. Eleven hundred of them. Five hundred more from the Third Infantry backed them up."

Kang watched the stranger draconians marching past. They wore leather jerkins embedded with studded armor plates and carried large swords and shields on their backs. Yes, they were draconian infantry, as he remembered them. But he hadn't seen draconian infantry for over thirty years. He thought back to the Chaos War, to the last army the engineers had joined. That army had been made up of humans, Dark Knights of Takhisis they called themselves. No draconians, other than his regiment.

"Where did they come from—Fonrar," Kang said suddenly, memory returning. "Fonrar brought them. She and Thesik. But how—"

"The females saw flashes of metal down in the canyon. Fonrar and Thesik went to investigate, sir."

"I remember now." Kang smiled grimly. "They didn't tell anyone because I don't listen to them." He rested his aching head in his hands. "I try, Slith. I really try!"

"Yes, sir." Slith was sympathetic. "It's tough being a father, sir. Or so I've heard." He cleared his throat. "The females saw flashes of light and went down into the canyon on the other side of the ridge. They ran into a draconian patrol, who had spotted our signal fire and gone out to investigate. The draconians almost attacked, but once they got a look at Thesik, they couldn't do enough for her."

"Why Thesik?" Kang was confused.

"She's an aurak, sir," Slith said. He waved a hand at

the passing draconians. "They're all scared to death of her. Or should I say *him.*" He winked.

"These other dracos don't know they're females?" Kang asked in a low voice.

"No, sir. I figured you'd be the one to decide if and when we passed on that bit of information. The other dracos noticed that the females were different—they aren't wearing armor, for instance, and they have their own separate unit. Wasn't much I could do about that. But I made up some mumbo jumbo about them being a special guard for the aurak. Fortunately," Slith continued, "our females aren't like the females of the Softskins. The anatomical differences are not that noticeable, if you take my meaning. But the differences are there and they'll be spotted soon enough. The females are shorter and"—he shrugged—"they smell funny."

"They do?" Kang was startled. "I never noticed that."

"We've been around them too much, I guess. But these boys picked it up right off. One of the baaz asked Fonrar about it."

"What'd she say?" Kang asked worriedly.

"She's got a good head on her shoulders. She said she smelled strange to him because she came from the south of Krynn, whereas he came from the north. Pretty lame, but the baaz bought it. If one draco noticed, though, others will, too. Others smarter than the baaz. I've ordered the females to keep to the rear, back with the supply wagons. And I've ordered them to stay away from the new dracos." Slith looked uncomfortable. "They wanted to know why. I think you should talk to them, sir. We've . . . uh . . . never really gone into . . . you know. Females and eggs and . . . uh . . . all that."

Kang frowned. "The females didn't say anything about *that*, did they?"

"Well, no, sir, but—"

"Then we will not mention it." Kang was stern. "Is that understood? They're just children, after all."

"Yes, sir." Slith looked back out at the column of marching draconians. His wings twitched, a sign that he disagreed with his commander but knew better than to argue.

"What do you know about these troops, Slith?" Kang asked in a conciliatory tone. "Where do they come from? I thought most of our people died when Neraka blew up."

"There were more survivors than we heard, apparently, sir." Slith was never one to stay angry long. "When the War of the Lance ended, those who had survived the Neraka disaster fled east to hide out in these mountains. A few joined the Dark Knights and fought during the Chaos War, but most thought better of it. These dracos are like us, sir. They've had their fill of human commanders, who either considered them disposable and assigned them to all the suicide missions or treated them worse than pack animals."

Yes, Kang could understand that. He and his engineers had signed on with a human army, proud to lend their skills and talents. They'd been ordered to dig crap holes.

As Slith was speaking, the command group came marching over the rise, near the end of the column. Ahead of the officers were three standard bearers, each carrying a different banner. The first was the banner of the Ninth Infantry, the second the banner of Third Infantry and the third was Kang's own banner, the First Engineers. When Granak saw Kang, he hoisted the Engineer banners high, higher than the banners of the other two regiments.

The sight of the three banners once more flying

together, his own highest among them, was exhilarating. Thinking how near they'd come to total annihilation, Kang struggled to regain his feet.

"Are you sure you can make it, sir?" Slith asked worriedly, assisting his commander, who was still wobbly and weak.

"I can make it," Kang said. If he died in the attempt, he would salute his flag.

The other draconian officers, seeing Kang conscious and standing upright, came over to meet him.

Prokel, the kapak subcommander of the Ninth Infantry, saluted, and then turned to introduce the other draconians with him.

"Sir, may I present the commander of the Ninth Infantry, Vertax, and Yakanoh, the commander of the Third Infantry."

Both draconians extended their hands, and Kang shook each hand in turn. He then introduced Slith, his subcommander.

"Do you feel up to marching with us, Kang?" Yakanoh asked.

Kang nodded. "I'd be honored, sir."

Technically, Kang held the same rank as Prokel, the subcommander of the Ninth Infantry. An infantry regimental commander outranked a specialist unit commander, however, due to the fact that an infantry regiment had, at full strength, fifteen hundred warriors. An engineer regiment, supply regiment or even a field artillery regiment had at most three hundred.

"We don't stand on ceremony here, Kang," Vertax said. "All senior officers call each other by name. We remain separate from the junior officers and from the ranks, of course. Still, after you've lived and fought together for forty years, the 'sir' part starts to get a little old."

There wasn't much Kang could say, so he kept silent as he took his place behind the standard. He and Slith were the only senior officers in their regiment and had been for nigh on thirty years. Kang's leg wound was stiffening, causing him to limp, but walking felt good, warmed his blood. Slith broke apart the poles that had formed the battle-field litter and fashioned one of them into a crude walking stick, which he handed to his commander. Kang noted that the other draconian officers politely slowed their pace to accommodate him.

"I don't want to slow you up," Kang said.

"It is an honor, Kang, to match our pace with so gallant a warrior," Prokel said gravely.

"We saw the numbers you were prepared to face," Vertax added.

"Better still,' said Yakanoh, grinning, "we saw the bodies of all those slimy gobbos you killed. A remarkable feat, considering how few of you there were."

"If it hadn't been for you, there would have been a lot fewer," Kang said fervently. "I have to thank you, both of you," he added, indicating the two Infantry regiment commanders, "for saving our hides. Another ten minutes, and you would have found two engineers, not two hundred."

Slith interrupted. "The number is one hundred sixty-seven, all ranks, sir."

Kang stared at Slith. "Lady of the Abyss!" He shook his head, the warmth gone out of the sunshine. The battle had cost the regiment a quarter of the men they had.

"We've all been wondering, sir," Vertax asked. "Why were the gobbos after you?"

"Damned if I know," Kang said.

"Did you raid one of their villages?"

"No, and even if we had, you know gobbos. They would have made a few sneak attacks, stabbed a few of us in the back, and then gone on their way satisfied. These gobbos were different. These bastards didn't know when to quit." Kang told his tale of his year-long running battle.

"Well, you obviously did something to make them mad," Yakanoh said, as he looked at Kang intently.

Kang paused to readjust the bandage on his leg, giving himself the opportunity to avoid meeting the eyes of his fellow officers. When he was finished, he exchanged covert glances with Slith, who very slightly shrugged.

Kang turned to Vertax. "My subcommander tells me that you and your two command groups have been living up here in the hills ever since Neraka?"

"Effectively, yes, although there are more than two regiments. We also have the Second and Fourteenth Infantry, the Third Artillery and Belkrad's Reconnaissance Squadron with us. They're almost at full strength. General Maranta commands the army."

Slith groaned. He looked stricken. "Not *the* General Maranta, sir! The aurak general?"

"Yes, of course," Vertax replied. "He was the only draconian ever to be promoted to the rank of General. Why, do you know him?"

Slith's scales clicked nervously. He ducked his head.

"You might say that, sir," he mumbled. He looked at Kang. "You remember, sir? The stockades . . . That little incident . . ."

Kang thought back. "The stockades . . . " Memory returned and he began to laugh. "Oh, *that* incident."

Slith groaned again and shook his head.

Vertax nudged Kang. "Go on, tell us!"

Kang grinned. "General Maranta was doing a tour

of Lord Ariakas's army in the field. Subcommander Slith had killed a beautiful elf maid earlier that day. He'd taken the pointy-eared floozy's form during the battle—you know how sivaks operate—and he was still in that form when General Maranta strolled into the Regimental rear area. The general sees a beautiful elf maid doing a little dance to entertain the troops. Maranta orders his bodyguard to bring 'the elf maid' to his tent for 'interrogation.' "

Prokel began to chuckle. "Let me guess. The general wanted to ensure that this elf maiden didn't have any concealed weapons on her lovely person, right?"

Slith's scales clicked loudly, sounding like a plague of swarming locusts. "Yes, that's about it," he said hurriedly.

"Well, not quite," Kang said with a wink. "Let's just say that General Maranta got quite a surprise during his search."

"Please, sirs." Slith's usual silver-green color had deepened to the shade of a pine forest in midwinter. "It wasn't funny! I spent two months in the stockade over that!"

"I'm sure the general will be very glad to make your acquaintance again, Mistress Pointy-ear," said Prokel. "Maybe ask you to do a little dance . . ."

Seeing that the jokes were only going to continue, and probably get worse, Slith said stiffly, "I think I should go check on the supply wagons and the wounded. With your permission, sir."

"Permission granted, you cute little elf wench, you," Kang said.

Slith saluted sullenly and, with an aggrieved expression, departed, his tail twitching in irritation.

"We're only a two hour march from our fortress," Vertax remarked, when the laughter had died down. "I think you'll be impressed, Kang, with what we've been able to do out here in the wilderness."

"I'm already impressed," Kang said. "I have to admit that I was extremely surprised to find more of our people alive after so many years. I was beginning to think we were all there were."

All one hundred and sixty-seven of us, he said to himself, and his cheerful mood evaporated. There had been over three hundred draconians in their home in the Kharolis Mountains, before they had headed north over a year ago. Kang fell silent, no longer joined in the laughter or the conversation. The others left him alone, figuring, perhaps, that his wounds pained him.

* * * * *

The column continued on at a march for another two hours. Climbing over a bluff, Kang looked down into the small valley. The other officers came to halt. They all turned, watching him expectantly, waiting to see his expression.

"That's our fortress," said Vertax, waving his hand proudly.

"It is?" Kang said. He was so astonished, he spoke before he thought. "What happened to it?"

"What did you say?" Vertax moved closer to hear over the clank and rattle of the column passing by. "I didn't catch what you said."

Kang came to the sudden realization that he was not looking on the site of a natural disaster. Or perhaps he was, but the disaster wasn't natural. Someone had worked at it.

"I said . . ." Kang gulped. "That's quite a fort, sir. Quite a fort."

Kang exchanged glances with Slith, who had returned

to report that the supply wagons, the wounded and the "special unit" were fine, just slow-moving. The sivak rolled his eyes and changed whatever he had been going to say into a cough.

The structure—Kang hated to dignify it with the term fortress—was a quarter-mile square. It was completely surrounded by a tall curtain wall made of wood. Every so often, at irregular intervals, some sort of odd-looking protrusion thrust up from the wall. Kang spent several moments trying to figure out what these protrusions were, eventually decided that they were meant to be watchtowers. Two tilted perilously and a third was actually propped up with poles or it would have tumbled down.

The curtain wall was broken—operative word—in two places by gates to the south and west. Made from timbers sharpened to a point at the top, the wall had evidently been built in sections of thirty feet in length and then assembled. The result was that no two sections were the same height, same construction or even the same design. He'd seen goblin teeth that were straighter, albeit in a similar state of decay.

In the center of the encampment stood one large building. That single large building was surrounded by a jumble of smaller buildings that had apparently been thrown up whenever and wherever, according to the whim of their makers. Dirt streets curled among them like a goblin's entrails. All the structures, with the exception of the massive building in the center, were constructed of wood with thatched roofs made of straw. A single spark would start a blaze that would make a red dragon proud. By the looks of one large charred and blackened area near the curtain wall, one structure had already gone up in flames.

The other officers were waiting for his reaction, waiting

for him to express wonder and admiration. Kang could manage the wonder. He wondered how this mess remained standing.

"What do you think?" asked Vertax.

"It's like nothing I've ever seen before," Kang said and that was the gods' honest truth.

Slith coughed again. "Sorry, sirs. Dust in my throat."

Vertax saw their carefully manufactured expressions and began to laugh.

"Don't worry, Kang. I know what you and your Second are thinking. You're thinking that our fortress looks like something built by drunken gnomes from plans drawn up by gully dwarves."

"Well, I do tend to view things from an engineer's perspective . . . " Kang began awkwardly.

"We know it's not pretty," Yakanoh said. "But the fort is stronger than it looks. And it's done right by us, saved our scaly hides on more than one occasion. There was that attack by those human mercenaries." He glanced at Vertax for affirmation. "We held them off for three days and nights before they gave up and went home."

Kang had to admit that now he *was* impressed. Astonished, but impressed.

"A word of warning, Kang," Vertax said, lowering his voice. "Don't criticize the fort to General Maranta. He thinks it's the Tower of the Suns and the legendary Halls of Thorbardin all rolled into one."

"The rest of us realize it's not perfect," Prokel admitted. "We can use you and your engineers to help us improve it and strengthen it. The only engineers we have are a dozen or so Pioneers. They're good at tearing down, not building up."

Each infantry regiment maintained a troop of Pioneers—soldiers with some engineering experience. Their job was to clear away obstacles from in front of advancing troops or create obstacles behind retreating troops. As the saying went, Pioneers either blew stuff up or made stuff fall down. They knew little about the construction or design of proper buildings.

"It's good to have you and your men, Kang," Prokel added. "You'll fit in well."

Kang didn't answer. He wouldn't mind helping them fix up their fort, offer advice and assistance, but just exactly how he was supposed to effect changes without the support of the general was beyond him. Kang faced another problem, too. He viewed this as a stopover, a way station, a place for his people to rest and heal before continuing on. He was not planning to remain in this ramshackle fort the rest of his life, as these draconians appeared to assume. He was still intending to reach his dream city, the city marked in red on his worn and tattered but very precious map.

Too many had given their lives for his dream. He was not going to let it die for the sake of convenience.

* * * * *

Flush with their victory over the hobgoblins, the draconian infantry marched proudly through the main gate on the south wall. Up close, the wall looked more solid than it had from a distance, but Kang gazed with admiration at the draconian guards walking the ramparts. They had more guts than he did.

"What's that laughing?" Kang demanded.

"The men, sir," said Slith. "Can't say I really blame them."

"Well, I can!" Kang was furious. "Go back and tell them to shut the hell up! These dracos may not be much in the way of engineers, but they saved our tails!"

Slith departed to return the First Dragonarmy

Engineers to a proper state of decorum. Under Kang's glaring eye, the draconian engineers marched past the tumble-down wall without so much as grin, although more than a few rubbed sore heads. Slith had been known to emphasize his orders with a few well-placed thwacks.

When Slith returned, Vertax motioned for them both to join him.

"Yakanoh and I will introduce you to General Maranta. Prokel will take your Second to find your troops some food and lodging. We'll make provisions for your wounded, as well."

At the word *food*, Kang's stomach rumbled. A trace of drool slid out of Slith's mouth.

"I'll take care of the special unit, sir," Slith said, as he marched off with Prokel.

Kang watched Slith leave with envy. He could have eaten a troll at one sitting and asked for seconds, but he knew the protocol. He would have to wait for his meal until after his meeting with the general.

Kang was about to follow Yakanoh and Vertax when he heard a cracking sound. He looked back to see a section of the wall give way. Frantic wing flapping was all that saved the baaz guard who had been standing on top of it from crashing down among the rubble.

"This beats the alternative," Kang reminded himself. "You'd be dead by now if it wasn't for this fortress."

His only hope now was that the fort didn't fall down on top of him.

* * * * *

"The troop's mess is over there," Prokel told Slith, pointing to a ramshackle building from which floated wonderful smells. "You can put your wounded under

81

that awning we've rigged. We used to have a field hospital, but it burned down about a month ago. As for the rest of your troops"—Prokel looked concerned—"we're short on space. But perhaps—"

"Don't concern yourself with us, sir," Slith interrupted. "We'll build our own shelter. We're used to doing that. What I need from you right now, sir, is a separate dwelling for the aurak and the special unit. We need one right away. Now, if possible."

Slith jerked a thumb at the group of female draconians, who had gathered near the supply wagons. Their guards, led by the disgraced Cresel—whose punishment had not been forgotten, merely deferred—kept the females under close observation.

So far, the females had been well behaved. As Slith had remarked to Kang, Fonrar had a good head on her shoulders. She knew that this was no time to go larking about. Still, Slith could guess that the females were intensely curious about this new place and these new draconians. They would be eager to explore—they were always eager to explore—and he could foresee trouble down the line if he didn't act swiftly to corral them.

"A separate dwelling?" Prokel was amazed. "I have to tell you, Slith, that only the general himself has a separate dwelling around here. As I said, we're limited on space. The rest of us share and share alike."

Slith was prepared for this. "It's that aurak, sir," he said, lowering his voice confidentially. "Difficult to get along with." He leaned in closer, lowered his voice another notch. "A couple of the boys . . . said the wrong thing . . . the aurak took it the wrong way. I'm not really supposed to discuss it, sir. Commander Kang's orders."

"I see." Prokel rubbed his chin with his hand. "But these other draconians who stay with the aurak . . ."

"Hand-picked, sir. They're the only one he gets on

with. The aurak likes his guards short," Slith added. "Can't abide a tall draconian."

Prokel, who was rather on the tall side, looked uneasy. "I have heard about auraks who have . . . well . . . a certain cold-blooded quality. General Maranta is an aurak, but he is perfectly normal. He's one of the very eldest draconians, came from the first clutch of eggs. Perhaps that explains it."

"Probably does, sir," said Slith.

"We do have a storage shed," Prokel said, considering. "It's got some ale barrels in it, but we could shift those—"

"It would only be temporary, sir," Slith hastened to assure him. "Until we can build a suitable shelter ourselves. And we'll take care of moving the barrels. Just tell me where to find it—"

"I can take you there myself," Prokel offered.

Slith shook his head. "You must be tired and hungry, sir. We can manage on our own."

"Very well," said Prokel, not particularly wanting to have anything more to do with the mysterious aurak. "You'll find the shed located at the end of that street. The street sort of twists and winds around itself, but keep following it and you'll come across it."

"Yes, sir. Thank you, sir. I'll send the troops in to eat now, sir, if that's convenient."

"Certainly. I'll go ahead and alert the cook. What about the special unit? Do they eat—"

"—with the others? No, sir." Slith was grave. "Not *anymore*, sir. If you know what I mean. I'll arrange for food to be brought to them, if that's all right, sir."

"Yes, quite all right." Prokel left with alacrity, obviously glad to be rid of the special unit.

Slith chuckled to himself, reflected with some pride that the tale of the bloodthirsty aurak engineer would circulate through the fort by nightfall and that it would undoubtedly grow in the telling. He trusted that for a time, at least, the females would be safe from the other draconian soldiers.

Now he just had to make certain the draconian soldiers were safe from the adventuresome females. A task that Slith freely admitted might be far more difficult.

Chapter Six

Vertax and Yakanoh led Kang to the large building
he'd seen from the ridge, the building located in the
very center of the fortress. The building was perfectly
square, standing about twenty feet in height. It had
been built of hand-hewn wood beams and large stones
gleaned from the rock-strewn canyon, all slathered
over and held together with mud that had hardened in
the hot sun until it was rock solid. The only windows
were narrow arrow slits and not many of these. The
double doors were of oak, massive, iron bound. Kang
was impressed. The rest of the fort might tumble
down—probably would tumble down—but this building would remain standing. Kang doubted if even a
direct hit from a second fiery mountain would take it
down.

"What is this place?" Kang asked, awed.

" 'The Bastion,' " said Vertax proudly. "General Maranta's quarters are inside."

The doors stood closed. Two sivaks, wearing black tabards emblazoned with the emblem of a five-headed dragon, stood guard. Sighting these, Kang's jaw dropped. He turned an amazed stare on Vertax.

"The Queen's Own?" Kang asked in a low voice.

Vertax nodded.

"I thought they were destroyed in the fall of Neraka!" Kang whispered, eyeing the guards.

The sivaks stood unmoving. Not so much as a wing flicked or a tail twitched.

"Come to think of it, though," Kang added, "I thought General Maranta died in Neraka."

"He never speaks of his escape," Vertax said, his own voice quiet. "And I would advise you not to do so either. He much prefers to talk of his victories, not his defeats."

"Can't fault him there," said Kang. "We were assigned to shore up the structure of a castle the Black Robes planned to use for a floating citadel or we would have been involved in that debacle ourselves. Would you believe it? The first few citadels the Black Robes tried to send up into the air, the blamed magic-users just yanked out of the ground. No regard at all for structural integrity. They were completely amazed when interior walls collapsed and bits of ceiling tumbled down on their silly heads. Wizards!" He shook his own head gloomily at the memory.

"At least," he added, "no one can blame the general for the Neraka disaster."

"True," said Vertax, his tone ironic. "Truer than you might imagine." He glanced at Kang from the corner of his eye.

Kang understood immediately, although it was

something he had never before considered. Maranta had been made a general in Lord Ariakas's army, but the title had been a hollow one. As a draconian, General Maranta had not been allowed to give orders to any human, not even the lowest private in the worst company of scraggly reserve foot soldiers. General Maranta had not been given a field command, he had not been trusted to lead armies. He'd been sent out on show, to keep the draconians content, thinking one of their own was a high ranking officer.

In reality, General Maranta had been assigned to meaningless duty, plotting strategies that were never used or ordering the dispositions of equipment and supplies that had already been ordered by some lower ranking human. As an aurak, a powerful magic-user, General Maranta had probably even been warned he was not to use his magic. General Maranta had knuckled under and had held his post throughout the war.

But perhaps General Maranta had not been the obedient, subservient draconian he had appeared. General Maranta had survived the fall of Neraka, whereas his commander, the proud and puissant Lord Ariakas, had perished. Kang felt suddenly proud of the cunning old aurak, who had been shrewd enough to foresee disaster and make his own plans accordingly, plans that not only saved himself, but many hundreds of his loyal troops. Kang would have given a great deal to know the true story of what had transpired at Neraka, doubted he ever would. There are some war stories that old soldiers keep locked in their hearts, never to tell.

The three officers approached the sivak guards. Kang had assumed that discipline might be good, but informal, considering that these draconians had slept, fought, eaten and worked together for over thirty years.

He was therefore considerably astonished to see both Vertax and Yakanoh pronounce name and rank and even give the password for the day. He was more astonished to see the sivak guards look them over suspiciously, intently.

Satisfied, one of the Queen's Own said, "You may enter. The general is expecting you." The sivak turned cold eyes upon Kang. "This is the officer of the engineering regiment?"

"Commander Kang, First Dragonarmy Engineers," Kang said, thinking it best to salute.

The sivaks looked him up and the sivaks looked him down, inside-out and sideways. Kang had never before undergone such intense scrutiny, even the one time he'd been briefly held prisoner by Solamnic Knights. He was starting to get a bit angry—they were all the same species for gods' sakes—when one of the Queen's Own gave a nod.

"You may enter, Commander Kang. However"—the sivak halted Kang as he started to walk toward the double doors—"I must ask you for your weapons, sir."

"What?" Kang was on the verge of blowing up like one of Slith's keg bombs.

Vertax laid a warning claw on his arm. "We all do it, Kang," he said quietly. "It's the general's custom. A hold-over from Neraka."

Recalling what he'd heard of the end of Neraka— draconians turning on draconians, killing each other— Kang reached behind his back and removed the battle-axe he wore on a harness between his wings. He'd worn the axe in that place for so long that, like his wings, it had become a part of him. He felt as if he'd lost a limb when he handed it over to the sivak guard. The Queen's Own knocked a certain way on the doors. Kang heard what sounded like a heavy bar being lifted.

The double doors swung open on well-oiled hinges and the officers entered.

Kang, glancing up, was astounded to see a crudely made, rickety and rusty portcullis hanging over the doorway. Kang cringed. If that portcullis was as poorly designed as the rest of the fort, he wouldn't have been one of those sivak guards standing beneath it for all the jewels in the Dark Queen's crown.

The doors shut behind them with a boom. Inside, the guards slid the massive solid oak bar back into place. No one and nothing was going to come inside that door if they didn't want it to, not without a struggle at least. The interior of the building was cool and dark, so dark that Kang had to wait for his eyes to adjust. No torches burned, no lamps were lit. When he had gained his night vision, he stared around him in astonishment.

He would later describe the interior to Slith.

"I'll swear, Slith, that they built the entire structure in one solid block of mud and stone and then they went inside and tunneled it out!"

"Sir," Slith said, moderately disapproving, "have you been dipping into the draco spirits again?"

"Even if I had, I couldn't have dreamed this one up," Kang retorted. "It's a maze. A goddamned honeycomb. Arched tunnels lead every which way, except the way you want to go seemingly. I would have never found the path that led to the center if it hadn't been for Vertax and Yakanoh. And the place is huge! I don't know how many rooms are inside it. No one knows. Vertax couldn't even tell me. The number changes. Sometimes rooms are blocked up for no reason and new ones opened. And you know who lives inside that massive building, Slith? Just General Maranta."

"Just him?" Slith was surprised.

"Just him," Kang said. "The Queen's Own have their own quarters near the HQ, but not inside it."

"So General Maranta lives in his own fort inside his own fort," said Slith.

Fort inside a fort. The very thought Kang was thinking as he walked deeper into the hollowed-out interior of this extremely strange building.

Kang never entered any building, but that he marked the entrances and the exits. He never went in a place where he could not quickly find his way out, should that become necessary. Instinctively, he began to take note of the various turnings: one right, one left, two left and so on. But after the twenty-eighth right turn and the thirty-seventh left, not counting the weird corkscrew tunnel and the serpentine corridor that doubled back on itself, he was forced to admit that he was thoroughly confused. The only way he could have escaped this place was to fly straight up and punch his head through the ceiling. And since the ceiling was some ten feet above his head and was, according to Vertax, shored up by heavy wooden beams with another layer of stone and mud on top of that, Kang figured he better stick closely to his guides.

It was then that Vertax told him, still keeping his voice low, for this entire cavelike structure must be a veritable echo chamber, that General Maranta lived and worked here *alone*.

"He's not a recluse or anything like that," Yakanoh hastened to add over his shoulder. The corridor was too narrow for them to walk side-by-side. "He inspects the troops periodically. Officers report to him on a daily basis—you'll be doing that, too, Kang."

"Here?" Kang couldn't imagine coming into the Bastion every day. He didn't like it. He felt cramped and stifled, as if the mud walls were closing in on him. His wings would have brushed against the walls on either side if he hadn't kept them tightly folded. He scratched at an itch on his back. He missed his axe.

"No, not here. This is a rare honor you're being accorded, Kang," Vertax said. "The general has a command tent set up outside. We meet there. He keeps abreast of what's happening in camp, knows what's going on with everyone and everything."

At this Yakanoh coughed into his hand, cast Vertax a significant glance. Looking uneasy, Vertax quickly changed the subject, launching into a discussion of how many months it had taken to build this place, what tools they'd used, how the general himself had designed the building.

So, Kang thought, the general has spies even among his own troops. Not surprising, he thought sadly. The aurak had seen treachery enough in Neraka.

Kang was wondering if they were going to walk all night. His empty stomach made protesting sounds, demanding to be filled. The officers rounded a bend, climbed a set of five stairs, and there, at the top, was another set of massive iron-bound doors and two more sivaks.

This time, however, the Queen's Own asked no questions. After a brief inspection to make certain that the officers carried no weapons, the sivaks knocked on the door.

"Commanders Yakanoh and Vertax and Commander Kang of the First Dragonarmy Engineers here to see the general," said the Queen's Own to his counterpart on the other side of the door.

A moment passed for the message to be relayed and permission granted and then the door swung open. Accompanied by the other officers, Kang stepped inside.

Light, bright light, dazzling light, struck Kang a physical blow, as if he'd been hit between the eyes. The light might have come from the sun itself, had that orb been able to tunnel its way inside the Bastion. Half-blinded, Kang had to wait for his eyes to once again adjust to his new surroundings. He felt himself vulnerable at that moment. The feeling made him nervous.

At the back of his mind, he was thinking how difficult, if not impossible, it would be for an enemy to penetrate the Bastion. Narrow corridors forcing the troops to walk single file. Twisting corridors where they would easily find themselves lost. Undoubtedly there had been slits in the walls for archers, although he had been too discombobulated to look for them. Dark halls one minute, brilliantly lit rooms the next would leave an enemy blind for critical seconds. The general was very well protected, not only by the Queen's Own, but by the building he had himself designed.

"This is the Audience Hall," said Vertax.

General Maranta could have held audience with every draconian in Kang's regiment and have room to spare. The chamber was completely round, open, unfurnished with the exception of a single chair that stood on a raised platform at the far end. The Queen's Own remained by the door, unmoving. No other draconians except themselves were in the room. The walls were smooth, windowless. No doors besides the one they had entered. There was only one way into this chamber and one way out. The brilliant light came from an enormous censer, an ornate lamp in which incense was burned. The censer was suspended twenty feet over his head. Forgetting himself, Kang stared.

The censer was certainly huge and must have been heavy, for it hung from an iron chain whose links were as big around as Kang's fist. The censer was made of wrought iron that shone black against the brilliant yellow light of the aromatic gums that burned inside.

The ironwork had been formed in the image of dragons that circled the lamp. Silhouetted against the glow, their wings extended to touch on either side, their tails coiled to meet at the base.

"I see you are admiring my lamp, Commander," said a voice, echoing across the vast chamber.

Kang gave a start. He looked toward the raised platform. A moment ago, that platform had been empty, he could have sworn it. Now an aurak sat in the chair, very much at his ease, as if he'd been sitting there for the last few hours. The Queen's Own thumped the butts of their spears on the floor, called everyone to attention. The officers snapped a salute. Kang's scales clicked, a reaction to his surprise. He drew himself to stiff attention.

"Begging the general's pardon, sir," Kang said, wondering if the aurak had dropped out of the ceiling. He could find no other explanation for this sudden appearance. "I meant no offense."

No one said a word. The silence was awkward. Kang saw them all staring at him, felt some sort of explanation was due. "The lamp is truly remarkable, sir. I've never seen workmanship like that—"

"Nor will you again, Commander," General Maranta said pleasantly. "The making of such beautiful and magical artifacts is a lost art. I am pleased that you appreciate fine quality workmanship. The censer came from the Dark Queen's temple at Neraka. One of the few pieces to be salvaged after the explosion. I found the censer lying several miles away from the wreckage of the temple. The ironwork was bent and twisted, but easily restored. The magical spell that creates the light remained. Remains to this day." The general glanced up at the lamp. "I thought the magic might vanish with the gods, but, as you see, it glows as brightly as it did before our Queen deserted us."

"Yes, sir," Kang said. He was never comfortable discussing his Queen's departure. He still felt the wound in his soul, still felt betrayed. He hoped the general would change the subject.

General Maranta sat on his dais like a king on his throne, Kang thought, wondering uneasily: does this aurak consider himself a king? As Kang looked more closely, however, the concern left him. The chair on which General Maranta sat was just that—a chair. Plainly made and unadorned, the chair appeared to have been designed for comfort rather than to impress or intimidate. The chair had to be large, because General Maranta was large, the largest aurak Kang had ever seen.

General Maranta was a draconian elder, the only elder Kang had ever met and probably, by now, the last in existence. The elders were the very first draconians produced from the stolen eggs of the good dragons. After that initial batch, their creators, the black-robed wizard Drakart; Wyrllish, a cleric of Takhisis; and the red dragon Harkiel, had waited some time before conjuring up more. They wanted to see how the experiment turned out.

The experiment was a success, providing a race of warriors, fierce, intelligent and capable. When this became apparent, the corruption of the good dragon eggs proceeded apace. The difference in ages between the first hatching and those that followed would not have been reckoned much in human terms—a few months at most. But among the draconians, the distinction was there and they respected it.

And perhaps the difference in age was more drastic than any might have imagined. The aurak that Kang looked upon was large and obviously still hale and strong. But Kang noted signs of aging, signs that unnerved him. Kang wondered in dismay if this is what he would see in himself if he looked into a mirror.

General Maranta's scales still retained their golden sheen, but it was not the brilliant sheen of Thesik's scales. She shone in the light like a new minted coin. By contrast, General Maranta's gold appeared dull, dingy. He was slightly stooped, as he sat in the chair. His head thrust forward from between hunched, rounded shoulders. The muscles in his arms were starting to sag, probably from disuse, and he had developed a slight paunch around his middle. The skin around his eyes was wrinkled and pouchy.

General Maranta's eyes were like the glowing censer. They hit Kang a blow that punched through clear to his soul. His first fleeting feelings of pity for the aging aurak were knocked away, replaced by awe, respect, and a quite natural and proper fear.

Kang remained standing awkwardly at attention. His shoulder wound itched and burned beneath the bandage. He couldn't put his full weight on his injured leg and was forced to shift position every so often to maintain his balance. All the while, he was being studied by this formidable aurak. Had Kang's military demeanor been less rigid, he might have flinched. He had nothing of which to be ashamed. He was proud of his men, proud of their accomplishments, proud of himself. As for secrets, he had only one, but he intended to reveal it and once that was done, he would have laid himself bare to these probing eyes.

Seemingly satisfied by his inspection, General Maranta rose from his chair and returned the officers' salute.

"Welcome, Commander Kang. Welcome. Welcome to my fortress."

This draconian was a true leader, one who could not

only intimidate but inspire, one to be feared and at the same time admired. Kang could understand how these draconians had survived Neraka. The General had willed it would be so.

"Sir, thank you," Kang said. "The First Dragonarmy Engineering Regiment is at your disposal, sir."

"Very good, Commander," said General Maranta. "I am, of course, glad to be able to add two hundred new warriors to our ranks, but that is not the only reason I am pleased to welcome you. You represent hope. You are proof of what I have been saying all along—other draconians remain in this world. In large numbers, perhaps. You and your men are the first we have found. I have long said there are others," General Maranta repeated, "but some have disagreed."

His gaze went to Vertax and Yakanoh, still standing at attention.

"I am glad to have been proven wrong, General," said Vertax.

"Yes, well, let this be a lesson to you," the general said. He waved a clawed hand. "At ease, gentlemen. At ease." Seating himself again in the chair, he beckoned Commander Kang to advance.

Kang marched forward three paces, halted at the foot of the dais. He was quite close to the general, uncomfortably close to the jabbing eyes.

"I have received unsettling news about you, Commander," General Maranta said. "I require an explanation."

"If this is about my second, Slith, sir," Kang said uneasily, "I can assure you that he deeply regrets his actions and that he will not cause—"

"Slith?" General Maranta was puzzled. "I don't recall any Slith. No, no. What I have to say regards the fact that you have an aurak among your ranks. And, yet, *you* are the commanding officer. Please explain."

Kang understood. Draconians maintained a social strata, just as did dragons, humans, elves, and all the other races. In the normal scheme of things, an aurak would rank far above a bozak. And although experience had come to dictate that bozaks made the best field commanders, Kang would have been required to defer to an aurak, much as a human general would defer to a human king. Kang definitely had some explaining to do.

He had been going to wait to reveal his grand news, perhaps request an audience alone with the general, but if his ability to command was being questioned, he needed to clear up the confusion immediately. The best way, he thought, was to be straightforward, forthright.

"Sir, I am in command because the aurak, although she appears full grown, is only recently hatched. She is little more than a child." Kang made his statement and then shut his mouth on it, saying no more, waiting for the reaction.

The implication of what he had said was of such amazing import that the three draconians looked as if they had been struck by a lightning bolt from a cloudless sky. "She" and "child." Words never before used in association with draconians.

Vertax and Yakanoh forgot their discipline and openly gaped. General Maranta drew in a sharp breath. The red eyes narrowed to the surgeon's knife, slit Kang's head open, sliced up his brain. Kang almost winced with the pain. He stood his ground, confident in himself, secure in the truth.

General Maranta sank back in his chair, regarded Kang with an expression that was thoughtful and troubled.

"You don't believe him, do you, sir?" Vertax demanded. He turned to Kang. "I do not mean to call you a liar, Commander, but I think it is probable that you have been deceived. No draconian females were ever produced."

"Yes, they were," said General Maranta suddenly and unexpectedly.

"Sir?" Vertax turned his astonished gaze upon him.

"They were produced in the first batch, at the same time that we elder males were made. But the females were not permitted to hatch."

"But, why, sir?" Yakanoh asked.

"Can't you guess?" General Maranta said. His voice was stern, his tone bitter. "Drakart and Wyrllish saw the creatures they had created and they were proud and pleased, but they were also afraid. We, the creation, proved to be more powerful than our creators. The Soft-skins feared us, feared what might happen to them should our numbers grow. And so they arranged it so that our numbers would never grow. We would live to serve them, live to die for them. And when all of us were dead, there would be no more to rise up to threaten or accuse them.

"The eggs bearing the future of our race were taken away and, so we supposed, destroyed. Those of us who knew were made to swear an oath never to reveal our knowledge to anyone. The curse of Takhisis was laid upon us if we broke that oath and, to my knowledge, none of us ever did. To what purpose? What good would there be in speaking of what had been irrevocably lost?"

"Not lost, sir," Kang said softly. "Hidden. Hidden where they would never be found until they were meant to be found."

"And how did you find them, Commander?" General Maranta's red eyes glittered.

"Takhisis led us to them, sir," Kang said simply. "Perhaps one of her last acts in this world."

"And why would Takhisis grant this valuable gift to you, Commander?"

The general was displeased, jealous. Kang guessed what he was thinking. Such a gift should have been granted to an aurak of General Maranta's rank and stature, not to a lowly bozak engineer. Kang couldn't blame the general. It is what he himself would have felt under like circumstances.

Kang explained how he had come by the discovery of the females. He told about how the dwarves were intent upon reaching the eggs first and destroying them. He told about the wild race through the caves of Thorbardin. He skimmed modestly over the battle with the fire dragon and the collapse of the cavern on top of him, dwelt instead on the thrill of the discovery of the box of cherished eggs. The tale took some time, but no one appeared in the least bored. At the end, General Maranta was grudgingly satisfied.

"So it was simply a matter of being in the right place at the opportune time," he said.

"Yes, sir," said Kang, glad to leave it at that.

Vertax and Yakanoh were regarding Kang with open admiration. Kang fidgeted, embarrassed, wished they wouldn't. General Maranta had taken notice and it was obvious to Kang that the general was annoyed. He was accustomed to being the one admired and he apparently did not like to share.

Kang sighed inwardly. Without meaning to or intending to, he had incurred the general's wrath and he done so in his first few hours in the fortress.

"And so, Commander Kang," General Maranta was saying, "it appears that in opening our gates to you, we have opened the gates to our own doom."

"Sir?" Kang looked up, startled.

"Her Majesty's gift, which you are so *proud* of having

acquired—" General Maranta began, laying cold emphasis on the word.

Kang winced. That charge was unjustified. He had been a faithful worshiper rewarded for his faith. He thought he had made that clear. He held his tongue, however, kept it curled tight between his clenched jaws.

"—is, as are most of Her late Majesty's gifts, extremely dangerous to the recipient," General Maranta continued. "I had been wondering why an army of goblins and hobgoblins would bother attacking a small and insignificant force of draconian bridge builders. Now that question is answered."

"Yes, sir," was all Kang could say. "I am afraid that perhaps you are right, sir. I can't help but wonder why—"

"Because we are a threat, Commander!" General Maranta thundered. "We were a threat fifty years ago and we remain a threat today. That is why they want to kill your females. And you have led the enemy here, to us!"

Kang ventured to protest. "But the goblins ran away, sir. They're probably still running! And, anyhow, they wouldn't attack this fortification. Gobbos are cowards, all know that. They dared to fight us because our numbers were few and we were half-starved and worn out and they thought we would be easy pickings. But to attack a position that is well-fortified and well-defended is not their way, sir."

"It didn't use to be, perhaps," General Maranta returned coldly. "But apparently that has changed."

He gestured to one of the sivak guards, who had been standing silent and unmoving. The Queen's Own removed a scroll of vellum and walked forward to present it to the general.

"I have here," said General Maranta, brandishing the scroll, but not opening it, "a report from my Reconnaissance officer. The goblins have not *run away*. Far from it.

They are regrouping, resupplying! Their ranks are increasing in number. In my opinion, the only reason they haven't attacked us before now is that they are waiting for additional reinforcements."

General Maranta leaned out of his chair, thrust his head forward. Kang had to hold himself rigid to keep from taking an involuntary step backward, away from the anger in the red eyes.

"Make no mistake, Commander Kang. *You* have brought your war to us."

"I am sorry, sir," Kang said. "I had no such intention, I assure you. If you will grant us this night to rest, we will be on our way before dawn. I had not planned to remain here, in any case. Basically, we're on our way to Teyr, a city we discovered on a map—"

"Not so fast, Commander Kang," General Maranta snapped his teeth. "You're not going to leave us to face goblins while you run away with the females!"

"You misunderstand me, sir," Kang returned with dignity. "We have placed you in danger. My only thought in suggesting that we depart was to draw the goblins away from the fort. They would leave you in peace. We ask only that the females could remain under protection—"

General Maranta waved him to silence. He glared at Kang a moment, then the general's outrage appeared to dissipate. The aurak's shoulders sagged. Sinking back in his chair, he shook his head.

"Perhaps I did misjudge you, Commander," General Maranta said, with a rueful smile. "You must forgive me. We have lived here in relative peace for the last thirty years. It grieves me to think that we might lose all that we have worked so hard to build."

"My men and I will be glad to use our skills to strengthen the fortifications, sir," Kang said, mollified by the general's conciliatory tone. Kang could understand the aurak's feelings of apprehension. He recalled his grief and sorrow when the dwarves had burned his own town to the ground. "If you want us to, we will man the walls and help defend—"

"Good, Commander, good," said General Maranta. He cast an oblique glance at the Queen's Own, who marched forward. Apparently the interview was coming to an end.

"—*so long as the threat remains*," Kang finished his sentence, laying emphasis on the words. He was not going to abandon his dream. "Once the goblins are destroyed, we plan to continue on north to Teyr, sir." He wanted there to be no misunderstanding about that.

"We will see, Commander," said General Maranta in placating tones. "You might come to like it here. We may be only five thousand strong now, but those numbers will grow. Our ranks will swell."

Kang was considerably alarmed. "Sir," he said, "the females are, as I have said, little more than children. And even if there were . . . um . . . little draconians"— he could feel his blood burn beneath his scales—"it would be years, maybe many years, before they were grown—"

"What do you take me for, Commander?" General Maranta interrupted with a chuckle. "Some lame-brained gully dwarf? I wasn't counting on your blasted females to provide me with warriors. We found *you*, didn't we? There are probably more units like yours, perhaps whole regiments, wandering around out there. They've been lying low, but now that the Chaos War has decimated the ranks of our enemies and left them weak, more lost draconians like yourselves will arrive here." General Maranta nodded sagely. "You can bet steel on it."

He rose to his feet. The officers came to attention, saluted. Turning on their heels, they marched out the way they had come, led by the sivak guard wearing the colors of the Queen's Own.

"Damned odd," was Kang's comment to himself regarding the interview. "Damned odd."

Chapter Seven

"Damned odd," Kang repeated again, except this time he said it out loud and he said it to Slith.

"What's odd about it, sir?" Slith asked.

Kang took a moment to respond, due to the fact that his mouth was filled with goat meat. "This is good," he mumbled.

Slith nodded. The wild goat was tough and stringy, but tasted as good to the half-starved draconian engineers as beef steaks served at a Palanthian lord's feast. The cooks had watched in admiration, disbelief, and some alarm to see Kang's troops gorge their way through a week's rations at one sitting. Slith's offer to form a hunting party to replenish the fort's supply of goat meat had been accepted with pleasure and relief.

"What's odd about it?" Kang repeated, chewing and thinking. He'd been trying to sort it out himself. "I'll tell you what's odd. General Maranta hasn't seen a strange draconian in this fort in over thirty years until we show up, and now he's talking about expecting more to arrive at any time. Where's he expect them to come from? Rain down out of the skies?"

"Well, sir, the general does have a point. The world is in a state of confusion. Everywhere we go, some new rumor springs up about who's in control of what where. There was that tavern keeper who told us that the Dark Knights are in control of both Palanthas and Qualinesti! The Dark Knights ruling the capital cities of both their greatest enemies—the Solamnics and the elves! Who would have believed it?"

"I'm not sure I do," Kang muttered.

"Then there was that bizarre story we heard from the drunken kender Gloth captured, about monster dragons fighting and killing and eating other dragons. If even half of what we've heard is true," Slith concluded, "then the world's turned upside down and maybe the turmoil will shake out a few draconians who've been in hiding all these years."

"Maybe." Kang was unconvinced. "If there are draconians on the move, why would they show up here in this out-of-the-way place? We would have marched right past it, not twenty miles away, and never known of the fort's existence if the goblins hadn't dumped us in General Maranta's lap. 'Bet good steel on it,' the general had said. I'd be glad to take that bet, except that I haven't seen a steel piece in more than a year now."

Kang shoved his plate aside and heaved a deep sigh of satisfaction. His belly was full. He would sleep the night undisturbed by someone waking him to tell him that gobbos were attacking.

"Maybe it is odd," Slith admitted. "But then generals have a right to be odd, sir. Considering everything

General Maranta's been through, it would be strange if he wasn't."

"I suppose you're right. Make your report," Kang said, washing down the goat with a mug of sour, tepid ale. He poured a mugful for Slith, slid it across the table.

"The troops are bivouacked on the parade ground over by the west wall. Prokel offered to let our troops bunk with the others in the fort, but I figured you'd want to keep the regiment together."

Kang swallowed, nodded, indicated his approval.

"I set the watch," Slith said in an undertone. "Not on the walls, of course. Prokel said that we should rest tonight and he'll work our men into the guard detail roster tomorrow. But I thought it would be best if discipline was maintained."

"Quite right," Kang said.

Discipline be damned. The real reason Slith had set the watch was that he didn't trust his fellow draconians. Kang sighed inwardly. In some ways, Slith was as bad as General Maranta. But then, Kang reminded himself, he hadn't survived this long by taking anything for granted.

"I told them to be discreet," Slith added.

Kang approved. No sense in offending Prokel or any of the other officers.

"And, get this, sir," Slith said. "There're no taverns in this fort!"

"I believe it," said Kang, grimacing at the ale. "This stuff is horrible."

"Yes, sir. First Infantry raided a granary and brewed this from the wheat. Horse piss would taste better! As it turns out, they're down to their last keg. We're going to need supplies when we leave and, as you say, we don't have the steel to pay for them. But we could barter. I could set up the distillery. Make some dragon's breath liquor."

"But there's nothing to distill," Kang protested. "We used up the last of that stolen corn."

"I've been thinking, sir," Slith said. "One thing we have a lot of around this fort is cactus. With your permission, I'd like to try to see if we could use cactus to make our brew."

"Cactus?" Kang was doubtful, but he could think of no better solution. "Well, I guess you might as well try it. I don't suppose cactus could taste any worse than fermented mushrooms."

"Yes, sir. I'll harvest some first thing tomorrow."

"You said that the females are bedded down safely for the night," Kang said. That was the first question he'd asked on his return from his meeting with the general. "Did they get enough to eat?"

"Yes, sir. I saw to that myself, sir. I've doubled their guard." Slith poured himself another ale, shrugged and shook his head. "They're not very happy with me, sir. Can't say that I blame them. That shed is small and they're crowded in there nose to wingtip. They were all set to go out and explore the fort—"

"You didn't let them?" Kang demanded, alarmed.

"No, sir!" Slith was offended. "Of course, not, sir! I told them they had to stay inside for their own good. Might be goblins lurking about."

"Inside the fort?"

"Yeah, I know, but it was all I could come up with," Slith said. "They were mad as hell. Shanra tried to bite me. Or maybe it was Hanra." Slith grinned. The sivak twins were favorites of his, though he could never tell them apart. "I thought this time they were going to rebel for sure, sir, and there was only me and Cresel to stop them and half the time he takes their side. But then Fonrar stepped in and told them that if they went roaming about you'd be worried and that you needed your rest, what with your wounds and all. They settled right down after that. Before I left, Fonrar wanted to know how you were, if you'd fainted again, if you were going to have a good meal. She really thinks a lot of you, sir. They all do."

"I know," Kang said, embarrassed and humbled. "I wish I deserved it. Everything I've tried to do for them seems to turn out wrong. This dream of founding our own city. It's cost so many of the boys their lives. Maybe I was foolish to even consider it. If we'd stayed where we were, up in the mountains—"

"We'd all be dead by now, sir," Slith said flatly. "If it wasn't dwarves trying to kill us, it would have been elves or humans. You know that, sir. You made the right decision. When we reach Teyr, we'll turn that city into the most impregnable place on Krynn. No one'll dare attack us, then. We'll be able to live in peace, like we've planned."

There had been a time when Kang had wondered if draconians could ever live peaceful lives. Born and bred to be warriors, draconians might be doomed to fight and claw their way through life until death came to them in the form of spear or arrow or sword thrust. But this past year, watching his troops tend to the young females, laughing at their antics, taking pride in their accomplishments, teaching them and protecting them, Kang knew for certain that he and other draconians could live in peace.

"*If* we reach Teyr," he said gloomily.

"We'll make it, sir. This stop-off is only temporary."

"I'm not so certain, Slith."

Kang glanced around. The two were the only draconians in the mess hall. The cook and his helpers were in the back, rattling pots and banging pans, cleaning up. They made a considerable racket, but Kang guessed that they were keeping him and Slith under surveillance. He kept his voice low.

"And it's not gobbos I'm worried about—at least for the time being. You didn't see the gleam in the general's eye when he started talking about us getting to like it here. He wants us to help strengthen the fortifications and you and I both know that there's a good six months work to be done around here, if not longer. Once the gobbos are settled, I plan to leave. And I don't think General Maranta's going to like that one bit."

"He's a general, sir," said Slith softly. "But he's not *our* general! Not anymore. The war's been over a long, long time."

"You're right," said Kang uneasily. "But I'm afraid that the men won't see it that way and how will it look to them if I defy a superior officer? What kind of example am I setting? If I refuse to obey him, how can I ask them to obey me the next time I issue an order? No." Kang shook his head. "That's not the answer. We'll have to figure out something else. In the meantime, first light, have the troops start building temporary quarters. Just make sure everyone knows that they're temporary. If we say often enough that we're leaving, maybe they'll start getting used to the idea. And now I guess I better go check on the females—"

Kang stood up, but his knees buckled and he unintentionally sat right back down again.

"No, sir," said Slith. Sliding his arm underneath his commander's, he helped Kang stand. "I'll check on the females. You're going to bed, sir. No arguments."

Kang might have argued, but he was too tired. Bed sounded too good. He allowed Slith to help him to the bivouac area, where his troops lay sleeping on the ground. Kang had to look hard to see those on guard duty, but he found them eventually, crouched in the deep shadows cast by the rickety wall.

As for Kang, he would not have to sleep on the

ground. Slith had seen to it that the commander's tent was pitched, the commander's cot set up. Kang hobbled inside. He collapsed onto the cot on his belly and didn't move.

Slith removed his commander's battle-axe. Unstrapping it from between his shoulder blades, Slith stood the axe beside Kang's bed, within easy reach.

"Good night, sir," Slith said quietly and left the tent.

The only answer was a gentle snore.

* * * * *

The draconian engineers were up ahead of the sun. They ate an early breakfast and began building their quarters before the break of day. Fonrar was the first of the females to wake up, shaken out of her sleep by the bellows of the bozak smithy, badgering his assistants as they set up the portable forge. She recognized Slith's voice, calling out the work details, assigning each to a particular task. The sounds of hammering, sawing, thudding and the rhythmic chanting of the work crews rose with the sun.

The storage shed in which they were quartered had no windows, but there were several knotholes in the planks. Fonrar placed her eye to one of these and peered outside. The day had dawned fine, not a cloud in the blue sky. The breeze was fresh and clean, crisp and cool and made her nostrils twitch.

"What's going on?" came a voice at her side.

"They're setting up camp," Fonrar reported.

"Let me see," Thesik said.

Fonrar moved aside obligingly and Thesik put her eye to the hole, only to stumble backward with a cry. She tumbled over a sleeping baaz, who grumbled and lashed out with an irritated kick.

"What is it?" Fonrar asked, alarmed.

Thesik gasped, pointed at the knothole. "Someone is looking in!"

Putting her eye to the knothole, Fonrar found a red eye peering back in. More eyes appeared at other knotholes. The sounds of whispers and grunts and shuffling feet could be heard clearly. Then came shouts. Gloth's angry voice lifted above the others.

"Clear out, you dracos! What do you think you're doing? You look like peeping kender, the lot of you! Shove off before I put you all on report! Cresel, I'll have that trooper's name!"

"Wake everybody," Fonrar ordered Thesik.

Thesik roused the other slumbering females, shaking and kicking them awake, Climbing over her grousing sisters and cousins, Fonrar managed to reach the door to the shed and banged on it urgently.

"Yes, ma'am," came a voice.

"What's going on?" Fonrar demanded.

"Nothing, ma'am," said the voice. "Everything's under control, ma'am. Go back to sleep."

Fonrar drew in a seething breath. One would think she was newly hatched! She was about to lose her temper, start shouting, then realized that there was an easier way.

"I have to go to the latrine," Fonrar said, looking back at the other females to make certain they were listening. "We all do."

The other females caught on quickly. "I have to go!" they piped up. "Hurry! I can't wait!"

Fonrar gave the door an experimental shove, found it barred. She sighed deeply and in anger. They were little better than prisoners. The guard was one of the new guards Slith had assigned and he was not prepared for this crisis, apparently, for she heard him ask distractedly

111

what he was supposed to do now. There came a sound of thumps and shouts and confused scuffling. The eyes disappeared abruptly from the knotholes.

After a moment, Fonrar heard Cresel's voice, slightly out of breath.

"I'll take over now. What's the problem?"

"We have to use the latrine," Fonrar said sternly.

"We have to go! We have to go!" The baaz were chanting loudly now, causing the walls of the rickety shed to rattle and shake.

"You can go in groups of five under guard. When five come back, the next five can go."

"Cresel!" Fonrar growled threateningly.

"I'm sorry, Fon," he said. "But it has to be this way. You'll see why."

Fonrar made a motion with her hand. The baaz ceased their chant. The females waited expectantly for further orders.

"Shanra, you and Hanra are with me. You, too, Thes."

"I'm coming, too, ma'am," said one of the baaz.

"Very well, Riel," Fonrar said.

Riel was the commander of the baaz, who made up the largest number of the females. She had appointed herself Fon's bodyguard, in imitation of the baaz who guarded Commander Kang.

"All right, Cresel," Fonrar said. "The first five are ready to go."

A bar scraped, a key rattled. Fonrar kept tight control on her resentment. No use lashing out at Cresel. He was just obeying orders. The door swung open. Fonrar stepped out into the fresh air, took a couple of steps, and halted, staring in amazement.

The shed was surrounded by hundreds of strange draconians. They had been peering into the shed, apparently, but had been driven back and were now being kept at a distance. Engineers formed a cordon around the shed, using spears or the flat of their blades to whack anyone who tried to venture in too close.

Completely taken aback, Fonrar looked questioningly at Cresel. "These dracos have never seen females before," he said quietly. "They're curious."

Daunted by the hundreds of pairs of staring eyes, the other females clustered around Fonrar.

"I don't have to go *that* bad," said Shanra uneasily.

"Me, neither," said her sister.

"We're going," said Fonrar sternly. She might need to use this ruse again and didn't want it weakened. "March."

The females formed up in line and marched in step to the area where Slith had, with admirable foresight, ordered the engineers to dig latrine pits for the females and throw up a screening wall around them. Their guards accompanied the females every step of the way and so did the hundreds of watching eyes. The males didn't hoot or shout or make any sort of disturbance. They simply stared.

"I don't like this, Thes," said Fonrar sharply, on their way back to the shed. She glowered at the staring draconians. "It's . . . insulting."

"Is it?" Thesik had been traipsing along idly beside her friend, a dream-laden gaze fixed on the distant mountains. Now Thesik came out of her dream and glanced around. Fonrar had the annoyed feeling that her friend had only just now noticed something was out of the ordinary. "I don't have that feeling, Fon," Thesik said seriously. "I see it as a tribute."

"I'm starting to think it's fun!" Shanra whispered with a smothered giggle.

"Me, too," said Hanra. "Don't they look silly!"

"They do, indeed," Fonrar said coldly. Quickening

her pace, she caught up with Cresel, who was marching ahead of them. Fonrar knew she was wasting her time, but she had to ask.

"Cresel," she said, "we can't stay cooped up in that shed all day. We'll go out of our minds with boredom. Let us work. We can help set up the camp. Please."

Cresel was already shaking his head.

"We can't do any of the skilled labor, of course," Fonrar continued, pleading, "but we're strong, especially the sivaks, and we can all dig trenches. And the baaz are wonderful organizers. They like nothing better than to stack and sort, catalog and count. They could have the supply wagons emptied out and everything stowed away in proper order before the commander wakes for breakfast. Please, Cresel, let us do something to make ourselves useful!"

"You know I can't, Fon," Cresel said and he sounded truly sorry. "Look at those numbskulls!" He gestured to the gawking draconians. "If you were on work detail, this lot would be hanging around staring and getting in the way and who knows what might happen? I'm sorry, Fon. But it's only for today. The men are working on your quarters first thing. Commander's orders. Just be patient, will you?"

"I guess we don't have much choice," Fonrar snapped.

She knew she shouldn't take out her irritation on Cresel, this wasn't his fault. But he happened to be the only one in range.

"Can you at least bring us some boards, nails and a hammer," she asked coldly. "So we can plug up those knotholes?"

"Sure, Fon," he said, glad to be able to say "yes" to something. "I'll have them sent over with breakfast."

Our quarters, Fonrar thought, falling back to walk

114

with the others. They're working on our quarters. Which means they're working on another prison, this one with thicker walls and a better lock on the door. I've had all I can take. I won't be coddled and doddled any longer! I'll show them!

"Show them what?" Thesik asked, and Fonrar realized she'd been muttering out loud.

"Whatever we can, whenever we can," Fonrar vowed. "We just need to be ready." Pausing before they were all herded back into the storage shed, she looked around at the others. "Are you with me?"

"We're with you, Commander!" said Shanra and Hanra with simultaneous giggles.

"The baaz are with you, ma'am," said Riel.

"I'm definitely with you, Fon," said Thesik with a smile. "The others will be, too."

"What do we do?" Shanra asked softly, her eyes alight with eager mischief.

Fonrar glanced back to make certain no guards were in earshot.

"I've made a decision," she said. "A decision I should have made a long time ago."

Chapter Eight

Cresel was as good as his word. Along with breakfast, he brought boards, nails and hammers.

A worried Gloth accompanied him. "Are you girls sure you don't want us to do this? The commander says that we can't spare the men yet, but I'm certain that by this afternoon—"

"We don't want to be gawked at all morning, sir. And we're perfectly capable of hammering a nail in a board," Fonrar added. She stood in the doorway, blocking entry with her body.

"But you might smash your finger," Gloth said anxiously. "Or break a claw!"

"We'll be careful, sir. Thank you for your concern," Fonrar said and slammed the door on him.

For once, the sound of the key turning in the lock was reassuring.

She turned around to find that the efficient and well-organized baaz were distributing the hammers, counting out the nails, and beginning to mount the boards in position. At Fonrar's nod, the hammering began and within minutes, every single knothole was covered.

"Is everyone all right in there?" Gloth demanded.

"Yes, sir," said Fonrar. "Except for the loss of one eye, sir."

"What?" Gloth wailed.

"I'm kidding, sir." Fonrar said.

"I'll want the hammers back," Gloth said angrily. "And the nails."

Glancing over her shoulder, Fonrar twitched one nostril. The others understood. Gloth turned the key, opened the door.

"Here, sir," said Fonrar, handing him two hammers and a batch of nails.

"Where's the rest?" Gloth demanded.

"Here, here!" The baaz gathered around, thrusting hammers at him from left and right.

"I'll help hold these, sir," said one, taking a hammer from Gloth and handing him two others in its place.

"Let me help!" cried another and took that hammer from Gloth and gave him three more.

Gloth juggled hammers, nearly dropping one on his foot. Turning his head, he shouted for Cresel to come assist him. At that point, one of the baaz accidentally dumped all the nails onto the floor, resulting in a mad scramble to collect them. Gloth fumed and fussed and handed over hammers to his assistant.

"This is why you females shouldn't be trusted with tools," he said, shaking a finger.

"We're sorry, sir," said Fonrar meekly.

Gloth stomped off, grumbling, no doubt going to complain about them to Commander Kang.

Let him, Fonrar decided. She had an earful to give the commander anyway. Not that he ever took time to listen to her. She put him out of her mind, straightened her back. They had work to do. Now that the knotholes were covered and no one could see inside, Fonrar took her place in the center of the shed and motioned her troops to gather around her.

"All right, what's the news?" she asked. "Anyone hear anything?"

One of the kapaks rose to her feet. "Yes, commander. I overheard Slith telling Cresel last night that Commander Kang told him that according to the general the goblins weren't driven off. They're regrouping and the commander expects them to attack the fort. Not right away, but soon."

Fonrar nodded. "Good work, Kasi. Anyone else hear anything?"

One of the bozaks raised her hand. "I heard Gloth tell Fulkth that Slith told him that we were going to stay around here just long enough to help them rebuild and whip the gobbos and then we're moving on to Teyr as the commander planned."

"Well done, Ogla. Anything else to report? Nothing?"

Fonrar looked to the baaz draconians. "How're our supplies?"

Riel reached into a bedroll, withdrew a piece of flat stone on which she'd made notations, and stood up to report. "We had a good haul yesterday, ma'am. The males stowed all the armor and weapons from the dead in the supply wagons and so we were able to add quite a bit to our stash. We have harnesses and dirks enough for everyone now and almost enough helms, though two of them are badly battered and will require work to repair. We're still short on swords. The males took the good ones for themselves, but we managed to snag one that has a notched blade and two goblin swords for a total of ten. We have one battle-axe with a cracked handle and four hammers—newly acquired." Riel grinned, showing her teeth, and resumed her seat.

"We have to have more weapons," said Fonrar. "That will be our first priority. We can't do much about it while we're cooped up in this damn shed, but once we have our own private quarters, we'll be able to resume foraging. With all the draconians in this fort and all the weapons lying about, it should be simple for the sivaks to slip out and pick up what we need."

"Why do the sivaks get to go all the time?" one of the bozaks complained, particularly offended by Shanra's smirk of triumph at being allowed to go into the fort. "Why can't one of us go?"

"Because for some reason the sivaks can walk about among the males and no one pays them the least bit of attention," Fonrar replied. "And it only seems to work for sivaks. The one time I tried it, Gloth spotted me immediately. I had to do fifty push-ups. Besides, I'm going to want you bozaks to work on your magic."

Now it was the bozaks turn to smirk and the sivaks turn to sulk. This resulted in some good-natured shoving and jibing, giggles and laughter.

Fonrar watched them, let them be children for a moment longer. When she next spoke, their childhood would end, as hers had ended out in that canyon when she had realized that, for the first time, she had been on her own, with no males around to protect her.

"Listen up, all of you," Fonrar said, her tone sharp. "This isn't playtime. Not anymore."

The females ceased their antics, looked at her in astonishment, startled at her tone.

"I've made a decision," Fonrar said. "We're going to start military training."

"With the commander?" Hanra asked excitedly.

"No," said Fonrar, shaking her head. "The commander won't teach us. We have to face that fact. We're going to start training on our own."

The females watched her, eyes wide. They understood the import of what she was saying. Understood that from this moment on, their lives would never be the same.

"None of the males will teach us," Fonrar continued bitterly. "They think they have to take care of us, like they did when we were little. That was fine when we couldn't take care of ourselves. Someone had to watch over us, just like someone watched over the males when they were little. But that ends now. Today."

She looked around at her troops. Thesik was grave, serious. Shanra and Hanra exchanged glances and moved closer together. Some of the baaz lowered their heads.

"I understand how you feel," said Fonrar, her tone softening. "This is frightening. I'm scared myself. But this is a step we have to take. Do you realize how close we came to dying out there? If the males had all been killed, what would have happened then? The gobbos would have come for us next. And we could do nothing to defend ourselves! Nothing!"

"What made you decide this, Fon?" Thesik asked.

"It was when you and I were out there in that canyon," Fonrar answered. "We had no weapons and no training to use weapons even if we'd had them. We were lucky. Damned lucky," Fonrar emphasized. "Lucky that we ran into more of our own kind. That could have easily been a patrol of hobs out there and then neither Thes nor I would be here today. None of us would. We would all be dead.

"You heard Kasi's report. You heard that the goblins

are regrouping. They're going to attack again, this time in greater numbers. We have to be ready to defend ourselves. We can't count on the males being around all the time to keep us safe. And so each of us should be ready to face any challenge that might come. Are you with me?"

The males would have answered with a rousing shout. The females could not. A shout would have brought Cresel inside to see what was going on.

"Yes, Fon," they said softly.

"One by one," said Fonrar. "Each of you say it back to me."

"I'm with you, Fon," said Thesik.

"I'm with you, Fon," said Shanra and Hanra together.

One by one, the others gave their affirmation.

"So," Fonrar continued when all had replied, "no more fun and games. This is for real. But we're going to keep our training secret. We don't want to worry the commander," she emphasized. "He's got enough on his mind. Agreed?"

All nodded solemnly.

"Good. Now, orders for the day. I will lead the baaz and kapaks in sword drill. We don't have room enough in here to use weapons—I don't want to skewer anyone. But we'll make do as best we can. You bozaks, I want you to practice your magic spells. You better not cast any fire spells inside this shed. But you can practice some of the less incendiary. You sivaks start turning those extra boards into wooden swords for future drills. And Hanra, stow that damn rabbit pelt! I don't want to see it again! Ever!"

Hanra and Shanra exchanged glances. This was a new Fonrar, a serious Fonrar, a Fonrar who wasn't going to put up with any nonsense. Hanra stuffed the contentious pelt in her bedroll. Shanra, who would have ordinarily offered an argument, kept her mouth shut.

The baaz and kapaks began clearing out a space that they could use for the drill.

"Let me know when you're ready," Fonrar said to Riel, who nodded.

Fonrar pried loose one of the nails on a board and peeped out the knothole. A few draconian males still lingered, hoping to get a glimpse of the females, but most had departed. Either they had assigned duties to perform or they had decided that the females weren't all that interesting. From her vantage point, she could see their own troops working busily to construct the temporary quarters. She tried to spot Commander Kang among them, but couldn't find him. She hoped his wounds weren't troubling him.

Some kapak spit would have cured him right up. The females had discovered that the saliva from the kapak females could heal wounds quite miraculously. They'd found out accidentally, when one of the kapaks had been playing too near the fire—after being told not to— and had badly burned her hand. Fearing she would get into trouble, she'd hidden the fact that she was hurt from the males. She'd licked the wound to ease the pain and was amazed to see the burn immediately heal. Since then, when the females were hurt, they used "kapak spit" to mend the cuts, scrapes, burns or wounds.

Fonrar had tried to tell this to Slith, but the sivak had said sternly that the commander wasn't to be bothered.

"His wounds are bad enough," Slith had said. "You're not going to make him worse by slobbering on him."

"What do you want me to do, Fon?" Thesik asked,

coming to stand beside her. "You didn't give me any orders."

Fonrar couldn't explain why, but she found it difficult giving Thesik orders.

"You could practice your magic spells," Fonrar suggested.

Thesik shrugged. "I really don't need to practice. The magic's all so easy." She wasn't bragging, merely stating a fact. "I've memorized all the spells the bozak males taught the others. From the very first day I could cast them perfectly. Thanks to one of them I can make you believe you're seeing anything I want you to see. It's lots of fun. I was thinking of trying it on Gloth. You know how terrified he is of snakes. Anyhow, Guelp said that I could probably learn really difficult spells—male auraks are powerful magic-users seemingly. But I'd need someone to teach me." Thesik eyed her friend. "You could practice *your* magic, Fon. I'd be glad to help."

Fonrar shook her head. "No, thanks, Thes."

"But you really should," Thesik argued. "You might need to use magic someday. It could save your life."

"Commander Kang doesn't rely on magic," Fonrar said. She put her eye back to the knothole, hoping to see him.

"But he used to use magic," Thesik said. "Guelp told me so. He told me how the commander would pray to the Dark Queen for his spells before battle and how he used them more than once to save himself and his men."

"He prayed to the Dark Queen," Fonrar responded, turning from the knothole. "When she left, his magic left with her. That's why he doesn't use it, Thes. The magic was part of his faith and now that his faith and trust in the Queen are gone, so is his magic."

"But it's not!" Thesik argued. "The other bozaks thought that, too, but then they found out that they can still cast magic spells!"

"And not one of them has ever told the commander," Fonrar said gravely. "Right?"

Thesik didn't answer.

"Right?" Fonrar repeated gently.

Thesik gave a shrug. "Yes, you're right."

"They haven't told him because they know it would hurt him, Thes. That's how I feel. I know it would hurt him. And so I'll never use the magic. Never."

"But you let the bozak males teach it to the others," Thesik felt called upon to point out.

"Because, as you said, it might save their lives someday."

Thesik regarded her friend in exasperation. "I give up. You're every bit as stubborn as the commander."

"Thank you!" Fonrar smiled, pleased with the compliment.

Riel saluted. "Troops ready, Fon."

Fonrar looked back, saw the baaz all standing at attention in the first row, as they'd seen the males. The kapaks stood at attention in the second row.

"Very good, Riel," Fonrar said. "Take your place."

Fonrar walked up to the front of her troops, turned to face them. She stood at attention in front of them.

"Now, when I give the command 'draw,' I want each of you to drop your right hand to your left side, wait for a count of three, then draw your sword and hold it in front of you."

She took hold of one of the baaz's swords, demonstrated the move, then gave the sword back.

"Right! You know what it looks like. Now we try it." Fonrar took a step back. "Squad, draw!"

The females reached for their swords. After considerable

fumbling, they eventually managed to draw their weapons and most hung onto to them. Fonrar shook her head.

"No, no! Together! We draw together! This time, we're going to try it with everyone calling out the time. When I say draw, you drop your hand to the hilt and say 'One.' Then you wait, count 'two, three,' and then draw your sword and say 'One!' You perform actions on the count of 'one' and prepare for actions on the 'two, threes.' Got it?"

Some nodded. Others did not. Fonrar kept them at it for two hours, non-stop, first with the draw, and then with the thrust.

At first, she had been worried about the noise they were making—claws scraping on the hard-packed dirt floor, wings rustling, swords clattering, the females grunting with exertion. But the daily business of the fort apparently masked the sounds the females were making, for no one bothered them.

Drill continued.

* * * * *

The draconian engineers had chosen as the site for their temporary quarters the charred and blackened spot where the field hospital had once stood. The draconians in the fort had kept meaning to clear away the debris and rebuild, but somehow never managed to find the time to get around to it. They had even cut and stacked the logs, but nothing had been done after that.

Kang wisely kept to himself what he thought of such slovenly and slip-shod behavior. Had he been in command, clean up and rebuilding would have been started before the debris was cool to the touch. As it was, he said that undoubtedly the draconians had more important matters to attend to. Prokel agreed, though he seemed to be at a loss as to what these might be.

Prokel's procrastination proved to be a blessing for Kang. The supply of logs was already on hand and the wood was well seasoned. He drew up plans for an H-shaped structure that would be quick to build and suitable for their needs. One vertical side of the **H** would be barracks for the troops, the other officer's quarters. The horizontal bar would be the common area with the mess hall. He added a separate building off the horizontal bar for the females. While Kang and Fulkth drew up the architectural plans, Slith and the officers had the men clear away the debris and clean up the building site.

They had to halt briefly to deal with the crisis created by the fort's draconian males mobbing the area to gawk at the females. An irate Kang sent a respectful but firmly worded request to General Maranta asking for help in dealing with the situation. Soon, the Queen's Own arrived, and the other draconians disappeared like so many rats racing back to their holes. Vertax came around to Kang's tent to offer his apologies and assurances that nothing like this would occur again.

"The boys were just curious to see the females. You can't blame them, really," Vertax added defensively, having taken a quick peek himself. "Most of us had no idea that female draconians even existed. Now that we've seen them, I've no doubt that will put an end to the curiosity. After all, the females don't look any different from us, do they?" He sounded disappointed.

"They smell better," Kang said dryly.

"They do?" Vertax was perplexed.

"Never mind." Kang went back to his drawing.

Vertax bent over the half-finished plans. "Is this what you're building?"

"A simple design," Kang said. "But adequate for *temporary* quarters."

"Temporary," Vertax repeated, smiling. "Oh, yes. Right."

He walked out, chuckling.

"Damn right, they're temporary," Kang said with a growl, but only after he was certain Vertax had departed.

After the fiasco with the gawkers, Kang was now even more convinced that the moment the goblins were disposed of, he would leave the fort, continue to pursue his dream. He was putting the finishing touches on the drawing, when he was interrupted by Gloth.

"Sir," Gloth began, "it's about the females—"

"What about them?" Kang reared his head. His hand jerked, adding a line he'd not intended. "What's happened? What's wrong?"

"They don't respect me, sir," Gloth said in a whining tone. "Not like they ought. I think you should have a talk with them."

"Oh, for the love of—" Kang began, glaring at Gloth impatiently. "Do you mean to tell me that you interrupted—" He paused, counted to ten, then said, "Answer me this, are the females safe? Secure?"

"Yes, sir," Gloth said.

"Fine. Now get the hell out of here and leave me alone!" Kang roared.

Gloth slunk off. Kang muttered imprecations on the unfortunate draco's head and rubbed out his mistake.

He had the plans completed by the time his troops had the construction site cleared, the logs in place, ready to start. Kang and Slith went over the plans with Pol'lard, the bozak smithy, made a few changes and improvements. Slith started everyone to work.

"We'll have it up by tomorrow, sir," Slith said.

"Excellent," Kang replied. "The females are getting restless."

"Can't blame them, sir. Cooped up in that shed."

"Yes, well, tomorrow they can move into their new quarters. They'll like that."

"You're still keeping them cooped up, sir," Slith observed.

"What else can I do?" Kang demanded. "I can't let them go roaming about on their own. You saw what happened this morning?"

"Yes, sir," said Slith. "The sooner we leave this place, the better, sir."

"I know," said Kang. "After we whip some gobbo butt, I'll ask the general's permission for us to leave. I don't think he'll stop us. What reason would he have?"

"He's a general, sir," said Slith. "They don't need reasons."

"Well, there's nothing I can do about it now," Kang returned irritably.

"No, sir," said Slith and, seeing that the commander was in a bad mood, the sivak wisely left to go about his work.

Kang realized that he was taking out his frustrations on his men, but at the moment he didn't much care. He watched his troops set to work with envy. A few hours of swinging an axe or heaving logs about would ease the tensions that were gurgling inside his stomach and tightening his muscles into knots. He knew better than to try, though. His wounds were just starting to heal. Any physical labor would break them open.

Kang thought he might go check on the females, but he didn't want to do that either. He guessed that they would be in a terrible mood, sulking and quarrelsome. He would have to be calm and patient with them and he just couldn't manage that right now. He had decided to go eat breakfast when Pol'lard the smith appeared with a question, followed by Rohan the quartermaster with a question of his own and then came Brattbak, one of the baaz subcommanders. By the time Kang had dealt with them, Fulkth returned, having discovered a problem in the architectural design.

Kang never did manage to get breakfast.

The morning passed in a fury of hammering, heaving, hoisting, and hauling. The engineers stopped work only for a trip to the mess hall and that was done in shifts, so that some continued working while others ate. The females were marched out to the latrine again and Kang was pleased to hear Gloth's report that the females were docile and well behaved. Probably they had been frightened by the turmoil this morning. Kang felt a bit remorseful, decided that he would stop by in the evening to reassure them.

Of all the draconian males, only Cresel noted that the females were a bit too docile, a bit too well-behaved. He had heard some very odd sounds emanating from the shed, sounds that were familiar to an old campaigner. Cresel guessed immediately what the females were doing and, thoroughly approving, he kept silent.

* * * * *

Fonrar worked her troops hard all that morning. She allowed them a break for lunch, and then started at the drill again. At first, she'd despaired of them ever succeeding and began to wonder uneasily if perhaps the commander was right. If any one of her troops had been holding a real sword, Fonrar guessed that half her force would be dead or wounded by now, slain by themselves or by their comrades. They fell over their own feet. They tripped each other up with their tails and batted each other in the face with their wings. They thought it was all funny, at first, but after each had done a few hundred push-ups, they weren't laughing anymore.

Fonrar grit her teeth, kept her patience, ran them through the drill. She performed the movements with them until her arms ached and she feared she might not be able to pry the sword hilt loose from her cramped fingers. Weary, exasperated, frustrated, she was just about to give up on them when the females performed the drill right. Not only right, but perfectly right.

Fonrar stared.

For a moment, the baaz and the kapaks were too tired and dispirited to realize what they'd done. And then, noting that Fonrar wasn't swearing at them, they looked at each other and began to realize what they'd done.

"Again," Fonrar said, not daring to believe.

They ran through the drill again. And again. They got it right every time. Fonrar had to strongly repress an urge to hug them all.

"Dismissed," she said instead. "You did well, troops. Very well."

Dead tired, the draconians collapsed onto the floor and ginned proudly.

"Tomorrow," said Fonrar, "we do this all again."

The grins vanished.

Fonrar went to check on Thesik and the bozaks. Spellcasting was going well. They'd memorized all the spells that Guelp had taught them and could recite them forwards and backwards, even when Thesik tossed things at them, poked and prodded them with a stick, and tried other means to distract them.

While she was talking to the bozaks, Fonrar became

aware that Shanra and Hanra and the other two sivaks were attempting to gain her attention. They lurked about in the background, giggling into their hands and making cunning little winks and nods at her and each other. Fonrar realized, with a sinking heart, that she'd given them nothing to do after they had completed making the wooden swords. No telling what mischief they'd done in the interval. She resolved that tomorrow, they would join the sword drill.

"Come here, Fon!" Shanra said, beckoning.

"Come see what we've done, Fon," Hanra added. "We've been using our engineering skills."

"Yes, you'll be proud us," Shanra said.

The sivaks led their commander to the door of the shed, pointed proudly at the top.

Fonrar saw that they had rigged some sort of contraption above the door, a contraption that involved a barrel placed precariously on the cross-beam. The barrel was held in position by a small stick jammed in between the door and the frame.

Fonrar had no idea what purpose the contraption served or why it was there, but the sivaks looked so proud and pleased with themselves that she thought she should issue cautious praise.

"That's . . . interesting," she said. "Quite good, the way you have . . . um . . . caused the barrel to stay in place like that. Quite good. But I'm afraid you're going to have to take it down. It's about time for Gloth's inspection and—" Fonrar paused. She looked more intently at the barrel, looked back at the sivak sisters.

"We know!" Hanra whispered, giggling.

"The barrel's filled with water!" said Shanra softly.

"When Gloth comes through the door—"

"—splash!"

Fonrar knew that she should be stern. She should

make them take down the contraption immediately. She should probably punish them, assign them fifty push-ups each. But just as she was about to open her mouth, the mental image of Gloth standing inside the door, dripping wet, with a barrel over his head, was too wonderful to relinquish.

The troops had worked hard all day. They deserved some reward. She deserved a reward.

"Attention!" came Cresel's voice, a bit louder than necessary. He always gave them warning, when he could.

"Hurry!" Fonrar said in a smothered whisper. "Take your places."

The females hastened to form ranks for the daily head-count. They did so quickly, without the usual scuffling and confusion. Waves of suppressed laughter rippled through the ranks as they heard the key turn in the lock. Fonrar found it hard to keep her countenance. Glancing at Thesik beside her, she saw her friend's eyes gleaming. The females were so excited that not one of them caught the odd note of tension in Cresel's voice.

The door opened.

The barrel fell. The contraption worked perfectly. The engineering lessons had been put to good use. Except that it wasn't Gloth who opened the door.

Water dripped from General Maranta's snout. The barrel lay smashed at his feet.

Chapter Nine

"Sir! Come quickly!"

Kang recognized the shout of one of the guards posted over the females. The guard was racing toward him, panting and waving his arm. If a draconian could have turned pale, he would have been white as a pail of milk.

"Sir! The females . . ." The draconian gasped for breath. "General Maranta . . . "

That was as far as he got. Kang began running for the shed. Had he known what had happened, he might have turned and run for the front gate. As it was, he figured he was in trouble when he heard gales of laughter emanating from the shed. Cresel wore the stricken expression of a draco who has just taken a spear in the gut.

"Sir," Cresel began, gulping.

Pushing the hapless Cresel aside, Kang entered the door. He found General Maranta sopping wet, the females prostrate with laughter.

"What is the meaning of this?" Kang roared.

At the sight of him and the sound of his voice, the laughter ceased abruptly.

"Attention!" Fonrar shouted.

The females straightened, stiffened. Eyes shifted forward. Heads jerked up. Hands fell to their sides.

Kang cast them all a single glance, a glance expressive of his fury, a fury they were not accustomed to feeling turned on themselves. The females withered in the heat of his anger. They shrank, hung their heads, cast each other sidelong glances.

Kang turned to the general, who was wringing water from his cloak. A glance at the smashed barrel on the floor told Kang all he needed to know.

"General Maranta, sir," he said, "I am sorry. Deeply sorry. Please . . . is there anything I can do, sir?"

At the word "General" horrified gasps and soft groans came from the ranks of the females.

"So *these* are my sisters," General Maranta said in a cold tone. He turned a narrowed, red-eyed gaze on Kang. "What are you teaching these females of yours, Commander?"

Auraks are proud, arrogant, always mindful of their standing and their dignity. They do not like to see either diminished. Most especially, they do not like to see those they consider beneath them receive more respect than they do. Kang realized at that moment that General Maranta was more offended by the fact that the females showed a lowly bozak more respect than they did an aurak. Perhaps General Maranta thought that Kang had put them up to this. His words certainly implied as much.

"Again, I ask you to pardon them, General," Kang said awkwardly. "They're young. They've never been introduced to anyone of your rank before. They had no idea who you were—"

Fonrar, gulping, stepped forward. She had gone cold all over. She could not feel her feet or her hands. But these were her troops, she was responsible for them. She wasn't going to let the commander take the blame. She was grieved to the heart to hear him forced to grovel and beg forgiveness for an act that not been his fault.

"Excuse me, General," she said, trying to keep her voice from shaking, "but if you're going to be angry at anyone, you should be angry at me. I'm the squadron's leader. Their poor behavior is my fault. Commander Kang didn't know anything about it. We were going to play a joke on . . . on one of the subcommanders."

At General Maranta's baleful gaze, Fonrar's courage almost failed her, but she kept talking valiantly, more for Kang than for herself.

"We're extremely sorry, General." She lifted her chin, braced her shoulders. "We await any punishment you think is fitting for our offense."

"Sir," Kang began.

"Enough!" General Maranta raised his hand. One corner of the aurak's mouth twitched, showing the tip of a yellow fang. "Well, well, Commander, boys will be boys, eh. Especially if they're girls." The general began to laugh.

Kang burst out with a guffaw and a swift glance sent Cresel and the other draconians into fits at the general's humor. The females remained uneasy and quiet. They were in disgrace. They saw nothing to laugh at. Personally, Fonrar felt she lacked the heart to ever laugh again.

"No wonder they are given to mischief, cooped up

like this!" General Maranta said, when he could contain himself. "Remember how we grew up, eh, Kang? Like warriors! Raised to battle." He rubbed his clawed hands together. "We fought over every scrap of food they tossed to us. There was never enough. The strong ate, the weak went without. Remember, Kang?"

"Yes, sir," Kang said, carefully keeping his tone expressionless. "I remember."

"These females look too well fed to me. Not enough exercise. You should let them out more. Let them tussle and scrape."

"Begging the general's pardon, but I don't see how that is possible, sir, considering what happened this morning. There was a near riot."

"Bah!" General Maranta erased the incident with a gesture. "That will not happen again, Commander. The men were curious. One can't blame them. But their curiosity is satisfied. You will have no more trouble." He cast Kang a shrewd glance. "Have you had any more trouble today?"

"No, sir," Kang said. "We have not."

"Nor will you. I might as well inspect the . . . er . . . troops while I'm here." General Maranta chuckled.

The females stood as motionless and rigid as if they'd all been dead baaz turned to stone. General Maranta passed among them, eyeing each intently. At a nod from Kang, Fonrar accompanied him and the general, walking silently some paces behind the commander. The general said no word to any of them until he reached Thesik, who stood at the back of the line.

He paused before her, stared at her long and hard.

Fonrar felt for her poor friend, who looked so nervous it seemed likely she might pass out. Her wing tips shivered, her tail curled to a tight ball.

"What is your name?" General Maranta asked.

"Thes . . . Thesik, sir," Thesik answered in a half-whisper. She did not look at him, kept her eyes straight forward, staring at the back of the head of the draconian female in front of her.

"Another aurak. The first I have seen in many long years. We might have come from the very same golden dragon parent, Thesik," General Maranta said. "You and I might be brother and sister."

"Yes, sir," Thesik said faintly, completely bewildered. She seemingly had no idea what the draco was talking about.

"Are you powerful in magic, my dear?" General Maranta asked benignly.

Fonrar's heart leaped into her gullet and lodged there. She couldn't say or speak a word.

"Magic, sir?" Thesik turned wondering eyes upon the general. "There is no magic, sir. Magic left the world with Her Majesty, Queen Takhisis."

General Maranta appeared taken aback. "So you practice no magic?"

"Practice? No, sir," Thesik replied.

No, sir, Fonrar thought, her heart sliding down her throat to where it belonged. Thesik had told the truth. She hadn't lied. She doesn't *practice* magic. She doesn't need to practice.

"The loss of our great Queen is most regrettable," General Maranta said. He looked at Kang, who stood silently beside him, and then, with a slight shrug, the general turned away. The inspection was concluded.

General Maranta left shortly after, treading on the remnants of the smashed barrel. Water dripped from his cloak.

Outside the door, General Maranta paused to tap Kang on the chest with a sharp claw. "Teach them to fight, Commander. They may be females, but they are draconian females. Not namby-pamby woodsy elf maids. Teach them to be warriors."

Kang might have mentioned that it was a namby-pamby woodsy elf maid named Laurana who had been responsible for defeating the general and his entire draconian army, but he wasn't prepared to spend the rest of his time here in the stockade. The thought of Slith and the elf maid also came to mind. Kang firmly banished that picture.

"Begging the general's pardon"—Kang was doing a lot of that this day—"but if the females become warriors, if they fight and die, then our race is no better off than we were before we found them. They are the future of our race."

General Maranta leaned close to Kang. "The future of our race is well in hand, Commander. Well in hand." He winked. "Teach them to fight."

General Maranta departed, accompanied by six of the Queen's Own, his bodyguards, who fell into step, two behind him and two before him and two walking on either side.

* * * * *

As it happened, Slith was sampling the first output of the new distillery when the alarm over the females was raised. The cactus juice had a bite to it. He'd thought at first he mistakenly mixed in the razor sharp needles, but after the initial discomfort the cactus juice slid smoothly down the throat, left a pleasant burning sensation in the belly.

"We're ready for business," he announced to his assistants. "One steel piece a snort. If they don't have steel, we'll take trades. Use your own judgment." Slith raised a warning finger. "And don't drink up the profits."

The two baaz nodded, grinning. Slith was about to have another sample, just to make certain that it tasted as good as he had thought, when he heard the guards cry out and saw Kang bolt for the female quarters. Slith was about to chase after, to find out what was wrong, when one of the distillation tubes, made from deer intestines, sprang a leak. Once this emergency was dealt with, Slith departed to see if he could offer assistance. He arrived at the scene just as General Maranta was leaving it.

Slith had thus far been successful in avoiding the general. Maranta had most likely forgotten the elf maid incident and Slith intended to make certain that the sight of him did not jog the general's memory. A group of draconians had gathered nearby, hoping to catch a glimpse of their general, who was well liked among the troops. Slith stepped in among these, planning to blend in with the crowd and take a look at the general himself.

General Maranta was talking to the sivak who walked alongside him.

"Entirely unsuitable," General Maranta was saying. "Remove them from consideration. The remainder of Kang's troop are satisfactory. Most satisfactory."

The sivak said something in reply. Slith tried to hear, but couldn't. Detaching himself from the crowd, Slith headed over to the shed, wondering idly as he walked what the general had been discussing.

Whatever it is, we're satisfactory, Slith said to himself. The commander will be pleased. Things couldn't have gone *too* wrong.

* * * * *

"Things could not have gone *more* wrong!" Kang groaned. He heaved a sigh that came from the claws on his toes and then he sagged into a camp chair. "First the females decide they're going to play a prank on Gloth. They rigged up the old water barrel drop. I'd like to get my hands on the draco who taught that to them!" Kang added savagely.

Slith, who recalled having related a story to the females about the old water barrel drop involving Dragon Highlord Verminaard, looked sympathetic and innocent.

"Only it wasn't Gloth who walked through the door," Kang growled, "it was General Maranta!"

"The females dropped a bucket of water on top of General Maranta?" Slith asked, amazed.

Kang nodded dismally.

Slith jumped out of his chair and headed for the tent flap.

"Where the hell do you think you're going?" Kang demanded angrily.

"Excuse me, sir," Slith said, "but I'm going to laugh and I know that if I laugh where you can see me you'll probably bust me lower than the lowest baaz—"

"Damn right I will!" Kang glared at his second.

Slith ducked out the tent flap. Whoops of laughter came from outside. Kang might have been tempted to join in. Whenever he recalled the image of the general wiping water from his snout, a corner of Kang's mouth twitched. But the laughter died when Kang remembered the look General Maranta had given him, a look of detestation that had been hot as a red-hot poker.

Slith returned. Composing himself with difficulty, he sat back down.

"Yes, sir. What happened next, sir."

"After the general mopped off the water—"

Slith covered his mouth, half-choked.

Kang glowered.

"No, sir. I'm all right, sir." Slith gasped. "Just a momentary lapse. Won't happen again."

"He made an inspection of the 'troops,'" Kang resumed, sighing again. "He stopped when he came to Thesik."

Slith wasn't laughing anymore. He sat forward.

"Yes, sir," he said. "What happened?"

"General Maranta said something about he and Thesik having come from the same parent, the same *golden dragon* parent."

Slith eyed his commander. "The females had to find out sometime, sir."

"I suppose." Kang slumped in the chair. His tail wound around his feet. His wings drooped. "I kept hoping . . . maybe the subject would never come up."

Slith was sympathetic. "I know that, sir. But now it has and they need to be told. They need to know the truth, sir. Otherwise they might start to feel like it's something they should be ashamed of."

"Shouldn't we, Slith?" Kang asked wistfully. "Shouldn't we be ashamed of our so-called 'birth'? Did you ever look up into the sky and see a silver dragon, see it so beautiful and deadly and magnificent and think that because of you, that dragon lost her child? Not only that, but the children turned out to be hideous and ugly perversions of something beautiful. Did you ever think that?"

"No, sir," said Slith stubbornly. "And neither should you and neither should the female draconians. We didn't ask to be brought into this world, but now that we're here, we're here and there's nothing you or I or the silver dragon can do about it. I look at it this way, sir. I'll be accountable for my own actions, but I'll be damned if I'm going to take responsibility for things that happened before I was even born! No, sir. I don't have anything to be ashamed about. And I don't consider myself hideous, sir. And I sure don't consider the females ugly. Do you, sir?"

Kang softened. "No, you're right, Slith. I have to say that I never in my life saw anything more beautiful than those tiny little creatures we carried out of that cave. And they've grown more beautiful every day. Thank you, Slith." Kang leaned forward to shake his second-in-command by the hand. "Thank you. I'll talk to them right away. Tonight, after supper.

"There's just one more problem," he added, feeling more cheerful, "but that's easily handled. General Maranta asked Thesik if she was powerful in magic. She didn't understand what he was talking about, bless her heart. Thank goodness we don't have to worry about them using magical spells!"

"No, sir," said Slith, avoiding his commander's eyes.

"I was sorry to lose the magic," Kang continued, "but now I'm glad it's gone. Can you imagine the problems we'd face if the females knew magic?" Kang shuddered. "It gives me nightmares just to think about it."

"Sir—" Slith began.

Kang closed his eyes, leaned back in his chair. He was worn out. He felt worse than after his battle with the hobs. His wounds hurt, his body ached. He had been so pleased to come to this fort, saw it as a safe haven, a place to rest and relax and forget his problems. But his problems were multiplying, not diminishing. General Maranta, the females, the goblins . . . But he'd been proud of Fonrar. She'd stood up to the general.

"What is it, Slith?" Kang asked, opening his eyes with a guilty start. He'd caught himself dozing off and he remembered that his second had been about to say something.

"I was going to say . . ." Slith paused, looked at his weary commander and changed his mind. "Never mind, sir. It can wait. We're going to be finished with the temporary quarters tomorrow. The females can move in tonight, sir, if that's acceptable."

"Excellent. Yes, see to it." Kang said. Stifling a groan, he rose to his feet. "I'll come inspect the site."

"The men have done good work today, sir. I'm sure you'll be pleased."

"I'm sure I will, Slith."

"Also, we're taking our turn in the watch rotation for the fort tonight. Do you want me to assign the men?"

"Yes. But see to it that we set our own watch, as usual." Kang grinned, nudged his friend. "By the gods, Slith! You should have seen General Maranta standing there soaking wet! I have to admit—it was damn funny."

"I'm sorry I missed it, sir," Slith said. "Oh, by the way, I passed the general on the way out. He was talking to one of his sivaks."

Slith related the conversation he'd overheard.

"Satisfactory?" Kang was pleased. "He said we were most satisfactory?"

"Yes, sir."

"Perhaps I jumped to conclusions," Kang said. "I didn't think he thought much of us. That's good to know, Slith. Very good!"

"Sir." Granak rapped on the tent pole. "Runner from General Maranta to see you, sir."

The runner, a baaz, entered the tent, saluted.

"Commander Kang, Subcommander Slith, General Maranta has called a Command Conference, this evening, sundown."

"Where?" Kang asked with trepidation, fearing he'd

have to fight his way through the maze of the General's private fort.

"Command Center, sir. Outside the HQ."

"I know where it is, sir," said Slith.

Kang was not surprised to hear that Slith already knew his way around the fort. Slith made it his business to get know his environs.

"Tell the general I'll be there," Kang said.

The baaz saluted again, and departed.

"Something's up," said Kang.

"That would be the scout's report, sir," Slith said.

Kang cocked an eye at his second. He could always count on Slith knowing the latest scuttlebutt. "Yeah? What have you heard?"

"Prokel dropped by to see how things were going with the temporary quarters this afternoon, sir. Just before the . . . er . . . emergency with the females. The scouts had just returned and, according to Prokel, they reported to the general that the goblin army is massing in numbers we haven't seen since the War of the Lance. Thousands of them. And they're well armed *and* well trained. Someone's put a lot of effort and a lot of money into this campaign, sir."

"Into wiping us out," Kang said grimly. "The Solamnics. It's got to be the Solamnics."

"But since when do they work with goblins?" Slith argued.

"It's these modern times," Kang said. "You can't trust anyone. Maybe the Solamnics have figured that once Paladine left, there's no one around to care what they do."

"Maybe so, sir," Slith said, but he sounded dubious.

"Not that it matters," Kang said gloomily. "You're just as dead no matter who kills you. When does Prokel figure the goblins will attack?"

"According to what he heard, more goblin troops are arriving daily and they're digging in as if they mean to stay a while. They can't even think of launching an all-out assault against this fort with fewer than ten thousand troops. And they only have half that number."

"I'll have to think this over. And now"—Kang rose to his feet—"I better go hear what General Maranta has to say. Is what you told me general knowledge among the men?"

"If it isn't now, sir, it will be," Slith predicted.

"I'll want to speak to them. The gods only know what rumors will be flying."

"Tonight, sir?"

Kang hesitated. He thought of waiting until the troops were assembled, waiting for the officers to bring them to order, thought of standing in front of them, making a speech. Thought of trying to be reassuring when what he really wanted was someone to reassure him.

He thought of all this and then he thought of his nice, warm, comfortable bed. He shook his head.

"No, everyone's exhausted. Myself included. First thing tomorrow morning. While I'm gone, have Gloth see to it that the females move into their new quarters. Oh, and you better warn Gloth that the females have it in for him. That bucket was meant for his head."

"Yes, sir." Slith grinned.

"Now," Kang said, exiting his tent, "tell me how to locate this Command Center . . ."

* * * * *

Kang learned nothing more during the meeting than what Slith had already told him. He brought up the subject of who was hiring and training the goblins, but

General Maranta refused to speculate. He left it to his officers to form their own opinions.

Kang was pleased by one statement the general made. When an officer—a bozak Kang didn't know— suggested that the goblins were attacking them due to the presence of the females and that if the females left, the goblins would leave, as well, General Maranta told the officer in no uncertain terms that he was an idiot. Did the officer really think that the goblins would mass thousands of soldiers just to wipe out one small regiment of draconian engineers, females or no? General Maranta doubted if the goblins even knew that draconian females were present among Kang's troops.

The goblins were being paid to destroy draconians. *All* draconians. True, Kang had inadvertently led the goblins to discover this fort, but they would have found it soon enough as it was. In fact, perhaps they had been dogging Kang, hoping he would lead them here. Everyone—goblins, hobgoblins, humans and elves—knew the name of General Maranta. They knew him and feared his power. If anyone was the target of the goblins' ire, it was General Maranta, not some lowly bozak engineer.

Not very flattering to Kang, but since it took some of the heat off him, he was more than happy to let General Maranta consider himself the target. In fact, General Maranta undoubtedly had a point. The goblins may have stumbled on this fort, but if they were being hired to wipe out draconians, this was an opportunity to do so in one fell swoop.

Following the meeting, Kang ate a quick meal in the officer's mess, then made his inspection of the building site. He was pleased with the progress. The new barracks would be ready for the males to move into tomorrow. The females had already moved into theirs. He had one more task before he could turn in. He would visit the females, inspect their quarters, see how they were getting along.

The move had gone smoothly, according to Gloth. Chastened by the fiasco involving the general, the females had been unusually cooperative. They had their bedrolls packed and were ready to leave the shed the moment Gloth gave the word to move out. Gloth had doubled the number of bodyguards, but he needn't have bothered. The fort's draconian males gave the females no more than a mildly curious glance and hastened on to whatever duty they had been assigned to perform.

Kang was pleasantly surprised. The fort may have looked a ramshackle mess, but apparently its inner workings were much better constructed. Discipline was strict, well enforced. The troops seemed in good spirits, respected their officers. He saw no harsh punishments being meted out, such as he'd been sorry to observe in the old dragonarmy. The few prisoners locked up in the brig were there on ordinary charges: drunk and disorderly, fighting in the barracks, petty theft. Unlike the goblin army, the draconians did their duty because they were proud to do their duty, not because they were being driven by officers wielding whips. He gave General Maranta credit.

According to the account of the fort's history, the general had escaped Neraka with the Queen's Own and the Ninth Infantry. Guessing that with the fall of their Queen, draconians would be hunted down and slaughtered by the victorious Forces of Light, Maranta had searched for an isolated, desolate place to establish a defensible position. They had thrown up the fort's walls and the first few buildings, then set about constructing the more permanent Bastion.

Once settled, General Maranta sent out scouts to find other troops of draconians who might be in a similar plight, urged them to join him. One of those scouts might have found us, Kang thought, if we had not been hidden away in the mountains.

He speculated briefly on how his life and the lives of his men might have been different. More of his troops would be alive today, he reflected, but they would not have found the females. Kang would be like Vertax and Yakanoh and the other commanders, respectful, obedient, unquestioning, looking to Maranta for both questions and answers. Kang had been on his own too long, he realized. He had developed an independent spirit, a bad thing in a military officer. Kang took himself to task over this. He would not have tolerated such an attitude from one of his own subcommanders and he vowed to shape up, view General Maranta with more respect. He deserved it.

Still, Kang was forced to secretly admit that he was glad the scout had not found them.

The night was bright with stars. Torches flared on the walls at the guard posts. A group of draconians returning from the mess hall laughed and talked, saluted Kang as they passed him. He fully intended to speak to the females, relate to them the true circumstances of their birth. He'd put this unpleasant task off far too long, like having a decayed tooth yanked. But when he arrived at the females' quarters, he found the area dark and quiet.

"I think they're asleep, sir," said the night guard. "Shall I wake them?"

"No, no!" Kang said hastily. "I'll just take a peek."

The guard slid aside the bar that held the door shut. Kang opened the door quietly, looked inside. The females lay on their newly built cots, fast asleep. Only one was awake, Fonrar. She was pacing the floor, walking from one of the small windows to another, looking out in the night. Kang was about to slip away, but she had sharp hearing.

She made a quick motion to him and he stepped inside, not sorry to have a chance to talk to her.

She came to stand at attention in front of him, saluting.

Kang smiled, shook his head. "At ease," he said softly.

"Sir," Fonrar began, "I just want to say again how sorry I am—"

"I know," he said. "I know. What's done is done." He regarded her with concern. She looked worn out, he thought, and desperately unhappy. "You shouldn't dwell on it, Fonrar. You mustn't let it keep you from your sleep."

"It was my fault," she said miserably. "I knew what they were doing. I didn't stop them. The worst of it is that we got you into trouble with the general, sir. We never meant for that to happen."

"It wasn't the first time I've been in trouble with a general," Kang said dryly. "And I'm certain it won't be the last."

"Still, sir, we'd feel better if you gave us some sort of punishment—"

"The purpose of punishment is to reinforce the lesson," Kang said, smiling. "I think you've learned your lesson, haven't you?"

"Yes, sir," said Fonrar, but she sounded subdued and she did not meet his eyes.

"I was very proud of you today, Fonrar," Kang said. "The way you admitted your wrong to the general. That took real courage."

"Don't praise me, sir," she said, still avoiding looking at him. "I don't deserve it."

He was pleased with her modesty and humility. "I

hope that the others weren't too upset about what the general said. Thesik, in particular."

"What about, sir?" Fonrar looked at him now, warily.

"About . . ." Kang was uncomfortable. He'd been rehearsing his speech all the way over here, but it sounded much too grandiose for an audience of one. "About coming from . . . the eggs of dragons."

"Oh, that, sir." Fonrar seemed relieved. "No one was upset. Why should we be? We've known about that for a long time."

"You have?" Kang was astonished.

"Yes, sir. Cresel explained it all to us. How we came from the eggs of the metallic dragons, eggs that were magically altered to produce draconians instead of baby dragons."

"Huh? Cresel explained . . . But that . . . that doesn't bother you?" Kang stammered.

"No, sir," Fonrar said, blinking. "Should it?"

"No, no," he said hurriedly. "Of course not. It's just . . . Thesik didn't appear to understand what the general was talking about. I thought—"

"Oh, that's just Thes." Fonrar smiled indulgently. "She's like that, sir. Keeps herself to herself. You never know what she's thinking unless she wants you to know and then half the time I don't understand. To tell you the truth, sir, Thesik was mad at the general. She didn't like the way he singled her out, as if she were different from the rest of us. And so she played dumb, didn't let on that she understood what he was saying. I think it has to do with wings, sir."

"Wings?" Kang was mystified.

"Thesik doesn't have wings, sir. I think that upsets her."

"I . . . I see." Kang didn't see, not in the slightest.

"Will that be all, sir?" Fonrar asked, stifling a yawn.

"Uh, yes," said Kang. "Get to bed. That's an order."

"Yes, sir." Fonrar saluted.

Kang watched as the guard slid the bar back in place, then he walked to his quarters, more than ready for his own bed.

"Wings!" he repeated, scratching his head.

Chapter Ten

A rapping on the tent post, followed by the sound of wings scraping on canvas interrupted Kang's dream, a pleasant dream this time. He opened his eyes to find a draconian standing over him.

"Hunh?" Kang grunted, the most intelligent sound he could make at this hour, whatever this hour was. What it obviously wasn't was morning. The tent was pitch dark. The draconian's body heat provided the only light. Kang recognized Slith.

Thoughts filtered through the remnants of a dream into Kang's brain. Slith had knocked, but he hadn't waited for Kang to yell "enter." Slith had barged into his commander's tent in the middle of the night. Slith—who should have been asleep as well. Something was wrong.

Kang sighed deeply and swung his clawed feet over

the side of the cot. Why didn't emergencies happen at noon? Why did disaster always wait to strike while a fellow was peacefully sleeping?

"Sorry to wake you, sir." Slith began.

Kang waved his hand, indicated that Slith was to skip the apology, get on with the bad news. Kang knew it was bad news. No one ever woke him up in the dead of night to give him good news.

"Whas'it? Goblins?" Kang mumbled, rubbing his eyes.

"Two of our troopers are missing, Sir. Urul and Vlemess, both baaz, both from One Squadron."

"Huh?" Kang stared at his second. "*Missing?* Two of ours? When? Where? How?"

"The two were among those assigned to stand sentry duty on the wall, sir. When their shift ended, all the sentries who were relieved of duty lined up inside the front gate. All except ours. Our two turned up missing. The fort's sentry commander put our two on report, but didn't bother to tell any of us that two of our own were gone, sir. After the rest of our sentries returned to barracks, Celdak did a head count and came up two short. He went to see the fort's sentry commander, who told him that the guards who were supposed to relieve our two had found them missing at their posts." Slith paused, then said quietly, "They're going to be listed as deserters, sir."

"Deserters! No! That doesn't make any sense," Kang protested vehemently. "Damn it, we've ventured hundreds of miles together over mountains, across rivers, through blood and fire and not a single draco has deserted. Died in battle, yes. Died of sickness. One killed by wolves and one committed suicide. But not desertion, Slith! Not desertion!"

Kang tried frantically to come up with a plausible

explanation. "Did you try the latrine? Maybe they've got the trots?"

"Yes, sir. First place we looked. Celdak reported to Gloth, who called out the whole squadron. Gloth thought maybe our two didn't know they were supposed to report to the fort's sentry commander and, when their duty ended, they left to find a drinking hole or maybe went to the mess hall. No sign of them. Gloth also ordered that the squadron search the section of the wall the men were patrolling. They found this lying on the ramparts, sir."

Slith held up a boot knife. "You probably can't see in the dark, sir, but it's one of ours. Made by our smith. I recognized it and so did Pol'lard, when Gloth rousted him out of bed. That's when Gloth woke me up and that's why I'm here waking you up an hour before sunrise, sir."

Kang absorbed all this. "Do *you* think they deserted, Slith?" He shook his head. "Maybe I should have talked to them last night—"

"They didn't desert, sir." Slith was emphatic. "Why should they? Where would they go? To join up with the goblins? For gods' sake, sir, we're *inside* the only safe haven that exists around here for miles! Why would they leave?"

Kang had to admit this made sense. "Has anyone checked outside the wall?"

Slith shook his head. "We've been told that no one goes outside the fort after dark—General's orders. He figures the goblins have patrols out to try to pick off any stragglers. We were going to wait until dawn."

Kang reached for his field harness and equipment and began to strap it on.

"At first light, I want the regiment in fighting order at the front gate. We'll do a full sweep of the area. Give the orders, start the troops moving, then go and see Prokel. You two seem to have hit it off well. Ask him if he'll lend us some bodies to help search. Got it?"

"Yes, sir." Slith started to leave, turned back. "What is it we're searching for, sir?"

"Blamed if I know!" Kang snapped, concern making him irritable. "Piles of dust, the rest of their equipment, blood, signs of a fight. Maybe some damn goblin archer got them during the night and they tumbled headfirst off the wall. Or maybe they saw something and decided to fly down and go check it out."

"Not likely, sir," Slith said. "They would have reported—"

"I'm aware of that, damn it!" Kang shouted. He hadn't meant to shout and he drew in a deep breath, annoyed with himself. He shouldn't be seen losing control. "Just go, Slith! There has to be an explanation."

Slith saluted, and dashed from the commander's tent. Kang exited the tent to find Granak already up and moving, the company standard in his hand. The body-guard was already assembled, waiting for him in parade order. Granak had foreseen his commander's need and prepared for it accordingly. Kang was comforted by the sight of the enormous sivak, solid and steady, undisturbed by the turmoil, ready for whatever might come.

The air was cold. There was no wind. Clouds blotted out the stars. The predawn darkness was thick and oppressive.

Kang's engineers were forming into troops and squadrons on the parade ground in front of the partially completed barracks. When all was ready, Gloth, Yethik and Fulkth, the two commanders of the line squadrons and the commander of the support squadron, marched up to Kang, saluted, and reported.

"Sir, First Squadron ready to march, sixty officers and other ranks." Gloth paused a moment, the next words hard for him to say. "Two missing, sir," he added harshly.

The next officer, Yethik, spoke up. "Second Squadron, ready to march, forty-eight officers and other ranks, two too ill to fight, Sir."

"Support Squadron, fifty-four officers and other ranks, ready to march," said Fulkth, "Two cooks and two orderlies staying behind to provide food for when we return, and two asssigned to security for the females, sir. Speaking of the females, what should we tell them, sir? They're bound to know something's up if they see us all march out the gate. And you *know* that they'll see us, sir."

Kang nodded gloomily. He'd come to learn that the females were highly observant. He was often amazed and occasionally dismayed at how much they knew about what was going on in the camp.

"Tell them we're going out on maneuvers," he said, after a moment's thought. "Don't mention anything about the missing men or about the goblin army massing. I don't want to upset them. And I don't want them to think that we all might . . . might . . . might abandon them." He couldn't bring himself to even say the ugly word "desert."

"Yes, sir." Fulkth saluted.

Kang turned back to the other officers. "March your squadrons to the front gate and wait for my command to move out."

The officers saluted again and shouted orders in unison. Although the babble sounded confusing, the soldiers knew which voice to listen for, and responded only to their squadron commanders. They marched in step to the front gate, halted, stood ready to move out the moment the sun had climbed over the mountains. They would not have to wait long. The sun would not make an appearance this morning, due to the clouds, but the black of night was giving way to a sullen gray. With first light, Kang ordered the gates to be opened. The squadrons departed, fanning out to explore the territory surrounding the fortress.

"You're with me," Kang said to Slith.

Accompanied by the bodyguard, the two examined the area beneath the wall where the draconians had stood watch. Kang had hoped to find the piles of dust that would mean his draconians had died on duty. Better death than dishonor. But they found nothing. There had been no wind during the night. The dust could not have blown away. Cautioning the bodyguard to keep their distance, Slith investigated every bit of ground minutely, crawling on his hands and knees.

"Nothing, sir," Slith reported, rising and wiping the dirt from his claws. "No dust, no blood. No broken scales or scraps of torn leather."

"No sign of footprints?" Kang asked.

"No, sir. But the ground is hard-packed and rocky. Wouldn't show much. Still, look at this sir." Slith indicated some scrub bushes growing at the base of the stockade. "See how brittle and dry these are? If the baaz had been shot and fallen from the wall, they would have landed in those bushes. No sign of that, sir."

The bushes were intact. Their small brown leaves scraped against the wood with an annoying dry rustle.

"So we know that they didn't jump from the wall. They weren't killed. They're not lying dead drunk in the latrine. Where in the Abyss are they?"

Slith gazed out across the barren ground that surrounded the fort. "I suppose they could have made a run for it, sir. Figured they'd head north. There's talk around camp of a fortress of Dark Knights of Takhisis not too far from here."

"Is there?" Kang looked up at Slith sharply. He was about to ask where, but they were interrupted. Kang turned to see Commander Prokel.

"Men deserted in the night, eh?" Prokel said, adding, with a shrug. "Well, it happens to us all."

Not to me, Kang was about to say, but he shut his mouth with a snap.

"Especially," Prokel continued, "with these reports of the goblin army preparing to attack. I lost two men last night. We'll lose more, I'm afraid. I'll recommend that the guard be doubled."

Kang made no comment. Another regiment of draconians—Prokel's regiment—marched away.

"I've sent out my troops to help capture the deserters. I ordered them to take them alive." Prokel rubbed his hands. "We'll make an example of them. Might deter others." He glanced up at the stockade with interest. "What did they do? Jump off the wall?"

"We can't find any signs of that," Kang said morosely. "Excuse us a moment."

Drawing Slith aside, Kang said in a low voice. "Find out from Prokel who that blasted sentry commander was and why he didn't report this disappearance to us immediately. And I also want to know more about that fort of Dark Knights. How close is it? How many men does it have? You have to talk to him, Slith. I'm afraid if I do, I'll lose my temper and say something that will get me into trouble."

"Whereas if I say something to get me into trouble—" Slith began, grinning.

"—I can always give you hell for it later," Kang said.

Muttering his thanks to Prokel for his assistance, Kang departed.

"Your commander's taking it hard, isn't he?" Kang overheard Prokel say. "You'd think he never dealt with deserters before."

"He hasn't," Slith said, adding companionably, "Say, I was wondering if you could introduce me to that sentry commander? I'd like to ask him a few questions—"

* * * * *

"There they go, off on maneuvers," said Fonrar, staring gloomily out the window of their new quarters. "And here we sit, doing nothing."

"Don't you think it's sort of odd?" Thesik asked, joining Fonrar.

"What's odd? That we're doing nothing? It's what we always do," Fonrar said bitterly.

"No, I mean that the commander's sending the men out on maneuvers. Yesterday they worked like ogres were driving them to finish the barracks and now, with the barracks only half-finished, they're off with first light to go on maneuvers. Why not go on maneuvers after the barracks are finished? Why waste the time? Doesn't make sense to me."

"You're right," Fonrar said, considering. "Something's wrong."

"I saw you talking to the commander last night. Did he say anything?"

"Just to ask if we were moved in and comfortable and to commend me for the way I stood up to that creepy old general." Fonrar sighed. "The commander commended me! He didn't punish me, like I deserve. I wish he would have, Thesik. Then I could be angry and resentful at him. As it is, he was so kind and understanding that it made me feel wretched and guilty. I hate deceiving him."

"I know." Thesik was sympathetic. "But remember that we're keeping this from him so as not to worry him. It's for his own good. And with the men gone and the barracks only half-built, this is a perfect time to go on some maneuvers of our own. We should take advantage of the situation."

"You're right," said Fonrar. Like any good commander, she put her personal feelings aside. "An opportunity like this might not come again."

The females' quarters were much roomier than the shed had been, provided more air and light through the small windows cut into the wall. The main door opened off a corridor leading to the common room that was located between two barracks. When the common room was finished, the females would be protected by male draconians on either side. The only access to their quarters through the common room. As it was, that section was only half-built. A second door led to their own latrine—a slit trench enclosed by a wall of logs.

Fonrar assembled her troops.

"Report."

Riel, the baaz commander, stepped forward. "The roof of the latrines is not yet completed. The wall can be easily scaled. A pile of wood outside will screen anyone climbing over the wall. After inspecting the construction, we have determined that with the proper tools, we could alter some of the logs so that they could be removed and put back into place without anyone noticing. *If* they didn't look too hard," she added.

"Right. And that will provide us with a way to get outside. Will they post guards there, do you think?" Fonrar looked to Thesik.

"I shouldn't think so," Thesik said. "They have guards on the main door, of course, but why guard the latrines if there's a wall around them and a roof over them?"

"Agreed. Sivaks, front and center."

Shanra and Hanra marched forward.

"The males are gone on maneuvers, or so we've been told. Thesik will take care of distracting the guards at the door. You two will exit through the latrines. Buckle on the armor, as usual. We need weapons. Don't talk to anyone, but keep your ears open. I think something's up and I'd like to know what's going on. And I'll expect you to map the fort on your return, so keep your eyes open, as well. Any questions? Good. Dismissed."

The sivak sisters departed to put on their armor. Thesik went to the main door, planning to find out what she could from Cresel, as well as keep him from hearing any suspicious sounds that might come from the direction of the latrine.

"I doubt if I can get much out of him," she confided to Fonrar. "He's shut up tighter than an oyster since the commander put him on report."

"Do what you can," Fonrar said and left to supervise the sivaks' escape.

Having seen them over the wall and safely away, with no alarms being raised, Fonrar returned to put the rest of her troops through sword drill.

* * * * *

Kang went back to his tent, planning to wait there for the reports to come in. He would have much preferred being out on the hunt or prowling about the fort, searching in sheds and under tables, but he had to restrain himself. To do so would give the appearance that he didn't trust his own men and officers, when, in fact, he knew that if the two missing dracos could possibly be found, his troops would find them. But the waiting was hard, the hardest task he'd ever set himself. He was hungry and he considered going to the officer's mess, but the thought of running into Vertax or any of the other officers, of having to listen to them discuss the incident and know that they held him in disdain for his dracos' desertions effectively ruined Kang's appetite.

He faced another difficult task. He would have to write out a report for General Maranta. He figured he might as well get that over with and started to write. He had not put down a single sentence before he stopped. Nothing could convince him that his men had deserted. Nothing. He would wait until nightfall, wait until all squadrons had reported in.

Meanwhile it was going to be a long day.

* * * * *

About two hours later, Slith appeared.

"Sir, I'm back," said Slith, ducking inside the tent. "And . . ." He paused to watched his commander, who was vigorously polishing his battle-axe. "Sir, I think if you keep rubbing the blade like that, you're going to be able to see through it pretty soon."

Kang looked up, somewhat shamefacedly. "Goblin blood eats away at the metal," he muttered in a gruff voice. He set the axe aside. "What did you find out? Anyone report in yet?"

"No, sir. All squadrons are still searching. But I found out something interesting."

At Kang's gesture, Slith sat down on the commander's bunk. He kept his voice low. "The commander on the sentry detail last night was a sivak. One of the Queen's Own."

Kang grunted. "Well, that's a first. The Queen's Own doing something useful for a change besides posting guard duty for a general. I'm surprised. They might actually get their pretty tabards dirty."

"Yes, sir. I said as much to Prokel, but he acted like he didn't know what I was talking about. According to him, General Maranta makes every draconian in the fort take his turn at sentry detail. Of course, the Queen's Own don't stand watch like the rest of us. They're in command. And one of them was in command last night."

Kang scratched his head. "I'm damned if I can see how that makes any difference. Did you talk to him? Why didn't he report the loss to any of our officers?"

"No. He just came off duty and he's asleep." Slith read his commander's thoughts, forestalled them. "I spoke to one of the Queen's Own officers, told him this was really important, and asked if he'd wake him."

"No luck, eh?" Kang said.

"No, sir. The Queen's Own have their barracks near that great hulking fort-in-a-fort, so I couldn't even give the fellow his own private reveille, like I considered. I told the Queen's Own officer that we were respectfully wondering why we were the last to hear about our own guys disappearing and the Queen's Own looked amazed that I'd even ask such a stupid question. Said the sentry commander had followed 'standard procedure.' *Is* that standard procedure, sir?"

"It wouldn't be if I were in command," Kang growled. "But it may be around here."

"I did wake up some of the other poor bastards who were on sentry duty last night," Slith said, adding with a shrug. "No one saw anything strange. No one heard anything out of the ordinary."

Kang shook his head, stared gloomily at his battle-axe.

"I did find out about those Dark Knights, though,

sir," Slith said. He was worried. He'd never seen his commander so cast down, so glum. Not even when it looked like they were all going to be goblin-fodder. "There's a keep held by Dark Knights near here. I brought a map."

He spread the map out on the floor, indicated the position of General Maranta's fort, and drew a line with a claw that led northward about thirty-five miles. "Here, sir. No one seems to know much about them, except that they think its an entire Wing—cavalry and foot. Prokel says the Knights may not know that this fort is here."

"The hell they don't," Kang grunted. "You can bet your silver wings that some blue dragon rider has spotted this fort and relayed the message to them. They may not *care* that we're out here, but they know. And I'll lay even money that General Maranta knows how many men the Knights have down to the last shit-hauling stable hand." He rolled up the map. "Is the general in his command tent?"

"I don't know, sir, but I can find out. Do you think our boys really headed that way, sir?"

"No, I don't. No one will ever convince me they deserted, Slith. But they're gone and there's nothing more we can do about it except what we're doing. Meanwhile, we have ten thousand goblins out there to worry about."

"I get it!" Slith said, intrigued. "You're figuring on asking the Dark Knights to help us."

"They may be human," Kang said. "But we're all on the same side. Once they hear that the cursed Solamnics are behind this, they'll jump at the chance to get into the battle. I'm just surprised the general hasn't thought of this before."

"Good luck, sir," Slith said.

Kang snorted. He hoped he didn't have to depend on Lady Luck. He and she just didn't seem to be on speaking terms these days.

Chapter Eleven

Shanra and Hanra strolled through the fort's small community, looking purposeful and confident, taking care not to gawk or stare, although there was much they wanted to gawk and stare at. They had never been inside a fort or any type of town or city. They had never seen so many of their kind in one place at the same time.

Being hungry, they decided their first stop should be the mess hall, of whose wonders and glories they'd heard about from Cresel. In any event, the mess hall—filled with male draconians—would be a good place to find out if they could blend in with these males as easily as they did the draconians of their own regiment. They had some difficulty locating the mess hall, but eventually Hanra—the bolder of the two—found the courage to step up to a draconian and ask for directions. The draconian glanced at them, glanced at the emblem on their leather armor, which was the emblem of the First Dragonarmy Engineers, and pointed down the right street.

"That was easy," said Hanra.

"So far so good," said her more cautious sister.

"Do you suppose what Cresel said is true?" Hanra asked, as they made their way through the crooked streets lined with ramshackle buildings. "That there's so much food spread out that you can eat and eat until you're stuffed and then keep eating?"

"No," said Shanra. "I think Cresel's making it up."

"You're probably right." Hanra sighed. "Still, it's nice to dream."

The two found the mess hall and, not knowing what else to do, joined the line that had formed outside. The delicious fragrance of roasting goat meat wafting from the mess hall made their stomachs gurgle.

"When was the last good meal we ate in camp?" Hanra asked.

"I think it was that kender," Shanra said. "And there wasn't much to him." She sniffed. "This smells absolutely wonderful."

A draconian in front of them in line turned to stare at them. The sisters froze in terror, fearing they'd been discovered. But he only growled and asked if they were crazed or what.

"Beans and goat again," he grumbled. "Burned at that. How do they expect a guy to fight when they feed him swill like this?"

"Yeah, how?" Shanra said, hardening her voice.

"It's disgraceful," Hanra agreed.

Inside, they followed the example of the other draconians, picked up large, square wooden platters and, when they came to a draconian standing over a huge kettle, ladling out food, they held their platters in front of him, as did the others. He dumped a ladle full of beans and meat onto Hanra's platter. She stood staring in astonishment. She'd never seen so much food.

He looked at her. "You want more?"

"Can I have more?" She gasped.

"Glutton for punishment, ain't you?" the cook said and dumped out another ladle.

The two found places at a table—a long board stretched across trestles. The food was every bit as wonderful as it smelled. They began to shovel in the beans and meat until they noted that their table companions were staring at them.

"They must be those engineers we rescued from goblins," said one. "I heard they were near starving."

"That explains it," said another with a disgusted glance at his own platter.

"Say, I hear you got females with you?" said the first, turning to Hanra. "What are they like?"

"Oh, just like us," said Shanra, winking at her sister.

"Only more intelligent," Hanra added. "Stronger, wiser, better looking—"

"I saw them," said one. "Nothing special. They are just like us, in fact. And what's the fun in that? I'll take human females any day."

"Yeah," said another, "hugging one of those female dracos would be just like hugging one of you guys!"

The males laughed. Hanra spluttered, so furious she couldn't speak.

"We have to go," said Shanra, jumping up. She caught hold of Hanra's arm and began dragging her toward the door. "Time for inspection."

Hanra's fists were clenched. "I'll give them a hug they'll never—"

"No, you won't. Not today." Shanra herded her volatile sister out of the mess hall.

The two walked aimlessly about for a little while,

kicking at stones in glum silence.

"Do you suppose they all feel like that?" Hanra asked at last. "The commander and . . . and Slith?"

"I don't know," said Shanra. "We've heard some of the others talk about human females before. You know, when they think we're asleep."

"But not Slith," said Hanra hopefully.

"No, not Slith," Shanra agreed. "We'll ask Fonrar. She'll know. Meantime, we have work to do. I wonder where they store the weapons?"

"I'll ask," said Hanra.

"No, it's my turn," said Shanra sharply. "You asked the last time."

"Yes, but you—"

"Something I can help you fellows find?" A draconian officer stopped.

"Uh, yes, sir," said Shanra in some confusion. "We . . . uh . . . lost our swords—"

"Broken," Hanra said. "In the fight—"

"—with the goblins. And we need—"

"Replacements," said the officer, who happened to be Prokel, although they did not know it. "Just have Commander Kang fill out a requisition form and take that form to the quartermaster in that building over there. He'll fit you up with everything you need. I guess Kang's wanting to make certain everyone's prepared for the big goblin assault."

The two sisters exchanged glances. "Yes, sir," said Hanra.

"Thank you, sir," Shanra added.

"Any luck on finding those two deserters?" Prokel asked.

"Deserters, sir?" Hanra gaped.

"Those two men from your regiment who left in the night. I guess they're not officially deserters yet."

"Uh, n-no, sir," Shanra stammered. "Not that I know of."

"Well, good luck with the hunt. Give my regards to your commander." Prokel strode off.

"Deserters!" Hanra said bleakly.

"Goblin assault," Shanra said.

"Requisition," they said simultaneously and looked at each other in dismay.

"Maybe Fonrar could write us a requisition," Hanra suggested. "You know, forge the commander's name."

"I don't see how," Shanra argued. "Do you even know what a requisition is?"

"No," Hanra admitted.

"Me neither."

The two stood there, staring at each other.

"Well, it can't hurt to go take a look at this quartermaster place," Shanra said. "Maybe we'll get an idea when we see it."

"And at least we'll be able to tell Fon where it is," Hanra agreed.

The two followed Prokel's directions, losing themselves twice amidst the tangle of streets. By this time, they realized that their unique ability to blend in with their surroundings was working yet again. The other draconians in the fort took them to be newcomers with Kang's regiment and were helpful in showing them the way they needed to go.

The sisters found the weapons supply warehouse. Unlike the rest of the buildings, the warehouse was made of the same material as the general's quarters—stone, wood, and hard-baked mud. It had no windows and a heavy wooden door barred the entry. If the fort was penetrated by enemy troops, the draconians did not want their enemies arming themselves with draconian weapons. The door stood open this day. A large and corpulent draconian sat at a table just inside the door, in the shady coolness. Two bozak guards sat inside with him, playing at some sort of game. Shanra and Hanra hung about at a safe distance, trying to see inside, but without much success.

As they watched, a baaz carrying a scroll came hurrying up. Entering the building, he saluted.

"Requisition for three broadswords, sir," said the baaz and handed over the scroll.

The sivak sisters looked at each other, nodded.

The quartermaster unrolled the scroll, glanced over the requisition. Turning, he shouted to someone inside the building and made a notation in a large ledger. The baaz left, lugging three broadswords with him. The swords gleamed in the sunlight. The sisters gazed at them with longing.

"We have to have one of those requisitions," said Hanra emphatically.

"Agreed," said Shanra. "But I haven't a clue how to get one, do you?"

Hanra shook her head.

Shanra sighed. "Well, there's no use hanging around here. Someone's bound to see us and get suspicious. Nothing left but to go back and make our report."

The two walked disconsolately down a street that ran alongside the warehouse. This street, which was one of the few wide, straight streets, led straight to the Bastion. Other streets branched off this main road, some actually going somewhere, others simply dead-ending, as though having come this far they had forgotten why they wanted to be here.

The sisters walked with bowed heads, kicking irritably at loose rocks. Hearing voices nearby, the sisters looked up to see two of the grandest, most splendid sivaks they had ever seen. The sivaks wore chain mail

171

armor that gleamed in the sunshine. They carried huge, ornate, curved-bladed swords thrust into jeweled leather belts. They each wore a tabard made of cloth bearing the emblem of a five-headed dragon.

"That's one of the Queen's Own!" Hanra said, awed.

"The ones Cresel told us about. They once served Her Dark Majesty!"

At the sight of these wondrous beings, the sisters forgot their injunction not to gawk and stare and did both. Only when the officers were almost upon them, did the two remember themselves. They came to attention, standing stiff and straight, saluting as they had been taught. The two officers never even glanced at them, made no acknowledgement of them. The officers continued chatting as if no other creature of consequence was in the area.

"I'm off to the mess hall. Will you join me?" said one.

"Later, when I'm off-duty," said the other. He flourished a scroll. "Right now, I have to fill this requisition for twenty swords put in by the general's aide."

The two parted company, one heading down a sidestreet, the other continuing toward the arms warehouse.

"Twenty swords!" Hanra whispered, awed. "Just our number!"

"Maybe the commander's wrong," Shanra whispered back. "Maybe there is a god."

They both stared after the departing sivak officer, stared especially at that precious scroll he held in his hand.

"What do we do?" Shanra asked urgently.

"This!" said Hanra.

She scooped up a large rock and began to pad soft-footed down the street. Reaching the sivak officer, Hanra lifted the rock and clouted him over the head.

To be fair to the Queen's Own, he considered himself as safe from attack in this fort as he would have been inside his own eggshell. The thought that he might be ambushed by two members of his own race certainly had never occurred to him. The Queen's Own were honored, revered, feared. If he heard the pattering of footsteps or the nervous giggle coming up behind him at all, he paid no heed to them. He went down like a lightning-struck oak tree.

"What have you done?" Shanra cried, racing after her sister.

"Found us twenty broadswords," said Hanra coolly.

"Suppose someone saw you?" Shanra gasped.

Hanra glanced around belatedly. The street was, fortunately, empty.

"No one did," she said. "Grab his feet."

The two dragged the sivak into one of the many alleyways that meandered through the town. Hanra plucked the blessed requisition from his hand. Shanra pulled the tabard off over his head. The two eyed his sword with longing.

"Better not," Shanra advised. "Someone would be sure to recognize it and know where we got it."

"I suppose you're right," Hanra said. She held out her hand. "I'll wear the tabard."

"You will not!" Shanra said, clutching it. "You got to hit him over the head! It's my turn to do something!"

"*I* have the requisition," Hanra said, waving it in the air.

"I'm wearing the tabard," Shanra said stubbornly and settled matters by popping it over her head.

"You will not—" Hanra began angrily.

Footsteps sounded down the street.

"Someone's coming!" Shanra whispered. "Give it! Give it!" She gestured frantically at the requisition.

"Oh, all right!" Hanra said. With an ill grace, she shoved the scroll into her sister's hand.

Two baaz draconians passed by the alleyway. Neither looked down it. Neither saw either the sisters or the body of the unconscious member of the Queen's Own. Shanra straightened the tabard. Hanra, sulking, brushed off the dirt. Heads high, the two marched out of the alley.

"You're not as high-ranking as I am. You should walk a few steps behind me," Shanra said out of the corner of her mouth.

"Like hell I will!" Hanra hissed.

The two strode up to the arms warehouse.

"You wait outside," Shanra said in an imperious tone to Hanra.

Hanra glared at her sister, but, under the eyes of the quartermaster and his assistants, she could do nothing but obey.

"Yes, sir!" she said, saluting with a snap of her hand and her teeth.

The quartermaster peered uncertainly at the apparent member of the Queen's Own. The sun outside was bright, the warehouse dark. He wasn't sure who this one was.

"Can I help you, sir?" he asked.

"Requisition for twenty broadswords," said Shanra, tossing the scroll down on the table in bored fashion.

"Yes, sir," said the quartermaster. He glanced at it and, finding it all in order, said, "I'll have these delivered. The usual place?"

Shanra stiffened. Behind her, she heard Hanra make a smothered sound.

"Uh, n-no, that won't do. We . . . That is the general . . . wants them now. Immediately. I brought my aide . . ." Shanra gestured behind her. "We'll carry them," she finished weakly.

"Well . . ." The quartermaster looked dubious. "If you say so . . ."

"General's orders," Shanra said desperately.

The quartermaster shrugged. He had the requisition, complete with the general's official seal. If the Queen's Own wanted to lug twenty broadswords through the streets, who was he to argue? No scales off his snout. He ordered his assistants to fetch the weapons.

Hanra, outside the warehouse, looked nervously up and down the street, expecting fifty members of the Queen's Own to come swooping down on her and her sister, declaring them imposters, outlaws, murderers and thieves. Inside the warehouse, Shanra tried to appear casual and nonchalant. She had just about succeeded in this when it occurred to her that perhaps one of the godlike Queen's Own should look stern and impatient.

"Let's hurry it up there," she said imperiously, staring down her nose at the quartermaster.

"Yes, sir," said the quartermaster. "Here they come now, sir."

Two baaz assistants came out of the darkness of the warehouse's interior, bearing between them a large wooden box. From the depths of the box came a most satisfactory sound of steel clattering against steel. The baaz plumped down the box with a thump.

Shanra looked at the box, looked at her sister. The two knelt to lift it.

The quartermaster stared, rose to his feet. "Sir! You shouldn't be having to carry that! I'll send my assistants—"

"No, no!" Shanra said. "Quite all right. I . . . need the exercise! Um, er, punishment for getting my tabard muddy! Let's get a move on, there!" she said sternly to her sister.

"Yes, sir!" said Hanra enthusiastically. For once the two were in complete agreement.

The sisters hefted the heavy box with ease and were out of the warehouse and dashing down the street before the quartermaster had fully recovered from the shock.

"I never saw the like!" he said, amazed.

"Me neither, sir," said one of his assistants.

"Did you recognize that sivak?"

"I've seen him around, sir," said the baaz.

"Yes, me, too. I can't seem to remember his name, though."

"I wonder what the general's doing with all those swords," the baaz said. "Forty swords a week ago. Twenty two days ago. Twenty more today. We're starting to run low. Maybe it's something to do with those damn gobbos."

"Maybe," said the quartermaster. He stared very hard at the requisition. All was in order. That was the general's seal. He shook his head. "Maybe."

* * * * *

General Maranta was inside his command tent and agreed to see Commander Kang. Two of the Queen's Own standing outside the tent closely scrutinized Kang before he entered. He had not worn his battle-axe or any other weapon and so he was passed through without difficulty.

The command tent was large enough to accommodate not only the general but several aides, who were busy at various occupations. In addition, the tent held a large table on which was spread out an enormous map of the area, a large desk occupied by the general, and smaller desks for his aides.

Kang waited near the tent flap until General Maranta should take notice him. The general was not one to make an officer cool his claws just to show that he could do so. General Maranta waved Kang over almost immediately.

"Any sign of your deserters?" General Maranta asked.

Kang set his jaw, looked over the general's head at a spot on the tent. "I don't think they deserted, sir," he said.

"You don't?" General Maranta's eyes narrowed. He pointed to the south. "There's eight thousand goblins out there right now, Commander. And more coming. I hate to say it, but we have to face facts. Vertax lost three men from his regiment the night before—"

"*My* men wouldn't desert, sir," Kang said proudly. "We've been in tough situations before this and my troops haven't run. They wouldn't do so now, sir."

"I see," said General Maranta coolly. "You consider yourself a better commander, your troops more loyal—"

"No, sir," said Kang, embarrassed. "That's not what I meant. It's just—" He floundered, helpless to explain. How could he make this aurak understand the community they had built, the hard times they'd endured, the good times they had celebrated. All of them together. He couldn't and so he gave up. "I don't believe they deserted. I think there's some other explanation. I think something happened to them and I mean to find out what. Perhaps there'll be word when my squadrons return this afternoon, sir."

"I hope so, Commander," said General Maranta, his tone cold. "I hope you find them and that your faith in them is justified." He started to turn away. "Now if there is nothing more—"

"There is, sir." Kang cleared his throat. "I was just informed that there is a Wing of Dark Knights not far from here. I was thinking that we could send a messenger to the Dark Knights asking for their aid in battling the goblins, sir."

"Out of the question," said General Maranta shortly. "I wouldn't ask a human for help if I was falling off a cliff and his was the only hand that could save me."

"I know how you feel, sir, believe me," said Kang, "but I've had some dealings with the Dark Knights and I think that they—"

"The answer is no, Commander," said General Maranta, his red eyes glinting. "You are dis—"

A commotion at the front of the tent distracted the general. He turned to look, as did Kang and everyone else. Two of the Queen's Own came inside, carrying one of their comrades. The sivak sagged in their arms. He looked ill and dizzy, his feet dragged. He was not wearing his tabard.

"Is that Corak?" General Maranta stared at the sivak. "What is wrong with him? What happened?"

"He was beaten and robbed, sir. A couple of bozaks found him in the alley behind Signal Regiment's latrine."

"Who did this to you, Corak?" General Maranta demanded.

The sivak shook his head weakly. He made a sort of croaking sound.

"He doesn't remember anything about the attack, sir. All he remembers is that he was taking a requisition to the armaments. He doesn't remember anything after that."

"What did the thieves steal from him?"

"The requisition, sir. That and his tabard. I spoke to the quartermaster. He said that shortly before lunch, two sivaks arrived with a requisition for twenty swords. One of them wore the tabard of the Queen's Own."

"Yes, I gave Corak that requisition," the general said, mystified. "Did the quartermaster fill it?"

"He had no reason not to, sir. Yes, he filled it. The two

sivaks left carrying the box of broadswords. He did think that was odd, sir, but they said that they were following your orders and he didn't want to question them."

"Strange, very strange." General Maranta eyed Kang. "Nothing like this has ever happened before. Not until you and your draconians arrived."

Kang stiffened at the insult, so angry he could barely contain himself. He remained in control, though he allowed his perfectly justifiable anger to be heard.

"Sir," he said, his voice grating, "my men do not steal. And may I remind the general that every one of my troops has been out of the fort the entire day searching for our missing men with the exception of myself and two *bozak* draconians left to guard the females. Commander Prokel will testify to this, sir."

"These *were* sivaks, sir," said one of the Queen's Own. "The quartermaster was sure about that. He also thought they looked familiar. He's seen them about here before."

"None of my sivaks have been anywhere near the arms warehouse, sir," Kang stated.

"Well, well," said General Maranta and he cast a sidelong, conciliatory glance at Kang. "Perhaps I was mistaken, Commander. You can understand my initial reaction."

"Yes, sir," said Kang, which was all he could say.

"We must work to clear up this mystery. I want a complete search of all living quarters, shops, stalls, warehouses. Twenty swords will be difficult to conceal. You will have no objection if we search your troops' quarters, Commander?"

"Certainly not, sir," said Kang. "So long as everyone in the fort is searched."

"They will be," said General Maranta dryly. "Thoroughly.

Dismissed, all of you." He waved his hand at the injured Queen's Own. "Take this man to the healers."

* * * * *

That night, Kang sat alone in his tent. He had a great many things he was supposed to be doing, but he did none of them. All squadrons had returned and reported in. No sign of the missing men. He would have no choice. He would have to list them as deserters. His only small amount of grim satisfaction came from the fact that the Queen's Own had made a thorough search of the half-completed barracks and had not turned up the missing swords. They had even insisted on searching the females' barracks, although Kang pointed out that they had been locked inside all day, with their own guard to keep watch over them.

The females stood for the inspection, each at the end of her bunk. The Queen's Own did a thorough job, though they must have felt there was little likelihood of success. They did not appear surprised that they found nothing and even apologized to Fonrar for the intrusion.

Fonrar had wanted to know what was going on, what they were searching for, but Kang was too upset to talk to her. He was too upset to talk to anyone. He sat in the dark, going over and over in his mind the few clues he had regarding the disappearance of his troops.

A knock came on the tent pole.

"Leave me alone," Kang muttered.

"Commander Vertax to see you, sir," said Granak in apology.

Vertax entered. Kang lurched to his feet, fumbled to light a lamp and find another chair. "Sorry, Commander. I—"

Vertax was sympathetic. "Don't apologize. I know

how you feel. I lost a couple of mine a few days ago. Good men, too. I wouldn't have thought they had it in them to run. But you never know what will drive someone over the wall."

Kang sat in silence.

"But that isn't why I've come." Vertax made himself comfortable. "General Maranta likes your idea."

"My idea, sir?" Kang asked, puzzled. "Which idea was that?"

"Your idea about sending a message for help to the Knights of Takhisis."

Kang's jaw dropped. General Maranta had so thoroughly discounted that idea that Kang had forgotten all about it. "But . . . this afternoon. He wouldn't even consider . . ."

Vertax shrugged, smiled. "The Old Man's like that. You'll learn his ways after you've been here long enough. He's quick to make up his mind, that's true. But he's not afraid to admit when he's been wrong. He's been considering this plan of yours and, although he doesn't like going to the humans for help, he thinks that it may be our only alternative. As he says"—Vertax grinned—"he likes the notion of humans dying to save *our* hides for a change."

"I'm pleased, naturally," Kang replied in some confusion.

"Good!" Vertax rose from his chair. "You'll leave first thing in the morning."

"Me?" Kang was astonished. "But I'm . . . I'm an engineer. He should send . . . an infantry officer—yourself, sir . . ."

"General Maranta wants you, Kang," said Vertax. "You've had dealings with these Dark Knights before. You know how to talk to them, what to say. He thinks you're the best man for the job."

181

"I'm glad the general has confidence in me, but I have too much to do to leave. There's these missing men. The troops have our living quarters to finish building. I need to make an inspection of the fort to determine what repairs—"

"Your second-in-command can do that," said Vertax. He looked at Kang gravely. "You have your orders, Commander."

There wasn't much to say in answer to that and Kang said it.

"I guess I'm going." He shrugged.

"Good. I'll tell the general. Do you require an escort?"

"I have my own bodyguard, sir."

"Requisition any weapons and supplies you'll need for the road."

Kang said he would and stood up to shake hands. "Speaking of requisitions, did those missing swords ever show up?"

"Not to my knowledge," said Vertax. "The Queen's Own turned the fort inside out. General Maranta's hopping mad. He even sent men down into the latrines."

Kang shook his head. "I'm thankful I didn't have that job."

"You and me both!" Vertax laughed, and departed.

* * * * *

"Hoist it up," said Fonrar, peering down into the slit trench. "Carefully, carefully, steady now . . ."

The baaz had tied ropes around the box to lower it. They were now hauling on the ropes to drag the box up from the females' latrine. Fonrar had meant to leave the stolen swords down there, but having heard from Cresel that the Queen's Own had ordered all latrines to be searched, the females panicked, all except

Thesik, who said that no one would search theirs. No one would think of it. As it was, there was nothing Fonrar could do. She didn't dare bring the box up while it was still daylight.

Thesik proved to be right. Apparently, no one remembered that the females had their own separate latrine. They might well remember by morning, however. That night, Fonrar ordered the box removed. The swords were distributed, one by one.

"Hide them beneath the mattresses," Thesik suggested.

"But that's the first place they'll look," Fonrar protested.

"Exactly. It's the first place they did look. They searched our bunks already. This is perfect."

"I suppose," Fonrar said.

"Come on. Cheer up! Twenty swords! This is what you've always wanted."

"Do you realize what kind of trouble the commander could get into, Thes?" Fonrar said miserably. "He'd take the blame. He always does. The general might even court-martial him!"

"I told you she'd complain!" Hanra said in an undertone to her sister. "We can't do anything right!"

"No one's going to find out. You'll see," Thesik said confidently. "And now you have real swords for drill tomorrow."

"What do we do with the box, Fon?" asked one of the baaz.

"Break it up—quietly! We'll hide the slats in with the slats of the bunks."

"Phew! It stinks!" protested a bozak.

"Look at this way, now the men won't say we smell different!" Thesik said.

"Here, ma'am," said Riel, presenting Fonrar with a sword. "You have the first one."

The barracks were dark. The females didn't dare risk a light. The lambent light of the stars formed silver slit-shaped patches on the floor. The argent light ran like quicksilver down the length of the fine blade. Fonrar wrapped her hand around the hilt. It seemed to have been made for her.

"It is beautiful, isn't it, Thes?" Fonrar said softly.

"Beautiful," Thesik agreed.

Chapter Twelve

Kang and his small escort force consisting of Granak and two baaz left the fortress before dawn, slipping out in the half-light, hoping to avoid goblin patrols. They had no trail to follow, but Kang and his men made good time through the canyon, running easily across the flat, rock-strewn ground. A ridge of ancient mountains cut across their path. The once-jagged peaks were rounded, like worn-down teeth, and covered with scrawny pine trees and a jumble of bushes that appeared to thrive in crevices. No pass led through the mountains. Humans would have found the going difficult. Kang and his men used their wings to carry them over deep fissures and rock falls, lift them up out of cul-de-sacs.

Topping a ridge, Kang paused to catch his breath. Granak tapped him on the shoulder.

"Look there, sir."

Kang looked. An enormous brown blob was crawling slowly across the landscape far to the east. At first he thought he was seeing a large herd of animals—bison, perhaps, or antelope. And then he understood. Goblins. Thousands more goblins, coming to join the already vast goblin army.

Kang shook his head. There wasn't much to say that hadn't already been said. But the draconians did run a bit faster.

The trip over the mountains cost them a day's hard labor and everyone was glad to rest when night came. They camped out in a slit between two jagged outcroppings, lit no fire, kept two men on watch. They were up before the dawn, came down out of the mountains to find themselves on a sea of tall, rolling grass whose rippling waves lapped against a shoreline of thick forest. Slith's map showed the Knights' keep north and east of their present location. The draconians continued on.

About noon, clouds rolled in and a light, chill rain began to fall. Reaching the forest, they searched out animal trails leading in the general direction they wanted to go.

"You've noted we're being followed, sir?" Granak asked in low tones when they stopped to drink at a stream.

"I've seen them," said Kang.

He had detected the scent of horses and humans about an hour past and guessed that he and his guards were being observed by a squadron of light cavalry. This gave him his first indication that he was near his objective, heading in the right direction. The cavalry was on his left flank. They took care to keep out of arrow range, but they made no secret of their presence. He could occasionally see one of them moving through the trees. He could hear the clank of armor, the jingle of harness, the crack of a branch snapped by a horse's hoof.

The trail led out of the forest and onto a man-made road cut through the trees. The road was hard-packed dirt and some care had been taken to maintain it. Ruts from wagon wheels, hoof prints and foot prints were further indications that the road was heavily trafficked, convincing Kang that this road led to his destination. The draconians had followed the road for only about a mile when their way was blocked by a mounted patrol of six soldiers. They wore oiled canvas capes against the rain. The folds of the capes fell partially across their swords, leaving enough metal showing to make certain the interlopers saw that the patrol was well armed.

Kang brought his party to a halt.

The patrol leader rode forward. His horse, unaccustomed to the scent of the draconians, balked, shied. Kang remembered a time when mounted warriors of the Dark Queen trained their horses to remain calm around draconians. This young officer had not even been born then.

The officer was evidently a good horseman. He was understanding about his horse's fright, not flustered or embarrassed. Summoning an aide to hold the horse, the officer dismounted and approached Kang on foot.

Kang advanced, the tall, imposing Granak solid at his back.

"This road is under the jurisdiction of the Knights of Takhisis," said the young human, speaking Common. "Please state the nature of your business in our territory."

"Kang, commander, First Dragonarmy Engineers. I'm on my way to see your commander," Kang replied.

The officer looked skeptical. "First Dragon . . . army, sir?"

Kang chuckled, although he felt a pang of regret.

How quickly they were forgotten. "First Dragonarmy. It was formed during the War of the Lance and was long gone by the time you were born. But our regiment was never disbanded, so we've never dropped the name. It's a name we're proud of," he added.

The officer studied Kang, then drew himself up, saluted. "Yes, sir. Can you state the nature of your business with our commander, sir?"

"I'd rather not," Kang said. "I don't have the authority. I'm acting under orders from my superior officer."

"Very well, sir, I will send a rider ahead to notify the Division Headquarters of your coming."

Kang nodded. The officer called out a soldier, gave him the message. The cavalryman galloped off down the road.

Kang exchanged glances with Granak. The general had guessed there was a Wing of Dark Knights here, not an entire division. The Dark Knights must be the dominating force in this part of the world. Humans have no love for goblins and they would not be pleased to hear of a large force of goblins massing nearby. An entire division! Between the Dark Knights and the draconians, they should be able to destroy the goblin army with relative ease. Especially if these Knights had dragons.

"So my men and I must be the first draconians you've ever met," Kang said to the young officer as they proceeded up the road together.

"Yes, sir, you are," said the young officer.

Kang sighed.

* * * * *

The chill rain strengthened to a downpour by the time they reached the keep, shortly after dusk. The keep was not pretty to look at. A hulking gray slab of stone, wood and mortar, surrounded by a moat, the keep stood on the highest promontory for miles about, overlooking a river landing below and guarding a pass beyond. Kang approved both the construction and the location.

Kang, his bodyguard, and his cavalry escort marched through the outer dirt ramparts that were the keep's first line of defense. Here, the young officer saluted Kang, who saluted him in the manner taught to him so many years ago in the dragonarmies.

"Good luck, sir," the young officer said.

He remounted his horse, who had by this time become somewhat reconciled to the draconians, though the beast still watched Kang with a suspicious eye and was obviously not sorry to depart. The cavalry troop wheeled in unison and galloped down the road. Kang watched, admiring the precision of their moves, then turned and proceeded on.

A wet and shivering sentry halted them at the drawbridge. The cold and pelting rain had little effect on the draconians, whose body temperature lowered to accommodate the chill. The water slid off their shining scales.

Kang gave his name and rank. The sentry nodded. Rain washed off his helmet and trickled into his eyes. He blinked the water away. "They're waiting for you, sir, in the keep. You can go on ahead. Someone will meet you on the other side of the drawbridge."

The soldier saluted again. Kang returned the salute and walked across the drawbridge, Granak and the two baaz trudging stolidly behind. Below, the brown water of the moat rippled as sheets of rain swept across it.

The draconians entered a tunnel that passed through the keep's outer ring wall, twenty feet thick at the base, and guarded by a portcullis at each end. Walking along the dark, rain-damp tunnel, Kang noted the murder holes set in the walls, so-called because during an attack on the keep, archers would be stationed on either side of the tunnel, ready to catch the enemy in deadly cross fire. Kang's skin twitched and his scales clicked nervously at the thought.

Leaving the ring-wall, Kang entered an open courtyard. An officer in a black tabard stood silently, waiting for the draconians. His tabard was soaked through. Rain poured down his face, yet he stood still and unmoving. He waited until Kang took his first step onto the stones of the courtyard, then brought his hand up in salute.

"Sir, I am Wing Commander Vosird of the First Wing, Wolf's Talon Division. I am to escort you directly to Groupcommander Zeck. He commands here."

Kang nodded, said nothing. The wing commander waited a moment, eyeing Kang, thinking that perhaps he might feel called upon to state his business. Kang did not and the wing commander had no authority to question him. The wing commander, looking slightly annoyed, turned and marched toward the main building of the keep. Kang looked back at his bodyguard, shrugged, then followed. The four draconians grinned and marched after their commander.

They entered a wooden door that was a foot thick. Guards were posted here and at the entrances to the outbuildings. A garrison troop stood on the ramparts. It was an impressive show of force for a keep located in the middle of a relatively peaceful region ruled by an army that wasn't at war with anyone.

The wing commander escorted Kang and his party inside the central building, along a series of hallways. They were passing through these corridors when they encountered a group of black-armored and helmeted

Knights. The Knights stepped aside to allow them to pass. All stared at the draconians before continuing on with their duties. Kang would not have taken particular note of any of this except that one Knight in particular stared at Kang so intently that the Knight almost walked into a stone pillar. The Knight was hooded and cloaked against the rain, so that Kang could make out nothing of the man, but he had the oddest impression that something about the Knight was familiar and that the Knight also seemed to recognize Kang.

By now they had reached their destination—another closed door. Here Kang's two bodyguards were asked to follow two of the guards, who would take them to their quarters. The draconians looked to Kang, who nodded, and the two obeyed. Kang and Granak continued on to the manorial hall, but before he left the hallway, Kang glanced back. The hooded Knight was still standing there, still staring at him. And then the door opened, they were being ushered inside, and Kang lost sight of the Knight.

Kang was introduced to Groupcommander Zeck and his officers and in the flurry of salutes, returning salutes and introductions, Kang forgot about the strangely familiar Knight.

Groupcommander Zeck offered refreshments for the visiting officers.

"Wine, ale? Or perhaps dwarf spirits?" The groupcommander smiled.

He was an older man and he had worked with draconians before, he told them. He apparently knew of their weakness for this particular fiery liquor.

"No, thank you, sir," said Kang, who wanted a clear head for this encounter. "We have traveled long and hard to reach you. The matter is of the utmost urgency."

"Of course, Commander," said Groupcommander

Zeck gravely. "I am all attention. Please state the reason for your visit."

Kang had gone over what he planned to say a thousand times while on the road, but being inside this impressive keep and in the presence of these high-ranking human officers, wearing their shining black, superbly crafted armor, momentarily confused him. Kang had been raised to think humans were only slightly lower than gods. Years of human blunders and failings had at last disabused him of that notion. He was astonished and somewhat amused to find a residue of the old adoration still lingered.

"Groupcommander Zeck, my commander, General Maranta sends his kindest regards, and wishes you and your command every success on or off the battlefield."

"Maranta," Groupcommander Zeck repeated, amazed. "You don't mean *the* General Maranta? The aurak?"

"Yes, sir, that's the one."

"I didn't even know he was still alive. Well, well." Groupcommander Zeck glanced around at his officers. Some of the older ones looked impressed, the younger ones blank. "What's he doing these days?"

Kang explained, gave the location of the fort of draconians and concluded by saying, "We need your help, sir. We need it badly. Our force of five thousand warriors is penned up in the fortress. We are besieged by an army of what we believe may be as many as twenty to thirty thousand goblins and hobgoblins. For reasons we are as of yet unable to fathom, they are bent on our destruction. We think that perhaps they are in the pay of the cursed Knights of Solamnia."

Groupcommander Zeck frowned. "Solamnics, is it? I wouldn't put it past them. What smattering of honor they once had is gone with their wretched coward of a god. I am familiar with your fortress out in the foothills.

I didn't know General Maranta was in charge, however, or I might have dropped by for a chat about old times. Goblins and hobgoblins, you say. Interesting. Seems damned improper for former allies to turn on you, doesn't it, Commander?"

Kang agreed that it did seem most improper.

"And you're here for our help?" Groupcommander Zeck asked.

"Yes, sir. Although we draconians and the Knights of Takhisis no longer work together in a combined army, my General has asked me to request that you come to our aid. In return, we offer diplomatic ties and the strong friendship of our race."

Groupcommander Zeck appeared impressed. "Your numbers are small, to be sure, but the history of the draconian race is rife with glory. We certainly would not want to lose such a staunch ally." The groupcommander turned to a waiting orderly.

"Dagot, I want you to have the Second and Third Wings prepared to ride out to do battle with the goblins in two days." He turned his attention back to Kang. "Is that satisfactory, Commander?"

Kang had expected the groupcommander to take the request under advisement, ask for several days to study the situation, promise to send General Maranta an answer within a week if they were lucky. He had not expected to have the matter settled in three minutes.

"Yes, sir," Kang said, recovering himself. "Most satisfactory."

"Excellent. Then our business is concluded. I would ask you to dine with us, but you are no doubt tired from your long journey. May I offer you and your companion officer a room for the night, supper and a hearty breakfast before you set out tomorrow?"

Kang's first inclination was to get back on the road

immediately, to return to his command. Then he thought of his men. He'd pushed them hard, he'd pushed himself hard. They would all travel faster on the morrow for hot food in their bellies and a good night's sleep.

"Yes, sir. I would appreciate that. We will be on the road in the morning. I look forward to meeting your warriors and officers on the field of battle."

Groupcommander Zeck nodded. "So it shall be." He turned away. The interview was at an end.

Wing Commander Vosiard, who had stood silently during this meeting, escorted Kang and Granak from the manorial hall, led them along a back corridor that was lined with doors. Halfway down the corridor, he opened a door, indicated a room with two beds—human-sized—and a table with a wash bowl and a pitcher of water.

"I'll have food sent up," said Voisard.

"Where are my men being barracked?" Kang asked.

The wing commander motioned with his thumb to an adjacent room. "Right next door, sir."

Kang dismissed the man, sat down on the bed, and gave a cavernous yawn.

"I'll go check on the troopers, sir," Granak offered.

Alone, Kang thought things over. Within twenty minutes of arriving at the keep, he had accomplished his goals. He didn't have any idea why, but this fact made him uneasy. Perhaps it was because he was so used to things going wrong, particularly when dealing with humans.

"By the law of averages, it's about time something went right," Kang reflected. "It's not surprising Group-commander Zeck made such a quick decision. He knows about our fort, his scouts would have told him. And since he knows about our fort, he might know about this build-up of goblins in his territory. He's probably not any happier about it than we are. Maybe he didn't know why they were here or what they were doing. Now that we've told him, he's going to act to get rid of them."

Granak returned to report that the two baaz body-guards had been well-fed and were already asleep. A human soldier brought a heaping platter of roast mutton to the room an hour later, along with a large jug of ale. Kang and Granak made short work of both. His belly full and his mind pleasantly fuzzy from the ale, Kang stretched out on the floor. He feared that if he lay down on the bed, he might smash it to kindling.

"If you want to sleep, sir, I'll keep the first watch," Granak offered, settling himself in a chair beside the door. "Did you notice? There're no locks on these doors."

Kang grunted. "I doubt if they're much bothered by thieving. There's no need to stand watch tonight, Granak. We're either in a powerful friend's camp, or a powerful enemy's. There's nothing we can do about anything they decide to do to us."

"If it's all the same, sir," Granak said respectfully, "I'll stand the first watch."

Kang closed his eyes. "If you insist. Wake me for the second."

* * * * *

Granak woke Kang, as promised.

"Anything to report?" Kang asked sleepily.

"No, sir. All quiet," Granak said.

Kang nodded and took his place in a chair by the closed door. Granak stretched out on the floor and was soon asleep, to judge by his dish-rattling snores. Kang's sleep had been uneasy. He was glad to have a chance to sit and think in solitude, if not silence. He was running over the groupcommander's words in his mind, reassuring himself that all was well, when he thought he heard, outside the door, the creak of a floor board.

The sound was soft, stealthy. He might have been mistaken. Hard to tell over Granak's snores. He recalled Granak's warning about no locks on the door and his own glib reply. Cursing himself for a fool, Kang eased himself out of his chair. Under the cover of Granak's rumbling, he crab-walked sideways, taking up a position that would put him behind the door if and when it opened.

Another crack of the wooden floorboard, this time accompanied by the creak of leather and the very soft jingle of harness. Outside, the rain was falling in torrents to judge by the drumming against the wall. A hand turned the door handle, gave the door a gentle shove inward. Kang crouched. A human entered the room, moving quietly on the balls of the feet. The human approached the slumbering form of Granak.

"Kang?" the human said, reaching out a hand.

Kang jumped, enveloping the human in his strong arms and covering the human's mouth with his hand to prevent him yelling for help.

Granak was on his feet at the same instant, a knife in his hand, moving to the door.

Their captive struggled briefly, instinctively, perhaps, and then relaxed in Kang's hold. The human was wrapped in a cloak and soaking wet, as if he had just come from outdoors in the rain.

"Check the hall!" Kang whispered, holding fast to his prisoner.

Granak peered out the door. "Empty, sir," he reported. Shutting the door, he put his back against it.

The human made some sounds, lips moving against

Kang's palm. He couldn't tell for certain, but they sounded like, "Let me go, Kang! You bloody fool! It's me!"

And then he knew her. Then he remembered.

"Huzzad!" He gasped, released her.

"Hush!" she said warningly, with a glance toward the door. Huzzad threw back the hood of her cloak and turned to face him. "You don't know your own strength. I'll be bruised for a week," she added, rubbing her forearms and twisting her neck.

"Huzzad, I didn't know—" Kang protested.

"You weren't meant to," she said crisply, cutting his apology short. "No harm done. I should have realized you wouldn't be caught napping. You were smart to set a watch."

"Granak's idea," Kang said, nodding to the large sivak. "You two haven't met. Granak, this is Huzzad, Knight of Takhisis. Huzzad, Granak. Huzzad and I met during that brief time we worked for the Dark Knights."

"I remember," said Granak, growling. "Digging latrines."

"If this is about our abrupt departure—" Kang began uneasily.

Huzzad shook her head. "You had every right to leave the Knights. You were treated shabbily. Not the first time. And it wasn't the last time, Kang."

Huzzad eyed him intently. He could see her as a warm-blooded entity in the darkness, brought her to mind as he had known her during the summer of the Chaos War. He saw her again on the back of her red dragon, a proud warrior. The two had become friends during their brief time together as allies. They had come to trust and respect each other.

"This will have to be quick and short," Huzzad said, speaking in a low voice. "I've just come from a Wing

Commander's Order Council and I don't have much time. You've been betrayed, Kang. Groupcommander Zeck isn't going to send the troops he promised."

Kang felt his disappointment as a dull ache inside him. "He has rescinded the order? What was his reason?"

"He didn't have to rescind the order, Kang. His officers knew he was lying to placate you so that you wouldn't cause trouble."

Huzzad leaned close, put her leather-gloved hand on Kang's arm. "The reason he lied to you. Can't you guess, Kang? Can't you figure it out?"

Seeing his blank look, Huzzad smiled sadly. "No, it would never occur to you. You—the 'monster,' the 'lizard-man,' the 'perversion.' We—the so-called 'civilized humans.' Surely you must have asked yourself who is arming and training these goblins, Kang. Paying them—and paying them well—feeding them, supplying them."

Huzzad sighed, her tone was bitter. "Now you have the answer. The Knighthood, Kang. Not the Solamnic Knighthood. The honorable Knighthood of her late Majesty, Queen Takhisis."

Kang took the blow in the gut. Her words drove the breath from his body. "I don't understand," he said bleakly. "Why? Because we refused to dig latrines for them?"

"The females, Kang," Huzzad said. "They know about the females. One of those dwarves, the runty one who gave you the map . . ."

"Selquist," said Kang.

He remembered the scrawny runt of a dwarf thief. An outcast from dwarven society, Selquist had been the one to find the map that led to the draconian females. The slimy dwarf had no idea what the treasure was, but it looked valuable and so he set out to claim it and Kang and his draconians had set out to reach the treasure first. The escapade had nearly gotten them all killed, but all's well that ends well. Or at least Kang had thought it had ended well. Apparently, he'd been wrong.

"Yes, that's it. Selquist. He sold you out. He went to the Knights and told them everything in return for a rich reward. The Knights are scared. Now that you have females, you can propagate. An all-male race could be controlled. Male draconians are strong and powerful, certainly, but you revered us. You were content to obey our orders, to live by our rules. And if there were rebels among you"—she shrugged—"they would be few and they could be easily removed. But now that you have the ability to reproduce, the Knighthood fears that you and your people will seek to determine your own destiny. And that makes you a threat."

Determine our own destiny. The words shot across the darkness of Kang's despair like a blazing star. Suddenly, all his thoughts, his dreams and plans were illuminated. He could see them clearly, give them a name. Destiny. His own destiny. The destiny of his people. He was enchanted, so enthralled and so moved that he lost track of what Huzzad was saying.

"Why are you telling us this now?" Granak was asking. He sounded suspicious.

Huzzad lifted her head proudly. "When I joined the Knighthood, I was given the Vision by our Queen. I believed in the Vision. I have led an honorable life, and have been promoted and decorated for it. I am true to the oath of loyalty I took, both to my fellow Knights, to our Queen and to those who fought with us as allies. I have ensured that those under my command do the same. But times are different now. I think I am the only talon commander in this entire Knighthood who still believes in the Vision.

"As for Groupcommander Zeck and the rest"—

Huzzad sneered—"they are nothing more than thieves and bullies. They fight among themselves. They wrestle for power. They terrorize the populace. And for what? Not for glory. Where is the glory in slaughtering peasants? In betraying our allies? They are in it for themselves. For power, for wealth. The only Vision they see is one made of shining steel.

"Leave first thing tomorrow, Kang, and don't take the main road. Keep to the woods until you reach the Endrikseen Pass Bridge. Zeck won't murder you inside the keep. There are still powerful draconians in the world, some serving Malystrx and the other new dragon Overlords. This place is rife with their spies. Zeck would be forced to answer for your deaths if you were killed here. But if you're waylaid on the road . . ." She shrugged.

"I understand. Thank you, Huzzad," Kang said quietly. "You are an honorable ally and a true friend. If you ever need help, you can call on me and my regiment. That's a promise."

She drew the hood of sopping wet cloak up over her head. "I have to leave now. I'll be missed."

She started for the door. Granak, at a nod from Kang, stood aside to let her pass. Pausing, her hand on the handle, she turned to him. "You don't think I'm going soft and weak like some sugar-coated Solamnic, do you, Kang?"

"Do you dream of growing old by the fire, Huzzad?" Kang asked. "Old and wrinkled, white-haired? Bouncing grandchildren on your knee?"

"No, I don't," she said. "But you do, Kang." She reached out her hand to him. "Good-bye. Good luck."

He grasped her hand, squeezed it warmly. "Thank you, Huzzad. More than I can say."

She was gone, shutting the door behind her.

"Should we leave now, sir?" Granak asked urgently. "I can go wake the others."

"No," said Kang, considering. "If we left now, it would look suspicious. We might get Huzzad into trouble. We'll wait until morning. Try to get some sleep, if you can."

"I don't think that's very likely, sir," Granak said and settled himself with his back against the door.

Kang sat down to think and watch for the first signs of the cold, gray dawn. Destiny, the blazing star, was still there, still shone bright in his mind. But it was far distant, more distant than any real star in the cloud-covered heavens.

Standing between him and his dream of a future for his people was an army of goblins, an army trained by some of the best warriors in all of Ansalon.

Chapter Thirteen

Kang and his men left the keep in the gray dawn. They were offered breakfast, but Kang refused, saying quite truthfully that they had a lot of territory to cover and that they would eat the trail food they had brought with them on the road. His stomach clenched at the thought of the mutton they had devoured so carelessly last night. A bit of poison slipped into the meat and no one would have been the wiser. Yes, they would have, Kang reflected. If he died, Groupcommander Zeck would have had to explain the shattering explosion when Kang's bones blew up. Much quieter to kill them on the road and blame the goblins. Not even Slith would think to question their disappearance. Certainly General Maranta would not.

"He'd probably figure we deserted," Kang muttered to himself.

He wondered briefly what Huzzad had meant about new dragon Overlords, served by powerful draconians. He wished they'd had more time to talk, but he didn't propose to hang about and discuss world politics.

He and his escort took the main road for as long as they were visible from the walls of the keep. Rounding a curve, they continued on the road down a steep hill. When they could no longer see the towers of the keep, Kang was certain that the watchers on the walls could no longer see them.

"Do you think we're being followed?" Kang asked.

Granak and the others sniffed the air.

"No, sir," Granak said.

"Of course, they wouldn't," Kang answered his own question. "Why should they? They know where we're going. They're down the road waiting to ambush us."

At this point, the road ran alongside the river. Kang continued on a short distance until he found a place where the river narrowed slightly. The water was ice cold and ran swift after the rain, but the draconians were all strong swimmers. Taking care to obliterate any tracks they had left on the muddy ground, Kang plunged into the water and swam ahead, using his powerful arms to fight the current that sought to carry him back in the direction of the keep. They reached the other side, hauled themselves out, and proceeded along the riverbank. They could keep the road in sight and yet not be seen.

The pass Huzzad had mentioned was beyond where they had met up with that mounted patrol. Kang figured that they should reach the bridge some time late that afternoon. Once there, they could safely return to the road.

They traveled along the river's edge, screened from the road by the trees and the expanse of the river. They could hear and sometimes see people traveling along the road, Knights on horseback and once a company of pikeman. They saw no signs of any ambush, however, and Kang was starting to think that Huzzad had been wrong. Not about Groupcommander Zeck. Kang had no doubt the groupcommander would be happy to be rid of him. But ambushing a few draconians probably just wasn't worth the effort.

"After all, the goblins are going to kill us anyway," Kang said to himself.

Having made up his mind to this, he was considerably astonished to hear voices coming from the direction of the stone bridge at Endrikseen's Pass.

The bridge was high above them, screened from their immediate view by some overhanging willow trees. Kang raised his hand, brought his group to a halt. They could all hear the voices now, as well as horses' hooves making a hollow drumming sound on the wooden slats of the bridge. The draconians crept closer to where they had a good vantage point.

Kang still couldn't see all that well. He recognized one of the voices, however.

"What do you bastards mean by drawing swords against a superior officer?" the voice raged. "Put your weapons away and stand aside. I have no time for such nonsense. I ride on urgent business from the group-commander."

"That's your human friend!" Granak said softly to Kang. "The one who warned us."

Kang nodded, waved Granak to silence, trying to hear.

"On the contrary, Commander," said a deeper voice in return, "I happen to know that Groupcommander Zeck issued you no such order. You were seen in the corridor where the dracos were housed last night and, when this was brought to the groupcommander's attention, he remembered that you had once been on friendly terms with these same dracos. As it has turned out, the draconians were apparently warned that they were in danger, for they have left the road and no trace can be found of them. You are being taken back on charges of treason—"

The Knight's words were cut short by a battle cry and the sound of ringing steel.

Kang waited no longer. Huzzad was in trouble and on his account. He would stand by her, as he had promised. He relished the chance to take his revenge on these treacherous Knights. Drawing his battle-axe from its harness, Kang bellowed a roar, to let Huzzad know that she had friends and to let his enemies know they were now facing five warriors, not just one. He and Granak and the other two draconian guards clambered up the bank. Huzzad was on the north side of the bridge. Kang and his draconians ran onto the bridge from the opposite direction. One Knight, the officer, and eight men-at-arms occupied the center of the bridge, caught in the middle. Kang and his group were outnumbered two to one.

Huzzad was already fighting four of the soldiers, striking to the left and the right with her sword, forcing them to keep their distance. She was holding her own until one dropped his sword to pick up a large rock. He threw the rock at her, striking her on the forehead, beneath her helm. The blow did not fell her, but it left her dazed and disoriented. Her attackers closed in, dragged her from the saddle.

Roaring a challenge, hoping to distract them from Huzzad, Kang thundered across the bridge. Behind him, Granak raised his voice in a murderous howl. The two baaz added their shrieks. At the terrifying sight of rampaging draconians, two of the human soldiers promptly dropped their weapons and fled. The Knight bellowed orders. Four wavered, but stood their ground, torn between fear of the draconians in front and their officer behind. The four who had attacked Huzzad were attempting to haul her off the bridge and into the woods beyond.

"You take the Knight," Kang ordered Granak.

The huge sivak descended on the line of guards, swinging his enormous sword with deadly effect, intent on reaching the Knight who stood behind them. Two of the guards went down in spatters of blood, bone and gore. One, seeing death upon him, chose his own way out and jumped from the bridge into the river. Granak knocked down the fourth with a blow of his fist, trampling the man beneath his feet. He and the Knight met in a deafening clang of metal.

Kang dashed after Huzzad's captors. Hearing his clawed feet behind them, the four dropped their burden to draw their weapons. Huzzad lay slumped on the wooden planks. Kang had no time to check to see if she was breathing. He slid his sword through one soldier's body, yanked it free, and—taking care to hop over Huzzad—attacked the next. He caught a glimpse of metal flashing behind him, but he was intent on his opponent and could not turn around. The two baaz had their commander's tail covered, however. Kang heard a shriek and a splash. The man he was facing dropped his sword and fell to his knees.

"Mercy!" he cried, staring at Kang with terror-filled eyes.

Kang recognized the cowardly cur who had thrown the rock at Huzzad.

"We're monsters, remember? Lizard-men, uncivilized." Kang grunted and lopped off the man's head. He kicked the still-quivering body into the river.

Turning, he was startled to see the Knight officer breathing down his neck. He raised his sword, about to attack, when the Dark Knight began to wave both hands and jump up and down in the air.

"It's me, Commander!" Granak's voice came from the Knight's mouth.

Kang relaxed. A sivak can take on the form of the person he has just killed, a fact Kang knew as well as he knew his sivaks but which he occasionally forgot in the heat of battle.

"Should I keep the illusion of Dark Knight, sir?" Granak asked. "In case there are any more."

Kang looked up the road and he looked down. Seeing no signs of anyone coming, he shook his head. "No, I don't see anymore. Change back. You give me the willies looking like that. Everyone all right?" he asked, glancing swiftly at his small troop.

The two baaz grinned, Granak nodded his head that was now once more the head of a sivak. No one was wounded. They had all enjoyed the fight. Satisfied that his troops were well, Kang knelt beside Huzzad, eyed her worriedly. He had no idea what was wrong with her. What little he knew about human anatomy came from seeing it leaking out of their ripped up corpses. Huzzad's face was covered with blood, but profuse bleeding was typical of humans, who had such soft, thin skin, and did not necessarily mean she was dead. He reached out a clawed hand, gently shook her shoulder. She didn't waken, but she was warm to the touch and breathing.

"What do we do with her, sir?" Granak asked, puzzled.

"We take her with us," Kang said. "She saved our lives. We would have walked right into that trap if it hadn't been for her. We owe her one."

Kang started to lift her, but Granak respectfully

elbowed his officer aside. "I can manage her, sir," he said and scooped her up effortlessly in his arms.

The four draconians set off at a run. Kang was determined to continue into the night. They would not rest until they had returned to the fort. He might have begrudged the time he'd wasted on this fool's journey, except that now he knew the nature of this new foe.

"Just what I need," he muttered as he ran. "Another enemy."

* * * * *

Kang and his small band traveled through the night and encountered no further trouble, except from Huzzad. She regained consciousness about three hours into their journey and ordered Granak to set her down on her feet. She could walk, she maintained. She could keep up. She managed a few tottering steps, at which point Kang told her that she was slowing them down, She had two choices. They could either leave her here, to make her own way through the goblins, or they would carry her.

Huzzad glared at him. "I won't be hauled about like some precious elf princess!" she said.

"Don't think of it that way, ma'am," Granak said politely. "Think of me as your horse."

Huzzad stared at him, then she began to laugh. Grudgingly admitting that Kang was right, Huzzad allowed Granak to pick her up again, but she insisted on riding "piggy-back," with her hands clasped around Granak's neck, giving him more freedom of movement. The draconians set off again.

The journey was not a pleasant ride for Huzzad. She grew increasingly pale and bit her lips against the pain the jarring was causing her. She said no word of complaint however, just gritted her teeth and did what she could to make the trip easier for Granak.

Kang's admiration for her, already high, increased.

The draconians arrived back at the fort just as dawn was breaking. The guards at the gates gaped in wonder at the bloodied human accompanying them, but passed them through on Kang's word that she was a friend. He noted that they dispatched a runner and guessed that within a few moments General Maranta would know that they had returned and brought a human with them.

"Where should I take her, sir?" Granak asked.

Huzzad had lost consciousness again, much to Kang's relief. He'd been sorry to see her suffering.

The answer was obvious to Kang. She was a female. He would take her to the females. Kang hoped that the female draconians would know how to care for this injured human, although he no longer possessed the illusions he had once held on that subject.

Kang entered his troop's newly completed barracks. He was proud to see that this building—erected in two days—was far better constructed than any other building in the fort. His engineers were now busy repairing and strengthening the wall of the stockade. Slith waved a hand and came loping over.

He regarded the comatose Huzzad with startled curiosity.

"Who in the Abyss is that— Wait! I remember her. That Dark Knight dragonrider. Where'd you find her, sir? What happened?"

"I'll tell you in a minute," said Kang. "First let me get her settled. Then I want a full report of what's been happening while I've been gone. Any sign of our missing troopers?"

Slith shook his head. "No, sir. But some more draconians have arrived. Another regiment."

"What?" Kang halted, amazed. "How? Who? Where did they come from?"

"I'll fill you in later, sir," said Slith. He nodded at Huzzad, limp in Granak's arms. Draconians were gathering around to stare. "You better take care of her."

"Oh, yeah, right," said Kang and made his way to the female's barracks.

* * * * *

"Commander's coming!" reported the baaz female who was standing look-out at the window. "And Granak. He's carrying something in his arms."

Fonrar ended sword drill in mid-thrust. "Put those weapons away!" she ordered. "Hurry up there! Douse that fire!" she added irritably to a spell-casting bozak.

"Sorry, Fon," the bozak said guiltily, stamping out the flaring sparks with her foot. "I didn't mean for the magic to work."

After a flurry of activity, the swords were all hidden away inside mattresses. The sparks were put out. A few of the baaz grabbed brooms and began industriously sweeping the floor of their barracks. Some of the others laid down on their beds.

Shanra gave a nervous giggle. "I wonder what he's bringing us. A present, maybe?"

"I hope it's another juicy kender," said Hanra. "They're starting to serve the most awful slop in the mess hall. They say it's because the men can't go out hunting—"

Cresel knocked on the door. "Commander," he said and paused just long enough to give the females time to quit doing whatever it was they might be doing that would almost certainly get him into trouble.

"Please come in, Commander," Fonrar said, opening the door herself.

Behind her, she heard the females jumping to their feet, scrambling to form ranks.

"Fonrar," Kang greeted her formally, stepped inside. "Girls." He nodded awkwardly at the others.

At Fonrar's command, the females saluted, rather belatedly. Twenty pairs of eyes were focused not on Kang but on the thing Granak was carrying.

"A human," Hanra growled out of the side of her mouth.

"A female human," Shanra growled back.

Kang acknowledged their salutes with a nod of his head. Moving to one of the beds—it happened to be Fonrar's—he ordered Granak to place the human female down on the bed with gentle tenderness.

Kang fussed over Huzzad, making her comfortable, telling the females to bring him blankets, arranging them around her carefully.

He lifted his head to give further orders and confronted twenty pair of eyes staring at him. The eyes were disapproving, if not downright hostile.

Kang was considerably taken aback. The females were obviously angry. He couldn't imagine what he had done to so infuriate them.

"Who is this, Commander?" Fonrar asked coldly.

"Her—her name is Huzzad," Kang said, rattled. "She's a Knight of Takhisis, a valiant warrior. She saved my life."

"What happened, sir?" Fonrar asked fearfully, her anger melting with her concern. "Are you all right?"

"Fine, fine!" Kang said, waving his hand. He was eager to leave this burden to others, eager to hear Slith's report. "She was hurt in the battle. I was thinking that you females might take care of her."

"She saved your life, sir?" Fonrar asked softly.

"Yes, she saved my life," Kang said, striving to be patient. "And the lives of Granak and the others."

Fonrar sighed deeply. "We'll take care of her, sir. Don't worry."

"Excellent," said Kang, mystified. "That's fine." He paused a moment. He knew that something was wrong, but for the life of him he couldn't figure out what it was.

None of the females said anything more. Thesik was gazing sadly at Fonrar. Hanra and Shanra were glaring at him irately, but that was preferable to Fonrar, who refused to look at him.

"I . . . have to go now," said Kang. Baffled, unable to comprehend what he'd done to upset them, he started for the door.

"Sir," Fonrar said wistfully, as he was leaving, "do you like her? The human female?"

"Like her?" Kang repeated. "Of course, I like her. She's an old friend. I knew her back when we worked for the Dark Knights."

"That's not what she means, sir," said Thesik. "She means do you 'love' her, sir." Thesik spoke the word in Common. The word did not exist in draconian.

"*Love?*" Kang repeated. If those twenty pair of eyes had been twenty goblin spears aimed right at his heart, he would not have felt more helpless than he did at this moment. "What is this nonsense?"

"We heard some of the guards talking, sir," said Thesik, seeing that Fonrar was too upset to respond. "About how they loved human females."

"Better than us, sir," Shanra added, pouting.

At this juncture, Kang would have preferred the twenty goblin spears. "I don't have time to explain right now," he said, his voice harsh to cover his embarrassment. "But, no, I don't . . . er . . . like her *that* way. She's *human*. She's squishy and lumpy." He looked back at them blankly. "What more can I say?"

"Nothing, sir," Fonrar said, smiling. "Nothing at all. We'll take good care of her, sir. You can rely on us."

"I hope you will," said Kang sternly.

But he had the feeling his sternness was lost on them. The females were grinning and nudging each other. He heard Hanra giggle.

"It's good to have you back safely, sir," Fonrar said.

"Thank you," said Kang. He departed in haste and utter confusion.

The twenty females gathered around the bed, stared down at Huzzad.

"Squishy," said Thesik, prodding the human with a clawed finger.

"*And* lumpy," said Fonrar happily.

Chapter Fourteen

"You are telling me that it is the Knights of Takhisis, our allies, who have hired the goblin army, trained them, equipped them and sent them to destroy us?" General Maranta stared, narrow-eyed, at Kang. "All due to the fact that *you* have discovered female draconians."

"So it would appear, sir," said Kang. He was dead tired, stupid with weariness, and yet he had to keep his wits sharp to hold his own with General Maranta's verbal sparring.

"So we would not be preparing for war against the goblins if we had not taken in you and your cursed females." General Maranta held up a hand that glistened with a golden sheen. "I'm not saying that we should have abandoned you and your troops, Commander. I just want you to consider what you owe us."

"I do, sir," Kang replied. "My troops are already

214

working to strengthen the fort. We will defend it to the end, to last drop of blood. But may I say, sir, that although our destruction was the Knight's primary objective, the destruction of this fort was next. Talon Commander Huzzad told us that you and the forces under your command have long been worrisome to the Dark Knights."

"Because I operate outside their control. Because I lead an army of skilled soldiers, born and bred for battle." General Maranta nodded sagely. "It is only right that they fear me."

"Yes, sir," said Kang.

"And our numbers are growing. I suppose you heard about the new contingent of draconians who arrived. They won't be the last. I'm convinced of it."

"Yes, sir," said Kang, too tired to make sense of this.

"Thank you for the information, Commander," General Maranta said, rubbing his hands together with a smile, his good humor restored. "And for bringing back this human prisoner. I look forward to interrogating her. Good looking, is she?"

"She is not a prisoner, sir," Kang returned. "She is my friend. She saved our lives. We owe her respect and honor, sir."

"She is a human, Commander." General Maranta eyed Kang, then said crossly, "Oh, very well. I am too busy to enjoy her. Keep her for yourself, if you like—"

"Sir!" Kang began a shocked protest.

General Maranta cut him off. "Return to your duties, Commander. We will defend you and your females. We will defeat this goblin army and give the Dark Knights even more to fear." General Maranta waggled a finger. "But no more talk of you leaving us, Kang. We saved your lives. You owe us those lives." General Maranta rose to his feet. "There will be no further talk of your leaving for this city of yours. Your place is here, Commander Kang. And here you will stay."

"Yes, sir," said Kang.

* * * * *

"You told him we'd stay?" Slith said, so amazed that he actually paused in the act of shoveling the last of the goat meat into his mouth. "But, sir—"

"It doesn't matter, Slith," Kang said. He was too tired to eat. All he wanted was sleep and he had duties to perform before he allowed himself that luxury. He shoved his half-full plate aside. "We can't defeat the goblin army. We can hold out for a week, maybe longer, but in the end—" He shook his head. "What we have to do now is to figure out how to save the females— What is it? Why are you shaking your head?"

Kang had to wait for Slith to swallow a mouthful.

"I'm not so sure, sir. You know I mentioned that more draconians had turned up."

"Yes, that's right. What about them? How many? Ten, twenty?"

"Five hundred, sir," said Slith, grinning, enjoying his commander's surprised reaction.

"Five hundred! Where'd they come from? How did they get through the goblin lines?"

"Good question, sir," said Slith. "They marched in the morning after you left, sir. General Maranta was on hand to welcome them. Made a speech and everything. Next thing I know, Prokel comes along and asks if we could use some help. I say 'sure' and he hands me a whole damned company of these new troops."

Slith finished his goat. Kang silently shoved his plate across to his second. Slith ate his commander's meal, relating his story between mouthfuls.

"I assigned them to Fulkth's squadron, who were detailed to bolster the ramparts. Later that day, Fulkth comes to me with a complaint. 'It's those new dracos,' he says. 'What about them?' I say. 'Are they insubordinate? Giving you trouble?' 'Oh, no!' says Fulkth. And he gets this strange expression. 'I almost wish they were. You better come see for yourself, sir.'

"So I take a look. Our men are working like gnomes with their pants on fire, hammering and sawing and lifting planks into place. I find these dracos just standing there, doing nothing. I'm ready to thump a few heads, when Fulkth stops me. 'Watch this,' he says. He goes over to one of them. 'Hammer these nails into this wall,' he says. The draco picks up the nail and he picks up the hammer and he hammers like there's no tomorrow. Then, when that's done and there isn't a unhammered nail left in sight, he quits. He goes back to just standing there.'"

Kang massaged his aching neck. "As I understand it, these draconians obey orders and you and Fulkth think there's something wrong with them?"

"It's not that, sir," Slith argued. "You see, there was no reason to hammer those nails into that wall. The draco did it because he was ordered to do it. He didn't ask what he was doing, which was nothing useful. He didn't look at us like we were nincompoops." Slith dropped his spoon onto his plate, leaned over the table. "It's that way with all of these new dracos. I think that if Fulkth ordered them to hammer those nails into each other's heads, they would do it."

"So we have troops who respect their officers." Kang grunted. "Might be a welcome change."

Slith shook his head. "You have to see these guys, Commander. There's something strange about them. They don't even look like draconians."

"Hunh?" Kang blinked.

"Oh, they're draconians," Slith hastened to assure his commander. "There's no doubt about that." He paused, tried to come up with an example of what he meant. "You know the other day when you were polishing your battle-axe to such an extent that you damn near rubbed a hole in it? Well, that's what they look like. Like someone's taken a cloth to them and rubbed all their features until they're sort of blurry and dull-looking."

"Blurry draconians," said Kang. He heaved himself up from the table. "That does it. I'm going to bed. By the way, where *did* they come from?"

"They say they come from the Khalkist Mountain region, sir," Slith answered.

"Well, that makes sense," Kang said. "The Khalkists aren't that far from here."

"Yes, but when you ask them *where* in the Khalkists, they only say 'the Khalkists.' "

Kang waved a hand. "I'm too tired to deal with this now. Anything else happen that I should know about?"

"No, sir," said Slith. "All progressing smoothly. Except that the scouts report that the goblin army is up to twenty-five thousand."

"Fine," said Kang, heading for the barracks. "If they show up, wake me. If not, don't."

"Yes, sir." Slith grinned, and went to see if he couldn't wheedle more food out of the cook.

* * * * *

Kang slept through all of the next day, all of the following night. The growling of his stomach woke him or he might have been asleep yet. After breakfast, he reviewed the repair work on the fort, found all proceeding well. At Slith's insistence, Kang observed the new troops and although he thought them rather slow and stupid, what else could one expect from draconians that had been skulking about the mountains for years in total isolation?

"If it hadn't been for us having to keep our wits sharpened to constantly battle those blasted dwarves," Kang said, "we might have ended up just like that."

"If you say so, sir." Slith was obviously not convinced.

Scout reports indicated that the size of the goblin army continued to grow. The goblins continued to train and exercise. Roving patrols had begun picking off any draconians who dared set foot outside the fort. Several scouts had not returned and now no one was allowed to leave the fort, including hunting parties. Kang waited all day for General Maranta to call a meeting of his officers to discuss the worsening situation, but the call didn't come.

Huzzad improved rapidly under the care of the female draconians. So rapidly that Kang was astonished.

That night, after dinner, Huzzad came wandering into the Common Room area where the draconians were relaxing after their labors. Kang and Slith invited her to join them for a private drink in Kang's quarters. Here, Slith introduced her to his special cactus brew. Huzzad was approving.

"Tastes better than dwarf spirits," she said. "But then so does horse piss."

She asked about the goblins. Kang gave her the latest scouting report.

"Twenty-five thousand!" Huzzad gave a low whistle. "Even for you dracos, the odds are little steep, aren't they?"

"Naw," said Slith. "Just starts to make things interesting."

"Yes, very interesting," Kang said dryly. "Much too interesting, if you ask me."

"And how does your general propose to deal with this?" Huzzad asked.

"He hasn't chosen to share that piece of information with us, as yet," Kang responded. "More cactus spirits?" He reached for the jug.

Huzzad held out her mug. Kang filled hers, filled his own. Slith had just topped his. While the three drank in silence, Kang eyed Huzzad's injuries. The cut on her head had almost completely closed. He could see only a white scar, looking like a streak of white lightning against her sun-browned skin.

"Are all humans such fast healers?" Kang asked.

"We would be if we had your kapaks around," Huzzad replied.

"What do you mean?" Kang was puzzled.

"You know. Their saliva. I have to admit it was a good thing I was unconscious, or I would have fought like three kobolds with their tails tied together before I let one of your dracos lick me, but it worked."

"Licked you!" Horrified, Kang was on his feet. "Huzzad—a kapak's saliva is poison! We have to do something." He looked at Slith, who shook his head gloomily.

"Nothing to do, sir. There's no antidote that I know of. She ought to be dead by now, in fact."

Huzzad was looking from one to the other in wonder. "You mean, you really didn't know?"

"Know what?" Kang asked uneasily.

"That the saliva of *female* kapaks isn't poison. On the contrary, it appears to have healing properties."

Kang and Slith both stared at her.

"You didn't know." Huzzad shook her head. "I'll be damned. I've been around men who were dumb about women, but you boys beat anything."

"It's just . . . well, I never thought about it."

Kang took a deep drink. He wondered what else he didn't know about the females. He was afraid to ask Huzzad, afraid she might tell him. He decided it was time to change the subject.

"Huzzad, Groupcommander Zeck said he had reports on this fort. Do you know what those reports entailed?"

"The usual: troop strength, fortifications, availability of food, water, and"—Huzzad added pointedly—"information on your general."

"Make sure that door's shut. What sort of information?" Kang asked.

Slith tested the latch, refilled their mugs all around. The two draconians hunched forward, eager and interested.

"When the Knights found out General Maranta was the one in command here," Huzzad said in a low voice, "the groupcommander wanted information on him. I saw the report. It was circulated among the officers. Did you know that General Maranta never once held a field command? He never led troops in battle?" She lowered her voice still further. "He was never even involved in a battle, in fact."

"Wasn't he in Neraka at the fall?" Slith asked.

Huzzad shrugged. "You might say that. If you count being in the tunnels underneath the city. He and the Queen's Own had their escape neatly planned. The minute things started to go wrong, they left. Some say to this day that if General Maranta and the Queen's Own had stayed, they would have prevented the destruction, saved the day for Her Dark Majesty. I doubt it, though. Not enough of them to really make a difference. It doesn't matter now, of course. What does matter is that if General Maranta fights this battle, it will be his first."

She sat back, looked at Slith and at Kang.

Kang and Slith looked at each other. Kang heaved a sigh.

"Damn! This is just all we need!" Kang shook his head. "I've been waiting for the general to call us together, present us with a plan for the defense of the fort. He hasn't done it so far and I'm beginning to think he doesn't have a plan, except some vague notion that draconians are going to drop out of the skies to save us."

"And if they're as bright as this last lot, then they'll fall out of the skies and land on their heads," Slith said morosely.

"If only I had my dragon," said Huzzad with a wistful sigh. "Flarion and I would have made short work of those vermin. I really miss her."

"What happened?" Kang asked.

"Some Solamnic Knight with a dragonlance killed her." Slith guessed.

Huzzad shook her head. "I could have understood that," she said, frowning. "She was killed by her own kind. She and her mate both. Another red."

"Since when do red dragons turn on red dragons?" Kang asked, amazed.

"Since these huge, bloated dragons arrived from some other part of Krynn," Huzzad said. "Or at least, that's what we assume. No one knows for sure where they came from. The one my partner and I fought calls herself Malystrx. She's enormous. Three times the size of my red. We never had a chance. I wouldn't have survived, if she hadn't protected me. Flarion might have escaped, but she wouldn't leave me." Huzzad clenched her fist. "I took a vow over her mangled body that I would avenge her."

She gave a bitter laugh. "Of course, I'll never have

the chance. No one can stand against Malys. Not the entire Solamnic army, not our own Knighthood. She'll rule Krynn and the Dark Knights will end up allying with her. Mark my words. It's only a matter of time."

"Still, you do have an idea," Kang observed thoughtfully. "If there's one thing that scares the crap out of gobbos, it's a dragon. I don't suppose there's any way we could get a message to a red or a blue? Ask one of them to help us?"

"Not that I know of," she replied. "I wouldn't even know where to begin to look. Most dragons are in hiding, terrified of ending up as one of the skulls on Malys's totem."

"Skulls?"

"According to rumors, Malys saves the skulls of the dragons she's killed and has used them to build a monument to herself. She believes that they give her magical power."

Kang was appalled, disgusted. "It's sad to see the state the world's come to. What do you say, Slith? Slith?"

The sivak gave a start. "Sorry, sir, I wasn't listening. I was thinking."

"Thinking what?" Kang asked, interested.

"Thinking that if we can't find a real dragon, maybe we could make one, sir," said Slith. "You remember that time we built that wicker dragon?"

Kang chuckled. "I'd forgotten about that. Tell Huzzad."

Slith was glad to comply. "We decided to play a joke on the . . . who were they, sir?"

"The Thirty-third," said Kang.

"Right. The Thirty-third Infantry. It was made up a bunch of new hatched baaz. They thought they were hot stuff. Wouldn't obey orders, weren't respectful to the officers. We decided to teach them a lesson and so we made this dragon out of wicker. It was a huge contraption. Amazing design. The wings flapped, the jaws opened and shut. You should have seen it.

"Anyhow, during the dead of night, we hauled this dragon over to where the Thirty-third was bivouacked and we hoisted it into the trees. The next morning, the baaz woke up, all hung over after a night drinking dwarf spirits and they saw this dragon and—this is no lie, I swear it—they all fell flat on their bellies, scared out of their wits. They began to groan and wail. Some fool cleric even started praying to it. We laughed— Do you remember, Commander? I laughed so hard I thought I hurt something inside."

"I remember," said Kang. "And then from out of nowhere, some fool kender climbed into the dragon and began to make it 'talk'—"

"—and that sent the baaz into a panic!" Slith laughed again, just at the memory. "And then, to make matters worse, a bunch of prisoners the baaz had caught escaped."

"I'd forgotten about them," Kang said reminiscently. "There was a half-elf and a Knight and a sickly mage. They'd been captured in that furor over a blue crystal staff. Those prisoners were as stupid as the baaz. Do you remember that adle-pated Solamnic challenging the dragon to a fight?"

"Ha! Ha!" Slith was pounding the table with his mug. "And then the dragon caught fire and the geniuses figured out it was wicker after all. The baaz lost the prisoners in the confusion. I wonder what ever happened to them?"

"They probably drowned in the swamp. You know," said Kang after the laughter had subsided and he could breathe again, "that's not a bad idea, Slith."

"What? Drowning in a swamp?" Huzzad eyed Kang.

"No, building a dragon."

Slith was nodding. Huzzad started to laugh, then she saw that Kang wasn't.

"You're serious!" she exclaimed.

"Damn right I am," said Kang. "Goblins are stupid, more stupid than even the Thirty-third Infantry."

Huzzad shook her head dubiously.

"And not only are goblins stupid," Kang persisted, "they're short-sighted. Look, a fake dragon doesn't have to fool them for long! Just long enough to throw them into confusion, panic the front ranks."

"We could tie keg bombs to it, sir!" Slith said, excited. "If we could figure out some way to make it fly, we could send it over the goblins and—"

"Boom!" said Kang gleefully.

"Boom, sir," said Slith. "Boom it is!" He gulped down his drink, stood up. "By the gods, sir, I think we may still have those plans. I think they're in The Chest, sir."

There was only one chest in the regiment that was mentioned with such emphasis. The Chest was a large box made of solid oak reinforced by iron bands. The Chest had been with them ever since their inception as a unit and it had remained with them throughout their years of exile and wanderings. The Chest held plans, all the plans the draconian engineers had ever made. Plans for bridges, plans for dams, plans for stockades, guard towers, siege engines, plans for their ill-fated village, plans for Kang's dream of a city, and, buried near the bottom, plans for a wicker dragon.

While Slith went off to investigate, Kang refilled his mug. "What do you think?" he asked Huzzad.

"I think you're both crazy," she said. "Totally insane. I've known gnomes who made sense compared to you."

"Yes, well, it's worth a try," Kang growled. "I don't

see anyone else coming up with anything brilliant to save our skins."

"You have a point there." Huzzad yawned, stretched. "I think I'll be turning in. I have an early morning tomorrow. Which reminds me. I'd like permission to take the females out onto the parade ground. They're progressing well in their sword drill, but they're finding the quarters a little cramped—"

"They're what?" Kang bellowed, leaping to his feet.

"Sword drill," said Huzzad, staring at him. "What did you think I said?"

"I thought you said sword drill," Kang repeated grimly. "What the hell do you think you're doing, Huzzad? Giving them military training! I won't have it! You're to stop this nonsense at once. Do you hear me? At once!"

"I would stop it, only I didn't start it, Kang," Huzzad retorted. "They've been training themselves now for quite some time. They're getting pretty good, too, and they'll be better now that someone's taking the time to show them what they've been doing wrong. They're born fighters, Kang. Born and bred to it, just like you males."

"I don't believe you!" Kang stated, glowering. "I think you put them up to this."

"Oh, yeah?" Huzzad said, her voice frost-rimed. "The scuttlebutt around camp is that twenty swords went missing a few days ago. A sivak was attacked— one of the Queen's Own. The attacker stole a requisition from him. Twenty swords, Commander. Now where in this fort might you find twenty draconians who were in need of twenty swords?"

"Are you saying—" Kang felt a tightness constrict his chest. "These children—"

"They are *not* children," Huzzad snapped. "They are adults. And if you don't accept that and start treating them like adults, you're going to lose them. You have a soul, Kang. Your own soul. You have rights, duties, responsibilities. You have the right to be wrong, to make mistakes. I have the same. And so do these females. Each one has her own soul. Each has her own destiny. Each has the right to achieve her own destiny. You can't take away that right. They look to you for guidance, Kang, for leadership and counsel. But they won't for long. Eventually, they'll start to hate you.

"All except Fonrar, of course," Huzzad continued. "She loves you too much to ever turn against you. But even she is struggling with her love for you and her need to be true to herself."

Kang sat down very suddenly. Fortunately, his bed was beneath him. He stared blankly at Huzzad.

"What are you talking about?" he demanded, his voice strained. "We can't . . . that word you said."

"Love?" Huzzad was amused. "Tell me, Kang. Don't you love Slith?"

"Of course not!" Kang practically roared.

"No? How would you feel if Slith died?"

Kang pondered. Slith dead. A world without Slith. He'd always known it was possible. They were soldiers. Death was part of the job. But the thought of Slith not being there filled Kang with a great sadness, a vast emptiness.

"I'd feel bad," Kang admitted, adding defensively. "We've been together a long time. We're . . . comrades."

"Comrades." Huzzad rested her hand lightly on Kang's shoulder. "Well, my friend, Fonrar feels very 'comradely' toward you. How's that? And sometime soon, you know, you 'comrades' are going to have to get together and make little 'comrades.' So it's not such a bad thing to have happen."

"I . . . I guess not." Kang mumbled.

"The females know about the goblin threat, Kang. They know that this is going to be a tough battle. They want to do their part."

"Out of the question," Kang said shortly.

"Why? Because they might get hurt? They might die? What happens if all of you die, Kang? What happens if every last male draconian is wiped out and these females are left trapped in their barracks, alone, weaponless, untrained?" Huzzad stood over him, stared down at him grimly. "What happens, Kang?"

He lowered his head, didn't look at her.

"I'll tell you what happens," Huzzad went on relentlessly. "The lucky ones will be killed. The unlucky ones will be captured and taken prisoner. Maybe the goblins will torture them and then kill them. Maybe not. Maybe since they're females they'll be sent to some sort of wizard laboratory for experiments—"

"Enough!" Kang shouted.

"How would you want to go out, Kang?" Huzzad asked. "Would you want to die fighting alongside the comrades you care about? Or would you want to die alone, in torment—"

"All right, damn it!" Kang glared at her. "You've made your point."

"Then Fonrar and I can take them out on the parade ground tomorrow?"

Kang looked back. He looked back to crawling on all fours around the campfire, pretending to be a bear, growling playfully as the little ones squealed and laughed. He looked back to the terror he'd felt when Thesik had wandered off and was discovered playing happily with a pack of wolf cubs. He looked back to holding Fonrar as she slept in his arms, her small fingers curled tightly around one of his large ones. He looked back . . . and he let go.

Kang cleared his throat. "Tell Subcommander . . ."—he gulped slightly—"Fonrar that she is to have her troop ready for inspection on the parade ground an hour past dawn tomorrow morning, in fighting order with weapons."

"I will, Kang," said Huzzad. "You'll be proud of them," she added as she left.

Kang lay down on his bed. He felt all wobbly and trembly, worse than when the goblins had hacked him open.

Destiny. There was that word again. *Each has her own destiny,* Huzzad had said. *Each has the right to achieve her own destiny.*

"Twenty swords!" he said to the darkness. "They snatched twenty swords right out from under the snout of the Queen's Own. Hit him on the goddamn head with a goddamn rock! Proud of them?"

Kang smiled. "You're damn right I'm proud of them!"

Chapter Fifteen

Kang went to the mess hall the next morning in anticipation of breakfast, only to find that rationing had been imposed. The presence of the goblins had meant that the hunting, foraging and raiding parties had not been able to hunt, forage or raid as usual. Consequently, food supplies were now running low.

"What is this?" Kang asked, watching the cook's mate shovel a wet and slimy brown gooey substance from a large vat onto his plate.

"Think you're funny, don't ya?" The cook's assistant glared at him.

"No, really, I'd like to know what it is," Kang said in respectful tones.

"Venison steak," said the mate. "Beef rump roast. Tenderloin of pork. Leg of kender. Either eat it or don't. Makes no difference to me. Sir," he muttered as an afterthought.

Having lived on grass and rodents for a month, Kang ate the brown goo and found that if nothing else could be said for it, the stuff stuck to the ribs. Stuck there in a solidified mass for the next twelve hours, in fact.

Kang had to give the cook credit. The brown goo would save on rations, due to the fact that it completely killed the appetite. Feeling as if he had swallowed a small boulder, Kang returned to the barracks, where he gave orders that the troops were to form up for inspection. All the troops, females included.

That day for the first time, the female draconians took their places alongside the males. The moment was a proud one for the females. They had spent the night polishing their weapons and harnesses and whatever shields and helms they had managed to obtain. The metal shone in the sunlight, their scales gleamed as if they had polished themselves into the bargain.

Commander Kang reviewed his troops—all his troops—casting a stern eye over the females as well as the males. He winced at the sight of the twenty shining new swords, was only momentarily taken aback at the sight of the stolen harness, helms and the shields, particularly when he recognized a cast-off leather belt that had once belonged to himself and that was now being proudly worn by Fonrar. But he recovered himself and, dismissing the rest of the regiment back to their duties, watched the females go through their sword drill with outward calm, if inward dismay, certain that one of the baaz—who handled her sword with particularly reckless abandon—was going to chop off a wing.

This trial over with no casualties, not counting the fact that he was a nervous wreck, Kang retreated to his quarters to restore his shattered nerves with a fortifying mug of cactus juice. He then took Slith's initial plans for what he termed the Drunken Dragon and began refining them, preparing them to show to the general. As to the theft of the twenty swords, Kang considered writing a report, but then decided not to. What General Maranta did not know would not hurt him.

He was working on the plans for the dragon when Granak knocked, reporting that Commander Prokel wanted to see him.

"Goblins are on the march," Prokel told Kang. "General Maranta's called an officers meeting in the command tent in an hour."

"Right," said Kang. "I'll be there."

He paced about inside his room during the intervening time, glancing at the plans whenever he passed the table. The more he looked at them, the crazier the idea seemed. How could he present a Drunken Dragon to the general? General Maranta was likely to get nothing more out of it than a good hearty laugh and Kang wasn't sure he would blame him.

The time came for Kang to depart and still he lingered, dithering, undecided. Eventually, he walked to the door, leaving the plans on the table. He knew very well that if he presented the plan, he would fight for the plan, no matter how much the general mocked or disparaged him. Kang didn't want to argue. He didn't want to end up being placed in a position where he would have to choose between a superior officer's orders and his own convictions. Kang reached the door, but he could not open it. He could not walk out.

He thought of Huzzad's report. General Maranta had never been in battle. Not once. He had been stationed in Neraka, the Queen's flunky, the Dragon Highlords' pet draconian, but that needn't have stopped him. Kang imagined what he himself would have done in that situation. He would have participated in the war. He would have fought with his troops, not just reviewed them. General Maranta had not done so. When battle had come to him, he had fled.

General Maranta wasn't a coward. Draconians did not have it in them to be cowards. But General Maranta wasn't a risk taker. That much was obvious by the Bastion he'd built himself. He wasn't a risk taker and, worse, he disdained the troops under his command. A typical aurak, he had no care for anyone but himself. Kang guessed that so long as one draconian was left alive in this fort—and that draconian was General Maranta—then he would happily expend the lives of all the rest. He had not built this fort as a haven for draconians. He had built it as a monument to himself.

Kang picked up the plans for the Drunken Dragon and proceeded to the meeting. He took his time. He wasn't looking forward to this.

"Kind of you to favor us with your presence, Commander," General Maranta said sarcastically, as Kang entered the tent.

"Yes, sir. Sorry, sir," Kang said.

"I was just saying that you and your men had done a splendid job of patching up the fortifications," General Maranta added magnanimously.

"Thank you, sir," Kang said, feeling worse, as General Maranta no doubt intended.

"Our scouts report that the goblins are on the march. They're moving slowly, of course. They're disorganized rabble and they're burdened with huge supply wagons. I anticipate that we have at least forty-eight hours to prepare against their attack. I have drawn up plans for the fort's defense," General Maranta said. "If you officers will approach the map."

General Maranta explained his plans quickly and concisely.

The walls would be manned by the Twelfth Infantry Regiment. They were the archer specialists, and could use their longbows to harass the goblin army as they formed up for the assault. Five of the six other regiments of infantry, and the two support regiments would all remain inside the walls, as would Kang's engineer regiment.

The Third Infantry would be held ready to launch a surprise attack outside the walls. They were equipped as heavy infantry with orders to hit the enemy flank during the battle, after the fight was joined.

Belkrad's Reconnaissance Squadron would send out small patrols to spy on enemy formations and report back. If they had the opportunity, they would try to hit the enemy's command post or supply wagons, but that was deemed a long shot.

Two of the other five regiments would be stationed at the base of the walls to mount a defense when the enemy drew closer. These draconians were expert at short-range shooting with bows and slings, and hand-to-hand fighting when the walls were threatened. Each regiment had a ballista supplied and crewed by the Third Artillery Regiment, which they would use against enemy siege engines.

The Ninth Infantry, along with the Fourth would be formed up in ranks, heavily armored, and posted near the front gate. When the goblins made a final rush against the gate, the draconians would fling open the gates and charge into the enemy. General Maranta's plan was to overwhelm the enemy with the size of the force and their tenacity. He had chosen well. These two regiments both had long lists of battle honors, and both knew how to operate in the heavy infantry role. Vertax, the commander of the Ninth Infantry, wagered a very handsome broadsword that he would cut off and bring back the heads of two goblin commanders. The other officers immediately took him up on the deal.

Kang's engineers, along with the remaining Tenth Infantry, would form the "Fire Brigade." It would be their task to move in to fill any gap, or stem any incursions into the fort. Also, as the name implied, they would be responsible for keeping fires under control.

Kang was surprised and favorably impressed. General Maranta may have never fought in a battle, but he had studied strategy and tactics and he knew the abilities as well as the limitations of his troops and officers. General Maranta asked for questions. His officers asked for clarification on only a few issues. Everyone understood what he and his troops were to do. Everyone knew where and how he would die. For that's what it came down to.

It was a good plan but in the end it must fail—to the weight of numbers, if nothing else. Five thousand draconians versus twenty-five thousand goblins, or possibly more. If the goblins sent in only half their army, the draconians would be fighting near impossible odds.

Which led Kang to his question. He wondered how the others could have missed it.

"Begging the general's pardon, there's a discrepancy here. You have an entire regiment manning this section of the wall and according to my calculations we don't have that many men—"

"On the contrary, Commander," General Maranta replied coolly. "I am expecting additional reinforcements."

The other officers looked at each other, smiled and nodded their heads. Kang recalled Slith's words about draconians raining down out of the skies.

"Might I ask, sir," Kang said respectfully, "where these reinforcements are going to come from?"

"I am keeping the location of the reinforcements and their numbers a secret. Regrettable, but necessary, considering the presence of a human inside these walls." General Maranta looked very hard at Kang. "Now if there is nothing more—"

"Sir, there is one more thing," Kang said. "I have here a plan for a weapon that might assist in the fort's defense. It looks a little strange, but if you'll bear with me—"

Kang spread out the drawings of the Drunken Dragon over the map of the fort. The officers gathered around, looked at it, looked at each other. At least no one laughed, for which he was grateful. They all glanced sidelong at General Maranta.

"What is this, Commander?" General Maranta asked.

"A dragon, sir. If I may explain—"

"I can see it's a dragon," General Maranta returned. "Commander, these men have urgent business to attend to, important preparations to make. If you have nothing better to do than to draw childish pictures, I am certain that we can find work for you."

"Sir," said Kang, keeping himself under control. The detailed and complex schematic could hardly be described as a "childish picture." "My idea for this dragon involves the defense of the fort. It will only take me a short time to explain."

He indicated how the dragon would operate. When he reached the part about the keg bombs, he could see Vertax looking less doubtful and Yakanoh was nodding slightly. All the officers kept their eyes on General Maranta, waiting his reaction.

His reaction was a snort.

"Apparently there is nothing of importance left to be decided," General Maranta said. "You are dismissed. Return to your duties."

The other officers cast oblique glances at Kang and filed out. Kang remained stubbornly in his place.

"Sir," he said, "may I have your permission to construct the dragon?"

"Why do you bother to ask, Commander?" General Maranta glared at him. "You have proceeded this far. You obviously intend to build the damn thing whether I give you permission or not."

"I would like your permission, sir," Kang said steadily.

"General Maranta, sir." One of the Queen's Own entered the command tent. He bent near, said something to the general in a low voice.

General Maranta listened, replied, "Very good. I will be there immediately."

"Sir?" Kang persisted.

"Do what you want, Commander," General Maranta said impatiently. "Waste time in whatever manner you and your slackers choose. Just so you're sober and ready to fight when the attack commences. That's all I care about."

General Maranta departed, stalking out of the tent. Kang retrieved his plans, rolling them carefully, then he followed. He saw the general heading for the Bastion. A troop of the Queen's Own marched after him. They disappeared inside. The heavy doors were bolted after them. More of the Queen's Own took up posts outside.

It occurred to Kang that General Maranta had not mentioned where the Queen's Own was going to be during the attack. Kang thought of the underground tunnels that had taken the general safely out of Neraka.

"He wouldn't do that," Kang said. "Neraka was a fight among humans. This is a battle involving his own people. He wouldn't leave us."

And at least, Kang had the general's permission to proceed with the dragon. Some might have said it was more insult than permission, but it was all Kang needed.

* * * * *

On his return to the barracks, Kang called a meeting of his officers, including Huzzad and Fonrar. He found it odd to talk to the males with Fonrar in attendance. He found that he was drawn to look at her and talk to her alone. Comrades.

Knowing that this would never do, he decided to handle the uncomfortable situation by ignoring her completely. He handed copies of the plans over to the officers, then ordered them to pull everyone off repairing the fortifications.

"We've done what we can short of tearing this fort down and starting over," he told them. "We built them a fort. Now we're going to build them a dragon. I know this looks odd," he added, waving his hand at the plans. His officers were looking extremely skeptical. "And we're going to have to make the contraption from whatever material we can scrounge up around this fort. We can't very well go outside to buy supplies. You've proven yourselves resourceful in the past. I have no doubt you will be this time. And I think we will be successful. We've done stranger things before."

"Like catapulting a dead-drunk minotaur into a dragon," said Gloth in an undertone to Fulkth.

"That worked!" Kang growled. "We killed the dragon, didn't we?"

"Yes, sir," said Gloth, looking guilty. He hadn't meant the commander to hear him.

"Fulkth, as Chief Engineer, you're in charge of checking

these plans, and of the construction. Slith, you'll be in charge of making the keg bombs."

"Yes, sir." Slith grinned. Making the keg bombs meant making a large supply of cactus juice.

"How long do we have, sir?" Fulkth asked, eyeing the plans. "A month."

"Forty-eight hours," Kang replied.

Fulkth's jaw sagged, his tongue lolling out from between his lower fangs.

"Is that a problem, Fulkth?" Kang asked.

"Well, sir . . ." Fulkth began.

"Good." Kang cut him off. "I didn't think it would be. If you have any questions, you'll have to find the answers yourselves, because I don't have them. Dismissed."

The other officers filed out.

"Sir," said Fonrar. "I would—"

"Dismissed," Kang repeated, not looking at her.

Fonrar hesitated a moment, then departed.

Kang sat down at his desk, dropped his head to hands. He knew he'd hurt Fonrar, but far better to hurt her feelings than to fail her and the others. Kang could see the situation deteriorating all around him. He felt as if he were holding a handful of sand. He had to keep his fist closed tight, not relax his concentration in the slightest, not allow himself to be distracted. If a single grain slipped through, the rest would follow in a torrent.

"At least there's one bright side to this entire mess," Kang muttered. "If we manage to live through this"— and Kang knew that this was a very big if—"General Maranta will undoubtedly change his mind about us leaving. To get rid of me, if nothing else."

* * * * *

Fulkth spread out the plans for the Drunken Dragon and regarded them thoughtfully. The enemy was on the march. He was trapped inside a fort with hopelessly inadequate supplies. He had to build a gigantic dragon with flight capabilities and he had forty-eight hours (hopefully) in which to do it. Faced with this, Fulkth's first trip was a visit to Slith's distillery to check on the cactus juice.

The original wicker dragon had been made of a light wooden frame covered by a wicker carapace. The wicker dragon had been intended for use to intimidate newly hatched baaz. That dragon had been stationary. This version had to fly.

Kang's plans called for the dragon to be covered with a skin that could be filled with hot air. Back in their village, Slith had once observed cinders being carried up a chimney on the hot air generated by the fire. He'd done some very nice calculations on the subject, with the result that when the female draconians had been little, Slith had filled pig's bladders with hot air and let them loose to float up among the trees, to squeals of delight from the females. Kang had put the same principle into action with the dragon.

The frame for the Drunken Dragon would have to be extremely light weight. Pine would be ideal and, fortunately, there was plenty of pine wood in the compound. As for the skin, pig bladders were out of the question. No one had seen a pig in months. Fulkth settled on canvas panels that would be sewn together, then covered by a pine tar compound that would cause the canvas to adhere to the wood, seal any leaks or holes.

Fulkth determined that this would work for the dragon's body, but he was worried about the wings. They not only had to look like wings, they had to be functional. They had to support flight, and they had to move in a convincing manner. Canvas would be too heavy. Paper would be ideal. For wing movement, Kang had come up with an ingenious solution. As the pressure in the central balloon grew from the expansion of the hot air, the pressure would force open two vents under the wings, one vent on each side. The escaping hot air would be trapped under the wings, causing the wings to rise. As the air cooled, it would dissipate, allowing the wings to fall. When the hot air built up again, the wings would lift, mimicking flight.

The final touch was a large cage in which they would stash what they were now calling the Cactus Keg Bombs and a fuse mechanism. Kang had added the cage to the front, but Fulkth recognized immediately that the weight would unbalance the dragon, cause it to tilt forward. After discussing this with his fellow officers, he came to the conclusion that this was a feature, not a design flaw.

As Slith pointed out, "If the dragon is tethered to the ground, it will rise and drift forward, until it pulls the rope taut. Once the rope is released, the dragon will sail forward in a glide that will carry it out over the enemy camp. Once there, it's supposed to drop down and—boom."

So that was the plan. All they had to do was assemble the parts and build.

Dremon, the Chief Supply Officer, was given the task of finding paper and canvas. Not only did he have to find them, he had to find them in large amounts. Dremon and his assistants hot-footed it to the supply center. He asked for paper and canvas. He was given several sheets of the first—enough to write a longish letter—and was told that they had none of the second.

Accustomed to improvising, Dremon asked for

permission to search the warehouse for canvas. The Quartermaster was extremely busy handing out weapons, shields, spears and arrows, and he told Dremon precisely where he could stuff his canvas. Taking this as permission, Dremon and his assistants marched into the warehouse, past the protesting Quartermaster, and commenced their search.

"What's this?" Dremon demanded, pointing to an enormous supply of canvas. "It looks like canvas to me."

"Well, it isn't," said the Quartermaster. "It's sails. You know, for a ship. You didn't ask for sails."

Twenty-two fully rigged sails to be precise. The sails had been made during the Chaos War, when General Maranta had planned an amphibious assault against some town somewhere, perhaps the very keep the Dark Knights now occupied. The war had ended before the assault could be carried out. Rats had chewed most of the rigging, but the canvas was in fine shape.

Dremon ordered his men to load up. He found no paper, but he did come across a supply of archery targets made of pasteboard. Since the draconians were going to be using goblins for archery practice, Dremon walked off with all the pasteboard. On his return to the barracks, he filled an enormous vat with boiling water, dumped in the pasteboard, and began cooking it to a pulp.

Fulkth ordered Yethik and Second Squadron to find pine wood and pine sap. Pine trees grew in abundance in the hills, but, unfortunately, at the moment, so did goblins. Yethik and his men prowled around the fort, looking over various wooden structures while their fellow draconians streamed past them, taking up positions on the walls.

"Found it, sir!" one of his men reported.

Ninth Infantry's Maintenance Shed was built completely out of pine. Ninth Infantry was using the shed, however, hauling supplies into it and carrying weapons out. Yethik and his dracos hung about impatiently. When Ninth Infantry was called to drill on the parade square, Yethik and his squadron attacked the shed, tore it down, carted off the lumber and any supplies they thought might come in handy.

Pine sap proved to be a problem. There was none to be found. Some sort of substance was necessary to adhere the canvas "skin" to the wooden skeleton. Yethik feared the project was doomed, but then a baaz, returning from the mess hall, arrived carrying two buckets.

"Lunch ration, sir," he reported.

Yethik peered into the buckets. He remembered this stuff from breakfast. "Take it away." Yethik paused, an idea forming in the pit of his stomach.

"Wait a minute, trooper!" Yethik yelled. "Bring that stuff back." He stuck a finger in the bucket. "Ideal!" he murmured. "Wonderful!"

"Sir?" The baaz stared at him.

"Go back to the mess tent," Yethik ordered, "and ask for seconds. And see if you can find out the recipe."

The baaz's eyes nearly rolled out of his head. He had to make Yethik repeat the order twice. Yethik never found out what the goo was, but it stuck to anything it touched and hardened rapidly. The goo was an ideal replacement for pine sap.

Gloth and his First Squadron were assigned to assemble the contraption. Using Yethik's stolen lumber, the draconians began building the frame of the body, the cage and the skull. Celdak, one of Gloth's Troop Officers, designed the fearsome head. It was his idea to add "fangs" made of old rusty broadsword blades. Not only would they add a touch of realism to the dragon, the fangs might impale a few gobbos if the wind was just right on landing.

Another squadron worked on the wing frame, laying out the wings side-by-side in the road in front of the barracks. Draconians stood guard, closing off the road to all carts and non-regimental draconians. They built the wing frame from the greenest of the pine wood, ensuring that it would be flexible and light. Once the frame was built, they planned to cover it with the wet pulp substance, mixing that with the brown goo. When the pulp mixed with goo dried, it formed a light-weight paper that stuck tightly to the frame, fingers, feet, tails and anything else it touched.

Fonrar and her troop were in charge of cutting up the sails to form large square panels of canvas that could be sewn over the central frame. They saved what rope was left from the rigging and tied it together to form one gigantic rope that would be used for the tether.

Once the central frame was complete, the draconians would sew the canvas over the central frame, then slather it with brown goo. Once the first coat of brown goo had dried, they would add a second. When it was dry, the skin would be rigid and air tight.

While the goo was drying, the draconians would mount three large vats in place under the central belly. When the dragon was ready for flight, they would build fires in the vats. The hot air would fill the dragon's body and cause it to rise. In what he considered a stroke of genius, Fulkth conceived the idea of funneling the smoke to the dragon's mouth. The Drunken Dragon would actually breathe fire.

Last they assembled the cage to hold the keg bombs, making the cage out of pine wood held together with twine. They could fit eight kegs filled with the explosive mash left over from the cactus juice in the chest area of the dragon. The kegs would be added at the last minute before the launch, due to the fact that they did not want the explosive kegs too near the fires while the dragon was still inside the fort.

Torches burned throughout the night. The draconian engineers did not sleep, but kept up their hammering and slathering, boiling and sewing. Slowly, inexorably, the Drunken Dragon began taking shape.

Chapter Sixteen

The females worked throughout the night cutting panels. The following morning, as they began sewing the panels together, Huzzad noted that they were missing two females—the sivak sisters, Hanra and Shanra. She said nothing, made no comment. She could guess where Hanra and Shanra had gone. The female bozaks required components to cast their magic spells. Although the females were now openly practicing sword drills, Huzzad and Thesik had opposed Fonrar's decision to tell Kang that the females were using magic.

"We're not lying to the commander," Thesik had explained. "We're just not telling him the whole truth all at once."

"It's like that brown goo," Huzzad had said. "After you've managed to choke down the first bite, the rest isn't all that bad. But we need to let him digest the first bite."

Reluctantly, Fonrar had agreed with them.

By dawn of the next morning, the wings were assembled and Dremon's troops were starting to mix the goo with the pulp. The frame of the body was halfway complete. The head was taking more time than had originally been calculated.

The rest of the draconians in the fort observed the dragon's progress with a mixture of curiosity, amusement and—in the case of the Queen's Own—disdain. The irate commander of the Ninth Infantry stomped over to angrily demand the return of his shed. This being impossible—the shed was now the dragon's skeleton—the commander was provided with cactus juice by way of payment. Several mugs later, the commander offered them Ninth Infantry's barracks in return for more cactus juice. Slith thanked him, but told him that they had all the pine wood they needed. The officer reluctantly and unsteadily departed.

As for the new draconians, those who had just arrived, they did what they were told, no more, no less.

Slith was growing more and more curious about these peculiar draconians and he decided that it might be entertaining as well as instructive to "pal around" with one of the new dracos for the day.

Leaving Gloth in charge of the distillery, Slith went in search of the new dracos, found one standing in front of a ladder, apparently waiting for someone to tell him what to do.

"Hey, you! Soldier!" Slith called.

The baaz turned his head. At the sight of an officer, the draconian snapped to attention, raising his hand to his forehead in salute and standing rigid.

It was fortunate he didn't have a hammer in his saluting hand, Slith reflected. Otherwise he might have clonked himself on the head.

"Sir!" the baaz said, eyes forward.

"At ease," Slith said with a friendly grin. "We don't stand on ceremony around here. Relax, will you?"

The baaz continued to stand at attention. "You are my superior officer, sir. I am to stand at attention in the presence of a superior officer."

"Not when the superior officer tells you to relax," Slith said.

"Is that an order, sir?" the baaz asked.

Slith was bemused. "Yeah, that's an order. Relax, soldier."

"Yes, sir." The baaz spread his feet, clasped his hands behind his back. "Relaxing, sir."

"Cripes," Slith muttered. "I hope the commander doesn't see this. Look, Soldier," he said aloud. "You shouldn't be all spit and polish like this. For one, you make the rest of us look bad and, for two, you'll unnerve the commander. Scare the hell outta him. Scares the hell outta me," he added under his breath.

Slith looked at the baaz closely, trying to figure out what was wrong with him. Nothing at first glance. Every scale was in place. He had all his fingers and toes, regulation tail and wings. The eyes. There was something odd about the eyes. A kind of lost look, as if searching for something that had gone missing. Slith couldn't make it out.

"What's your name, Soldier?" Slith asked in friendly tones.

And damned if the baaz didn't seem to have to stop to think about it.

"Drugo, sir," he said, after a pause.

"Drugo. You sure about that?" Slith joked.

The baaz paused again, gave the matter more thought. "Yes, sir," he said at last.

"Damn!" Slith muttered. "This bastard's starting to

creep me out. Very well, Drugo, I have to go pick up some stuff at the Quartermasters and I could use some help."

Slith started to walk off.

"Yes, sir," said Drugo, standing in place.

"*Your* help," said Slith, glancing around.

"Yes, sir," said Drugo and obediently fell into step alongside Slith.

Drugo was no conversationalist, as Slith discovered after bringing up several interesting and amusing subjects—battles fought, elves tortured, humans disemboweled. Drugo had nothing to say on any subject and so Slith eventually gave up and began concentrating on not getting lost. The two draconians plunged into the maze of crooked streets that wandered and meandered all around the fort. Slith had been to the Quartermaster's before and had some vague notion of where it was located, but although he had gone exploring several times, he never went anywhere in this rat's nest of a town but that he didn't manage to take a couple of wrong turns before achieving his objective.

Then he noted that Drugo appeared to know exactly where he was going. Slith discovered this when he turned left at a crossroads and Drugo continued going straight.

"It's this way," said Slith.

"If you say so, sir," said Drugo.

"Wait a minute." Slith halted. "Do you think it's the other way?"

"I wouldn't know, sir," said Drugo. "You are my superior officer."

"Have you been to the Quartermaster's before?" Slith asked.

"No, sir," Drugo replied. "I am new in the fort. I don't know my way around yet."

"But you certainly looked as if you knew the way to go," Slith said.

"If you say so, sir," Drugo replied.

Slith kept a firm grip on himself, otherwise he would have gone for a firm grip on Drugo's neck.

"We'll try my way," said Slith and, sure enough, after two more turns they were in a blank alley, brought to a halt by two sheds and the back side of the blacksmith's forge.

Drugo said nothing, just stood there.

"Drugo," said Slith. "Go to the Quartermaster's. That's an order."

"Yes, sir," said Drugo and off he marched.

He led Slith straight to the Quartermaster's.

"I'll be damned," said Slith.

* * * * *

Slith picked up the supplies, handing over a requisition that he'd written up himself with Kang's forged signature, acting on the theory that the commander would have ordered the supplies if he had known that he needed them. Slith and Drugo headed back to the barracks, following a different route, by way of experiment. Sure enough, Drugo never missed a turn. They carried with them two boxes of gear and equipment, including twenty pair of fine quality leather bracers.

"A little present for the females," Slith said, indicating the bracers.

Drugo made his customary laconic response of "Yes, sir." Clearly he was not impressed.

Two female draconians, standing unnoticed nearby, heard Slith's words about 'presents' and responded much more enthusiastically than the indifferent Drugo.

Shanra and Hanra were out on the town again, this

time in search of spell components. Huzzad had told them to look for a building called "mage-ware" supply. They had found it, had handed over the requisition, which this time Huzzad had made out, forging Kang's signature. Thesik had pointed out that the forgery didn't look anything like Kang's scrawling scribble, but Huzzad said that the mage-ware supply manager wouldn't know the difference since he had never seen Kang's signature and wouldn't know it from Paladine's and, indeed, that had proved to be the case.

Their packs stuffed full of bat guano, sand, and sulfur, the two were on their way back to their barracks when they happened to cross paths with Slith, accompanied by a baaz whose identity was unknown to them.

The two ducked into the shadows of an alley, where they could gaze at their hero adoringly.

It was at that moment that Slith, completely unconscious that he was being observed by the two females, made the remark about the bracers. The words "females" and "presents" carried clearly.

Shanra squealed, causing her shocked sister to grab hold of her and drag her farther down the alley.

"Shush! He'll hear you!" Hanra scolded.

"Sorry," Shanra returned meekly, then added, with an excited giggle, "Presents! He bought us presents!"

"He's so wonderful." Hanra sighed. "I wonder what they are?"

"Let's follow and see if we can find out," Shanra said.

The two slipped out of the alleyway, mingling with the draconians who were out in the streets in droves, going about the serious business of preparing the fort for war. The sivak sisters attempted to get within earshot of Slith and his companion, but the narrow streets were at times too crowded. Bumped, shoved and jostled, the two were never able to come close enough to hear anything more until Slith made a right turn and walked out into an open area that was relatively free of traffic.

Pleased with their success, the sivak sisters had almost caught up when Shanra grabbed hold of Hanra's arm, jerked her back.

"Look! Look there!" Shanra gasped.

"What?" Hanra asked, alarmed.

"That sivak standing in front of that big ugly building. Isn't he the one you knocked unconscious?"

The big, ugly building was the Bastion. The sivak under observation, a member of the Queen's Own, was inspecting the guards on duty.

"What do we do? What if he sees us?" Hanra said nervously.

"Let's head back the way we came," Shanra whispered.

The two were about to sneak off, when they heard Slith's voice. The sisters halted in the shadows, hoping he would say something about the presents.

"The commander was right," Slith was saying, observing the Bastion. "That's one ugly building. Well-fortified, though. I'll give the general credit. No one's gonna walk in on him unannounced."

Slith peered at the sivaks more closely. "I'll be damned! That's the bastard who was on duty the night our boys disappeared. I never was quite satisfied with his answers." He set the box down on the ground. "You stay here with the loot," he told Drugo. "I'm gonna go have a talk with my sivak brothers over there."

The sivaks of the Queen's Own were eyeing Slith in no very brotherly fashion, but that didn't deter Slith, who never minded making a nuisance of himself and who had a few questions he wanted to ask these dracos. Slith had taken a step in the direction of the Bastion, when he felt a hand clutch his arm.

"Eh?" Slith said, turning in astonishment. "What is it, Drugo?"

"Don't go there, sir!" Drugo whispered. He sounded as if he were being suffocated. His eyes were wide and terror-filled.

"Why not, Drugo?" Slith asked, interested in this reaction. "Why shouldn't I go there?"

"Pain," said Drugo, clutching Slith so that his claws dug in between the silver scales. "Pain and . . . and darkness. And fire. Terrible fire. Lost . . ." he murmured. "Lost . . ."

"Hunh?" Slith was startled. "What would pain and darkness and a terrible fire be doing inside the general's Bastion? You're not just feeding me one, are you?"

Slith stared hard at Drugo. The vacant eyes stared back at him.

"No," Slith conceded, "you have a hard enough time just feeding yourself." He looked back at the Bastion. "Pain and fire. Sounds like the good old days." He gently disengaged his hand from the draconian's slicing grip. "You stay here and guard the supplies. No, no! It'll be all right. I'm not going to go into the Bastion. Don't worry. I'm just going to go pass the time of day with the Queen's Own. Be sociable. Stay right here."

"Yes, sir," said Drugo, but he didn't sound happy.

Slith sauntered off. Drugo had been ordered to guard the boxes and guard them he did, seemingly prepared to lay down his life in their defense.

"Uh, oh," Shanra groaned, aghast. "Look there. Slith's going to talk to that sivak you hit over the head."

"Slith knows I was the one who hit him," Hanra said, horrified. "And he knows you were the one who stole the requisition. Maybe he's gone to report us!"

"Slith wouldn't do that," Shanra said, but she sounded uncertain.

"He would if the commander told him to. Move closer! I have to hear what he's saying!" Hanra urged.

Shanra hesitated. "What about that baaz soldier?"

"He's not one of ours. He won't know who we are. C'mon!"

The two females slipped out of their hiding place. Walking nonchalantly, they strolled past Drugo, who eyed them with deep suspicion, but since they made no attempt to steal the boxes he'd been ordered to guard, he said nothing. Arriving at another alley, this one nearer the Bastion, the sisters dove into it. They flattened themselves against a wall, stood panting with relief.

"Hullo, boys," Slith was saying companionably. "How's it going? Lose any more swords lately?"

Shanra gave a smothered giggle. Hanra clamped her hand over her sister's mouth, glared at her sternly, and Shanra subsided with a gulp.

The guards were not amused. "Do you have business here, sir?" said one.

"Nice place the general's got," said Slith, gazing at the Bastion. "Lots of room for him to spread out. I don't suppose you give tours, do you?"

"Please state your business, sir," said another of the Queen's Own. At a glance from him, one of the guards departed.

"My business." Slith rubbed his jaw. He jerked his thumb over his shoulder. "You see that soldier back there? He was saying something very interesting just now. He's terrified of that place." Slith pointed to the Bastion. "Downright terrified. Said it was a . . . let me see, how did that go . . . a place of 'darkness and pain and terrible fire.' Now why do you suppose he'd say something like that?"

"He's a baaz, sir," said one of the Queen's Own disparagingly. "Who knows what those wretches think?"

"If they think at all," added another.

"And *that's* my point!" Slith stated, triumphant. "I've known lots of baaz in my time and I've never known one to have an imagination. Not a creative bone in their bodies. Now you have to admit, it takes a real imagination to come up with something like 'darkness, pain, and a terrible fire' when you're talking about the general's quarters. Especially when this is one of those *new* dracos—from the Khalkists."

"What seems to be the problem here?" A sivak officer, wearing the tabard of the Queen's Own, emerged from the command tent. "Who's your commander?"

Slith came to attention, snapped a salute. "Commander Kang, sir!"

The officer glowered. "These men are on duty, as you should be, no doubt."

"Yes, sir. Perhaps you could tell me—"

"Dismissed!" the officer bellowed.

"Yes, sir." Slith whipped around, tail lashing, and marched back to where Drugo stood, still guarding the boxes. Slith hefted his box, Drugo picked up the other, and they left, slogging through the muddy streets.

"Time to scoot!" Shanra breathed into her sister's ear.

"Right!" said Hanra.

"Do you know, sir," said one of the Queen's Own in a grim tone, "I think that sivak who was just here may have been the one who stole the swords."

Hanra and Shanra halted, stared at each other. Acting on the same impulse, they both darted back to their hiding place, listened intently.

"What makes you say that, Troop Leader?"

"He made a crack about the swords, sir. And he said some other things that were suspicious. He was asking questions about the Bastion, sir. Claimed that one of the new baaz had been making up stories about what was going on inside."

"Indeed," said the officer, frowning. He gazed off in the direction Slith had taken. "What sort of stories?"

The sivak repeated Slith's words.

"I think we may have a problem there," said the officer. "See to it."

"Yes, sir," said the Queen's Own and immediately two of them departed, taking the same route as Slith and Drugo.

"Sir!" An aide came dashing up. "Sir, the lead elements of the goblin army are in sight, coming over the ridge."

"Very good," said the officer imperturbably. "I will inform the general."

He disappeared back inside the command tent.

Horns blasted, announcing time for the changing of the guard, and a troop of light infantry marched past. The light infantry almost immediately ran afoul a company of shock infantry heading in the opposite direction. There was momentary confusion, as the officers sorted out the situation and got everyone moving again. The sivak sisters took the opportunity to emerge from their hiding place and slip away.

"What do you think he meant?" Hanra asked worriedly.

"The goblin army's in sight," said Shanra.

"No, no," Hanra said, annoyed at her sister's stupidity. "What he said about Slith being the one who stole the swords. Do you think Slith will get into trouble with the general on account of us?"

"The general wouldn't dare!" Shanra returned. She had unsullied faith in her champion. "If that grubby old aurak tried anything, Slith would chop him into ogre meat. I just hope we get to see it."

"Speaking of seeing things, you didn't happen to get a look at what was in the box, did you? Our presents?"

"No," Shanra said, shaking her head sadly. "But we better get back to the barracks fast or we'll miss out on our share. The others will hog it, whatever it is. You know they will."

Now thoroughly alarmed, the two sivak sisters pushed and shoved their way through the crowded streets.

* * * * *

The sun made no appearance all that day, lurking behind a mantle of gray clouds that threatened rain, but never committed to more than an annoying drizzle. The engineers' barracks were filled with the sounds of hammering and the noxious smell of the brown goo pulp concoction. After what passed for lunch, Kang made the rounds, inspecting the construction. He was pleased with the progress.

Though the pulp was taking longer to dry than they'd anticipated, the brown goo had proven to be far more effective than they had hoped. But time was running out. Receiving the scout's reports that the first elements of the army had been sighted, Kang climbed up to the reinforced battlements to see for himself. Line after long line of goblin soldiers marched over the ridge, the very same ridge where Kang had first stood and looked down into the fort. He could smell their foul stench and he could even hear the occasional shout from their officers.

The goblins poured down the ridge and into the canyon like a flood of turgid water, roiling and boiling as various units detached themselves and took up positions on the field. The flood crept slowly toward the fort, the tide rising. Soon they would be surrounded, an island in an ocean of death.

The draconians could do nothing to halt the flow. The archers of the Twelfth kept watch on the walls, occasionally picked off the odd goblin here and there, to much cheering and shouting. But they might as well have been flicking grains of sand into that ocean of death for all the good it would do.

Kang descended from the wall with a heavy heart, to find a few of his men clustered around the walls, trying to see through the cracks.

"Yes, there're goblins out there," Kang told his troops, ordering them back to work. "No surprise to us. We knew they were coming. We're the ones with the surprise."

The men laughed and returned to their work with renewed vigor.

"Pass the word for the second-in-command," Kang told Granak.

Granak passed the word. Kang waited in his quarters for Slith to arrive, but the sivak did not show up.

Figuring that perhaps something had gone wrong with the cactus mash, Kang tromped over to the distillery. Slith was known to take great care with his brew, tasting it repeatedly to make certain of the quality. He sometimes tasted it so copiously that he could be found sleeping off this quality control. Slith was not around, however. Gloth was in charge. Under his direction, the draconians were filling the barrels with the pungent mass of cactus pulp. The fumes alone nearly rocked Kang back on his heels. He felt giddy just breathing them.

"Slith went to the quartermasters to requisition supplies, sir," Gloth said.

"When was that?"

"This morning, sir."

"Shouldn't he be back by now?" Kang demanded angrily. "It's mid-afternoon!"

"I couldn't say, sir," Gloth replied meekly.

Of course he can't say, Kang thought. It isn't his responsibility to keep track of Slith.

Angry at Slith for not being there when he was needed and further angry with himself for allowing his anger to show, Kang stalked off. He hung around the work crews, watching them construct the dragon until he realized that he was only getting in the way and making the men nervous. He made a brief inspection of the females, found them hard at work spreading the brown goo mixture over the wings. He successfully avoided speaking to Fonrar and, pleased with that at least, he retired to his quarters, leaving orders that Slith was to be sent to him the moment he returned.

* * * * *

"Men are all the same, Fon," Huzzad said in comforting tones. "Whether they have skin or scales, they're all the same."

Having been first viewed by the female draconians with jealousy and suspicion, Huzzad was now not only accepted by the females but looked upon as a kind of elder sister, one who has "seen the world" and could impart her knowledge to her younger naive sisters. Huzzad had taken care not to try to usurp Fonrar's place of commander, but was acting in the capacity of adviser. She had shown them where they were deficient in their training, undertaken to correct their mistakes and had done so in a respectful manner.

Having taught them how to be better soldiers in possible battles with the goblins, Huzzad was now teaching the females how to be better soldiers in that grand eternal struggle—the battle of the sexes.

"You'd think he would have at least looked at me," Fonrar said, slopping on brown goo with wet, irritated slaps of the brush. "He didn't. Not the whole time. He hates me."

"He doesn't hate you," Huzzad said. "In fact, if he was human, I'd say he likes you so much that he doesn't know if he's on his head or heels when you're around."

"Really?" Fonrar stopped work, looked up, pleased. "But then why does he act as if he can't stand the sight of me?"

"Men don't like change. Men like things to stay the same. Why? Because then they don't have to make any changes themselves. In Kang's mind, you are still the little hatchlings he rescued from the cave. All he had to do was feed you and protect you. He understood what was required of him. But now you're grown up and he doesn't have a clue what he's supposed to do or say or how to react around you. He's afraid, Fon. Afraid he's going to lose you."

"But why?" Fonrar was bewildered. "Why would he think that?"

"When you were little, you looked up to him. He was perfect in your eyes. He could do nothing wrong. But now you know different, Fonrar. You know he's not perfect. You know that he can make mistakes. That's why you feel so angry at him sometimes. That's why you rebel against him. So in a way he *has* lost you. He sees that every time he looks into your eyes."

"I like him better for not being perfect," said Fonrar loyally. "I feel closer to him. I wouldn't want him to be any different from the way he is."

"I know," said Huzzad, smiling. "And he'll figure it out. Someday. You just have to be patient. Give him time."

The two were interrupted in their conversation by

the arrival of the sivak sisters. They came clambering over the wall of the latrine, bounding through the door, panting with excitement and overturning a bucket of goo.

"Did we miss it?" Shanra cried.

"What'd he bring us?" Hanra asked. "Did you open the box yet?"

"Calm down!" Fonrar ordered. "Did who bring what?"

"Then he hasn't given out the presents yet?" Hanra said in relief.

"We haven't missed out on our share?" Shanra said, adding suspiciously. "You're not just saying that, hiding it from us?"

"What are you two talking about?" Fonrar demanded, exasperated. "Hiding what?"

"We saw Slith on the street," Hanra explained. "He was coming from the Quartermasters and we heard him say he had bought presents. For us."

"He was carrying two big boxes," Shanra added. "We tried to see inside, but we couldn't. He was on his way back with the boxes. We thought he'd be here by now. We would have been here sooner only we took a wrong turn."

"Well, he hasn't been here," said Fonrar shortly. "And this is no time to be talking about presents. We have work to do. Grab brushes, both of you."

* * * * *

The dismal afternoon darkened imperceptibly, so that it was difficult to tell where day left off and night began. Outside the walls, goblin campfires began blossoming to life like some sort of noxious weed. Goblin archers returned fire at the draconians on the wall, doing little damage, for goblin archers were notoriously poor shots. The draconians hooted and shouted and danced on the walls, urging the goblins to fire. When they did, they invariably missed and the draconians collected the spent goblin arrows for use when their own ran short.

An enemy officer finally figured this out and the goblin tactics changed. They began to fire flaming arrows into the fort. These had the potential for doing far more damage, not to people, but to the wooden fort. Kang had ordered barrels filled with water placed at strategic locations around the fort and he had the draconians to soak the thatched roofs with water. Thus far, the flaming arrows were few and the archers had not yet found their range. Most fell harmlessly into the streets. Those few that did hit a wet rooftop sizzled and went out. Kang pulled a group of draconians from dragon building and put them on fire detail, ready to handle any major conflagration. He had intended to put Slith in charge of this detail, but Slith had not reported back.

Kang put off going to supper. The draconians were now ready to fit the various parts of the dragon's body together and Kang was kept busy with questions, questions he would have liked to discussed with his second-in-command.

Kang ordered Granak to do a thorough search of the barracks, the streets around the barracks and the mess hall. No sign of Slith. No one could even say for certain when they had last seen him. No one knew what supplies he had gone to pick up or what he might be planning to do with them.

A sharp tooth of worry started to gnaw at Kang. He quickly yanked it out by reminding himself that Slith was quite capable of taking care of himself. Slith enjoyed intrigue, he loved spying things out, thought nothing of going off on his own to concoct some ingenious plan. Fond of surprises, Slith quite often kept his little expeditions secret, waiting for the proper moment to gleefully spring them on his unsuspecting commander. Slith figured that Kang would understand and usually Kang did. More than once, these forays of Slith's had proven to be of real value.

"I'm just jumpy," Kang said to himself. "It's these blasted goblins." And, although he wouldn't admit it, Huzzad's question—*How would you feel if Slith died?*—bothered Kang deeply. Until that moment, Kang had never realized how much he would miss Slith, if something happened to him.

"Go talk to the Quartermaster," Kang told Granak, after the search had failed to turn up any trace of the sivak. "Find out when Slith was there and what he picked up. Don't let on that anything's wrong. I'm certain nothing *is* wrong."

"Yes, sir," said Granak, and motioning to the two baaz, who were part of Kang's bodyguard, he left on his assignment.

"What's this I hear, Commander?" A voice came out of the darkness. "Another of your men gone missing?"

Kang turned to find General Maranta, accompanied by an escort of the Queen's Own, approaching the barracks.

"Sir," said Kang, "we are unable to locate Subcommander Slith. We are afraid that something might have happened to him."

"Fah! Nothing's happened to him. He's gone over the wall! Run for his miserable life," said General Maranta. "I have never seen a more undisciplined lot than these engineers of yours, Commander!"

Kang's anger was brimstone, his worry fire. Both combined to seethe in his belly and he knew, in that instant, exactly how one of the fire-breathing red dragons feels the moment before it unleashes its blazing attack.

"Sir," he said in a voice that was so tightly controlled he sounded half-strangled, "you obviously do not know Subcommander Slith or you would not say—"

"Desertion in the face of the enemy," General Maranta continued. "But it's no less than I expected from you cowards. Engineers." He sneered. "You weren't good enough for them to make regular soldiers of you and so they made you crap-hole diggers and shit-haulers! Don't worry, Commander. My men rescued you from the clutches of those nasty old goblins once and we'll do so again—"

Red-hot flame exploded inside Kang. The fire cooked his brain, boiled his blood. He could never afterward remember clearly what happened, but he knew that someone was bellowing and someone was battling in a rage and that draconians were shouting and his arms were being pinned in a grip like a vice.

The words "court-martial" filtered through the smoke and the flame in his brain.

"You can't court-martial me, General Maranta!" Kang roared, saliva flying from his mouth. "I'm not under your command and neither are my men!"

He heard cheering; his men were cheering, and the realization of what he had said and done struck him like a bucket of icy water dumped over his head. The water doused the flame in an instant, leaving him chilled and sick, with a suffocating feeling of despair.

"Let go of me," he mumbled.

"No, sir," said Gloth, his arms wrapped tightly around Kang.

"You can let go," Kang repeated. "I'm all right now."

"Yes, sir," said Gloth uneasily. Slowly, he loosened his grip.

Kang looked around to see Fulkth standing nearby,

along with Yethik and Huzzad. All had their swords drawn. Behind them were fully half the draconian engineers, holding swords, saws, hammers. General Maranta was nowhere in sight.

"By the gods, sir," said Fulkth, his tongue flicking from between his teeth, visible in a wide grin, "I thought you were going to kill him!"

"You should have sir," Yethik growled. "After what he said about Slith."

"And us, sir," Gloth added grimly. "Calling us cowards!"

The other draconians gave a angry rumble of agreement.

Kang felt weak all over, feared his legs were going to give way. He sat down limply on the Drunken Dragon's tail section.

"Tell me what happened."

"Don't you remember, sir?" Gloth asked.

Kang shook his head.

"You jumped at him, sir. General Maranta. You never said a word. Just bellowed and jumped at him. You should have seen his face, sir." Yethik chuckled. "He was so startled that he couldn't even move. Same with the Queen's Own. If it hadn't been for Gloth, here, General Maranta would have been one dead aurak. Gloth grabbed hold of you and hauled you back. By then, the Queen's Own had the general surrounded."

"They were going for their swords," Fulkth added. "But by that time Yethik had his own sword drawn and these boys and Huzzad showed up." Fulkth jerked his thumb over his shoulder, indicating the troop behind, armed and ready to fight. "I think the general had second thoughts about us being cowards. He spewed out something about court-martialing you, sir, and made a hasty departure."

"He's right," said Kang. "I deserve to be court-martialed. I attacked my commanding officer. Here." Unbuckling his harness with its command badges, he handed the harness to Fulkth. "I place myself under arrest."

"No, sir! No!" The draconians sent up a howl of protest.

Fulkth refused to touch the harness. He wouldn't look at it, pretended he didn't see it.

"I have something to say." Huzzad's voice rang out. She stepped forward. The draconians fell back to give her room.

After years of being denigrated by humans, used little better than slaves, the draconians had lost the respect and awe they had once felt about the race. Huzzad had earned their trust, however, and they shouted for her to speak.

"Kang," said Huzzad, "you can't do this. Not in this desperate situation with Slith missing and half the goblin nation out there. Your people are counting on you. You can't let them down."

"My people," Kang murmured.

He looked to see Fonrar and Thesik and the rest of the females, standing with the others. Their expressions were grave, serious. He looked at his troops, that he had brought such a distance at so great a cost. He thought of his dream, lying somewhere far ahead, a city of white stone beneath a bright sun and a clear blue sky. His people. Their destiny.

Kang buckled on the harness to resounding cheers. But in that moment, he made a decision. A decision he would not discuss with anyone. Not yet.

"Go back to work," he ordered. "The goblins will attack with the dawn. We have to be ready."

The draconians returned to their duties. Fonrar

lingered, regarding him worriedly. He managed a reassuring smile for her and she nodded and walked off. The other officers hung about until Kang glowered at them, then they hastened away.

Kang watched them go. He was numb. He couldn't feel his hands or his feet. He couldn't feel his brain. He couldn't think or move or do anything. He sat on the tail section, watching his troops work. The Drunken Dragon was now completely assembled. They were adding the finishing touches to the head and loading the kegs of cactus mash into their special cage.

Fulkth had rounded up every bit of rope the regiment could find, then tied the bits together to form one gigantic length of rope. They ran the rope through a pulley and attached the end of the rope to the dragon. When the dragon was filled with heated air, it would start to rise up off the ground. The rope would keep it tethered until it had risen high enough to fly over the walls. A single sword slash on the rope would cut the dragon loose and send it on its first and last glorious flight.

The Drunken Dragon was enormous. Fully sixty feet in length from snout to tail tip, its wing span was nearly a hundred feet. They had mixed in red clay with the brown goo to give the dragon a red coloring. The female baaz had come up with the idea of adding in metal shards gleaned from the blacksmith. When the shards caught the firelight, they glinted with the appearance of shining scales. The sword-blade teeth had been honed razor sharp. The eyes were shining silver meat platters that had been "borrowed" from the Quartermaster's shed. The platters were part of the loot General Maranta had carried with him from Neraka. Reflecting the light, the meat platter eyes looked truly fearsome.

As Kang gazed at the dragon, a feeling of pride—pride in his people—seeped in to fill the emptiness inside. They had done a magnificent job.

"You know," he said softly, "this just might work!"

"Sir," came a tense voice behind him.

Kang looked around, recognized Granak.

"What have you found?" Kang demanded, jumping to his feet. "Any sign of Slith?"

"Yes and no, sir," said Granak. "We haven't found him, but we did find that draco he went off with. A baaz named Drugo."

"Good," said Kang. "Where is he? I want to have a talk with him."

"That's going to be a problem, sir," said Granak. "His neck is broken. Drugo's dead."

Chapter Seventeen

Flaming arrows streaked overhead, falling thicker and faster. Fires were breaking out all over the fort. Here and there was an explosion—some goblin scoring a lucky hit, some bozak having been in the wrong place at the wrong time. Outside the walls, drum beats began a rhythmic and heart-thumping pounding. The goblins used drums to start their soldiers' adrenaline pumping and to dishearten and demoralize the enemy. The attack would come soon now.

"Report," Kang said in a voice he didn't recognize.

"We found Drugo's body in an alley six streets over, sir. He was alone. There didn't seem to have been a struggle. Drugo was attacked from behind, his neck twisted. My guess is he never knew what hit him."

"Wait a minute," said Kang. "He was a baaz. There couldn't have been a body. Nothing but a pile of dust!"

"I know, sir." Granak shrugged, helpless. "I don't understand it any more than you do, sir."

"And what about Slith? Any sign of him?"

"We found two boxes lying nearby. They were upended, their contents scattered all over the alley. And we found this."

Granak held out his hand. Four silver scales gleamed in the torchlight. Kang peered at them. They came from a sivak, there was no doubt about that. But there were lots of sivaks in this fort. There was no way to prove that these were Slith's.

"I suppose it's possible that Slith killed this Drugo," Kang said reluctantly.

"No, sir." Granak was firm. "If Subcommander Slith had killed this baaz, he wouldn't have made such a mess of it, sir. He wouldn't have left the boxes at the scene. And he wouldn't be skulking about hiding. If he had killed the baaz, Subcommander Slith would have had a good reason and he would have come back to tell us about it."

All the draconians within hearing distance distance had stopped to listen, including their officers, who should have ordered the troops back to work. The loss of yet another draconian from their ranks affected them all. They were especially worried about Slith, who had been their second since the formation of the company.

"Proceed with your report," Kang ordered.

"Yes, sir. We talked to the Quartermaster. He confirmed that Slith and Drugo had been there late this morning. They picked up several items, including twenty pairs of leather bracers. We found everything in the boxes in the alley, sir."

"I think you should talk to the females, Kang," said a voice at his elbow.

Kang turned to find Huzzad there, listening intently. Kang made an impatient gesture.

"Whatever the problem, it will have to wait," he said. He turned back to Granak. "Take me to where you found the—"

"This can't wait, Kang," Huzzad said insistently. "Two of the females saw Slith today at about noon. Outside the Quartermaster's."

Kang's head jerked. "They did? What in the Abyss were they doing there?"

Huzzad shouted for Fonrar. The two held a brief conversation, then Fonrar departed. Within moments, she returned with the two sivak sisters, Hanra and Shanra. As they approached, a flaming arrow streaked down from the sky, landed on the Drunken Dragon. Fire crews leapt to put out the flames, which, fortunately, did not spread. The brown goo was apparently not flammable. The same could not be said for the cactus mash.

"Make sure those keg bombs are under cover!" Kang roared.

He turned to find the sivak sisters standing at attention in front of him. The sisters looked meek, contrite, scared and extremely guilty.

"One moment," Kang said when Fonrar would have spoken. "Granak, finish your report."

"Yes, sir. The Quartermaster's assistant showed us the route Slith and Drugo took when they left. That route would have taken them past the Bastion, but apparently they turned off before they reached it. We located a couple of the Queen's Own who were on duty at the time. They weren't much interested in talking to me, but I insisted and eventually they agreed to cooperate."

Kang could well imagine the tall, imposing Granak "insisting." Kang smiled grimly.

"I described Slith and the baaz who was with him.

The Queen's Own said that they hadn't seen either of them—"

"That's not true!" the sisters cried simultaneously.

Startled, Kang looked at them.

"Very well," Kang said, "let me hear what you two know. And make it quick."

"Sir," said Hanra, "we saw Subcommander Slith today. This morning. We saw him by the Quartermaster's." She looked down at her feet. "We are . . . uh . . . very fond of Slith, sir. Subcommander Slith. And, well, we followed him."

"He said he had presents for us, sir," Shanra added. "We wanted to find out what they were."

"And what were you two were doing at the Quartermaster's?" Kang said sternly. "You don't need any more swords, I take it?"

"Oh, no, Commander," said Shanra, missing the sarcasm. "We have enough swords, thank you, sir. We were picking up the spell components Thesik and the bozaks need for their magic—"

"Shhh!" her sister hissed at her.

But it was too late. Horrified, Shanra put her hand over her mouth.

"Magic!" Kang stared at Fonrar.

"Please, sir," she said, stricken. "I can explain—"

"Yes, you will," he said tersely. "But first things first." He turned back to the sisters. "You followed Slith, you said."

"Yes, sir," Hanra said, seeing that Shanra was too mortified to talk. "We followed him and the stranger baaz. They came to that big ugly building—"

"The Bastion," Kang said.

"Yes, sir. Slith and the stranger baaz stopped to look at it. And then we saw that sivak. The one . . ." Hanra halted, looked confused.

"The one you hit over the head," Kang guessed.

"Yes, sir." Hanra was now looking at her feet.

"Go on."

Between the two of them, the sivak sisters related all that they had seen and heard between Slith, Drugo, and the Queen's Own.

"That stranger baaz talked about a 'terrible darkness' and 'fiery pain.' He was really frightened. He told Slith not to go in the Bastion. Slith said he wouldn't. He just wanted to talk to the Queen's Own. And he did. He told them what the baaz had said and he asked them what it meant. The Queen's Own said the baaz was just being stupid. Then an officer came out and told Slith he had better leave and so he and the baaz picked up the boxes and walked away. And that was all that happened—"

"—except for what the officer said after Slith was gone," Shanra added.

"What?" Kang asked sharply. "What did he say?"

The two exchanged guilty glances.

"You tell," Hanra muttered. "You brought it up."

"Well . . ." Shanra drew in a deep breath. "They said they thought Slith was the one who had . . . uh . . . stolen the swords, sir."

"Tell me exactly what they said," Kang ordered.

Shanra thought back. "It was something like: 'he'—meaning Subcommander Slith, sir—'made a crack about the swords. And he was asking questions about the Bastion.' "

"Yes, and when he said that, the officer looked really angry," Hanra added. "He wanted to know what the baaz had said and the sivak told him. All about the darkness and the fiery pain."

Shanra struck in eagerly. "I remember this part. The officer said, 'I think we may have a problem here.' "

"Yes and then he said, 'See to it,' " said Hanra. "And they left."

"Which way did they go?"

"The same way as Subcommander Slith, sir."

"And what happened then?" Kang asked, frowning. The two looked at each other doubtfully.

"Oh, yes. I remember," Hanra said. "Another sivak came running up and said that the enemy was on the move. We saw more draconians coming and so we figured we better leave."

"Yes, we didn't want to miss out on the presents," Shanra said.

"The presents," Kang repeated absently.

His mind was on these new draconians, on how they had come from the Khalkists, marched through the goblin lines to reach this fort unscathed. Slith had not believed the story and had decided to check it out. He'd spent the day with one draconian, who had told him that the Bastion was a place of "pain and terrible darkness" or words to that effect. The Queen's Own had deemed Slith "a problem" and had been told to "see to it." Now the strange draconian, whose body had not turned to stone as it should have, was dead and Slith was missing.

But why kill one and not the other? If Slith had tumbled onto something he shouldn't have, why not kill him too? He had mysteriously vanished, just like other draconians in the fort had mysteriously vanished. Kang had not believed that they were deserters and he was damn sure Slith would not have deserted. And then there was this talk about "pain and terrible darkness" in the Bastion.

Kang didn't have any answers, but he knew where to start looking. Looking for answers and looking for Slith. There was now no doubt in Kang's mind that his friend was in an extremely bad situation. If there had been a way out, Slith would have found it by now.

Kang began to issue orders.

"Support Squadron, you're with me. The rest of you remain here and keep working—"

Kang's words were obliterated by horn blasts, braying and raucous, coming from outside the walls. General Maranta had miscalculated. The goblins were not waiting until dawn to attack. They were launching their attack now.

"Damn!" Kang said, and added several more colorful words suitable to the situation.

Horns inside the fort began calling the troops to their positions. Officers were shouting orders, draconians were answering with cheers and battle cries. The ground shook with the tramping of many feet.

If Kang could have split himself in two, he would have done so in that instant. He would have sent half of himself clambering up the wall to see the disposition of the goblin forces, to try to figure out where they were going to strike first and hardest. He would have sent the other half of himself to the Bastion to find out what had happened to Slith.

He would have split his troops, as well. Support Squadron would be needed here. They were shorthanded, as it was. He needed men to finish readying the dragon for flight, men to protect it and in addition he needed men to maintain order inside the fort and continue fighting the fires.

His officers stood poised, ready to react, tense, worried, uncertain what their commander was going to do. A volley of arrows sailed over the wall. Fortunately, they had been fired from a great distance and were mostly spent. Rattling on the ground, they bounced off the draconians' scaly hides, doing little or no damage.

But they were a harbinger of things to come. The range would shorten, the flights of arrows would soon become more deadly.

Kang knew, of course, what he should do. Slith was one single draconian. His life was unimportant. Kang's responsibility was to the fort, to his fellow draconians. More lives than just Slith's would be lost in this battle. Kang could not let his personal feelings intervene. If their situations had been reversed, Kang would have expected Slith to make the same decision, would have given him hell if he had not.

"Belay that order, Support Squadron," Kang said calmly. "We can't spare the men."

"No, but you can spare our Squadron," Fonrar said suddenly and unexpectedly. "We'll find out what's happened to Subcommander Slith, sir."

Before Kang could find his voice to order them firmly to return to their barracks, Fonrar was herself shouting orders. "Female Troop! You will arm yourselves and report back to me on the double. Move! Riel, bring me my sword and webbing!"

The baaz saluted. The females dropped the wood they had been using to stoke the fire and dashed off, running toward their barracks in a disciplined, orderly manner.

"This will be a good training mission, Subcommander Fonrar," Huzzad remarked.

"Agreed," said Fonrar, adding with equal formality. "We would be honored if you would accompany us, Wing Commander Huzzad."

"I am the one who would be honored, Subcommander," said Huzzad, loosening her sword in its sheath.

By this time, Kang had recovered from his shock. "No," he bellowed. "Absolutely not! I won't allow it. You will return to barracks—"

He might as well have been talking to the Drunken Dragon. Neither Fonrar nor Huzzad was paying the least bit of attention to him. The female draconians returned, buckling on their harness as they ran. They began to line up in front of Fonrar. Riel handed Fonrar her sword. Thesik helped to buckle it on, as Fonrar continued to issue orders.

"Hanra, you and your sister know your way to the Bastion. You take the lead. The rest of us will follow." Fonrar looked over her troops. "Everyone ready?"

The females thundered back a reply.

"Good! Move out! Double-time, there, troopers!"

The squadron broke into a run. They were not in particularly good order, a few of them tripped over their swords, but they were setting a good pace.

Fonrar saluted. "We'll find Subcommander Slith, sir. Don't worry." She left at a dash, accompanied by Huzzad, who gave Kang a wry grin.

Kang sucked in a huge breath, ready to call a halt to the entire proceeding. And then he remembered Huzzad's words, heard them as clearly as if she were standing next to him.

Each one has her own soul. Each has her own destiny. Each has the right to achieve her own destiny. You can't take away that right. They look to you for guidance, Kang, for leadership and counsel. But they won't for long. Eventually, they'll start to hate you.

Kang shifted words in mid-bellow. "Fulkth! You're in charge! Have that contraption ready to launch at first light. If I'm not back, you take command. You know what to do. Granak, you're with me."

The streets were crowded, congested. Every draconian in the fort was on the move, each having to be somewhere he wasn't and all trying to get there at the same time. Nothing short of a fiery mountain falling down in

front of him could stop Granak, who at times bodily
lifted up draconians and tossed them out of his path
and the commander's. They soon caught up to the
females, who were also proving adept at bullying and
pushing their way through the streets.

Hearing Kang's shout, Fonrar looked around. Her
expression hardened. She eyed him defiantly, mar-
shalling her arguments, ready to march them out to do
battle.

Reaching her side, Kang raised his hand in a salute.

"I'd like to join you, Troop-Leader," he said gravely,
politely, one senior officer speaking to another. "If that
is agreeable?"

Fonrar smiled at him. Her eyes shone brighter than
the blazing fires.

"I'd like that, sir," she said. "I'd like it very much."

Running along at Fonrar's side, Huzzad glanced at
Kang and winked.

"Comrades?" she asked.

"Comrades," said Kang.

Chapter Eighteen

Two members of the Queen's Own stood guard outside the Bastion. They remained at their posts, seemingly oblivious to the noise and confusion inside the fort. The flaming arrows had not penetrated this deep into the interior. Even the sounds of the drumbeats and the first fierce yells of the advancing goblin army were muffled back here. The Queen's Own took note of Kang's advancing force, but the sight of armed draconians marching through the streets was nothing out of the ordinary, did not even rate a second glance.

Kang was counting on just such a reaction from the Bastion's guards. He didn't want a fight. The objective was to save draconian lives, not kill them. He gave Fonrar the signal, which meant that the plan they had hastily cobbled together on the way here was to be put into action.

The troop of draconian females, with Fonrar at its head, marched toward the Bastion. Fonrar gave the guards a salute. The Queen's Own were engrossed in talking to each other and didn't even bother to acknowledge her. The front ranks of the females drew near. The guards continued talking, discussing the upcoming battle.

Kang's orders to Fonrar had been to take the guards by surprise, subdue them. They hadn't had time to discuss how that would be accomplished, but Fonrar had assured Kang that she and her troops would get the job done. He expected the females to rush the guards, bear them down by sheer numbers, clunk them over the head a couple of times. Not elegant, but at least effective.

Kang marched at the rear. He had stationed Granak up front with Fonrar, with quiet orders to the large sivak to jump in and help, should the females get into trouble. Hearing Fonrar's sudden, sharp command, Kang raced toward the Bastion, the rear ranks of females racing back with him. Expecting a battle, he arrived at the Bastion to find the two members of the Queen's Own lying on the ground, having what appeared to be a peaceful snooze, while several baaz females bound them neatly hand and foot.

"What the—" Kang stared. "How did—"

"Magic, sir," said Fonrar, trying hard to sound casual. "Sleep spell."

"But the magic is gone!" Kang protested.

"Yes, sir," Fonrar answered. "We know, sir." She was clearly embarrassed.

"The magic's not gone for them, Kang," Huzzad explained hurriedly. "It's not gone for any of the rest of the draconians in your regiment. The male bozaks have been teaching the females."

Kang glared at them all grimly. "Why wasn't I informed?"

"We know how you feel about the magic being the Queen's gift and how when she left, the gift was lost," Fonrar said. "If you didn't use magic, the other bozaks didn't feel it was right for them to use magic. But we didn't know anything about any of this, sir. The males caught us using some spells, just fooling around. They told us that the magic was not a toy, that the spells might hurt us if we didn't know what we were doing. And so they taught us the right way. Don't be angry, sir. We didn't mean to deceive you."

"I know," said Kang. "I'm trying to understand. I'm not angry at you. Just angry at myself for being an idiot. Granak, break down that door. Unless," Kang added dryly, "one of you females has a magic spell that will work."

"I think I might, sir," Thesik offered. Warning everyone to stand back, she chanted several words, then held her hand out toward the double doors. Nothing happened at first. Then the sounds of rending metal came to their ears. The iron hinges turned to rust as they watched. The doors teetered unsteadily and then dropped to the ground.

The baaz dragged the two slumbering Queen's Own inside the Bastion, deposited them, bound and gagged, in a corner.

"What is that weird sound?" Kang demanded, entering.

He'd first heard it standing outside, but he'd discounted it, figuring it was goblins pounding on their drums. Once they were inside the Bastion, the sound was markedly louder.

Ka-thump. Ka-thump. Ka-thump. Ka-thump.

The rhythmic sound kept time, counted cadence. The thumping was loud and all-pervasive. They could feel it, feel the walls shiver in response to the beat, feel the sound pulse up from the floor through their feet.

"This is strange," said Kang, looking around the rock walls with their honey-comb lattice structure. "I was here before and I didn't hear this sound then."

"What do you suppose it is, sir?" Fonrar asked.

"It's like a thousand hearts, all beating at once," said Thesik.

"Creepy, that's what it is," said Huzzad from the darkness of the Bastion's interior. "Ouch! Son-of-a— I just walked into a goddam wall! Look, you dracos can see in the dark, but I can't. I don't suppose there's a torch around here anywhere?"

There wasn't. Not that being able to see will help us all that much anyway, Kang thought glumly, recalling the twisting, turning, confusing corridors they'd have to traverse to reach the underground rooms.

"If it's all the same to you," Huzzad said. "I think I'll wait right here, guard the rear."

"Good idea," said Kang. "If any more of the Queen's Own try to enter, you can lower the portcullis."

He gestured to the rickety-looking apparatus with its wicked teeth, flaring red in the light of the fires. The portcullis shivered with every thump of the strange sound. Huzzad glanced up at the portcullis, glanced at the frayed rope holding it in place, watched it shiver and shake and hastily took a step out from underneath it.

"I'll wait outside," she said. "Take my chances with the goblins. Good luck! I hope you find Slith. I want his recipe for that cactus juice."

"We'll have to walk single file," Kang said. "This place is a maze. It's got more twists and tangles than a pack of snakes all knotted together. And we've got to get through here fast!"

He felt a sense of urgency. He didn't like the strange drumming, didn't like Thesik's analogy. But the Bastion had been specifically designed to do exactly what it was doing—thwart an enemy's advance, slow him down, make him confused, cause him to lose valuable time.

Even Prokel and Vertax, who had been here before, had lost their way in the serpentine catacombs. Not only did Kang have to reach Slith swiftly, but he was needed back at the battle.

"Commander," said Fonrar. "May I make a suggestion?"

"Yes, what is it?" he said, trying to curb his impatience.

"You should let Thesik take the lead. She has a really good sense of direction. She never gets lost. Never."

"It's an aurak thing," Thesik added modestly. "You know, sir. No wings."

"No, it's too dangerous," Kang snapped. "I'll take the lead. But Thesik can come behind me, let me know if I'm headed the right way."

He did this mainly to humor the females, for he didn't really believe that Thesik had any better sense of direction than he himself. They wound around the corridors, turned this way and that. Kang walked with his sword drawn. Behind him, he could hear the footfalls of the females, their claws scraping against the floor, their wings brushing the sides of the walls. They were quiet, orderly, alert, halting when he halted, no bumping into one another. They had been well trained. He couldn't have done better himself.

I haven't done anything for them myself, he thought, ashamed. That will change. I'll make it up to them.

In the meantime, he was proud of them. He was especially proud of Fonrar.

"Sir," Thesik said, reaching out her hand to stop him.

"You don't want to go this way. If you take this corridor, you'll double back on your trail." She indicated another that branched off to the left. "This is the route you want."

Kang hesitated. Then he admitted to himself that he really was lost. He didn't have a clue about where they were going, except a gut feeling. Having come to the conclusion long ago that his gut wasn't the most reliable organ in his body, he decided to follow Thesik's advice. Immediately when he stepped into the corridor, he heard the sound of the heartbeat grow louder. He looked back at her.

"Well done, Thesik," he said.

"Thank you, sir." She smiled, pleased with his praise.

"What a fool I've been," he muttered as he hurried on. "What a big, blind stupid dope of a fool."

After that, he sought Thesik's opinion. She led them unerringly when, left to himself, Kang might have wandered the maze for days.

The sound of the strange thumping heartbeat had been an annoyance at first, but the closer they came, the louder the sound grew. The annoyance changed to dislike and soon Kang grew to actively hate the rhythmic thudding. He couldn't think for the pulsing that shook the floors and the walls, shook the very teeth in his head. He put his hands over his ears in an effort to block it out, but then he heard the beating of his own heart thudding in time with the drumming and that was more disturbing. He fumed, frustrated that they couldn't move faster, but he didn't dare, for fear that they would miss a turn.

"Sir," Fonrar said, behind him. "I think I hear voices up ahead."

The next moment, he heard them, too. He couldn't make out words. The thudding noise prevented that. His own heartbeat increased in excitement, for at the same time, he thought he was starting to recognize his surroundings. The maze of corridors ended at the entrance to General Maranta's Audience Hall. Kang recalled that when they had come near to reaching that point, the corridors no longer twisted, but ran straight and smooth, like the one they were in now.

"I think we're near the end, sir," said Thesik.

Kang thought so, too. He lifted his hand, motioned his troop forward at a run. They would not be able to take the Queen's Own by surprise this time. The sivaks would have heard the approach of Kang's force, heard their scraping footsteps, their whispered conversations, heard the rattle and jingle of harness. The Queen's Own who guarded the entrance to the Audience Hall would be waiting and ready for them.

Kang had no time to alert his troops to what he planned. He hoped that they would catch on, follow his lead.

"Ho, there!" he began shouting, as he tramped down the corridor. "Queen's Own! Don't fire! It's the First Dragonarmy Engineers! I'm acting on orders from your commander"—

Kang was blank. What in the name of the vanished gods was the name of their blasted commander?

He looked at Granak, who shrugged helplessly.

"—Commander Blxrkxzqur sent us!" Kang hollered, covering his mouth with his hand. The sound of his voice would be distorted by the corridors. He just hoped the commander's name wasn't something like Mog.

His words echoed through the corridor as did the tramp of many feet, the clash of metal. Glancing back at Fonrar, he saw that she had grasped his intent, if not necessarily what he planned to do. His one hope was that Commander What's His Name wasn't standing down here waiting for him, but that was a risk he had to take. He didn't think it likely. In General Maranta's position, Kang would have left the Queen's Own commander outside the Bastion with orders to defend it should the fort fall to the enemy.

Kang continued running. To stop would look suspicious. He raced around the corner. Granak had shouldered—politely—Thesik aside and was in position right behind his commander. Fonrar and her squadron double-timed behind.

Four of the Queen's Own stood guard at the door to the Audience Hall. They had their weapons drawn, but not raised. They were wary, tense, but anyone would be in their situation, stuck deep inside this cavernous building with no way of knowing whether it was day or night, no way of knowing what was happening in the fort outside.

"Are you men all right?" Kang thundered as he burst into their midst.

"Yes, Commander," said one, looking puzzled. "Why wouldn't we be?"

"We found a breach in the walls of the Bastion on the northeast corner," Kang said crisply. "We have evidence that a goblin raiding party is inside the Bastion. Your commander sent me to reinforce you. You men"—he motioned to his troops, who ran in after him—"deploy!"

Kang stood near the captain of the watch detail. Granak had taken up a position next to another sivak. Fonrar, standing beside a third, was loudly ordering her troops to spread out. At a nod from Kang, Granak socked his sivak on the jaw, knocking him out cold. He caught the draconian in his arms as he fell, gently lowered him to the ground.

Kang elbowed the captain in the gut, doubling him over, gave him a crack on the back of the head that sent him to the floor. The sivak near Fonrar stared at this. He opened his mouth, but at that moment Shanra, hissing to her sister, "It's *my* turn!" clouted him on the head with the pommel of her sword. The female baaz swarmed over the fourth, tied him up in his own harness.

"You better sleep 'em, just to make sure," Kang told Fonrar.

She nodded and, turning to one of the other bozaks, gave the order to cast a sleep spell.

Kang was disappointed. He'd wanted to see how she handled the spellcasting. "Why didn't you do it?" he asked in an undertone, not to upbraid her in front of her troop.

"I don't use magic, sir," Fonrar said. She gazed up at him. "You don't. I didn't want . . ." She paused, confused, and looked hurriedly away.

She didn't want to hurt him. Feelings—comradely feelings—warmed Kang's blood, more intoxicating than cactus juice. He had no time to express them, except for an awkward pat on her shoulder. He saw she understood, however. Her eyes were shining and she returned his pat with a shy one of her own.

"Weapons drawn," said Kang, facing the closed and barred door. "Those of you who have magic spells, be ready to cast them. Remember, we don't want to kill any draconians if we don't have to."

"What do you think we're going to find inside there, Commander?" Thesik asked nervously.

"I don't know," Kang answered. "So be prepared for anything. Ready?"

Each of the females gripped her sword, nodded.

"Thesik," Kang ordered. "Open the door."

The aurak cast her spell. The door fell inward with a crash.

Kang started to enter the Audience Hall, but this time Granak politely elbowed his commander aside, to be the first one into the chamber. Kang followed at a run, the females pouring through the shattered door behind him.

They halted, stared, amazed. Whatever they had been prepared to find, it wasn't this.

The Audience Hall was packed with draconian soldiers. Hundreds of them, sitting wingtip to wingtip. All of them were armed, wearing helms and body armor. They were seated on the floor in neat and orderly rows, their equipment beside them, apparently waiting for someone to give them orders. All of them turned their heads to stare at Kang and his troops as they burst into the chamber.

The thudding noise was very loud now. Kang had the eerie impression that it was coming from these draconians, that it was the sound of their collective beating hearts.

If this was more of General Maranta's bodyguard . . .

We're dead, Kang thought. He gripped his sword, prepared to go down fighting, but the draconians did not attack.

They continued to stare at him expectantly. Waiting.

"Sir," said Granak, sounding puzzled. "Don't you think . . . don't they look kind of familiar?"

"Which one?" Kang asked, returning their stares, wondering what in the name of all that was holy he was going to do.

"All of them, sir," Granak said.

Now that Granak mentioned it, the draconians did look familiar. Kang had the feeling he'd seen them—all of them—before. He didn't know how that could be possible.

"Urul, sir," said Granak, "and Vlemess."

Urul and Vlemess, the two draconians who had disappeared while on guard duty.

"Yes!" Kang said in relief.

He walked over to one of the draconians, thinking he was Urul, prepared to question him, find out what the heck was going on here. He paused, however, confused. The draconian standing next to Urul also looked like Urul. But the nearer he came, the less each did. It was as if someone had blurred Urul's features, erased them.

Kang stared closely into the eyes of each of the draconians. He saw that same empty, vacant and bewildered look he'd seen in the eyes of the new draconians. The oddest thought came to him.

The idea was ludicrous, crazy, demented, horrible. But if there was any possibility he was right, Slith was in terrible danger. And not only Slith, all draconians everywhere were in danger.

"You don't see Slith anywhere?" Kang demanded in a harsh voice. He glanced swiftly around the groups of draconians, fearing to find a group of sivaks, a group of sivaks with Slith's face and that lost and hopeless look in their eyes.

"No, sir," said Granak, after a moment. "All the draconians here are baaz."

"Then hopefully we're in time!" Kang said fervently.

The thudding sound wasn't coming from inside this chamber. It was somewhere close, behind the walls. He recalled General Maranta making his sudden, dramatic appearance, seemingly out of nowhere. There must be a door along those walls somewhere. Kang headed for the back of the Audience Hall, moving slowly around the draconians, who continued to stare at him as if their hundreds of brains had only one thought and one set of eyes between them.

"Don't do or say anything threatening," he warned his troops. "Fonrar, have your squadron spread out, search the walls. Look for a door. We need to locate the source of that thumping sound."

The thudding went on and on and just when Kang thought that hammering heartbeat was going to cause his own heart to burst, the sound stopped.

The silence was heavy, ominous. Kang was filled with a terrible foreboding that whatever horrible thing was going to happen to his friend was going to happen now.

"Slith!" Kang roared in helpless desperation, standing in the center of the vast Audience Chamber. "Slith, it's me! Where are you?"

Very faintly, he heard what sounded like, "Here—ulp!"

"That was Slith!" The two sivak sisters were jumping up and down. "That was Slith, sir! We know his—"

"Shut up!" Kang bellowed and they were all instantly silent.

He shouted Slith's name again, but no answer came.

"Where did that come from?" he demanded.

The two sivak sisters pointed to a place directly behind the dais on which General Maranta had first made his appearance. Tripping and falling over the feet of the draconian soldiers, Kang made his way to the dais. Fonrar's troops, who had moved around the chamber's walls, had already reached the area and were searching desperately for a door.

The wall was smooth stone, unbroken. But he could hear sounds coming from the other side—sounds as of claws scrabbling on the floor. And other sounds, a voice, chanting.

"Damn it!" Kang swore, frustrated, his fear for Slith twisting his stomach. "There must be a way back there! There must!"

"I see it," Thesik cried. "There." She pointed.

Kang looked. He saw nothing. Smooth wall. No door. No opening of any kind.

"It's there," Thesik insisted and she ran forward.

"Thesik! No!" Fonrar called, jumping to try to stop her friend, for it appeared to her—it appeared to them all—that Thesik was going to dash her brains out running straight into a solid stone wall.

They watched in astonishment, their cries dying on their lips, to see Thesik dash right through the wall and vanish from their sight.

"An illusion!" Kang realized. "It's an illusion!"

An extremely good one. Some illusions are immediately dispelled the moment the viewer ceases to believe in them. But even though he knew now that the stone wall wasn't real, he could still see it. He wondered how Thesik had seen through it, decided that must be another "aurak thing."

Drawing his axe, he barged through the door and nearly fell over Thesik, who was standing just inside the doorway. She caught hold of his arm, put her finger to her mouth, cautioning silence. Kang raised his hand to halt the rest of the troop, who were right behind him.

He was inside another vast chamber. The interior was lit by a extremely bright light—a "fiery light"— radiating from the center. He could not see its source, due to the fact that his view was blocked by a crowd of draconians. Perhaps as many as hundred stood between him and the light. Kang froze in place, waited for the draconians to turn and attack.

The draconians did not move. They were intent on watching whatever was happening in the center of the chamber. When his eyes had grown accustomed to the bright light, he saw that the draconians bore no weapons, they wore no armor. They made no sound.

They didn't move, except to breathe. They were kapaks, their scales had a faint brass sheen.

The chanting voice continued. Kang recognized the voice of General Maranta. A shadow passed back and forth in front of the fiery light, partially obscuring it. Kang motioned Thesik nearer.

"Do you know what's going on?" he whispered.

Thesik shook her head. "I can't see," she answered.

"I'm going to try to find out. Tell the others to stay where they are until I signal."

Thesik nodded and slipped back outside the illusionary door.

Left alone, Kang looked carefully around the chamber, searching for General Maranta's bodyguards, the Queen's Own. He could not see any of them, only row upon row of silent, watching kapaks.

Gripping his axe, Kang padded softly forward. Although he tried to move as quietly as possible, he clanked and rattled, his tail scraped the hard-packed floor, his claws clicked. He grit his teeth, expecting any moment for the kapaks to turn and see him and raise the alarm or for one of the Queen's Own to come bounding out from the crowd and confront him.

Nothing happened. Kang crept up so close to the kapaks that he could have breathed on their scales. Kang peered over the heads of the crowd in front of him.

General Maranta stood in the center of the chamber. He was alone, Kang was quick to note. No sign of the Queen's Own anywhere. The "fiery light" emanated from an object the general held in his clawed hand. The object was a black crystal globe that glowed with a inner light that was red at the edges, black at its heart.

General Maranta ceased his chanting. The globe's light dimmed.

"Bring the next," he said calmly.

Two members of the Queen's Own appeared, dragging between them a kapak draconian. The kapak was gagged, his hands and feet and even his wings tightly bound. He struggled in his bonds, to no avail. The Queen's Own dumped the kapak down on the floor in front of General Maranta.

The kapak stared at the general with wild, frightened eyes, shaking his head and trying, pathetically, to crawl away by inching his bound body along the floor.

"The sacrifice you make is for your people," General Maranta said in soothing tones. He held the black globe over the kapak. The red light shone on the draconian, who lurched violently, tried to wriggle out from beneath it.

The general removed his hand. The black globe hung in place over the kapak. General Maranta started to chant. The black globe began to spin, slowly at first, and then faster and faster. The fiery light shone down on the kapak. The strange thudding noise began and Kang realized that he was hearing the kapak's frantically beating heart, amplified a hundred times or more.

A scream bubbled up from the kapak's throat. He stiffened, then his body jerked in a spasm. Mist drifted up from the kapak's body. The globe drank the mist greedily, sucking it up. The globe spun faster and the mist that had been sucked into the globe spewed out of it in long, thin tendrils. Whenever one of these tendrils touched the ground, it gained mass and form. It became a draconian.

That's not mist! Kang understood, sick with horror and revulsion. What he had mistaken for mist was the kapak's soul. The black globe had taken the draconian's soul and split it up, giving birth to new draconians.

Draconians without a soul. Draconians with blurred

features. Draconians whose bodies lacked the magical power to alter after death. Draconians who would obey orders without question, mindless, mechanical.

The kapak on the floor had quit screaming. The thudding sound grew slower and slower and finally ceased altogether. The kapak lay limp and lifeless. Standing around him were a hundred new kapaks. Their features resembled his, but they were less distinct. They gazed down at the poor wretch that had died to give them life with empty, lost expressions in their eyes.

Kang's stomach wrenched. He was afraid for a moment he was going to vomit. He was shaking so he had all he could do to keep hold of his axe.

General Maranta seized hold of the floating globe. He stopped chanting.

"Go stand over there," he told the new kapaks in irritable tones, as one might speak to children who are underfoot.

The general looked tired. His shoulder slumped. He paused to rub his eyes. The magic of the spell must be draining his energy.

The kapaks marched obediently to take their places with the rest of what Kang now realized were to be the fort's "reinforcements." The Queen's Own came forward, lifted up the body of dead kapak. The corpse was drained of its magic. It could no longer turn to acid, as it was supposed to. The Queen's Own hauled the corpse away.

Kang fought the horror and his revulsion, forced himself to think. First, he needed to know how many of the Queen's Own were in this chamber and where they were located. He tried to see, but the kapaks were blocking his view. The Queen's Own were coming from somewhere in the back of the chamber.

Kang was debating within himself whether he

should try to sneak back to see how many of the Queen's Own they would have to deal with or whether he should return to tell his troops what was going on when the decision was taken out of his hands.

"Bring the next one," ordered General Maranta, straightening and shaking off his fatigue.

The Queen's Own came forward, dragging Slith.

The sivak was bound and gagged, as had been the kapak. But Slith had not been taken captive easily. His face was covered with dried blood and he continued to fight his captors every step of the way, lashing out at them with his tail, trying to butt them with his head. Blood flew from the bindings that cut into his scaly flesh. Four of the Queen's Own were required to haul him forward and they were scratched and bleeding. They appeared relieved to dump him at General Maranta's feet.

"Good riddance!" one said.

"A fighter," said General Maranta approvingly. "You will be my first sivak. The sacrifice you make is for your people."

The general lifted the black globe and began to chant.

"Slith!" Kang roared and slammed into the kapaks standing in front of him. "Here! I'm here!"

Distracted, General Maranta ceased his chanting and turned his head.

Slith looked up, gave a howl of triumph and, with a lurch, began to roll across the floor, straight into General Maranta. Upended, the general fell heavily on his back.

Kang's shout had been intended simply to distract General Maranta. Having once been a fairly adept magic-user himself, Kang knew that spellcasting requires intense concentration. His yell would break that concentration. What he had not intended was that his troops would take his yell for the signal to charge.

He heard Fonrar shout an order, heard the females respond with a battle cry.

"The Queen's Own!" Kang bellowed. "Stop the Queen's Own!"

He could not take the time to look to see if Fonrar had understood. He had to reach Slith. Fortunately, the mindless kapaks were not putting up any resistance. They stared at him stupidly, not moving, not attacking, not doing anything. He was reminded of a herd of cows. He elbowed and kicked and punched his way through the mass of kapak bodies.

Slith thrashed about on the floor, struggling to free himself. Kang glanced quickly around. Several of the Queen's Own were endeavoring to reach him, but they were being blocked by the kapaks. He looked for General Maranta. The last he'd seen, the general was lying sprawled on the floor. He was nowhere in sight.

"Where's Maranta?" Kang demanded, bending over Slith and helping him to a sitting position.

Slith glared at him, making furious, incoherent sounds.

"Oh, yeah, right." Kang tore loose the gag.

"About time!" Slith gasped. His eyes shifted to a point behind Kang. "Look out!"

Kang lunged sideways. The vicious sword slash whistled past him. Straightening, Kang struck the Queen's Own in the gut with the butt of his axe, driving the wind from the sivak's body. The sivak tumbled forward. Slith kicked with both feet, caught the sivak in the head.

"Untie me, damn it!" Slith shouted.

"Sorry, I can't," Kang grunted. He was fending off two of the Queen's Own. "I'm a little busy right now!"

One of the sivaks he'd been battling suddenly disappeared. Kang caught a glimpse of the sivak flying over the heads of the kapaks. His flight was not of his own volition. The large, stalwart figure of Granak came to stand beside Kang.

"Take over here!" Kang yelled. He had caught a glimpse of the general's head. "I have to deal with Maranta!"

Granak nodded and with one punch of his fist flattened the sivak Kang had been battling.

"Granak! Good! Untie me!" Slith said, scooting over to where Granak stood and holding out his bound hands.

"Just a moment, sir," said Granak calmly, grabbing yet another of the Queen's Own and turning him upside down, while still another leapt on his back.

"Damn it, someone untie me!" Slith howled.

Fighting his way through the kapaks, who had begun to mill about aimlessly, Kang tried desperately to keep General Maranta in view. Kang found the general and then he lost him, only to find him yet again, moving rapidly toward the rear of the chamber. The Queen's Own were back there, guarding a group of draconian prisoners. Fonrar and her troops were here ahead of him, having circled around the walls while he dealt with Slith.

The females were inexpert swordsmen, but they were fearless fighters and made up in enthusiasm what they lacked in skill. Fortunately, the Queen's Own had split their forces, leaving only a few to guard the prisoners. Thus the females faced only five of the experienced sivaks. Kang winced to think what might have happened if the odds had been even. As it was his heart nearly stopped when he saw the sivak sisters covered in blood. He soon realized, by their grins and Shanra's irrepressible giggle, that it probably wasn't their own. Their grins vanished when they saw him.

"Oh, sir!" said Hanra, looking guilty. "I think we killed one."

"It was an accident!" Shanra said. "We didn't mean to—"

Kang waved them to silence. "Where's the general? Did you see him?"

"Through that door," cried Fonrar, pointing. "What are your orders, sir?"

Kang looked back.

"See if Granak needs any help. He's in the middle of the confusion somewhere with Slith."

"Slith!" the sivak sisters cried and before he could stop them, they had plunged into the crowd.

Kang shook his head. "Go back and guard the entrance," he told Fonrar urgently. "See if you can figure out a way to block it off." If those hundreds of armed draconians in the Audience Hall took it into their heads to join the battle—stupid or not—they would finish the fight for Kang and his small force.

Fonrar nodded to indicate she understood. She started to leave, then turned back, looked at Kang.

"Be careful," she said.

"You, too."

Fonrar smiled, saluted and dashed off, yelling at her troops to join her.

Kang waited until they were safely away, then he started for the small door in the back of the chamber.

Chapter Nineteen

The arched doorway opened out from the main chamber. Kang approached cautiously, but not quietly. He did not want to appear to be sneaking up on Maranta. Kang doubted if he could sneak up on the cagey aurak. And so he walked steadfastly through the arch, just as he would have walked had he been on his way to confer with his general about plans of attack.

Entering the chamber, Kang was immediately blinded. Darkness, "great darkness," impenetrable darkness swallowed him up whole. Kang recognized a magic spell. He halted, keeping near the door. He dared not proceed farther. He listened intently for any jingle of armor that would betray one of the Queen's Own waiting to ambush him. He listened for the sound of steel being drawn slowly from a sheath or for the sound of an arrow being nocked. He heard none of this. He heard only breathing, harsh, shallow.

"General Maranta," Kang said, his tone respectful. "The goblins are attacking, sir. Your commanders have been searching for you. When they couldn't find you, we feared something was amiss. We need you with us, sir. We need your leadership."

"You lead them, Kang." The general's voice was soft, bitter. "You brought this doom upon us."

"Excuse me, sir," said Kang. "But I don't believe that. Yes, the goblins are out to kill us. But they needn't have massed an army of forty thousand to do that. The Dark Knights have been planning this assault for a long time. An assault against this fort. If we hadn't come along, the goblins would have attacked this fort just the same."

"You are clever, Kang," said General Maranta from the darkness. "But not as clever as you might think. I have known for some time that the Dark Knights plotted our destruction. I knew it when I sent you on that fool's errand. You were not expected to return. I knew that, too, Kang.

"But the Dark Knights will not destroy us," Maranta continued. "Not while I have Dracart's Heart—one of the few artifacts to escape the destruction of Neraka. One of the few and one of the most valuable. I brought it out with me, knowing what its powers were, knowing that I would need it when our race began to die out. Dracart was a far-thinker, you see. He had created the females, in order to perpetuate our race, but he was disturbed as he watched us grow. He had not counted on the fact that we would develop into creatures of such intelligence. That we would develop self-will. For us to breed, to propagate, would create a race of powerful, dangerous beings. One that could not easily be controlled. And so he hid away the females. And instead, he made this globe. Thus he would perpetuate our race. Thus he would keep us under control."

"Very interesting, General," Kang said, hoping to keep him talking. The general's voice sounded near, within reach. And it seemed he was alone. None of the Queen's Own around, or they would have attacked him by now. Kang slightly shifted his body. "And so Dracart's Heart will perpetuate our race but in so doing, reduce our mental powers, transform us into what the humans hoped we would become—slaves who will do what we are told mindlessly, with no thought of asking questions, no thought of rebellion. Slaves who will call every man 'master.' "

"Not 'every man,' Kang," General Maranta said. "Just one. Me."

Kang was confident he knew where Maranta was standing. He tensed, readied himself for the desperate lunge that would, he prayed, take the general completely by surprise before he could cast any of the powerful magicks of which auraks are capable. "Do you really want to be the ruler of this race of slaves, General?"

"Yes," said Maranta, "for it is the race that will continue."

Kang shifted his weight to the balls of his feet. "I swear by our lost Queen, Maranta, I would rather see every single draconian dead than alive as you would make them. I would rather have said of us that we fought courageously and died nobly. I would have that be our epithet. I would not have history look upon the last remnants of our race with sneers of pity—"

Kang leapt forward, but in that instant, powerful arms encircled him from behind and a strong hand pressed against the back of his head in a deadly hold that Kang recognized. One wrong move and the hand would break his neck.

"I have him, sir," said the Queen's Own.

Kang cursed himself for being a bloody idiot. He had thought himself clever, keeping Maranta talking. Yet, all the while, it had been the general who had been keeping Kang talking. The Queen's Own, devoid of their armor, had silently moved into position, captured Kang easily.

General Maranta lifted the darkness spell and now Kang could see. He was in an alcove off the main chamber—Maranta's living quarters, hidden deep inside the Bastion. The room was small and plain. A bed, a table, a chair. A few books, spellbooks, a wooden chest painted black, trimmed with gold, probably the repository for the cursed globe. Guarded by the Queen's Own, guarded by magic, guarded by the Bastion, a marvel of construction and design. And at its heart, fear.

Another of the Queen's Own took Kang's battle-axe and his knife. They bound him expertly, tying his hands and feet. Kang knew better than to fight them. The sivaks would have no compunction about knocking him unconscious and his wits were all he had left. That and the hope that his troops would soon secure the area and come to find him.

That hope died when he heard shouted orders coming from outside the small room.

"The Queen's Own are ordering the draconians you saw in the Audience Hall to attack," Maranta told Kang. "They won't harm the males. The males are useful to us. But the females are a danger. They will be killed, as they should have been killed long ago."

Kang struggled against his bonds now, struggled futilely. His struggles grew more desperate, verging on panic, when he saw the general reach into the gilt box and bring out the black globe. The sivak guards retreated to a safe distance.

Fear such as Kang had never experienced shriveled his heart. He had faced death in battle and he'd known despair and anger, but never this weakening, numbing, debilitating terror. The sivaks had shoved a gag in his mouth, and he was pitifully grateful, for he felt a scream welling up inside him and he could not stop it. He would die a shrieking, pitiful wretch. But he would not die. That was the horror. He would live in a hundred bodies, each of their hundred minds left with some dim, vague memory of what he had been and, most awful, what he could never be.

General Maranta lifted the globe over Kang's head. The general began to chant. Kang heard the frantic beating of his own heart fill the chamber.

A clang, as of a sword crashing down on a metal helm, rang out. One of the Queen's Own pitched to the floor alongside Kang, unconscious. His partner fell on top of him. Kang twisted around to see Granak and Slith, weapons in the hand. Beside them stood Thesik.

She raised her hand, pointed at Maranta and began to chant. Words of a magic spell twined around the general, words spoken in a voice that was higher pitched, musical, sweeter, and nearly as powerful.

Maranta's concentration broke. His chanting halted. He turned to see who had interrupted his spell and stared in wide-eyed astonishment. He recognized the spell Thesik was casting. He foresaw the danger. With no time for a counterspell, he flung at her the only weapon he possessed, the black globe.

His aim was wild. The crystal globe flew harmlessly past Thesik and fell to the floor. The globe rolled out into the chamber and was lost among the feet of the kapaks.

White hot flame flashed from Thesik's fingertips. The flame shot across the room in a breath-snatching wave of fire, engulfed General Maranta. Kang felt the heat of the flames burning his scales and then Granak had seized hold of his commander and began dragging him backward, out of danger.

Maranta screamed in pain. He danced and flailed about, batting himself with his arms, trying to put out the magical fire.

"Don't let him die!" Kang ordered frantically. "Do something! Put out the flames!"

"But, sir—" Slith protested angrily. "He tried to kill me!"

"You know what happens when an aurak dies!" Kang yelled over the roar of the flames.

"Oh, hell! Right, sir," said Slith, jumping to his feet. "Good point. Cut the commander loose," he ordered, handing the knife to Thesik.

General Maranta had fallen to the floor, was writhing in agony, flopping and thrashing and screaming. Slith and Granak tried to approach the general, hoping to beat out the flames, but the fire was now too strong, the heat too intense. They could hear his flesh pop and sizzle in the heat. The smell was nauseating. Maranta's shrieks were horrible to hear.

"I don't think there's much we can do, sir," Slith cried.

"Run for it!" Kang shouted. "Bring those sivaks!" He gestured to the two unconscious sivaks on the floor.

Slith shook his head. "C'mon, Granak! Grab one of these bastards."

Kang's feet were untied, if his hands weren't. He started to run, then he saw Thesik, frozen in horror, staring at the dying general.

"I didn't mean . . ." She whimpered.

Kang caught hold of her. "You did what had to do, Thesik! Now we have to run!"

She gulped, nodded. Granak lifted of one the unconscious sivaks, swept him up in his arms. Using his powerful wings and legs, he propelled both of them half-way across the chamber in a flapping leap. Slith was also using his wings, dragging his sivak along like a vulture with an overlarge kill.

Kang dashed after them. He was about to take to the air himself when he saw out of the corner of his eye something glitter in the flames. The black crystal globe lay on the floor near the wall, where it had rolled to a stop.

"Go on!" he roared.

Dodging sideways, he made a dive for the globe, clutching at it with both hands that were still bound at the wrists. He managed to snag it, but when he stood up, he staggered, nearly lost his balance. He would have fallen but there was Thesik's hand at his elbow, helping to steady him.

"You all right?" he asked Thesik.

She was wide-eyed, horror-stricken. Her eyes shifted in the direction of the flame-filled room.

"Don't look!" Kang could see the general's body withering in the heat. The general's screams were trailing away to a dying gurgle.

"Clear the area!" Kang bellowed. The chamber was still filled with kapaks. He could see his own troops at the far end, could see Fonrar looking for him and Thesik anxiously. "Get everyone out of here!" he shouted again.

Granak tossed the sivak through the illusionary door and then began herding the kapaks out of the chamber, into the Audience Hall. Kang grabbed Thesik and raced for the door, running and flapping his wings until he thought his heart would burst from his chest. He had ceased to yell, he needed all his breath. The females were gone from the chamber, with the exception of Fonrar. She had made certain her troops were safe in the Audience Hall, but she hadn't joined them. She was working to keep the kapaks moving, her gaze on Thesik and Kang.

The general quit screaming.

"Down!" Kang shouted and he plunged to the floor, dragging Thesik with him. He rolled over on top of her, covering her body with his own body and his wings.

He heard thuds and thumps all around him, those left in the room obeying his orders. And then another body was alongside his. Fonrar flung herself down beside Thesik, flung her own arm and wings protectively over her friend.

Green light flickered against Kang's eyelids. A wave of searing heat washed over him. The air was charged with electricity that crackled painfully through his body. Fonrar's hand found his arm, clutched him convulsively. A thunderous boom shook the Bastion. The floor dropped out from under Kang, then rose up to meet him, knocking the breath from his lungs. Debris rained down from the ceiling. If the building collapsed, they would be buried under tons of hard-baked mud and wood.

"Hold, damn you!" Kang told the building. "Hold, hold."

A crash came behind him. The general's quarters had become his tomb, if one could actually speak of entombing whatever ashes were left of the aurak. The Bastion gave a shudder and Kang's heart stopped beating. Fonrar's grip on his arm tightened, her claws gouging him painfully.

The building shuddered and then was still.

The Bastion held.

Kang took back all the nasty things he'd said about

the construction workers. They had not built a pretty structure, but, the gods bless them, they had built a secure one. He clambered to his feet, throwing off dust and the odd bit of chipped mortar. He looked over at Fonrar.

Her face was covered with rock dust. Blood trickled down past her eye from a cut on the head, but she smiled at him reassuringly. Between them, they helped Thesik to stand. She was trembling and wobbly, more from the shock of the horror she had witnessed than from the blast.

"I killed him, Fon," Thesik said thickly. "But what else could I do?"

"Nothing, Thesik," Fonrar said soothingly, putting her arms around her friend. "Nothing. Come along. Don't think about it. It's all over."

Thesik shivered and shook her head.

"Will she be all right?" Kang asked, managing to free himself from the bonds that bound his wrists. He stuffed the globe away safely into his webbing.

"Yes, sir," said Fonrar. "I'll take care of her."

"Sir!" Granak loomed up in front of him. "Subcommander Slith sent me to see if you were safe and to tell you that you're needed in the Audience Hall. Fast."

Several kapaks were jammed inside the door, trying to flee the terror of the inner chamber. Granak picked them up and tossed them aside, opening the way for Kang. He emerged into the Audience Hall to find all of the armed and armored draconians on their feet, weapons drawn, facing Slith and his small force of females.

One of the Queen's Own had regained consciousness. He was on his feet, pointing at Slith.

"They killed the general!" he was saying. "They are traitors! Slay them! That's an order!"

The draconians started to advance. Slith stood with his sword drawn, the females with their weapons ranged around him.

"You blasted lizard!" Granak swore, shaking his fist at him. "And to think I carried you to safety."

Kang gripped his battle-axe. He had worked so hard to save his people, and now his people were going to repay the favor by killing not only him but their own future.

"I have an idea, sir," Slith said.

"An idea would be much appreciated about now," Kang said in grim tones.

"Tell them to halt," said Slith.

Kang glared at him.

"I mean it, sir!" Slith was insistent. "You outrank that bastard. Maranta trained the draconians to strict obedience. Make it your best arrogant, you-sons-of-bitches-I'm-your-superior-officer-order to halt, sir. You do that really well."

Kang chose to ignore that comment. Walking forward, making himself an excellent target, should any one of these dracos choose to attack, he threw out his chest, raised his hand with an imperious gesture and shouted, "Company will halt. Halt!"

To his complete and utter shock and surprise, the company halted.

The Queen's Own, hissing in fury, opened his mouth.

Kang nodded to Granak, who gave the sivak a tap on the head. The sivak slumped to the floor, unconscious once again.

Kang breathed a sigh.

"Good to see you're still in one piece, sir," said Slith, grinning. "No offense, but I wouldn't want a hundred of you. I'd be saluting every time I turned around."

"And I don't think the world's ready for a thousand of you, either," Kang said, smiling back.

He looked out over the assembled troops, who were standing at attention, awaiting orders.

"Now let's go fight the real battle," Kang said.

Chapter Twenty

Kang had completely lost track of time below ground. Days might have passed or years. They might emerge from the Bastion to find the goblins had slaughtered every draconian in the fort and were taking possession. He had forgotten about the battle against the goblins during his terrible struggles with the general. He remembered it clearly enough now and wondered if all that had been for nothing, if he was destined to die ignominiously, a goblin arrow through his throat.

"Sir, if we thread this maze, it'll take us a year and a day to get all these troops out of here," Slith observed.

"You're right," said Kang. "And after that blast, some of the tunnels have probably collapsed. Don't bother to thread the maze. Put these kapaks to work bashing holes in the walls. I need them up there as fast as possible."

"Yes, sir." Slith ran off, shouting orders.

Kang turned to look for Fonrar, found her waiting at his shoulder, sword in hand, ready to stand or fall alongside him. He allowed himself a brief moment of pure pleasure, then wrenched himself back to duty. They weren't out of this yet.

"Where's Thesik?"

"Here, sir," said Thesik. She managed a wan smile. "I'm fine, sir. Thank you."

"I need you, Thesik," said Kang. "I have to get out of this maze and back outside fast."

"I can guide you, sir," said Thesik. "I know the way."

"Granak," Kang said, "stick to me like that brown goo." He looked at Fonrar. "I have no other bodyguard. Will you and your troop act as one for me?"

"We would be honored, sir!" Fonrar said, glowing so brightly that her scales seemed to shimmer.

"Let's move!" Kang gestured.

Thesik took the lead. She traversed the maze unerringly, never faltering, never losing her way. Kang and the females followed at a run. Behind them, they could hear the draconian army of dunderheads, as Slith had termed them, starting to claw through the walls like devouring rats.

Ahead, echoing down the tunnel, they heard the sounds of battle—the clash of steel, snarls and fierce growls.

"Huzzad!" Kang gasped. He'd forgotten about her in the excitement, forgotten that he'd left her alone to defend the entrance to the Bastion. If the goblins had broken through, she might be defending against an army . . .

But she wasn't fighting goblins.

Huzzad stood blocking the entryway, battling the Queen's Own, who were attempting to force their way inside. She had lowered the portcullis—one sivak lay groaning beneath it. Two others were attempting to rip the portcullis down, while four more, armed with pikes, thrust the pikes through the portcullis and fended off Huzzad, kept her from interfering with the work.

Huzzad bled from numerous wounds, but she grinned as she fought, taunting her attackers. Her sword flashed in the light of the fires burning in the fort beyond. She had sliced off the iron points of one of the pikes—the sivak holding that one was now poking at her with the end of the splintered pole. Several of the sivaks were bleeding from wounds, where Huzzad had darted in to slice at them with her sword.

"Get away from there!" Kang shouted down the corridor and he had the amazing satisfaction of seeing the Queen's Own obey. They vanished from in front of the portcullis.

I'm really getting good at this, Kang thought to himself.

Huzzad turned at his shout, lifted her sword and started to wave.

A bolt from a crossbow sliced through the portcullis. The shaft struck Huzzad in the chest with such force that it knocked her back against the wall. She crumpled to the ground.

That was why the sivaks had retreated, Kang realized. They were making room for the archer.

Kang gave a great bellowing roar of fury and started to run forward, but he was elbowed and shoved and nearly trampled in the rush of the female draconians, who surged around him and past him, shrieking in rage. Fonrar and Riel hit the portcullis with a rush, ripping it from the ceiling. Holding the portcullis in front of them, the two smashed into the front ranks of the sivaks. Hanra and Shanra came behind, Hanra pausing to skewer the sivak who had been pinned beneath the portcullis. The battle swirled out the entrance to the Bastion. Kang lost sight of what was happening, but he could hear Fonrar's voice shouting orders and Shanra's wild giggle.

"Go with them!" Kang ordered Granak. "Keep the damage to a minimum!"

"I think the women have it pretty well in hand, sir," said Granak, peering over Kang's head.

"Not them!" Kang swore. "The Queen's Own! I don't want them all dead!"

"I don't think they're any great loss, sir," Granak remarked, but he dashed ahead to carry out Kang's command.

Kang hurried to the entrance of the Bastion, where Thesik was holding Huzzad cradled in her arms.

Kang glanced at the bolt, saw only the tip protruding from Huzzad's breast. He could smell her warm blood, if he couldn't see it, black against her black armor. He knelt by her side. Her face was livid. Her eyes huge and misted with pain. Looking up at him, she swallowed and grimaced.

"I don't think . . . kapak spit . . . will heal this," she said.

Kang took hold of her hand. Soldiers know when death is upon them. He would not insult her with senseless lies or meaningless platitudes.

"Thank you, Huzzad," he said quietly.

"Comrades?" she said with a pain-filled smile.

"Comrades," he said and he held her hand tight as he watched the life drain out of her eyes.

Huzzad's head fell back limply in Thesik's arms, the red hair flowing around her shoulders, glistening in the firelight.

"Huzzad!" Thesik cried, giving her a shake.

Kang laid his arm on Thesik's arm. "Lay her down. There's nothing more you can do for her."

Thesik raised a stricken gaze. "She's not— No! She can't be. I liked her!"

The other females returned, gathered around. The females had known death since they were small. Draconians had died almost from the day the females had been saved. But those deaths had been far distant, removed from them. Kang had seen to that. This was the first death that really hit close. This was as if one of them had died. Perhaps right now they were coming face to face with their own mortality. And that of those they loved. Comrades.

Kang could not protect them from this. Nor, he realized, as he rose to face them, did he want to. They had grown up in a very short time, it seemed to him. But they had grown up.

"You avenged her death," he said to the twenty pairs of grieving eyes that were fixed on him. "That was right and proper. After this is finished, we will give her an honorable burial. But now we have to go on. We have to keep fighting. Otherwise her death will be meaningless."

He heard a whimper—Shanra. Fonrar ordered her to pull herself together. Emerging from the Bastion, Kang saw two more of the Queen's Own dead, including the one with the crossbow. His head had been cut off.

Well, as Granak had observed, no great loss. Kang wasn't certain he wanted little Queen's Own running about anyway.

The remainder of the Queen's Own stood in a group, glaring at Granak, who had appropriated the crossbow and had it trained on them.

"I thought you might want to have a word with them, sir," Granak said, catching sight of Kang. "I told them that if a wing so much as quivered, someone would have a bolt instead of an eyeball."

"Well done." Kang growled. "You men." He turned to the Queen's Own, addressed them in what he would now forever think of as his best arrogant you-son-of-bitches manner. "General Maranta is dead. I'm in command. What time of day is it? What's the status of the battle?"

The Queen's Own gaped at him. "We don't believe you," said one sullenly.

"Fine! Don't believe me! I still outrank you." Kang roared. "What's the goddamn status of the goddamn battle?"

Their eyes shifted to Granak and the crossbow.

"It's near dawn, sir. We held against the first assault," said the officer finally. "But we've taken heavy casualties. The goblins are regrouping. We expect them to attack at dawn, throw at us everything they've got."

"Report to your commanding officer," Kang told them. "There's nothing more you can do here."

The sivaks of the Queen's Own exchanged uncertain glances. They looked at Kang, grim, covered with blood and dust; at the squadron of tough, confident females ranged behind him; at the immense Granak, who stood holding the crossbow. Picking up their dead, the Queen's Own departed.

"This way," said Kang, and he and his troop headed back for the front gate at a run.

The fort was quiet, except for the moaning of those who had been wounded and for the occasional barked order from an officer. They passed charred, burned out buildings. One entire block of structures was gone. Several of the fires started by goblin flaming arrows were raging out of control, with too few left to fight them. The air was filled with smoke that made breathing difficult, stung the eyes. Kang tried to see the Drunken Dragon, make certain it was safe and ready to launch, but the swirling smoke was too thick.

Draconians lined the walls in silence, waiting to push back the next assault that would most likely be the last. They could not withstand a massive attack in force. Kang could not see from his vantage point, but he could feel a rumbling in the ground beneath his feet and guessed that the goblins were trundling forward heavy siege engines. He pictured huge stones smashing into the rickety walls or, worse, into the fragile Drunken Dragon. They had to launch soon. They had to get the contraption off the ground before those stones started flying.

A raucous blaring of horns announced the goblin advance. The draconians answered with their own horns and defiant jeers, urging the goblins to come on and be slaughtered.

Kang reached his own area. The females gathered around him, looking uncertain, wondering what was happening. Kang peered through the smoke until he finally caught sight of one of his officers. He let out a roar. Gloth turned, saw him, came dashing up.

"Sir! Thank the Queen! Do we let the Dragon loose now?"

Kang was about to answer when something buzzed past him with a sound like an angry hornet.

Thesik gave a cry and clutched at her upper arm. The shaft of an arrow stuck out from her scales, quivering. Blood welled up between her fingers.

The arrow had not come from over the wall. It had come from somewhere behind them. Kang whipped around to see two goblins crouched beside the wreckage of a storage shed, reloading short bows.

"Troop, charge!" Fonrar ordered.

Howling in rage at the injury done to one of their own, the females, led by Riel, dashed toward the goblins.

"Sir!" Gloth cried in agony. "Should they be waving those swords around like that? They might cut themselves."

Seeing death coming down on them, the two goblins dropped their bows and ran, but their short legs were no match for the draconians. Shanra sliced the head off one with a deft stroke. Riel spitted the other on the end of her sword, driving it clean through the goblin's breastbone. Lifting the goblin, she tossed the corpse onto a rubbish heap.

"I don't think they're going to cut themselves too badly," Kang said dryly. "Don't let the dragon go yet. I have to see what's happening outside the walls. Wait for my signal before you release the tether. When you see Granak wave the regimental standard, cut the dragon loose."

"Yes, sir," Gloth replied, and with an amazed glance at the females and a puzzled shake of his head, he dashed off.

Kang grabbed hold of a couple of passing draconian soldiers and was about to order them to find out where the goblins had breached the walls. But Fonrar was well ahead of him.

"Troop," she said, addressing the females, "we've got to find where these goblins have broken through. You bozaks and sivaks, prepare to follow me!"

The females ran off, heading for the section of wall near the barracks.

Kang's next concern was to make certain Thesik was all right and that she was removed to the safety of the barracks. He turned to issue those orders, only to see a detail of kapak females carrying Thesik in their arms, bearing her to safety under Fonrar's direction.

Fonrar turned to wave at Kang. "She's going to be fine, sir. You don't need to worry about us. You deal with the goblins. Good luck, sir!"

I'm to deal with the goblins, he thought. Like I dealt with monsters under the blankets and bears in the woods and nightmares and sniffles. They have faith in me. Please the gods, wherever they are, that I don't let them down.

He turned to Granak, standing at his side as usual, quiet, reliable, waiting for orders. "Fetch the standard and follow me. We're going to the gate."

Granak grabbed the standard of the First Dragon-army Engineers, which had been planted firmly at the base of the tether rope holding the Drunken Dragon in place. Four draconians under Dremon's command were straining to hang onto the tether, which was pulled taut, as if the ugly beast was eager to fly off and wreck havoc on its enemies.

"Not long now," Kang promised.

Granak returned, bearing the standard. Kang ran toward the front gate, Granak loping along behind. Their route took them down a narrow street that ran between two regimental barracks. Passing a side street, Kang saw a regiment of armored draconians lined up in ranks. He wondered what in the Abyss they were doing lollygaging down here when there was fighting to be done on the walls. Then he remembered. These dracos were the reaction force Maranta was holding back for a sally out the front gate. The general was no longer around to give them the order.

Kang found their officer, recognized Prokel.

"I'm going to need you," Kang hollered over the shrieks and clatter and the thudding of boulders down into the compound. The siege engines had arrived. "Wait for my orders!"

Prokel yelled back. "General Maranta—"

"—is dead," Kang shouted. "Wait for my orders."

Running off before the stunned Prokel could argue, Kang and Granak arrived at the gate to find the stairs leading up to the ramparts on the left side of the gate had caught fire, filling the air with flame and smoke and imperiling the draconians fighting on top of the wall. No one could go up that way and the draconians on top had no way down except flight. On the right, the staircase was clogged with baaz climbing up and other baaz trying to climb down. A baaz stood at the top, cursing and yelling at another baaz at the bottom. Every so often a dead baaz would pitch off the wall, turning to stone as he fell.

Kang wondered if these were veteran soldiers or some of Maranta's dunderheads. Not that it mattered. Without strong leadership, in the chaos of battle, discipline would almost certainly break down.

"I'll handle this, sir," Granak said, and waded into the confusion. "Move your tails, you damn dim-witted skinks!" he yelled, and when no one seemed either able or inclined to obey, he began pushing, shoving, elbowing and kicking his way up the stairs with Kang following close behind. "Move! Move!"

Baaz fell left and right, tumbling over the railing, slammed back against the sides. Order was restored. Reaching the top of the wall, Kang was at last able to see clearly what was going on.

Two goblin phalanxes had pushed to the walls and were attempting to raise scaling ladders. Two hobgoblin phalanxes had moved in to try to batter down the gate. One phalanx had a battering ram covered with an iron shield to protect the hobgoblins carrying it from archery and boiling oil. Behind the ram, another phalanx of several hundred hobgoblins carried the banners of the general. Kang saw the gigantic hobgoblin leader himself, laughing and joking with the members of his retinue as he watched the progress of the battle.

Arrows thick as locusts hummed around Kang and Granak. One smashed into Kang's breastplate.

"Sir!" Granak cried in shock.

"I'm not hurt," Kang yelled. Pulling the arrow out, he threw it down in disgust. He grabbed hold of a nearby sivak, who was screaming defiance at the goblins below and taking aim at them with a javelin.

"Who's in charge here?" Kang demanded, jerking the sivak around to face him.

The sivak looked startled. "Uh, I don't know, sir. Aren't you?"

Kang released the sivak, who tossed his javelin at the enemy. The next moment, the sivak fell back, an arrow in the eye. His shape shifted as he fell to the ground below and he landed looking like the goblin who had slain him. Kang glanced about, saw no other officer. He took a look at that hob general, took a look at the sky. Despite being obscured by smoke, the dawn was coming, the sun was starting to rise. In the smoky, dusky half-light, the Drunken Dragon might almost look real. He reminded himself again that goblins were shortsighted.

"Granak, now!" Kang yelled.

Granak took a pace back and turned toward the interior of the fort. He raised the standard above his head and waved it once, twice. Then the flag jerked, wavered.

A javelin hurled from a small ballista struck the huge draconian between shoulder blades. The blow carried Granak off the ramparts, sent him crashing to the ground right in the midst of a troop of baaz. The standard fell with him.

As Kang watched Granak fall, time slowed. Granak fell slowly, so slowly that it seemed to Kang as if he might reach out and snatch him back, snatch him back to his place on the wall beside Kang, snatch him back to life. The sound of battle died away. All Kang could hear was the flutter of flag as it spiraled down to land beside the body of the huge sivak who had carried it so proudly.

"Sir!" Someone was jostling him. "Sir! What are your orders?"

Kang turned his head. A group of veteran baaz was gathered around him. They clutched their bloody weapons in bloody hands, stared at him hopefully. Beyond them, he could see more of his people, fighting, dying. He looked back down to the ground, but he could not see Granak or the standard amidst the chaos below.

"Sir," the baaz said again, afraid and desperate. "Your orders?"

I'm to deal with the goblins. Please the gods, wherever they are, that I don't let my people down.

The noise of battle returned to him with roar.

He grabbed hold of the nearest baaz.

"You! You're now my standard bearer. Do you understand? Go and get that standard and bring it up here. Run, damn you! Run!"

The baaz blinked in surprise. This wasn't what he'd expected, but he'd asked for orders and he was quick to obey. He wasn't from Kang's regiment. Kang had no idea which regiment claimed ownership of the baaz, but right now, he was Kang's. He deployed the other baaz, sent them to plug up holes in the wall where other dracos had fallen, reminding them again that if they were next to a bozak who died they were to shove the corpse over the wall into the enemy ranks, so that the resultant explosion would take out the enemy, not friends. He wondered briefly if someone would shortly be tossing his corpse down in the melee below, dismissed that thought as being stupid and irrelevant.

"I have it, sir!" The baaz came running along the ramparts, carrying the standard. The flag was covered with blood and no longer looked like the regimental standard, but Fulkth would be watching for a flag—any flag—to wave four times.

"Lift up the standard," Kang ordered. "Lift it up high. As high as you can. This is the flag of the First Dragonarmy Engineers, son. We want everyone to see it."

"Yes, sir," said the baaz. Risking his life, making himself an excellent target, he climbed up on top of a post and balanced there, his wings flapping gently.

Arrows zipped around him, but none struck him.

"Wave it four times," Kang said. "Back and forth. Once, twice, three times, four. Excellent! Hop down, now, and stand there and do nothing until I tell you otherwise."

Kang waited, tensely. He peered through the smoke, trying to see the horizon. The mists swirled and parted and he saw blue sky. The day was going to dawn clear and fine. The sun's rays streaked across the sky in bands of purple and red, a spectacular sunrise, reminding him that the world he might soon be leaving was indeed a lovely place.

He looked down, blinking and trying to see through the smoke. The hobgoblins battered the gate with their iron-covered ram. Draconian arrows fired at them were having little effect, due to their heavy armor and the shielding. The gate trembled, but held. Kang's engineers had reinforced it, but it wouldn't hold long. He looked back over his shoulder. And there was the Drunken Dragon, lifting up into that glory-streaked sky.

Kang choked back a wild impulse to laugh hysterically. He knew he'd better, for the laugh might change in an instant to a sob.

The dragon looked like no dragon Kang had ever seen. The dragon looked like no dragon ever born. It was the color of brown goo mixed with red clay. Its wings creaked as they raised and squeaked as they lowered. Its tail looked broken, for it hung at an odd angle. Flames from the numerous fires burning in the fort were reflected in its sword blade teeth. Smoke coiled not only out of its nostrils but out of every gap where wood and goo didn't quite meet. The Drunken Dragon probably wouldn't fool the goblins. They would be more likely to fall down on the ground, prostrate with laughter. Yet Kang was proud, as he watched it creaking and squeaking and jerking on its tether. His men had done a good job against overwhelming odds.

"Look at that, will you?" one veteran draconian snickered to another. But his comrade was fighting for his life and dared not risk looking. Those who did manage to catch a glimpse of the Drunken Dragon, rising ponderously up out of the smoke, shook their heads, rolled their eyes and went back to the business of slaughter.

"That's all right," Kang told them. "Sneer if you want. So it won't fool the goblins. It doesn't have to. All it has to do is fall down on top of them—" He gargled, his words dying away in awe.

The clunky Drunken Dragon had vanished. In its place flew an enormous golden dragon, beautiful, awful. Gold scales flamed in the red-purple sunlight, dazzling the eye. Golden wings beat in a graceful motion. The gold's fearsome jaws parted in a terrible snarl of hatred and fury, showing its fangs, sharp and gleaming.

Kang staggered backward, nearly fell off the parapet. His first thought was that he'd gone mad. He was hallucinating. Wild ideas tore through his head. The Solamnic Knights had sent a gold to massacre them all. A gold had dropped out of the skies . . . but no.

Dragonfear! he thought. I should be falling down and peeing myself with terror. All of us should. But I'm not. I don't feel the dragonfear. Which meant that this gold wasn't real.

Rational thought took hold again, though with a struggle. He could still hear the wheeze and clack and rattle of the hot-air dragon. He could see the guy ropes falling away until only one rope remained—the fuse to light the keg bombs. The fuse was lit, flame creeping slowly along the rope.

The Drunken Dragon was still there. The Drunken Dragon was the golden dragon. It was all an illusion, Kang realized. Someone had cast a powerful illusion spell. Someone had transformed his brown goo-covered hot-air dragon into a beautiful, wondrous golden monster rising up out of the smoke and flame of battle.

Now from all around came shouts and cries of astonishment, terror, fear. The cries were in two languages, goblin and draconian. Friend and foe alike ceased their fighting and lifted their heads to stare.

"An illusion!" Kang shouted in draconian. "It's magic— Oh, never mind!"

He trusted that after their first surprise, the draconians would have sense enough to realize what was going on. And if they didn't, well, their fear would make it more realistic.

The dragon floated slowly over the gate, the flapping of its wings wafting away the smoke so that now it was clearly visible. A group of goblins had finally managed to plant one of their siege ladders and were starting to clamber over the side of the wall, swords gleaming, when the lead goblin looked up and saw a golden dragon hovering menacingly on top of him. He gave a shriek and fell backward, taking the ladder and all his comrades down with him. Up and down the ramparts, goblin battle cries changed to cries of terror.

At the sight of the gold dragon, goblins who had managed to reach the walls dived head-first over the ramparts. Others flung themselves from ladders or tried to scramble down, knocking off those beneath them. Goblin soldiers on the ground flung aside their weapons and turned to flee. Their shouts and screams and panicked retreat threw the ranks advancing behind them into confusion.

Oblivious to his own safety, Kang leaned over the ramparts, staring out onto the field, trying to see the hobgoblin general. Smoke swirled before his eyes. He cursed it and flapped his hand at it and then the smoke parted. The hobgoblin general was no longer joking and laughing. He was staring open-mouthed at the dragon. His retinue were pointing and, in some cases, starting to run for their lives.

The hob's mouth shut with a snap. Then it opened again, thundering orders. He had been fooled at first, but, like Kang, he had reached the same conclusion. He knew the dragon wasn't real and he was trying to quell the panic, stop the stampede. His officers advanced onto the field wielding whips and shouting commands. But for goblins mad with fear, the whips and shouting only increased the confusion.

Kang started to do a little victory dance, then he noted that the thudding sound of the battering ram against the gate had not ceased. Cursing, he looked down at the hobgoblins. Either they had heard the orders of their general or they were not intimidated by the sight of a golden dragon or they had seen through the illusion. Whatever the reason, they had not ceased their efforts to take the gate and the hobgoblin soldiers behind them held their positions.

Kang regarded them with grudging admiration and even saluted their commander. The hobgoblins would all be dead in a few moments. Kang could afford to be generous. He glanced upward. The illusion of the golden dragon was gone for him. He could see the wing-flapping, clunky contraption sailing ponderously out over the gate. It was heading straight for the hobgoblin troops, straight for their general. The fuse . . .

The fuse had gone out.

Kang stared at the trailing fuse with sickening horror. It shouldn't have gone out. Slith had assured him that it would never go out. Wind would not blow it out, rain would not soak it out. Yet, it was out. Kang stared until his eyes ached, searching for a glimmer of fire, a tiny spark. He tried to convince himself that it was still burning, but at last he was forced to admit in despair that Slith had made a mistake. The Drunken Dragon was going to fly serenely over the goblins and keep on flying until all the hot air had drained from it and it made an ignominious landing twenty miles distant, ending up as nothing more than a corpse of broken pine wood covered with brown goo.

Flaming arrows would do the trick. Kang searched about frantically for an arrow that might have been fired, but hadn't gone out. Of course, now that he wanted flaming arrows, the goblins had quit firing them. He would signal his troops, see if he could make them understand the problem. From their vantage point, they would not be able to see the dangling fuse. They would not know that it had gone out.

Kang turned to his new standard bearer to find nothing but a pile of dust and no standard. He had no idea where it had gone, guessed that it had fallen over the battlements and was lying somewhere on the wrong side of the wall.

The Drunken Dragon flew over the gate with a hundred-foot clearance.

Magic, Kang thought desperately. If I had my magic, I could cast a spell to blow up the dragon.

Other draconians had magic. He'd seen that for himself. The magic within them had not died with the departure of the Queen of Darkness.

Kang remembered very clearly how he would kneel before the altar, whisper his prayers to the Queen. He remembered her blessings falling on him, remembered the thrill that burned through his body as the magic filled him.

He closed his eyes and sought inside himself. But to no avail. Others might have magic still. He had lost it, as he had lost his Queen. As he had lost his faith. And though his Queen had abandoned him years before, he felt abandoned by her once again. Anger burned in place of magic. She would once more fail her people.

Or maybe not.

Kang's hand went to his webbing, pawed through it frantically. His fingers closed over the magical artifact, Dracart's Heart. He no longer possessed any magical power, but this artifact did. He had intended to destroy it anyhow.

"You'll fulfill your maker's design anyway," Kang told it, holding the black crystal in his hand. "If this works, you'll save the draconian race."

The Drunken Dragon's head was over the hobgoblin general. The hob was pointing up at it, laughing uproariously.

Gritting his teeth, exerting all his strength, Kang closed his fingers convulsively over the crystal.

The Heart of Drakart shattered. Shards of broken crystal pierced Kang's flesh. Blood streamed from his hand. Pain flooded his body and so did the magic. He was astounded at the power that was so bright and flaring it burned away the terrible pain. His heart beat frantically, his blood boiled. He feared that he had made a deadly mistake, that the magic would consume him, that he wouldn't be able to control it.

With a great cry, he concentrated on the dragon and on his desperate need. He began to chant the oft-recited, well-known and beloved words to a prayer that was a magical spell.

The magic gathered itself inside him into a ball of flame that burst out from the fingers of his bloody hand. The flame was like a meteor blazing through the air, trailing white hot sparks that burned through anything they touched, even the iron casing of the battering ram. The fireball struck the Drunken Dragon in the tail section, setting it instantly ablaze.

The magical fire raced along the pine wood frame, eagerly licked up the brown goo. Holes gaped in the wings. The Drunken Dragon began to descend rapidly. Now the hobgoblins, staring up at it, were afraid. They wavered in their attack.

The flames reached the keg bombs. A ball of light, blue-white, dazzling, consumed the Drunken Dragon. Kang, staring straight at it, was momentarily blinded. A boom as of a hundred thunderclaps shook the fortress and knocked Kang to his knees. A wave of heat struck him. He heard screams, screams of dying hobgoblins, screams of goblins being burned alive, terrible screams.

He staggered to his feet, rubbing his eyes, frantic to see what was happening.

The sight that met his eyes was appalling.

The dragon had exploded at a height of about ten feet above the hobgoblin phalanx. The liquid inside the keg bombs spewed out with explosive force and ignited, raining flaming death on top of the hobs. The hobgoblin general's retinue had taken much of the initial blast.

Kang caught a glimpse of the hobgoblin general. His chest and arms were on fire. He was shrieking impotent curses and then Kang lost sight of him as the burning undercarriage of the dragon came crashing down on the general and his staff.

Kang hoped to see that this had finished the hobgoblins around the gate. He cursed, swore. The goblins that had survived were fleeing, but the phalanx of hobgoblins—though their numbers were decimated—was still holding its position, still trying to batter down the gate. The death of their general seemed only to fuel their determination.

I'd like to meet whoever trained this lot, Kang thought savagely. I'd like to shake his hand. Right before I cut off his head.

Draconians were cheering on the walls. Kang ordered them to shut their damn mouths and start firing arrows. He told them throw spears, throw rocks, do anything they could to stop that advance.

He clattered down the stairs to where he had left the Ninth Infantry. Hopefully they were as disciplined as the hobgoblins. He found them standing in ranks, waiting.

"Prokel!" Kang shouted. "Follow me!"

Prokel hesitated. "You said General Maranta was dead. How—"

Kang shook his head. Even if he could, he didn't have time to explain. The troops would either follow him or they wouldn't. Ignoring Prokel, Kang pointed at the front gate.

"The hobs are trying to batter down the gate, men! They must not succeed! I'm going out there to fight them. Are you with me?"

He turned and started for the gate at a run. If no one followed, this last battle of his was going to be one for the bards.

And then he heard behind him Prokel's voice, "Ninth Infantry! Charge!"

The heavily armed and armored troops of the Ninth came pounding after Kang, chanting their regimental battle cry in deep voices.

"Open the gate! Open the gate!" Kang yelled to the troops manning the lower gate approach.

Looking behind him, the draconians at the gate saw the infantry advancing and understood. They pulled back the bracing bars just as the Ninth arrived.

The gate swung open, sending startled hobs tumbling inside the compound. The Ninth heavy infantry struck the hobgoblin formation like a hammer striking a block of ice. The hobgoblin formation shattered. They dropped their battering ram. Some turned to run. Others, seeing that there was no hope of escape, drew their swords and prepared to fight to the death.

Kang was in the vanguard of the charge. His momentum carried him through the hobgoblin ranks and outside the gates, watching the enemy retreat before him. He had no enemy to fight and he paused to catch his breath and take stock of the situation. A patch of color caught his eye. His regimental standard lay on the ground. He raced to snatch it up, hacking open the skulls of two goblins on the way.

Kang returned to the gate and found the Ninth Infantry swarming out onto the battlefield. The hobs and gobbos were on the run now. The Ninth was chasing down those who had the bad luck to be in the rear.

Kang stood in middle of the open gate, raised his voice in a loud bellow that sounded above the turmoil.

"Attack! The enemy's on the run!" Kang waved the banner as he yelled. "Attack!"

A cheer went up from the rampart's defenders. Many were so excited that they leapt off the wall, using their wings to carry them to the ground. They rallied around Kang and in less than a minute, he was leading over a hundred draconians.

"Charge!" he yelled, and ran forward.

Goblins and hobgoblins were fleeing in all directions. The burning wreckage of the Drunken Dragon belched black smoke into the air. The Ninth was hacking its gory way to the right. Kang took his formation off the road to the left, smashed into rear of the fleeing goblins.

Kang continued his charge another fifty feet, then he stopped with the realization that he was too weak to go any farther. His hand throbbed with a pain that seemed to lance up his arm and into his gut. He was astonished to see the hand was badly mangled, two of his fingers hanging by the tendons. The pole of the standard he had been waving was covered with his own blood. He tried to hold onto the standard, to keep it from falling to the ground, but he had no strength left.

"I've got it, sir!" said a voice and a hand reached out, took hold of the standard and planted it firmly at Kang's feet.

The voice was familiar but it was coming out of a hobgoblin's mouth. And then the hobgoblin disappeared and there was Slith, grinning so that he showed every single one of his teeth.

"Damn fine, wasn't it, sir!" Slith cried.

"Damn fine," Kang echoed. He was weak from loss

of blood, but he was determined to remain conscious. He wasn't going to miss the end of this.

"What in Abyss did you do to yourself, sir?" Slith demanded, seeing Kang's hand that was no longer recognizable as a hand but looked more like something that had come out of the end of a meat grinder. "We have to bandage that, sir. Stop the bleeding."

Slith searched about for material to use for a bandage, but he wore nothing but armor and webbing, the same as Kang. Slith's gaze fell on the standard. Ignoring Kang's shocked protest, Slith ripped the banner from its pole and began wrapping the stained and muddy cloth around Kang's hand.

"That standard has Granak's blood on it," Kang said.

Slith paused in his bandaging, looked up, alarmed. "Is he—"

Kang nodded, sighed heavily. "Javelin got him."

Slith lowered his head, went back to work. "Damn gobbos," Slith muttered. "Granak was a good soldier."

"Yes," said Kang. The soldier's epitaph, the best there could be. "Yes, he was. Huzzad's dead, too."

"Yes, sir. We found her body on our way out of the Bastion. I left an honor guard with her, sir. I thought you'd want that."

"She was probably the only human who ever gave her life for a draconian," Kang said. No, thought Kang, that wasn't quite true. Huzzad gave her life for honor, for a Vision given to her by a goddess, for faith in that Vision. That would be Huzzad's epitaph.

"There you are, sir," Slith said, finishing the bandaging with a neat knot. "Some kapak spit and you'll be good as new."

Kang smiled faintly. Slith continued talking, saying something about how he and his troop of dunderheads had managed to finally make their way out of the Bastion.

They had arrived at the gate in time to see the dragon explode. Hearing Kang's order to charge the gate, Slith had tried to reach him, but Ninth Infantry had been in the way.

"Once the Ninth cleared the road, we came out and saw you waving the standard. We chased after you, but you were too fast. There they go, sir," Slith added proudly. "Look at them."

The First Dragonarmy Engineers dashed past, shouting their battle cry, hunting goblins. Their officers saluted as they ran past him. Kang returned the salute, though his hand hurt like hell. He looked out over the battlefield. Dead goblins and hobgoblins littered the field for as far as Kang could see. Draconians could be seen in the distance, chasing small bands of goblins. They were meeting little resistance, taking no prisoners.

We won, Kang realized dazedly. The day is ours. We won.

"Slith," he said after a moment, when he could speak past the choking sensation in his throat, "do you have any of those keg bombs left?"

"Why, sir?" Slith looked around in consternation. "Do we need them?"

"I do," said Kang.

Slith caught his commander's smile and understood. "Yeah, I saved one, sir. And a couple of mugs to go with it."

The two turned and headed slowly back to the fort. Kang refused Slith's offer of assistance. Kang's hand throbbed so that he had to grit his teeth against the pain. He was light-headed from loss of blood and weak, but he'd be damned if he was ever again going to be carted around on any blasted litter.

He passed the charred carcass of the shattered dragon and gave it a fond nod and a salute. Smoke billowed up from the dragon's remains and from a hundred small fires still blazing inside the fort. The fort itself was in sad shape. Now that Kang looked at it, he was amazed they had held it for as long as they had. Parts of the wooden stockade were completely demolished.

Walking inside the gate, Kang saw piles of dust—dead baaz, pools of acid—dead kapaks. Some of the dead sivaks still wore the look of their killers, others had gone back to their original form. The draconians had won, but the cost had come high. The euphoria Kang experienced over the victory began to fade. He bowed his head. His walk slowed. He felt sick and faint. He was about to tell Slith to send for the litter-bearers, when the cheering began. Cheering and the clash of swords against shields.

Startled, Kang looked up. Draconians lined the ramparts. Other draconians thronged around the broken gate. They were all cheering lustily.

Kang glanced around. "What is it?" he asked in confusion. "What's all this for?"

Slith smiled. "You, sir."

"Me?" Kang was astounded. "No . . ."

At the sight of him, the draconians' cheers increased in volume, sending echoes booming from the surrounding mountains. He could have no doubt. All eyes were on him. They clashed their swords against their shields. Those holding spears began a rhythmic thumping of the butts into the ground. Others stamped their feet in time. They parted ranks to form an aisle, allow him a clear passage into the fort.

Slith fell back. "Go on ahead, sir. Congratulations. You've earned this."

Kang paused, overcome with emotion. "Not just me," he said. "They all—" He couldn't finished. He choked, cleared his throat. "Find Granak," he whispered hoarsely. "And see to Huzzad."

"Yes, sir," Slith replied.

Lifting his head, bracing his shoulders, Kang drew in a deep breath and walked among the rows of his cheering people.

Chapter Twenty-One

The barracks of the First Dragonarmy Engineers were among the few buildings still standing after the battle. Kang ordered that these now be used to house the wounded. He gave that order from his bed, for he had no sooner set foot inside the fort than the females, led by a concerned Fonrar, had cut short the festivities and hustled him off to be fussed over, treated and pampered, all of which he outwardly protested, inwardly enjoyed.

"How's Thes?" were the first words he asked, as they helped him inside.

"She's fine, sir," said Fonrar. "Just fine. She's right here, in fact."

Thesik appeared, leaned over him. "How are you, sir?" she asked anxiously. "Could I get you something to eat?"

Kang shook his head, stared intently at her and Fonrar. They both looked extremely innocent, a look he remembered from childhood. A look that meant that they had been doing something they shouldn't.

"*You* cast the illusion spell on the dragon," Kang said suddenly, weakly.

Thesik and Fonrar exchanged guilty glances. "I'm sorry, sir," Thesik said. "I don't know what came over me. It was a wonderful dragon, sir, but it just . . . just seemed to need a little something. I hope you're not angry."

"It did need 'a little something,' " Kang said. "You may have saved the day. I'm proud of you. Proud of you all. But tell me one thing, Thes, you've never seen a golden dragon. How did you know what one would look like?"

"Begging your pardon, sir," Thesik replied. "But I *have* seen golden dragons. I see a golden dragon in my dreams almost everyday. I'm not sure why. It's very strange. Do you understand, sir?"

"Yes, Thesik, yes, I do." Kang replied, who sometimes saw a bronze dragon in his dreams. He understood. He had hoped she never would.

Kang refused to be carried to his own room. He insisted on being in the center of operations, in order to see and supervise. As it turned out, he was left with little to do. The females took charge and within an hour after the battle, the wounded were being brought inside and attended.

Kang lay in his bed. He had a mug of cactus juice in one hand. The other was covered with kapak spit. Thanks to that and Rial's surprising skill with a needle, Kang's right hand retained the requisite number of fingers. Everyone assured him that the hand would be as good as before, but he knew they were lying to placate him. He had suffered nerve damage, severed tendons. Not even the miracles of kapak spit could restore these. He would never hold an axe again. That knowledge did not bother him as much as it might have. Once he would have been devastated, but not now. Not since he had made his decision.

Fonrar had removed the bloodstained standard and carried it off somewhere. When he asked about it, she told him to rest and leave the work to others. He was too tired to argue. He rested and watched with pleasure Fonrar directing operations. She was too busy to speak to him, but she smiled at him every time she passed him, a comradely smile that warmed his heart better than the mug of cactus juice.

Kang had just dozed off, when he felt a hand shake him.

He groaned and woke with a start. "What? What's wrong?"

"Sorry for waking you, sir," said Slith, "but I thought you'd want to see this."

Kang lifted his head. "Granak!" he exclaimed.

The big sivak lay on his stomach on the litter. He lay on his stomach because the javelin that had felled him was still sticking out from between his shoulder blades.

"We found him like that, sir," Slith said, regarding Granak in admiration. "He was lying on the ground cussing up a storm and shouting for someone to help him pull that toothpick out of him."

"Will he be all right?" Kang asked anxiously, propping himself up on one elbow.

"Yeah, he'll be fine," said Slith. "You know, a little kapak spit . . ."

Kang eased himself back down. "Thanks, Slith. You just disproved a theory of mine."

"What would that be, sir?"

"That no one ever wakes me up to tell me good news."

"Yes, sir." Slith grinned. "Go back to sleep, sir."

"I will. Oh, and Slith," Kang said, closing his eyes. "I want everyone in our regiment out on the parade ground tomorrow morning. I have an announcement to make."

*　*　*　*　*

The First Dragonarmy Engineers formed up in squadron ranks. Each Squadron second-in-command handed command over to the Squadron Commanders. Slith took the field and ordered the squadrons to report their strengths. Each, in turn, reported the number of active on parade, on light duties or wounded.

Other draconians from other regiments halted to watch, wondering what was going on. Smoke still hung in the air, although today the smoke was not from the burning fort—those fires had at last been put out—but from the huge pyre of goblin corpses. The stench was horrific, but wonderfully sweet to the draconians.

Kang marched onto the field. His hand was bandaged, but he returned Slith's salute with precision. Slith marched to the right side of the First Squadron, and took his customary position, that of the second-in-command. Kang paused to look out over the regiment, standing on parade at attention. The regiment looked far too small. Only one hundred and three soldiers stood on the field.

"Regiment! Stand at ease," Kang said. "I have an announcement to make, but first, I have a promotion."

The regiment rustled, scales clicked. There hadn't been a promotion in the regiment since Granak had become Standard Bearer at the beginning of their trek across the Plains of Dust, over a year ago.

Kang drew himself up. "Subcommander Slith!" he yelled.

Taken by surprise, Slith didn't move. He looked over at Gloth, thinking perhaps that he'd misunderstood.

Gloth hissed, "Yeah, you!"

Slith came to attention, saluted.

"Sir!" he said and marched smartly out to stand in front of the commander.

Kang returned the salute. He reached forward, as Slith stood at attention, and removed the sivak's harness. Placing Slith's harness on the ground, Kang unbelted his own and slung it around Slith's shoulders.

Slith continued to stand at attention, but he appeared absolutely dumbfounded.

Kang ignored him and addressed the troops. "Regiment, today's orders: As of today, Subcommander Slith is promoted to commander and is hereby placed in command of the First Dragonarmy Engineer Regiment. His post takes effect immediately. That is all."

Kang saluted Slith, and turned to leave.

Slith came to his senses. "Sir!"

Kang looked back, stopped.

"Sir," said Slith softly, "are you sure?"

Kang smiled. "Never more sure of anything in my life."

Slith lowered his gaze a moment, overcome. Then he lifted his head.

"Sir, we have something for you." Slith turned to the regiment and, in his best, arrogant, you-sons-of-bitches command voice, he yelled, "Standard Bearer, bring forth the standard!"

Granak lay on a litter beside the field, propped up on one arm. He couldn't stand yet, but he wouldn't have missed this for the world. Cresel held the standard on parade. The bloody flag had been hung on the battered, blood-stained pole. At a nod from Granak, Cresel marched up to Slith, lowered the standard to horizontal.

Slith took the standard from the pole, detaching the ties. Folding the standard, he turned to Kang. "Sir, this is for you. We thought you should have it. Especially now that you've promoted me to your position, sir."

Kang accepted the standard wordlessly. He couldn't say a thing.

Slith nodded again to Cresel, who reached inside his leather tunic and pulled out another cloth. He unfolded it and handed it to Slith. The flag was an exact replica of the one they had handed to Kang, except that below the twenty-three battle honors, a new one had been added. "Maranta's Fort" Anyone who saw the banner would know that this regiment had fought there and won.

Kang turned, and marched from the field, leaving Slith in command. He didn't look back to see what Slith did, what orders he gave. Kang knew that everything would be done exactly as he would have done it—or better.

* * * * *

Kang had yet another ceremony to attend, but this one he did not plan. At Subcommander Fonrar's request, Kang had permitted the females to offer Huzzad the final honors due to her. Fonrar asked Kang about the burial customs of humans. Were there special rituals they should follow? Kang told her that the customs varied widely. Some humans entombed their dead with treasure. Others burned the bodies, kept the ashes in urns. Still others built rock cairns over the body. Fonrar absorbed this information thoughtfully, then went to confer with the others.

Late afternoon, as the sun sank behind the mountains, smearing the sky with blood red, purple and gold, Kang and Slith and all the other draconians of the First Dragonarmy Engineers stood at attention as six baaz draconians, moving with slow and solemn step, bore Huzzad's body on a shield to a bier constructed of what remained of the Drunken Dragon.

They placed Huzzad's body on the wood bier. Carefully, they arranged her red hair around her shoulders. They had removed her armor, wrapped the body in cloth. Thesik stood at the head of the bier, holding Huzzad's helm in her hands. Huzzad's sword and armor lay at the foot of the bier. At a signal from Fonrar, the baaz poured incense taken from the Bastion over the cloth and over the bier. The smell of the incense was pungent, sweet.

Riel stood by, holding a flaring torch.

Fonrar said a simple eulogy. "She was our sister."

Kang said, in his heart, *She was my friend.*

At Fonrar's signal, Riel laid the torch to the wood. Flames crackled and soon the bier was engulfed in fire, the heat so intense that Thesik, holding Huzzad's helm, was forced to step back. Slith ordered the troops dismissed. The draconians left, returned to their duties.

The females remained with the bier. They would remain throughout the night, until the ashes cooled.

"We want to take her with us," Fonrar told Kang. "We don't want to leave her here alone."

* * * * *

A week after the battle, most of the wounded were now completely healed, including Kang and Granak, who had once again taken up his duty as head of Kang's bodyguard. Kang had tried to argue with the big sivak, saying that now that he was retired, he shouldn't have a bodyguard, but Granak was adamant.

On orders from Commander Slith, Kang was to have an honorary bodyguard. If Kang tried to argue, Slith had threatened to pull rank on him.

Kang was in his own quarters, studying a map of the territory, a map that had once belonged to General Maranta.

"Sir," said Granak, opening the door, "Commanders Vertax, Prokel, Slith, and Trok to see you, sir."

"Trok?" Kang looked up.

"He took over from Commander Yakanoh, sir," Granak replied.

"Oh, yes." Kang nodded. Yakanoh had been killed in the outset of the battle, impaled on a goblin spear.

"And Commander Mitrat, of the Queen's Own," Granak added. His voice held no inflection, but at this last, Granak rolled his eyes.

Kang rumbled deep in his throat. "Ask them to step in."

He rose to his feet to greet them, offering his left hand to shake. He invited them to sit down, sent Granak for a jug of cactus juice.

"Kang," said Vertax, "we'll get right to the point. We understand from Commander Slith that you've retired from the military. Is that true?"

"Yes," Kang answered. He frowned, cast a glance at Slith, who pretended not to see him. "It is."

Prokel shook his head. "A goddamn waste. Kang, we want you to take Maranta's place. We want to make you general."

Kang stared at them, taken aback. He looked at Mitrat, saw even the commander of the Queen's Own give a stiff nod. Kang started to speak, but Vertax struck in.

"You deserve it, Kang. I have to admit I thought your idea of that wooden dragon was ridiculous at first. Why didn't you tell us you planned to cast an illusion spell on it? I know"—he forestalled Kang, who would have spoken—"better to take us all by surprise. Our reactions were more realistic. I nearly lost my lunch when I saw that monster overhead. Brilliance. Sheer brilliance," Vertax raved, tapping his claws on the table in applause. "You saved us, Kang."

"From the goblins," said Kang, eyeing them.

"From the goblins," said Vertax, heartily enthusiastic.

Kang said nothing. He sat quite still, watching, waiting.

Vertax lost some of his enthusiasm. He and Trok exchanged uneasy glances. Prokel squirmed in his chair. Mitrat stared straight ahead.

"Did you gentlemen know Maranta had in his possession the Heart of Dracart?" Kang asked.

"No," Prokel began.

"We knew, Kang," Vertax cut in, not meeting Kang's stern gaze. "You knew, Prokel. Don't try to convince us otherwise. You had to know. The Ninth brought all sorts of loot and magical artifacts with them from the Temple at Neraka."

"I didn't know," Prokel insisted stubbornly. "The Heart was only a rumor, a legend. Like those blamed dragonlances. Remember how we laughed when we first heard about those?"

"I talked to dracos who actually saw it," Vertax persisted.

"Oh, sure you did. When you pinned them down it was always someone's buddy's friend who saw it."

Vertax finally looked at Kang directly. "Whether we knew about it or we didn't, I swear to you, Kang, we didn't know that Maranta was crazy enough to use it! I was like you. I thought my men had just deserted—"

"I never thought my men had deserted," Kang said.

He shifted his gaze to Mitrat. The commander of the Queen's Own had neither moved nor spoken.

"You knew about the Heart of Dracart? You knew Maranta had brought it safely from Neraka?"

"Yes, sir," said the commander stonily.

"Did you know what it did?"

"No, sir," said Mitrat. "It wasn't my place to know."

"And was it your place to help Maranta murder your fellows?" Kang demanded, his voice rising in anger.

"I was following orders, sir," Mitrat replied. "General Maranta was my superior officer. It was not my place to question him."

"Even when you saw him killing good men and using their souls to create mindless nincompoops who walk and talk and salute anything in a fancy tabard." Kang regarded Mitrat in disgust. "No, you didn't say a word. You know why? Because the poor souless bastards Maranta was creating were no different from yourself!"

Mitrat lunged to his feet, hand grappling for his sword.

Slith was on his feet, placing himself between Mitrat and Kang.

Vertax grabbed hold of Mitrat, jerked his arm. "Sit down, you fool! Kang's right. We're all to blame. I wondered where those strange troops came from—"

"We all did," said Trok, "but it was easier not to ask questions. It was easier to trust the general. Like Mitrat, here. We followed orders."

"That is the strength of the military, sir," Mitrat stated. "A soldier obeys orders. Remove discipline and you have anarchy, chaos."

"I am aware of that, Commander," said Kang. "The

lost gods know that when I was in command, I expected all my officers to obey my orders, even if they didn't understand them or didn't agree with them. I expected the same of myself." Kang gazed long at Mitrat. "But I could not have done what you did. Not without questioning, protesting, even resisting, if necessary. Discipline, orders—it used to be all so simple for me. It's not anymore. And that's why I have removed myself from command.

"I made a decision to retire from the military some time ago," Kang continued. "I'm not sure how to explain this, but it came to me that our people no longer need a military leader. We need someone who will help us take our rightful place among the other races in the world."

He felt embarrassed, spread his hands. "I know I'm not qualified for this position and I'm probably going to make a hash of it, but I'd like to give it a shot. I want to be a leader of people, now, not of soldiers. The First Dragonarmy Engineers are going to be moving out tomorrow morning. We're going on to the city of Teyr. We're going to build a new life there, raise our young in peace."

Vertax shook his head. "That won't be easy, Kang. There are those like the elves who don't want peace with us. Those like the Dark Knights who don't want us to take our place in the world."

"I know," said Kang. "But Commander Slith is the leader of our regiment. I have every confidence in his ability and in that of his troops."

"There's nothing we can say to make you change your mind?" Prokel asked.

"No, sirs. Thank you," Kang said.

The commanders finished their drinks, rose to their feet, and started to file out, all except Slith, who remained seated.

"Commander Mitrat," Kang said.

The commander halted, stiff-backed, and for a moment Kang thought he was going to be ignored. Then Mitrat slowly turned.

"Sir," said Kang, "I want to apologize for what I said to you. I was out of line."

Mitrat maintained his ice-rimed silence for long moments, then a tiny crack appeared. "I did what I was required to do and I do not regret it. Yet, there were times . . . At night, I could see their eyes. . . ."

He said no more. Looking at Kang, Mitrat nodded his head slightly, then turned and continued out the door.

Slith sat, staring at Kang.

"What is it?" Kang growled. "Have I sprouted feathers?"

"No, sir," said Slith. "I'm glad you turned them down, sir."

"Did you think I wouldn't?" Kang was astonished.

"I thought maybe when you heard their offer, you might change your mind. Not but what I think you'd make a good general, sir, it's just that, well, we've come all this way and we've lost a lot of good men—"

"We leave for Teyr in the morning. I want the First Dragonarmy Engineers to be ready at first light," Kang said, cutting Slith off. "Will that give you enough time to prepare, Commander?"

Slith grinned. "You bet it will, sir."

When Slith had gone, Kang poked his head out the door. "Uh, Granak," he said, feeling awkward and embarrassed. "I'd, uh, like for you to ask Subcommander Fonrar if she would like to, uh, share some dinner with me."

"Yes, sir," said Granak, taking care to refrain from smiling. "I'll ask her, sir."

Kang returned to his map. The road ahead would be difficult, but they would make it. Of that, he was certain.

* * * * *

The next morning, the First Dragonarmy Engineers lined up on the parade ground for the last time. Their wagons were packed. Each draconian, male and female, was well armed and well supplied with the stores they would need for the trip.

Inside her pack, Fonrar carried a silver urn recovered from the storehouse. The urn was decorated with dragons. It had come from Neraka and inside the females had reverently placed Huzzad's ashes. Their sister was coming with them.

Slith walked over to Kang, who was watching the proceedings from the sidelines. "Sir, would you like to march with us in the vanguard?"

Kang smiled, and nodded. "Yes, Commander, I would be proud to. Thank you for asking me."

At Slith's command, the First Dragonarmy Engineers marched out of Maranta's Fort. They marched past the large, black, greasy burned spot on the ground—the remains of the once-grand goblin army. Granak marched at their head, proudly waving the new standard. The engineers had traveled for perhaps a half a mile and were just climbing over a rise, when a baaz came dashing forward.

"Sir!" he yelled. "Commander."

Both Kang and Slith turned around. "Yes," both answered.

"Oops, sorry," Kang said. "I forgot."

"What is it, trooper?" Slith asked.

"Look, sir!" The baaz turned, pointed.

Draconians were filing out of the fort. Row after row

of them. The Ninth Infantry led the way. Behind them was the First. Behind them the Third. They marched up to rear the engineer column. They said nothing, but joined up behind the ranks of engineers, falling into line behind them.

Kang stared, puzzled. "What are they doing?"

"They're coming with us, sir," said Slith.

"All of them?" Kang was flabbergasted.

"Looks that way, Commander. Sorry, sir,"—Slith glanced at Kang, perplexed—"what do I call you now? What's your title?"

"How about—Your Grace?" Kang suggested, grinning.

Slith snorted.

Draconians continued to leave the fort. The last few, Kang saw, wore the tabards of the Queen's Own. Led by Commander Mitrat, they joined the line, but took care to leave a space between their ranks and the ranks of the ordinary soldiers ahead of them.

Slith frowned. "Do we really want those bastards, sir?"

"They're draconians," Kang said. "They're our people. We'll find a place for them."

Last, after the Queen's Own, a group of about one hundred draconians straggled out of the fort. They looked after their departing fellows, seemed confused, as if they couldn't figure out what was happening or what they were supposed to do about it.

"The dunderheads," said Slith. "Those that survived the battle. Not many did, the goblins be thanked. What do we do about them, sir? Do we want them along, too? You can't say they're draconians."

"Yes . . . they are. Maybe, in time, some part of them will remember what they used to be. Meanwhile, they're our responsibility. Send a messenger to Commander

Mitrat. Tell him that he and the Queen's Own are in charge of them."

"Yes, sir." Slith grinned, then said, "It will be a pleasure, sir. I mean—Governor."

Governor. Kang liked that.

As he had said, he would probably make a hash of it. He'd been trained as a soldier, not a political leader. But he would do the best he could.

Turning, his heart swelling, Kang led his people north. He led his people to their destiny.

A Brief History of Draconians

Draconians were created at end of the Age of Darkness to a serve as specialists and shock troops in the dragonarmies during the War of the Lance. They were created to provide the Dark Queen's generals with soldiers who were more predictable than humans and more tractable than the ogres and goblins that made up the bulk of the army. Although male and female draconians were created at the same time, the existence of the females was concealed for a long time.

Draconians are the result of twisted and evil magic. Their race was created using the eggs of metallic dragons that had been stolen and secreted under a temple devoted to Takhisis in the city of Sanction. The stolen eggs were subjected to a special ceremony (called "the corruption ritual") performed by Dracart, a wizard of the Black Robes; Wyrllish, one of Takhisis's most powerful priests during the War of the Lance; and Harkiel, a dark-hearted red dragon. This ceremony corrupted the embryo within the eggs, causing it to split into dozens of humanoid creatures.

Each breed of draconian draws its origin from a specific type of metallic dragon egg. Baaz were created from brass dragon eggs, Bozaks from bronze, Kapaks from copper, Sivaks from silver, and Auraks from gold. Until the time of the Chaos War, the world believed that draconians were sexless beings, unable to reproduce except through the corruption ceremony. The world was wrong.

Dracart knew from the earliest experiments in creating draconians that female metallic dragon embryos created female draconians while male embryos gave rise to males. As he watched the first generation of male draconians thrive and turn into fierce warriors, he feared that the draconians might become a threat to the other races of Krynn. The draconians were loyal to Takhisis and her priests *now*, but Dracart feared a future in which draconians might rebel against their masters. He decided that the best way to keep the draconians under control was to deny them a way to propagate except through the corruption ritual.

Dracart wanted to destroy all female metallic dragon eggs in the possession of the dragonarmy, but Takhisis forbade it. Instead, she decreed that the eggs containing females be hidden in a different location than Sanction. The eggs that contained the females were not allowed to hatch.

The *Heart of Dracart*: When the Whitestone Forces mounted a serious opposition to the dragonarmies, Takhisis decided that she need a more efficient method to ensure an ongoing supply of draconians than the corruption ritual. She ordered Dracart to create such a method, one that didn't depend on metallic dragon eggs or a union of powerfully evil beings. She was confident the draconians would remain loyal to her.

Through means known only to him and the Dark Queen, Dracart created the crystal that he called the *Heart of Dracart*. This artifact creates hundreds of new draconians from an already existing one,

Designers: Steve Miller, Don Perrin, and Margaret Weis
Editor: Julia Martin
Creative Director: Mike Selinker
Based on the DUNGEONS & DRAGONS® game by Monte Cook, Jonathan Tweet, and Skip Williams. Based on the original DUNGEONS & DRAGONS game by E. Gary Gygax and Dave Arneson.
DRAGONLANCE® material based on original designs by the original pioneers of Krynn: Jeff Grubb, Tracy Hickman, Harold Johnson, Doug Niles, Carl Smith, Margaret Weis, and Michael Williams.

shattering the spirit inhabiting the draconian and putting slivers of it into the copies. The process kills the donor draconian. The replicas are not as smart, powerful, or long-lived as the original, but they are docile, obedient, and able to fight.

Maranta's Ambition: Dracart never used his artifact. As the Whitestone Forces searched the ruins of Neraka after the city fell, they found the infamous wizard dead with his throat slashed. The *Heart of Dracart* was not recovered.

The *Heart of Dracart* was stolen by Maranta, an Aurak. He knew that any draconian created by the artifact would be little more than a mindless slave. He had every intention of destroying the artifact, but found he could not bring himself to do it.

As time passed, draconians began to age and die. Their species truly became endangered, and the idea of creating an army of mindless slaves that would continue the species, at least somehow, began to appeal to Maranta. By about twenty years after the War of the Lance, Maranta had already built a base of power, and he hoped that the surviving draconians would gather under his leadership. Now, he also started to consider the possibility of becoming the savior of the draconian species. In truth, he cared little for the draconians who served him and never hesitated to order his troops to defend him while he remained safe in his fortress.

Kang's Discovery: During the Chaos War, another draconian leader, a Bozak engineer named Kang, discovered Dracart's hidden collection of female dragon eggs. After a conflict with the dwarves of Thorbardin, Kang secured the eggs and allowed them to hatch.

Twenty female draconians emerged from the eggs: one Aurak, two Sivaks, three Bozaks, four Kapaks, and ten Baaz. With the knowledge that his race now would be able to reproduce naturally, Kang saw the need for a place where draconians could raise their young and that they could call their own. In the company of the females and the draconians who had been his companions since the War of the Lance, Kang set out to find such a home.

Kang Against Maranta: Kang and his group eventually clashed with Maranta. Despite their shared desire to see the draconian species continue, Kang and Maranta were motivated by two very different ideals. Kang wanted to find a secure place where draconians could thrive, while Maranta was interested in ensuring his own continued power. Maranta saw Kang and the female draconians as a threat. He feared that Kang's talk of establishing a city of draconians would cause those who had been loyal to Mantra to shift allegiance to Kang.

During a goblin attack upon Teyr, Maranta put his plan to save the draconians into action and used the *Heart of Dracart*. Appalled by Maranta's actions, Kang battled the Aurak, defeated him, and destroyed the artifact.

Draconians and the Nation of Teyr: With the defeat of Maranta, Kang became the leader of Teyr, a free nation inhabited by draconians. Most of the inferior draconians Maranta created were killed in the battle against the goblins, but a few survived. Kang took pity upon them and brought them with him to the new city he established. Unfortunately, these draconians were sterile. Maranta's dream of continuing the species could have actually ensured the end of it, since so few fertile draconians lived in Teyr that it would have been nearly impossible to sustain the species.

What the future holds for Kang and the draconians of Teyr has yet to be revealed.

Draconians in the D&D® Game

	Aurak	**Baaz**
	Medium-Size Monstrous Humanoid	Medium-Size Monstrous Humanoid
HD:	8d8+24 (60 hp)	2d8+4 (13 hp)
Init:	+6 (+2 Dex, +4 Improved Initiative)	+0
Spd:	40 ft.	20 ft.
AC:	20 (+2 Dex, +8 natural)	16 (+6 natural)

Atk:	2 fire energy rays +10 ranged touch; or 2 claws +12 melee; bite +7 melee	2 claws +2 melee; or halfspear +2 melee
Dmg:	1d8+4 fire energy ray; claws 1d4+4; bite 1d6+2	Claws 1d4; halfspear 1d6
F/R:	5 ft. by 5 ft./5 ft.	5 ft. by 5 ft./5 ft.
SA:	Spells, spell-like abilities, mind control, breath weapon	Death throe
SQ:	Spell resistance 18, divine grace, keen senses, disease immunity, low metabolism	Spell resistance 11, glide, disease immunity, low metabolism
Saves:	Fort +9, Ref +12, Will +12	Fort +2, Ref +3, Will +2
Abilities:	Str 18, Dex 15, Con 17, Int 18, Wis 15, Cha 18	Str 10, Dex 11, Con 14, Int 10, Wis 9, Cha 10
Skills:	Appraise +10, Diplomacy +10, Forgery +10, Gather Information +10, Hide +9, Innuendo +8, Intimidate +10, Intuit Direction +10*, Listen +2, Spot +4	Bluff +5, Disguise +5, Gather Information +5, Listen +5, Spot +4
Feats:	Alertness, Blind-Fight, Combat Casting, Improved Initiative, Spell Focus (Evocation), Spell Penetration	Alertness, Run
Clm/Terr:	Any land	Any land
Org:	Solitary or pair	Band (4d10)
CR:	8	1
Treasure:	Double standard	Half standard
Align:	Often lawful evil	Usually neutral evil
Adv:	9–24 HD (Medium-size)	3–6 HD (Medium-size)
	Bozak	**Kapak**
	Medium-Size Monstrous Humanoid	Medium-Size Monstrous Humanoid
HD:	4d8+8 (26 hp)	3d8+6 (19 hp)
Init:	+1 (Dex)	+1 (Dex)
Speed:	20 ft.	20 ft.
AC:	18 (+1 Dex, +7 natural)	18 (+1 Dex, +7 natural)
Atk:	2 claws +6 melee; bite +4 melee; or short sword +6 melee	2 claws +6 melee; bite +4 melee; or short sword +6 melee
Dmg:	Claws 1d4+2; bite 1d6+1; short sword 1d6+2	Claws 1d4+3; bite 1d4+1 and poison; short sword 1d6+3 and poison
F/R:	5 ft. by 5 ft./5 ft.	5 ft. by 5 ft./5 ft.
SA:	Spells, death throe	Poison or healing, death throe
SQ:	Spell resistance 14, divine grace, glide, disease immunity, low metabolism	Spell resistance 14, disease immunity, low metabolism
Saves:	Fort +5, Ref +7, Will +7	Fort +3, Ref +4, Will +4

3

	Bozak	**Kapak**
Abilities:	Str 15, Dex 13, Con 14,	Str 16, Dex 13, Con 15,
	Int 15, Wis 12, Cha 14	Int 12, Wis 12, Cha 10
Skills:	Bluff +8, Diplomacy +8*,	Disable Device +6, Hide +7,
	Hide +7, Intimidate +4,	Listen +6, Move
	Knowledge (religion) +6,	Silently +7, Open Lock +7
	Listen +3, Move Silently +7,	
	Spot +9	
Feats:	Alertness, Combat Casting,	Dodge, Multiattack, Run
	Multiattack, Run	
Clm/Terr:	Any land	Any land
Org:	Band (2d6)	Band (2d10)
CR:	4	4
Treasure:	Standard	Standard
Align:	Usually lawful evil	Usually lawful evil
Adv:	5–12 HD (Medium-size)	4–9 HD (Medium-size)

Sivak

Large Monstrous
Humanoid

HD:	6d8+24 (51 hp)
Init:	+1 (–1 Size, +2 Dex)
Speed:	20 ft., fly 60 ft. (average)
AC:	19 (–1 size, +2 Dex, +8 natural)
Atk:	2 claws +10 melee; bite +8 melee;
	or bastard sword +10 melee
Dmg:	Claw 1d6+5; bite 2d6+2;
	bastard sword 1d10+5
F/R:	5 ft. by 5 ft./10 ft.
SA:	Trip
SQ:	Spell resistance 15, shapeshift,
	blend, divine grace, spells, disease
	immunity, low metabolism
Saves:	Fort +8, Ref +9, Will +8
Abilities:	Str 21, Dex 15, Con 19,
	Int 13, Wis 12, Cha 15
Skills:	Bluff +7, Diplomacy +7, Disguise +7,
	Gather Information +7, Intimidate +7,
	Listen +8, Spot +7
	Sivak
Feats:	Alertness, Multiattack, Power Attack, Run
Clm/Terr:	Any land
Org:	Band (2–12)
CR:	6
Treasure:	Standard
Align:	Usually neutral evil
Adv:	7-18 HD (Large)

4

Draconians have short, stubby tails, lizard snouts, and scaly bodies. Their coloration serves as a dim reminder of the dragons from which they were spawned. Baaz scales have an unmistakably brassy coloration, Bozaks are the color of tarnished bronze, Kapaks are reddish with greenish tints like oxidized copper, Sivaks are a polished silver color, and Auraks are a deep golden hue. Female draconians tend to be shorter and more finely built than males, with female Bozaks being the only exception to this trend.

While all draconians except Auraks have wings, only Sivaks can truly fly. Draconians move either by walking upright, running on all fours while flapping their wings, gliding down from heights (for a distance four times greater than the height from which they launched), or running on all fours while flapping their wings. This latter form of movement is their fastest, and it kicks up an intimidating dust cloud on the battlefield. All winged draconians have the Run feat for free, allowing them a faster running speed while running on all fours and flapping their wings.

Draconians are drawn to evil dragons and revere them. They serve dragons willingly and eagerly, while only reluctantly serving leaders of other species. When a dragon commander is within line of sight or when entering a battle under the command of a dragon (in the chain of command), draconians receive a +1 morale bonus on all attack rolls and saving throws.

Draconians have an unknown life span. Draconians are reptilian and reproduce as other reptiles do. Female draconians lay 2d4 eggs per clutch. All draconians love ale and spirits.

When draconians die, the magical energies that are inherent in their bodies are released in a death throe with spectacular and catastrophic effects.

Draconians

Draconians are proficient with all simple and martial weapons.

Disease Immunity (Ex): Draconians are immune to all natural diseases.

Low Metabolism (Ex): Draconians can survive on one-tenth the food and water it takes to sustain a human.

Auraks

Auraks are the most innately powerful of all draconians. They are also the rarest. They often work as special agents and enforcers. They are arrogant, self-absorbed, and view themselves as superior to all creatures except dragons and the Dark Queen herself. Aurak males are about 7 feet tall, while females are slightly shorter.

Aurak Combat

Auraks hardly ever use their natural weapons in combat, preferring instead to rely on their ability to generate rays of fire energy from each of their hands that deal damage equal to 1d8 plus the draconian's Charisma modifier with each successful ranged touch attack. These rays can strike targets up to 60 feet distant. When using *change self*, Auraks appear to be using a weapon appropriate to their form, but they are really attacking with their rays. These rays are a supernatural ability.

Spells: Auraks cast spells as 8th-level sorcerers. Their preferred spells include the following: *enlarge, shocking grasp, emotion, stinking cloud, blink, lightning bolt, phantasmal killer,* and *wall of fire.* Female Auraks prefer Illusion spells.

Breath Weapon (Su): Three times a day Auraks can breathe a noxious cloud (5-foot cone). Victims caught in the cloud are dealt 20 points of damage and blinded for 1d4 round unless they succeed at Fortitude saves (DC 17). Those who save take only 10 points of damage.

Spell-Like Abilities (Sp): Auraks can *change self* three times per day to resemble any individual human or humanoid and to perfectly imitate its voice. This effect only lasts for 2d6+6 minutes.

Up to three times per day, Auraks can perform limited short-range teleportation. This ability functions exactly like the *dimension door* spell except that it has a range limited to 60 feet and Auraks can only transport themselves and their equipment.

5

Auraks can turn *invisible* (as the spell) up to once every 10 minutes. (The use of their *mind control* ability on another does not make them visible.)

Male Auraks can *polymorph self*, as the sorcerer spell, three times per day.

Mind Control (Su): An Aurak's most insidious power is the ability to affect the minds of others. Auraks can use *suggestion* once every 10 minutes at will, as the sorcerer spell. Once per day, they can also *mind control* one creature of 8 or fewer Hit Dice for 2d6 rounds (requires concentration). The draconian controls the actions of the subject as if the subject's body were his own. The target of a mind control must succeed at a Will save (DC 18) to avoid being controlled. The save is only rolled as the draconian attempts to take control of the target.

Death Throe (Ex): On the round that an Aurak reaches 0 or fewer hit points, its flesh transforms into eerie green flames. The Aurak enters a fighting frenzy that grants him a +4 morale bonus to all attack rolls and saving throws. Anyone adjacent to the draconian who attacks it in melee takes 1d6+the draconian's Charisma modifier points of fire damage each round from the flames (Reflex half DC 17). Six rounds later or when the Aurak reaches −10 hit points, it transforms into a whizzing ball of lightning that strikes with an attack bonus of +15 and deals 2d6+the Aurak's Charisma modifier points of electricity damage to those struck. After three rounds of lightning attacks, it explodes with a thunderous boom, stunning all within 10 feet for 1d4 rounds (2d4 if underwater) and dealing 3d6 points of sonic damage to all within 10 feet. A successful Will save (DC 18) negates the stunning effect. The explosion destroys any items carried by the draconian.

Keen Senses (Ex): Auraks' senses are so fine that they have low-light vision and can detect hidden and *invisible* creatures within a 40-foot radius. They can also see through all *illusions*.

Skills: *Female Auraks have 8 ranks of Intuit Direction for free. Male Auraks do not possess this skill.

Baaz

Baaz occupy the bottom rung on the ladder of draconian social order. They are often abused and treated as slaves by other draconians. In the past, the Baaz could do little to change this situation, so they remained aloof from others not of their kind. However, with the arrival of female Baaz, this is beginning to change. Baaz females are organizers who work well in groups. They are working to change the status of Baaz at large by refusing to cooperate with those who abuse them and encouraging the males to follow their lead.

Baaz are often encountered prowling through civilized lands in disguise. Their size and build is such that they can pass themselves off as human by wearing large hoods and masks and concealing their wings under robes. Baaz males serve as scouts and spies, while female Baaz are rapidly becoming highly prized managers and low-ranking military commanders.

Baaz are the physically weakest and most plentiful of all draconians. Male Baaz stand between 5 feet and 6 feet in height, with the majority of them being on the short side. Female Baaz tend to be lighter in build than males.

Baaz Combat

Death Throe (Su): On the round that a Baaz reaches 0 or fewer hit points, his body turns to stone. The creature that struck the deathblow must roll a successful Dexterity check (DC 13) or have his weapon fused to the draconian. The Baaz "statue" crumbles to dust after 1d4 minutes. Items carried by the Baaz are unaffected by the petrification and subsequent dissolution. Any stuck weapons can be retrieved after the Baaz crumbles away.

Glide (Ex): A Baaz can use his wings to glide, negating any damage from a fall of any height and allowing him to travel horizontally up to four times the vertical distance descended.

Bozaks

Bozaks are intensely spiritual beings. They sometimes organize religious services. Others have turned their need to believe in something to believing in draconians themselves. This has strengthened their already considerable leadership abilities.

Bozaks display no gender differentiation in height and build. They stand between 6 feet and 6 1/2 feet tall. Both sexes have keen organizational abilities. Males have served as leaders in draconian military units since the War of the Lance.

Bozak Combat

Bozaks of both sexes are cruel and cunning warriors who only rarely spare the lives of opponents.

Spells: Bozaks are natural sorcerers. They can master the mystic arts with only minimal instruction while young. The average Bozak casts spells as a 4th-level sorcerer. Few females advance beyond this level, while males have been known to advance as high as 8th level. Their favorite spells are *burning hands, enlarge, magic missile, shocking grasp, invisibility, levitate, stinking cloud,* and *web.*

Death Throe (Ex): On the round that a Bozak reaches 0 or fewer hit points, his scaly flesh shrivels and crumbles from his bones in a cloud of dust. Then the bones explode, dealing 1d6 points of damage to all within a 10-foot radius (Reflex negates DC 14).

Divine Grace (Ex): Bozaks add their Charisma modifiers to all saving throws (included in the numbers above).

Glide (Ex): A Bozak can use his wings to glide, negating any damage from a fall of any height and allowing him to travel horizontally up to four times the vertical distance descended.

Skills: *Bozaks gain a +4 bonus to Diplomacy checks when dealing with other draconians.

Kapaks

Kapaks are the backbone of draconian fighting forces. They are fierce warriors who possess an inherent love of battle. However, they also excel at performing quiet missions of sabotage and assassination. Male Kapaks stand between 6 and 7 feet tall. Kapak females are a little shorter, standing about 5 1/2 feet in height. Both are powerfully muscled.

Neither male nor female Kapaks show any aptitude toward original thinking, nor are they very perceptive. This makes them better followers than leaders. Another kind of draconian or a leader of a different species usually leads Kapak forces.

Kapak Combat

Poison (Ex): Bite or blade; Fortitude save (DC 13); initial damage paralysis, secondary damage 0. Paralysis lasts 2d6 minutes. Only male Kapaks have venomous saliva. Before entering combat, male Kapaks often lick the blades of their swords. The poison remains on the blade for 3 rounds.

Healing Saliva (Ex): The saliva of female Kapaks cures wounds. If a female Kapak licks a wound within 10 rounds of the injury, the wounded creature regains 2d6 hit points. The healing properties work especially well on draconians, curing 3d6 hit points. The saliva of a female Kapak does not heal when delivered by her bite.

Death Throe (Ex): On the round that a Kapak reaches 0 or fewer hit points, his body instantly dissolves into a 5-foot-radius pool of acid. All within this area suffer 1d6 points of acid damage each round they remain in the pool. The acid evaporates in 1d6 rounds. All items the Kapak was carrying are rendered useless by the acid.

Sivaks

Sivaks are the most powerful of the commonly encountered draconians. Both male and female Sivaks serve as elite warriors and infiltrators who are highly sought after by evil leaders and other draconians. The males' ability to perform covert operations is aided by their shapeshifting ability. The males stand close to 9 feet tall. Females are between 6 and 7 feet tall.

Sivak Combat

Both sexes prefer to wield large, ornate bastard swords. Sivaks' tails are long (for draconians), and they often use them in combat to knock foes off balance.

Trip (Ex): In place of his normal attacks in a round, a Sivak can use his tail to make a trip attack using his normal melee attack bonus (+10).

Shapeshift (Su): A male Sivak is capable of assuming the form of a humanoid of his own size or smaller at the moment he kills it. The Sivak does not gain the memories, skills, or spell use of its victim, but his appearance and voice is an exact match to its victim's. The Sivak can change back to his normal shape, but after doing cannot shapeshift again without killing another humanoid.

Blend (Ex): Sivak females cannot shapeshift like male Sivaks. Instead, they have a chameleon-like ability to blend in with their surroundings. This works just like a *robe of blending*, giving the Sivak a +15 circumstance bonus to her Hide checks and allowing her to *change self* at will.

Divine Grace (Ex): Sivaks add their Charisma modifiers to all saving throws (included in the numbers above).

Male Death Throe (Ex): A male Sivak changes shape when slain, assuming the form of the being that killed it. This death shape lasts for three days, and then the entire body decomposes into black soot. If the Sivak's slayer is larger than the Sivak or not humanoid, the Sivak instead bursts into flame, dealing 2d4 points of fire damage to all within a 10-foot radius (Reflex negates DC 17).

Female Death Throe (Ex): Female Sivaks do not assume the form of those who kill them. Instead, they burst into flames when killed, dealing 2d4 points of fire damage to all within a 10-foot radius (Reflex negates DC 17).

Heart of Dracart Draconians

Draconians created by the *Heart of Dracart* have life spans of only 1,000 days. These tragic creatures are the same as their normal counterparts, with the following exceptions:

Hit Dice: These draconians have 2 HD less than normal for their kind.

Armor Class: These draconians have only a +3 natural armor bonus, regardless of kind. Most have lower Dexterity scores than their counterparts as well.

Special Attacks: These draconians do not have the death throe ability.

Special Qualities: *Heart of Dracart* draconians do not have any shapeshifting or polymorph abilities, even if created from Sivak or Aurak stock. They also lack the divine grace ability and the draconian immunity to natural disease.

Abilities: Hear of Dracart draconians have the following ability scores: Str 11, Dex 10, Con 10, Int 5, Wis 5, Cha 5.

Skills: These draconians have only the following skills, regardless of Hit Dice: Listen +2, Spot +2.

Feats: These draconians have no feats except Run, which they have only if their donor draconian type possessed that feat.

Challenge Rating: As base type −2.

From the best-selling writing team of Weis and Hickman

Dragons of a Fallen Sun

The War of Souls • Volume One
Margaret Weis and Tracy Hickman

Change—for good or for ill—comes to the world of Krynn. A violent magical storm sweeps over Ansalon, bringing flood and fire, death and destruction. Out of the tumult rises a strange, mystical young woman. Her destiny is bound up with that of Krynn. For she alone knows the truth about the future, a future strangely and inextricably tied to the terrifying mystery in Krynn's past.

Sequel to
the best-selling *Dragons of Summer Flame*,
this is the first volume in a magnificent new epic trilogy
by the creators of the DRAGONLANCE saga,
Margaret Weis and Tracy Hickman.

Downfall
The Dhamon Saga
Volume One
Jean Rabe

How far can a hero fall?

Far enough to lose his soul?

Dhamon Grimwulf, once a Hero of the Heart, has sunk into a bitter life of crime and squalor. Now, as the great dragon overlords of the Fifth Age coldly plot to strengthen their rule and to destroy their enemies, he must somehow find the will to redeem himself.

But perhaps it is too late.

Don't miss the beginning of Dhamon's story from Jean Rabe!

Dragons of a New Age

The Dawning of a New Age
Great dragons invade Ansalon, devastating the land and dividing it among themselves.

The Day of the Tempest
The Heroes of the Heart seek the long-lost dragonlance in the snow-covered tomb of Huma.

The Eve of the Maelstrom
Dragons and humans battle for the future of Krynn at the Window to the Stars.